THE STACKED DECK

THE DEVIL'S OWN, BOOK 3

THE STACKED DECK

JD MARCH

FIVE STAR
A part of Gale, Cengage Learning

GALE
CENGAGE Learning·

Farmington Hills, Mich • San Francisco • New York • Waterville, Maine
Meriden, Conn • Mason, Ohio • Chicago

LIBRARY OF CONGRESS CATALOGING-IN-PUBLICATION DATA

Names: March, J. D., author.
Title: The stacked deck / by JD March.
Description: First edition. | Waterville, Maine : Five Star, a part of Gale, Cengage Learning, [2016] | Series: The devil's own ; book 3
Identifiers: LCCN 2015047692| ISBN 9781432832193 (hardcover) | ISBN 1432832190 (hardcover) | ISBN 9781432832117 (ebook) | ISBN 1432832115 (ebook)
Subjects: LCSH: Ranch life—Fiction. | Families—Fiction. | GSAFD: Western stories.
Classification: LCC PS3613.A7325 S73 2016 | DDC 813/.6—dc23
LC record available at http://lccn.loc.gov/2015047692

First Edition. First Printing: June 2016
Find us on Facebook– https://www.facebook.com/FiveStarCengage
Visit our website– http://www.gale.cengage.com/fivestar/
Contact Five Star™ Publishing at FiveStar@cengage.com

To the best of friends who have been unwavering in their continued support.
Whistle, CC, Shelley, and Anna, I owe you everything.

PROLOGUE

Not a drop of moisture remained in the baked red dirt. A lizard sheltered from the sun in the shade of some low-growing bitterbrush, its tongue flicking occasionally to catch an unwary fly. At least the lizard had some shade. It didn't have to sweat its guts out under a sun hot enough to burn your eyeballs. He wiped the sweat away from his forehead and looked forward to sundown. It would bring some relief from this stifling heat, so dry it was painful to breathe. The dust got in his nostrils and caught the back of his throat, making him cough.

He took a step back and looked at his handiwork. The small house was coming on well. And it was far enough out of town to suit his purposes. He smiled. It had no near neighbors and that was just the way he liked things. There was nobody to see when he came and went. And, even more important, nobody to hear anything. Yes, the house would do very well indeed. And the cellar . . . well, that was a triumph. He'd sweated buckets digging the damn thing, but nobody would ever suspect its existence. He laughed out loud. Things were panning out just fine. It had been time to move on and make a fresh start. People had been looking at him and whispering. They were starting to wonder about him and ask too many questions. But here, nobody knew anything at all about him. Yes—this new place would do very well indeed.

Turning to go in search of a cool drink, he tripped over a long-handled hoe discarded next to the newly planted vegetable bed. He stumbled against the fence, cutting his hand, even as he cursed Joshua, the handyman he'd taken on for a few days' extra help. The silly old fool was always leaving things lying around. Joshua would be halfway home before he'd remember the hoe and come shuffling back to collect it. He picked up the hoe and tossed it nearer the house. It would make it more difficult to find and force the old buzzard to have to look for it.

He pushed open the front door. It smelled of new paint. Still nursing his cut hand, he poured a glass of lemonade before stretching slowly. Hell, his back hurt from all the work. His muscles were unaccustomed to hard labor, but the house was almost finished now. Maybe tomorrow he'd start putting his plans into action. He'd waited long enough.

He turned to go into the living room and dropped the glass with a start. It shattered into a thousand shards. A kid, maybe seventeen or eighteen, was leaning against the door, a gun in his left hand. The kid didn't move a muscle, just stood watching him with a strange half-smile on his face.

"Who the hell are you? And what the hell d'you think you're doing in my house? How long have you been standing there?" His voice sounded more like a croak, and his palms were sweating.

"Long enough." The kid spoke softly and he didn't sound aggressive. That was a good sign. He was probably only some drifter who wanted money.

"I asked what you wanted, you little shit." That was better, his voice sounded stronger now.

The intruder continued to look at him, not moving. How could anyone stay that still? It was a pity the kid wasn't younger. He'd probably been pretty when he was younger. He pushed the thought away. He couldn't let some kid get the upper hand here. "I said what do you want? If it's money you're after, I've got damn all here." He smiled thinly. "I keep it in the bank so little pricks like you can't steal it."

"Steal it?" The kid sounded amused. The odd smile still seemed to play around his mouth but his eyes were icy. "It ain't your money I want. Although I guess, in a way, some of it's mine."

He felt a sudden stab of fear. There was something about this kid that disturbed him. It wasn't just that curious stillness. Maybe it was something about the eyes. Yes, it was the eyes. They were . . . predatory. There was something wild in them. Wild and dangerous. "What the hell d'you mean by that? Let me tell you, I've worked damn hard for my money. But I guess kids like you don't understand the idea of working hard. You want everything easy and you'll take whatever you want without doing a stroke of work. But I earned my money, dealing with shit like you." Yes, that was the way to act. Be aggressive and don't let the kid see he's got you rattled.

"Like I said, I don't want your money even though I earned some of it for you. Wouldn't even want to touch it. I guess it's dirty, just like you."

He could feel the sweat starting to trickle down his face. He swallowed hard. The kid just continued to watch him with those feral eyes. Who the hell was he? He'd swear he'd never seen him before. "If you don't want my money, what is it you do want?" His voice was croaky again.

The kid looked him up and down, real slow, like he was sizing him up for a suit. "You."

"Me? What the hell do you mean? And who the hell are you?" He brushed the sweat out of his eyes with his arm.

"You don't remember?" The intruder gave a short laugh, but his eyes looked even more remote. "You should remember me. I sure as hell remember you." He paused, his face older now. Harder. "Yeah. I remember you, every waking hour and every fucking night." He motioned to the living room with his gun.

9

"So you might as well go in there. Make yourself comfortable because I'm gonna be here a while. We're gonna take it real slow."

"Take what slow?" His voice was barely a whisper now.

"Killing you. I've waited a long time for this. And I intend to enjoy it. Every second of it. Every hour of it. By the time we're through, you'll be begging me to kill you."

He shuddered, suddenly chilled except for the gush of warmth as his pants grew wet. "Who the hell are you?"

The kid smiled again. "You'll find out. All in good time." He paused. "I'll tell you before you die. My name will be the last thing you ever hear."

CHAPTER ONE

The sun beat down on his bare head and the wind almost took his breath away as he urged the horse on. His hat drummed a crazy rhythm against his back with only the stampede string to stop it flying away. Laughing aloud, he crouched lower over Pistol's neck as they approached a gnarled oak tree blown down in a recent storm. Pistol sailed over it with distance to spare and Johnny let him have his head as they galloped on in their wild rush. At times like this, life seemed too damn good to be true.

As they crested the hill, overlooking the hacienda, he reluctantly reined in to an easy walk. If the old man saw him riding flat out down the hill, it would only make him mad. It seemed to worry his father and he'd drone on about how one of these days Johnny would kill himself. Johnny patted Pistol's neck. "Buen amigo, pero ahora lentamente." No point in irritating Guthrie just for the hell of it. The man couldn't help fussing. Johnny grinned. Fussing. Who'd have thought anyone would ever fuss over him? Not that the old man wanted him to know he was fussing. Usually just sounded real mad and yelled. But Johnny was getting to read him better these days, and he could see concern in those eyes even when the man was yelling. And it wasn't like he'd completely given up trying to wind up the old man. He still did it all too often. It was like he couldn't help himself sometimes. But there was no point when his father was just fussing.

He shook his head. He still couldn't believe how much had

happened these past seven months. To own a part of something like this. To have a compadre like Guy. And an old man. And maybe, just maybe, a future.

He urged Pistol forward, picking their way along a well-worn track back to the corral. Pistol's hooves sent the loose scree pinging down the hillside. As he approached the gates, Johnny pulled his horse to an abrupt halt. An unfamiliar buggy had been left at the side of the barn. Whatever horse had drawn it there had been unhitched and stabled . . . "Damn." Johnny grunted in irritation. He knew he was hopeless with visitors—he could never think of anything to say to them and he always looked dumb while Guy would talk to them with such ease, making it look so simple.

Sighing, he rode across to the barn, unsaddled Pistol, and gave him a swift rubdown before turning him loose with the other horses. Johnny narrowed his eyes, thinking hard. Maybe he could sneak in through the kitchen and slip up the backstairs without his father spotting him and insisting he meet their visitor.

He cat-footed across the courtyard and had almost made it to the kitchen door when his father's voice stopped him in his tracks. "Johnny, come on in! There's someone I want you to meet."

Turning toward the French doors that opened onto the courtyard, he forced a smile and slowly made his way over to Guthrie, who beckoned him inside. He gritted his teeth as his father placed a hand on his shoulders and pushed him into the living room.

Guthrie clapped Johnny on the back and smiled broadly at a heavily built, bearded man who slouched in Guthrie's favorite chair like he owned it. "I told you I had a surprise for you, Ramsey. You'll scarce believe it, but this is my son, John. He came home."

Something flashed in the man's eyes as he looked at Johnny. Shock? Whatever it was, the man didn't look none too happy. He got slowly to his feet. "Did you say, your son, Guthrie?"

Guthrie nodded, with an odd sort of lost look in his eyes. "Aye, my younger son, from my second marriage. I finally found him. All those years I spent searching . . ." He trailed off. Then he nodded again and smiled. "Johnny, this old reprobate is my friend, Ramsey Burnett. We've known each other pretty much all of our lives. From when we were boys back in the old country."

"I'm pleased to meet you, John." Burnett held his hand out to shake, but he sure didn't look too pleased and he didn't sound it either. Johnny eyed him thoughtfully. The man was tense now—certainly different from how he'd seemed when Johnny had entered the room. And although he was all smiles, the smiles never reached his eyes. Johnny glanced at Guthrie to see if he reacted to Burnett's tone, but his father was busy opening a new bottle of Scotch.

Burnett gave an oily smile. "I must say it's quite a surprise to find you here, John, after all those years with no word of you. It was as if you'd disappeared off the face of the earth."

Judging from the tone of Burnett's voice, he was wishing that had been the case.

Burnett rubbed at his beard. "So I dare say your father has told you lots of tales about the old days in Scotland. He and I go way back. We grew up together—partners in crime, you might say! He must have told you about me."

Johnny hesitated as he searched his memory, but then shook his head. "No, I don't think I recall him mentioning you, but I ain't been home that long."

Burnett raised an eyebrow. "Ain't? Oh my, I can tell that you weren't raised by your father! That sort of casual language wouldn't have been allowed in the Laird's home, would it, Guthrie?"

Johnny frowned. What the hell was the man talking about? What was wrong with saying ain't? And what was a laird? With a shrug, he gestured vaguely at his dusty clothes. "If you'll excuse me, I think I should go wash up before dinner. I'll catch up with you later."

Guthrie nodded, smiling broadly. "Aye, that's grand, Johnny. Ramsey will be staying for a few days, won't you, Ramsey? You'll be able to get acquainted over dinner."

He sure seemed happy to see his old friend. He was like a dog with two tails, and didn't even wait for Johnny to leave the room before he was talking about old times they'd known. And Burnett kept slapping him on the back and laughing at everything the old man said, like it was the best joke he'd ever heard.

Johnny left Guthrie to swap stories with the man, and headed off to wash the worst of the dust off himself before stretching out on his bed with a heavy sigh. It looked as if it was going to be a trying few days.

He was dozing when footsteps along the passageway jerked him awake. He'd recognize that measured tread anywhere. The footsteps paused at his door and then there was a short double rap on it.

"Yeah, come on in, Harvard."

Guy pushed open the door and came in, smiling in a kind of embarrassed way. "How did you know it was me?"

Johnny looked at him through half-closed eyes. "I recognize how you walk. Everyone walks different." He paused. "You met Guthrie's old friend yet?"

Guy nodded, but slowly, like he was thinking real hard about something. "Yes." He hesitated, chewing on his lip. "I met him just now. He seems very full of bonhomie."

Johnny shook his head. "What the hell is bonnomy?"

His brother shrugged. "Full of free and easy manners; cordial benevolence, if you like. It's a French word."

Johnny grunted. "Damned French. Arrogant sons of bitches."

Guy frowned before nodding. "Ah, yes. They ruled Mexico for a while. You obviously don't hold them in high esteem."

Johnny pushed himself into a sitting position and glared. "If that's a fancy way of saying I don't think much of them, you're right. They were real bastards. And they used to execute their prisoners of war. Let's just say they weren't the friendliest people."

Guy grinned. "The master of understatement, that's my brother."

Johnny rolled his eyes. Why couldn't Guy just act normal? Talk normal. He sighed. "So, what d'you think of Burnett?"

Guy stood at the window and rolled his head from side to side as if to ease a crick in his neck. "I have to say that I would rather spend an hour with him than a day."

Johnny laughed. Good old Harvard. He did have a certain way of saying some things. Sounded real fancy, but he managed to hit the nail on the head. "Yeah. He sure is full of himself, ain't he?"

Guy stared out of the window, frowning. "He says he knew me when I was young, but I don't recall ever meeting him. However, Father seems very pleased to see him."

Johnny inclined his head. That was true enough. Trouble was, the old man seemed to have lousy judgment when it came to friends. Look at those damn ranchers, Carter and Dixon, who his father called friends. Look what bastards they turned out to be. Hell, what about Donovan! Johnny had had to shoot that son of a bitch for pulling a gun on his old man. "So you don't think too much of Burnett then?"

"I don't know." Guy turned away from the window, with a

shrug. "He's probably fine, just not to my taste. I thought he was rather pompous. He certainly enjoys the sound of his own voice. But it's nice for our father to see his friends and have the opportunity to talk about old times."

"Nice?" Johnny raised an eyebrow, trying to think of old friends he'd like to meet. But then there were only one or maybe two people he'd call friends. "I guess. But keep him out of my way. I thought he was full of shit."

Guy grinned. "You really are a cynic, aren't you? OK. I will endeavor to ensure that he doesn't bother you." He paused and shook his head slowly. "It was strange though, when I met him, he seemed very surprised to find me here. And he assumed I was just visiting. He said he had believed I was going to pursue a career in business back in Boston. He looked almost put out to find that I was a permanent fixture here."

Johnny narrowed his eyes and shot his brother a sharp look. So Burnett had reacted the same way with Guy . . . "He was like that with me too. It was almost as if he was pissed to find out I was even alive." Johnny hauled himself off the bed. Yeah, there was something odd about Burnett. The man was after something. The only question was what? "You know, I reckon we should keep an eye on him. I don't trust him an inch."

Guy raised an eyebrow. "That's nothing new—you never trust anyone! But I have to admit, that on this occasion, I am inclined to agree with you." He turned toward the door. "I'll see you later. It might turn into an interesting evening."

Johnny wanted a drink. He padded down the stairs and paused near the living room. Damn! Burnett and Guthrie were still in there, knocking back whiskey like there was no tomorrow. Seemed they hadn't moved since he'd left them earlier. Mierda. He either had to put up with Burnett or go without. Maybe Harvard had a bottle in his room . . . He turned to head back upstairs when the old man spotted him. Waved a bottle at him, like he'd already had more whiskey than was good for him.

"Come on in and join us, Johnny. Whiskey? Tequila?"

Guthrie was full of that damned French bonnomy too. He'd definitely had too much to drink.

Burnett looked across the room, his eyes meeting Johnny's for just a second before glancing away, an odd expression on his face. Kind of resentful. And that made no sense. Wasn't like he knew about Johnny's past, about Fierro. All Burnett knew was that Guthrie's long-lost son was back home. A good friend would be pleased. So, maybe Burnett wasn't as good a friend as Guthrie thought. Wouldn't do no harm to sit awhile and listen to them talk. Maybe it would give him an idea of what Burnett was up to.

Johnny forced a smile. "Yeah, sure. I'll have a tequila."

Burnett laughed like Johnny had made a great joke. "Tequila! You don't drink that rotgut, do you? Guthrie, you're falling down on the job! It seems to me you should be educating him better, teaching him to appreciate Scotch and the finest malts. The boy obviously needs your good influence. Gabriela can't have brought him up right."

Johnny gritted his teeth and shoved his hands down in his belt. Burnett was lucky he didn't get a fist in the face for that. Nobody, but nobody, was going to criticize his mother. And what was wrong with tequila, anyhow? Fucking gringo.

Guthrie laughed. "Nothing wrong with this tequila, Ramsey. It's good stuff, and growing up around the border, it's hardly surprising that Johnny has a taste for tequila, is it, son?"

"The border?" Ramsey Burnett's lip curled. "That's rough territory. There are a lot of bad characters down there. The sort of men who should be locked up behind bars. Or hanged. Gunfighters, desperados, all sorts."

Johnny bit down hard on his lip. He wasn't gonna rise to this.

Say nothing. Just let the man talk. Seemed to be what he did best. He'd bet that Burnett would be good at letting other people do his work and then taking the credit while he talked and talked. Johnny glanced at Guthrie. His father had turned an unpleasant sort of red, like he didn't know what to say.

"When your father and I first arrived here from Scotland with my cousin Euan, we did any work we could find, and we even worked for a time as bounty hunters to raise extra money. That was one of our more rewarding jobs. We enjoyed hunting down law breakers. We made sure they were taken in front of a judge sharpish and then dealt with in the right manner. That's what we did with people like that, wasn't it, Guthrie?"

All of a sudden the old man seemed to find the contents of his glass real interesting and avoided meeting Johnny's eyes. But the tips of his ears were red too. Always a sign that Guthrie felt awkward.

Burnett took a swift swig of his drink. "So, Johnny, this place must seem like heaven to you, after growing up in those border towns. Filthy hellholes from what I've seen of them. What line of work were you in when Guthrie found you?"

Johnny tilted his head and eyed Burnett thoughtfully. What would Burnett say if he told him that he'd killed a guard and escaped from a Mexican jail before coming home? It was tempting, if only to see the man's reaction. Yeah, real tempting. Too tempting.

"Johnny had done some droving, some ranch work." His father sounded strained.

Ranch work. Johnny choked on the tequila and started coughing. Pretty much all of the ranch work he'd done was running range wars. And trust the old man to spoil a golden opportunity to shock Burnett.

The old man smiled thinly. "And Johnny's excellent with horses, he's got a great gift for that. He can ride anything and break anything. He's turning into a fine rancher."

Johnny looked at Guthrie, met his eyes. Could see the silent appeal not to say what he'd been doing before he came home. So, the old man was ashamed. No surprises there. And although he'd always suspected his father was ashamed of him, this pretty much proved it. And Guthrie didn't want his oldest friend to find out the truth about his long-lost son. Because people like Johnny should be behind bars or hanged. Maybe they were right. But leastways he was honest, not like fucking Ramsey Burnett. Yeah, there was something about the man that screamed that he shouldn't be trusted.

Burnett laughed. "No business experience then, but I guess that can come with time. Even so, this must be a bit different from life around the border, eh, Johnny?" He raised his glass, and smiled like Johnny was his oldest friend. "Ever see any gunfights down there? From what I hear the area is teeming with desperados, men like Panchez, and that Johnny Fierro people talk about. Your father and I had no time for men like that. Only good for hanging, aren't they, Guthrie? That's what you always said, isn't it? Oh the tales I could tell you, Johnny, about your old father."

Johnny tilted his head. It was kind of interesting to hear what his old man had thought of gunfighters, back when he was a bounty hunter. And kind of revealing that his father had never told him that he'd worked as a bounty hunter—that was obviously something he hadn't wanted Johnny to know about. "Only good for hanging? Is that what he used to say, Ramsey? What else did Guthrie used to say when he was a bounty hunter?" Johnny glanced at Guthrie, who was shuffling his feet and fiddling with the bottle. "I'd be real interested to hear what else he thought."

"That was a long time ago." Guthrie sounded strange, like he'd got something stuck in his mouth. Like his foot. "People's views change over time. We gain a new perspective on things."

Johnny narrowed his eyes. Yeah, the old man was wriggling like a fat, juicy worm on a hook. He was sweating, too—there was a sheen across his forehead. Guthrie took his handkerchief out, and mopped at his brow. Yep. He was real uncomfortable. Johnny could sense the tension in his father. Hell, it was coming off the man like waves crashing on a beach. Maybe he could play all of this out to his advantage.

Johnny smiled, enjoying the rush of power. He loved having an edge and he figured he'd just gotten the edge over Guthrie. And once he got the edge over Ramsey Burnett, life would be pretty much perfect.

The sound of Guy's footsteps ruined the moment. "Good evening, gentlemen, I thought it might be time for an aperitif."

Guy was all gussied up for dinner but somehow managed to look comfortable in his fancy clothes while he smiled around like there was no place he'd rather be. How the hell did Guy do that? Always looked relaxed, like he hadn't a care in the world. But then, maybe he hadn't. And always smiled like he meant it. But maybe he did. Like he always knew how to pass the time of day with the local ranchers when Johnny couldn't think of a single thing to say to them.

"You want a drink, Harvard?"

Guy grinned. "That was the general intention. I wouldn't say no to a small Scotch." He glanced at the two older men. "Actually, no, on second thought, I'll join you in a tequila."

Johnny didn't flinch. He knew Guy couldn't stand the stuff. Instead he just nodded and turned to pour Guy the drink. Good old Harvard, must have sensed the mood, or Johnny's mood, or maybe the crafty devil had been on the stairs listening . . .

"Don't tell me you drink that rotgut too, Guy." Burnett flashed another oily smile.

"Certainly. Cheers, gentlemen." Guy raised his glass to

Burnett, but as he turned to sit on the couch he winked at Johnny.

"Are we getting any dinner tonight?" Guthrie sounded tetchy. But then maybe he just wanted to move the talk onto matters away from the border.

"Don't be so impatient." Peggy stood in the doorway, red-faced, with her hands on her hips. "Dinner's ready if you'd all like to come and sit down."

The evening didn't get any better. He had to sit next to Burnett while the old coot droned on. Peggy bustled around like she was trying to make up for dinner being overcooked and late. She was certainly trying hard because she laughed at all Burnett's bad jokes and then asked him how long he was staying. "We're having a party tomorrow. Uncle Guthrie hosts one every year. He calls it our 'noblesse oblige' night." She stumbled slightly over the words and giggled. "It would be an opportunity for you to meet some of our friends."

Shit. He'd forgotten the damn party. And friends? That was a joke. An evening for the ranch workers and their families, and maybe a few folks from town, but most of the old man's rancher friends wouldn't be coming because they wanted to avoid contact with Fierro. Probably afraid they might catch something. Or worried that he'd attack their daughters. Like he'd be interested in their dull daughters. He'd take the girls at the bordello any day over all the local girls. They were far more fun and knew just how to please a man.

He dragged his mind back to listen to Guy asking Burnett for stories about when Guthrie was a boy in Scotland. The man needed no encouragement. He started to relate all sorts of improbable tales about their boyhood, most of which seemed to involve them stalking deer or catching huge fish. "My family lived on the Laird's estate. My father was the factor there, like his father before him. But thanks to the generosity and benevolence of Guthrie's father, I was allowed to share Guthrie's tutor. I used to go up to the big house for lessons with Guthrie. Of course, my family was very ordinary, we were nothing like as rich and grand as his."

Was it his imagination, or was there a hint of resentment in Burnett's words? Johnny shot Guy a quick glance, but his brother was listening attentively, and smiling encouragingly at their visitor.

"Ramsey . . ." Guthrie flushed as if not wanting the stories to continue.

"Oh, hush, Guthrie. It's only natural that your boys would want to hear about your roots. Surely you've told them how imposing your home was? Your father's clan has castles spread right across Scotland, boys. And surely, Guthrie, you've told them how your mother was an English lady with a title of her own? Her family was a very old one, with a distinguished lineage. They were from the southwest of England and one of the oldest families in the country. Oh yes, boys, she was a grand lady, so poised and full of airs and graces. Mind you, Guy, I daresay you met lots of ladies in the circles you moved in when you lived in Boston with your aunt and uncle. After all, your mother was one of the Boston Eliots, was she not?"

Guy inclined his head. "Yes, she was. And my uncle was connected to the Appletons."

Burnett glanced at Johnny. "Yes, I remember Guy's mother well. She was an exceptionally beautiful and cultured lady. Your brother has an impressive lineage, like your paternal grandparents. What a pity, Johnny, that you weren't able to enjoy the same social benefits as your brother. If I remember correctly, I don't believe that your mother was well connected. But maybe my memory is playing tricks on me."

Johnny sighed softly. Like the son of a bitch didn't know that Johnny's mother had been a half-breed.

Burnett took a sip of his wine. "Yes, a great pity. But perhaps the border territory has more attractions than I remember."

Guthrie's face turned a mottled red. He coughed and stretched to pick up the decanter. "More wine, Ramsey?"

Johnny pushed his chair away with a clatter. "If you don't mind, I got to go to town. I promised the sheriff I'd help him with something tonight." It was a lie, but he couldn't stand another minute of sitting next to this bastard, and ignoring his father's tight-lipped face, he headed out for some fresh air.

He breathed in deeply, trying to clear his head. Either Guthrie had a whole bunch of really shit friends, or Burnett had changed some over the years. People did change . . .

Damn it, maybe the best thing was to go into town and have an evening away from all of this crap. He could ride in to see Stoney, seeing as how he'd said he had to help the sheriff. Even better, he could visit Delice and the girls. He grinned. Yeah, that would make for a better evening than watching his old man and Burnett get drunk.

CHAPTER TWO

Darkness was rolling in as Johnny rode to town and he could smell the wood smoke long before he saw the buildings. He shivered and hunched down into his jacket. God only knew what the winters would be like in these parts—damn cold most likely. Maybe he should have stayed south, and then he wouldn't have to put up with oily shits like Burnett. Time was he'd have shot the man for insulting his mother . . .

He sighed. Soft. That was the problem. He was getting too damn soft.

He tethered Pistol and went in search of Stoney, but the sheriff's office was empty. A fire was laid in the potbellied stove but was unlit. Probably he was out on his rounds. Johnny swung on his heel and headed down the street to the bordello. The place wouldn't be busy so he'd have a choice of the girls. He grinned. Maybe Burnett had done him a favor after all.

He pushed open the heavy door and paused to scan the room. The girls were huddled together in a cloud of lace petticoats, deep in conversation. There were only a couple of customers at the far side of the room, too intent on fondling the girls perched on their knees to notice Johnny's entry.

Sadie squealed with delight and rushed to Johnny's side, pawing at him as she tried to drape herself across him. "Oh my, you do a body a power of good! And I thought we was going to have a dull evening."

Johnny grinned and batted her hand away. "Hey, Sadie, let a

fellow have a drink first." He quirked an eyebrow. "Anyhow, I thought Jeb Lutz came in midweek. Isn't this his night? He'll be pissed if you ain't free for him."

Sadie pouted and tossed her thick, wavy hair. "That's why we should get up them stairs now. Before he gets here." She tugged at Johnny's arm. "Come on."

He shook his head. "Now, that ain't fair to poor Jeb. Just because he don't bathe too often."

She stamped her foot and scowled. "Don't fun with me. You know I hate . . ."

"Sadie!" Delice's voice cut across the girl. "We do not discuss our customers. You are well aware of that rule. Now, run along and leave Johnny alone."

Johnny turned to her with a broad smile and swept his hat off with a flourish before bowing low. "Ma'am."

Delice rolled her eyes. "We don't often see you in here midweek." She gestured toward his usual table. "I'll get you a tequila."

He settled himself in the corner and watched as she reached for a bottle of the good tequila from under the bar, rather than the cheap stuff. She set the bottle and a glass in front of him and pulled up a chair for herself.

She eyed him curiously. "So what brings you into town this evening? You're normally firmly ensconced at the ranch during the week."

He huffed out a breath as he poured himself a generous measure. "Avoiding an old friend of my father's. I couldn't stand another minute of his company. Figured I'd shoot him if I had to listen to him any longer."

"So you walked out? I'll bet that went down well!" She shook her head at him, like he was some dumb kid. "For heaven's sake, haven't you realized by now that it's exactly that sort of behavior which annoys your father and causes trouble between the pair of you? Couldn't you have just put up with it for one evening? Surely the man wasn't that bad?"

Johnny bowed his head and pushed the glass in circles before glancing back at her. "He insulted my mother. It seems I ain't good enough for the likes of him."

She held his gaze. "And I'm guessing your father didn't say anything to this?"

Johnny shrugged. "Oh he was hitting the bottle pretty good. And he was all excited to see his old friend. Reckon he didn't even notice." Johnny stared down into the contents of his glass. Trouble was his father had noticed every single jibe. The man had become more red-faced and tongue-tied. Yeah, his father had known exactly what Burnett meant and not said a damn thing. So that showed what he thought of his younger son.

He swallowed hard, he didn't want to think of that. He forced a smile. "So, what's been happening? You been busy in here?"

She eyed him thoughtfully, and didn't say anything for a couple of beats. She sighed softly and then shrugged. "Oh, the usual customers. Miners and cowpokes. Although, we did have some excitement yesterday. I threw out a fellow who was cheating at faro."

Johnny grinned and fumbled in his pocket for a smoke. "Cheating? I thought that was what the house did. And I reckon it's a lot easier for the house to cheat than the gamblers."

Delice narrowed her eyes. "You really do like to live dangerously, don't you? Our faro games are on the square. We do not use gaffed boxes."

Johnny's smile broadened. He couldn't resist poking the bear. "You sure about that? Because I been around and from what I've seen, pretty much all places rig the box. You can buy them ready rigged, I heard. And as for the dealers . . ."

"I'll have you know that I run an honest establishment, and I do not employ crooked dealers," she hissed. She pursed her lips suddenly and sighed, her irritation fading as fast as it had come. "You devil! You already know that, don't you?"

He raised his glass to her in a mock toast. "Yep. I watched the dealers when I first started coming in. I know you deal a straight game in here—the only place in town that does, I reckon. But I don't get a rise out of you so often I could turn this chance down."

She glared, but her lips twitched, and he leaned back in his chair enjoying her reaction.

He took a drag on his cigarette and blew a perfect smoke ring. He grinned at her. "So tell me, how was the fellow cheating?"

She shrugged. "Sleight of hand. He was good, but not good enough. Not much gets past me. He took his game to the saloon across the street and, from what I hear, that's where his luck ran out."

Johnny raised an eyebrow. "You mean he got out-cheated? There's a bunch of highbinders in that place."

She nodded. "There certainly are—I won't have them in here! But I'll admit I was rather pleased when I heard he'd been fleeced. He owes money to a few people by all accounts. But he was quite a braggart. He was telling everyone that he's about to get rich. Oh, and this will interest you—he claims he's been given a share of one of the local ranches. Can you imagine that?"

Johnny laughed. "Given a share of a ranch? Just like that? It's crazy. Maybe he's inherited something. Although, I can't think of anyone who's up and died lately. Did he say where this ranch was?"

Delice shook her head slowly. "No, not that I heard. I have to say that it all sounded like idle boasts to me. He was the kind of man who liked the sound of his own voice."

Johnny tensed. A braggart? A big talker? He looked at her

27

uneasily. "What did this fellow look like?"

She frowned. "He was maybe in his fifties. Heavily built, bearded . . ."

Johnny jerked forward, jolting the table and splashing his drink across the polished surface "A red beard? And not American?"

"Yes, that's him." She sucked in a ragged breath. "Don't tell me that this man is your father's visitor?"

He nodded slowly. "It sure sounds like him. But what the hell does he mean, that he's been given a share of a ranch? He didn't say nothing about being given anything around here when he was droning on over dinner." Mierda. The ghost of a thought was forming. But no! Surely not? He leaned forward. "You don't think . . . I mean . . . My old man can't give him a share of Sinclair, can he? I thought it was all tied up legal."

Delice's eyes widened. "Surely your father wouldn't have done that? I would imagine he's far too shrewd to do anything so reckless." She chewed on her lip. "As to whether it's all tied up legally, I guess it depends on the terms of your partnership agreement. I suppose he could have given him a piece of his own share, but again, depending on the terms, he might not be able to do even that without your permission."

"If he's given him something, he can damn well take it back. He ain't giving that piece of shit nothing," Johnny snapped.

Delice sighed. "It might not even be the same man. Although it certainly sounds as if . . ." She hesitated. "But even if it is, it might be another ranch he's talking about. Or, much more likely, it's probably just idle talk because he owes money and he was trying to keep the wolves at bay."

"I don't know. I got the impression he'd come here to see my old man, not for any other business." Johnny ground out his cigarette, wishing it was his heel in Burnett's smug face. Should have known everything was too good to last. Nothing ever lasted. But he'd shoot Burnett before he'd let him have a piece of the Sinclair spread. Nobody took anything from Fierro. And if Guthrie Sinclair tried it, Fierro would shoot him too.

"Don't go storming back, losing your temper. That really won't help matters." Her calm voice broke into his thoughts.

He smiled thinly. "Oh, don't worry, I won't be losing my temper. I'll be totally in control. I'm always in control. Of everything."

They locked eyes, and she let out a whisper of a sigh. "Maybe it would be a good idea if you spoke with Stoney before you charge back looking for a fight. I believe he intervened to stop them shooting the man. But when you get home . . ." She hesitated, concern showing in her eyes. "You'd been getting along better with your father lately, and it would be a shame to jeopardize that. Just don't do anything foolish, honey."

Johnny laughed, but there was no mirth in it. "But you said yourself, I like living dangerously." He took a final swig of tequila and got to his feet. "Looks like the girls won't have the pleasure of my company this evening after all. I'm off to see Stoney."

She nodded. "And don't forget. Don't rush in assuming the worst and jumping to hasty conclusions. Try to stay calm."

He didn't reply, but gave her a mock salute and headed back into the street.

He strode to Stoney's office, hoping the sheriff would be back from his rounds. Peering through the grimy window, he could see Stoney lounging back in his chair, sipping from a steaming mug.

Johnny pushed open the door and raised a hand in greeting. Stoney frowned. "Johnny. What you doing in town tonight? We don't usually see you midweek."

Johnny bit back a grunt of irritation. Why did everyone think he could only find his way to town on the weekend? "How you doing, Stoney? Everything quiet in town?"

The sheriff nodded and raised his mug. "If you want a cup of coffee, help yourself."

Johnny shook his head. "No thanks. I wanted to ask you about some gambler you had trouble with yesterday. What can you tell me about him?"

Stoney surveyed Johnny through narrowed eyes. "Is that why you're here? To ask about some drifter? And exactly what is it that makes you so interested in this gambler that you came into town midweek to ask about him?"

Johnny shook his head, he was damned if he'd give too much information to Stoney. Wasn't his business. "I didn't come to town to ask about him. But I heard mention of trouble and wondered what it was all about."

Stoney eyed him suspiciously. "You sure like to play your cards close to your chest."

Johnny rolled his eyes. "When you're done griping, tell me about this gambler."

Stoney leaned back in his chair and put his feet up on his desk. Then he took out a large knife and started cleaning under his fingernails.

Johnny tapped his thigh with his fingers, right by his gun. He saw Stoney swallow hard but the sheriff kept cleaning his nails. "Damn it, Stoney, just tell me about the fellow. Did you get his name?"

Stoney huffed in a breath and very slowly laid the knife down on his desk. "And, I'll ask again, why do you want to know?"

Johnny leaned across the desk, so he was just inches from the sheriff. Stoney's coffee sloshed over the side of the mug, soaking a pile of wanted posters. The sheriff's mouth tightened.

"I don't reckon it's any of your business." Johnny spoke softly, knowing that Stoney would sense the menace.

Stoney swallowed again but gritted his teeth. "Don't try

intimidating me, Fierro. It won't work." He narrowed his eyes. "I reckon, seeing as how I'm the sheriff, it is my business when a man like you starts fishing around. For all I know you're figuring on calling him out."

Very slowly, Johnny stepped back. "I ain't planning on doing that, tempting as it may be."

Stoney folded his arms. "So, I'll ask again. Exactly what is your business with that man?"

Johnny threw his hands in the air, it would be quicker to give in. "I think he might be a friend of my old man's. He turned up at our place today, and it sure sounds like the same fellow. I reckon he's after something, and I'm trying to figure out what the hell he's up to. You happy now?"

Stoney grinned. "Now that wasn't so difficult, was it?"

Johnny ground his teeth. "Just get on with it."

"He got thrown out of the bordello after cheating at faro. You know what Delice is like, she sure wasn't standing for that. She gave him hell. Anyway, because she threw him out, he moved his game to the saloon on the other side of the street. Way I heard it, he got into a game of poker and was dealing off the bottom of the deck. But a couple of the boys decided to fleece him and outdid him at his own game. It took him a while to figure what they were up to and by the end of it, he was giving out markers and owed a lot of money. I figured I'd best get him out of there before they killed him."

Johnny shrugged. "Why bother? I'd have let 'em shoot him."

Stoney leaned back in his chair, smiling smugly. "That's why I'm the sheriff and you're not."

"Did you get his name?"

Stoney nodded. "Yep, course I got it. He told me he was going to settle all his debts because he'd be staying in these parts. Said he was cut in for a piece of a ranch." Stoney snorted, like he hadn't believed a word of it. "I didn't set much store by

31

anything he said. You know the type—a double-dealing con man. But his name? He said it was Burnett."

"Mierda!" Johnny's fists tightened. "That's the bastard."

Stoney rubbed his chin. "Well, *if* he's to be believed, he's been promised a share in a ranch. Or a job as foreman or something. The story varied a fair bit with each telling. But he wouldn't say which ranch when we asked. He was playing that close to his chest. So maybe your place, or someone else's. But to be honest, I figured he was full of bullshit and big talk."

Johnny grunted. "He ain't getting a share of Sinclair. Over my dead body. I'll fucking kill him first."

Stoney tensed. "Johnny, you listen, and you listen good. If you do anything to break the law, I'll throw you in my jail. That's a promise. It ain't one law for you and one for everyone else."

Johnny held his gaze. He bit back the words that sprang to mind, that Stoney wasn't a good enough gun to arrest him. Hell, it would take more than one lawman to take him. Because Fierro would go down fighting.

Stoney huffed out a sigh. "But I tell you what I will do. I'll send some wires and see what I can find out about this high-binder, because my gut tells me he'll have left a trail behind him, and I'll bet my badge there's some paper out on him somewhere. Leave it with me. And in the meanwhile, don't piss me off. I really don't want to throw you in a cell." He stumbled to his feet, wincing and rubbing his back. "Dang, but my back's aching—that's a sure sign the weather's on the turn. So, Johnny, have we got a deal?"

Johnny nodded. It was easier to play along with Stoney on this. But if Burnett pushed him, he'd kill him. "Yeah, sure, Stoney. If you can check him out, I'd appreciate it. I'll catch up with you later."

Stoney gave him a hard-eyed stare but Johnny slipped out of

the door with a casual wave before the sheriff could say anything.

He hurried over to Pistol and stepped into the saddle. He spurred the horse into a lope and rode out of town.

He could feel his blood surging through him. His fists were clenched tight around his reins and right now he had a powerful urge to smash one into somebody's face and he didn't much care whether it was Guthrie or Burnett. If Burnett was telling the truth, what the hell had Guthrie been doing offering a bastard like that a piece of their ranch or even a job? Could he do that? And if he'd offered him a share, could Guthrie welsh on the deal with him and Guy? Or had he done it some time ago and never told them? And if so, had Guthrie gone through with the deal?

The only thing Fierro had ever owned looked like it could be taken away. But hell, they'd signed an agreement. In front of a lawyer and all. Wasn't that agreement final? Maybe Guthrie couldn't take it away.

His mouth and throat were dry with the heat of the anger rising inside him, threatening to take over. He'd never owned anything 'til now. He'd kill to keep this land. And no son of a bitch like Ramsey Burnett was going to get a piece of what was rightfully Fierro's. He'd taken a bullet in the back fighting for this land. No way was Burnett going to waltz on in and have a piece without shedding a drop of blood for it.

Johnny gritted his teeth. Even so, his instincts had been right, he'd known that Burnett was after something, right from the start. But to find out that Burnett probably had his eye on Sinclair was too much. Why hadn't Guthrie come clean with him and Guy earlier in the day? Unless he was planning on springing it on them? Was Guthrie that devious?

Johnny slowed Pistol to a walk. Somehow, deep down, he felt his father wasn't that tricky. The man had seemed genuinely surprised to see Burnett. Maybe Delice was right and Burnett had invented the story . . . And Stoney had said that the story had changed with each telling. Oh shit, the only way to find out was to have it out with Guthrie. And he wanted to be calmer when he did that. He needed to be in control.

He finished the journey home at an easy lope. He unsaddled Pistol and turned him out into the corral. Johnny leaned over the corral fence, taking deep breaths. The night air was clear and the sky looked like it was painted with a million glittering stars. The moon was rising full and colored a brilliant orange, casting light over his mountain, making it stand out in sharp relief against the dark sky.

This was his land and nobody was gonna take it away from him. He straightened up and with measured steps walked towards the hacienda. He felt calm now, in control again. He smiled. Yeah, he was ready to do battle with Guthrie Sinclair and fight for what was his.

CHAPTER THREE

His spurs jingled. Shit, that would never do. He didn't want anyone to hear his approach. He stopped short of the studded oak door of the hacienda. Leaning down, he slipped the spurs off his boots and shoved them down behind one of the clay pots planted with Peggy's flowers. Usually he thought the flowerpots were damn stupid, but just this once they were useful.

The drapes were partially drawn but light flickered from the lamps in the living room. Moving into the shadows, he could just glimpse Guy and Guthrie sitting with drinks in their hands. Guy was hunched over, squatting on a low stool by the fire, and Guthrie was leaning back on the couch, waving his glass around as he talked. The old man looked comfortable. Johnny smiled. He was going to change all that. Nobody messed with Fierro. And there was no way on God's green earth that Fierro was going to be in partnership with a piece of shit like Burnett.

It wasn't like Fierro had gone begging Guthrie for a share. It had been offered and he'd signed the damn partnership agreement between the three of them, figuring that was final. He'd always thought he could choose to walk away but he couldn't be kicked out. And he'd figured the terms of partnership meant it couldn't be changed without them all having an equal say. Certainly not to include a bastard like Burnett. Could he have been wrong? Harvard would know. His brother seemed to know the answer to just about everything.

The sound of laughter dragged his attention back to the living room. Both of them were laughing at something. Looking relaxed, easy in each other's company, not knowing he watched from the shadows. Sometimes it felt like that was how he'd passed his life—always on the outside. Watching families play and eat together when he was a child, peering into their homes. Watching his mother as she fucked and bucked under a never-ending stream of strangers. Watching men through saloon doors. And now, here he was, watching again. Watching and planning his next move. Nothing changed. He used a different name now. But he wasn't any different.

He turned away, silent as a snake before it strikes. He was good at going unheard. It was one of his talents. And it always gave him the edge he craved. He eased the handle down on the heavy door, pausing halfway through the motion to avoid the creak it made if pushed in one swift movement. Must be losing his touch. He'd oiled the hinges just days before and forgotten the damn handle. He slipped into the house, softly pushing the door closed behind him. He padded across the hall and stood at the door. They still didn't notice him. Too busy drinking and jawing. Talking about the damn party.

"Thought you'd be telling Harvard about all those things you used to do when you was a bounty hunter."

Guthrie jerked forward, spilling his drink down his shirt, and Harvard almost fell off the stool he was perched on.

"Do you have to creep around like that?" The old man sounded real pissed. "You made me jump out of my skin."

Johnny shrugged. "Not my fault if you two are so busy jawing you didn't hear me come in."

His father gave him one of those looks. The kind that said he didn't believe a word of it. "You always do that. You creep around the place and I never hear you coming. One of these days you'll give me a heart attack."

"That would be a real shame. 'Specially when you haven't

told me all your stories about when you was a bounty hunter. And about all those gunfighters you couldn't wait to hang. I'm real excited about hearing those stories. What's that word of yours, Harvard? Agog? That's it. I'm all agog."

The old man narrowed his eyes. "That's not amusing, Johnny."

Johnny glanced at the floor, kicking at the rug before giving Guthrie a long hard stare. "Well, I guess the men you hanged didn't think you were amusing either. Hang many of them, did you? Just gunfighters? Or weren't you that choosy?"

"Johnny . . ." Guy's voice was tight and cold. Icy. Hell, it was enough to make a man feel chilled. "I don't feel that this is the time to discuss that. Why don't you come and sit down and help us plan the entertainment for tomorrow evening?"

Johnny laughed softly. "Sorry, Harvard, but I won't be joining the party tomorrow. I don't like people at the best of times, and I sure don't like a crowd of them all together. No, I'm much more interested in Guthrie and his old friend Burnett." He flexed his fingers and tapped a rhythm against his holster. "The charming Ramsey Burnett. Must have been a very good friend, the way you welcomed him today." He locked eyes with his father. "Yep. You were real pleased to see him. Expecting him, were you?"

Guthrie stared back, his brow furrowed, like he was puzzled. "No, Johnny, I was not expecting him. But it's always nice to see old friends, particularly ones I grew up with. I've known him since childhood and it's been a good few years since we saw each other last. We have lots to catch up on."

"Notice you didn't tell him what I used to do for my living. Droving? Ranch work? Pretty much the only ranch work I'd ever done was running range wars and we both know it."

Guy sighed. So soft it was almost a whisper. Shook his head, like he thought Johnny was being a damn fool. Maybe when he knew about the old man cutting Burnett in for a share of the ranch, he wouldn't be so calm.

Guthrie leaned forward on the couch. Looked pretty riled up now. The pulse was going in the side of his head. Same as it always did when he got mad. "No, I didn't tell Ramsey what you used to do for a living. As we were about to sit down for a family meal, it did not seem an appropriate time to do so. If you—"

"You ashamed of me? Is that it? Couldn't face telling your old pal that I'm one of those people you liked to see hanged. Hell, even my choice of drink ain't good enough for him. And he had the fucking nerve to criticize my mother for not bringing me up right."

The old man huffed out a sigh. Kind of exaggerated. Like he thought his son was being particularly dumb. "I am not ashamed of you, Johnny. In fact, I can recall at least two occasions when I have told you how proud of you I am. I believe Ramsey meant his remarks in a light-hearted manner which was not supposed to be taken too seriously—"

"Bullshit. He meant every damn word. I saw it in his eyes."

Guthrie snorted. "Oh for heaven's sake, how could you tell that from his eyes?"

Johnny tilted his head to one side and shot his father a cold smile. "How d'you think I stayed alive this long? I can read men. And I can smell bullshit when it's under my nose. And your friend Burnett is full of it."

Guthrie's jaw hardened. "I will not sit here and have you insult my oldest friend."

"Well, your oldest friend owes a lot of money in town. I bet he didn't tell you that. He's a gambler and a cheat."

His father jumped to his feet, moving real fast for a man of his age. "You've got a nerve, John, insulting my friends. You can damn well apologize. You're living with civilized people now—

not dishonest and murderous rabble."

"I ain't apologizing for telling the truth. If you don't believe me, go ask around in town. He was skinning suckers in the Golden Nugget, until they caught on and paid him back in kind. He's as crooked as they come."

"And you believe the word of the sort of people who frequent sordid gambling dens." Guthrie's lip curled.

"Before this degenerates into a fistfight or a free-for-all, can I suggest that you both simmer down." Guy glared at both of them. "Johnny, why don't you pour yourself a cup of coffee and calm down. Now."

Johnny scoffed. "Coffee? Is that the answer, Harvard? That'll make everything all right? You ain't heard nothing yet. The best bit's to come. But, fine, I'll go pour myself a cup of coffee. To keep you happy."

"What do you mean, I haven't heard anything yet?"

Yeah. That had got Guy's attention. He was rubbing his chin, looking puzzled. Johnny picked up the coffee jug, real slow. Poured a cupful. Stirred it slowly. Then stirred it again. Yeah. He'd sure got their attention now. Both of them.

"You sure you weren't expecting a visit from Burnett? You sure there's nothing you want to tell me and Harvard?" He looked at Guthrie. Looking for a flicker of guilt. But his father, although still red-faced from their argument, looked at him blankly.

"Why the hell do you think I was expecting him? If I'd known he was coming, I would have told you both. I had no idea he was coming by. It was only because he was passing this way that he thought he'd drop in. It's what civilized people do when they are traveling close to where old friends live."

Johnny snorted. "This ranch ain't on the way to nowhere! He ain't in the mining business, so he's got no reason to be heading to Elizabethtown. And there's sure as hell nowhere else he could be going around these parts."

Guthrie opened his mouth to say something, but stopped, looking puzzled, like that was something he hadn't thought of. "Well, no, when you put it like that, but the ranch isn't far from the Santa Fe Trail, maybe he has business along there somewhere."

Johnny raised an eyebrow. "If he was going somewhere on business, I reckon he'd have mentioned it. Seems like the man can't keep from talking. He sure as hell likes the sound of his own voice and he's been talking big in town. And if it's gambling he wants, he'd do better down in Santa Fe than Cimarron."

Guthrie glared. "He's not a gambler. I don't know who you've been talking to, but he's a respectable man. And an old friend. Not that you know much about respectable men! Who do you count among your friends? Killers and whores? Anything you've heard in town is rubbish."

"Killers and whores?" Johnny spoke softly. "You really don't think much of me at all, do you?"

His father flushed. "Everyone knows that you spend all your free time in that whorehouse. And if that's where you've heard this gossip, you should know better than to set any store by it."

"Maybe you'd believe Stoney. Seeing as how you don't set any store by all the killers and whores I know."

"Ramsey is a decent man who wouldn't get involved in gambling, and would certainly never cheat. It was probably an innocent game of cards and he got taken by a bunch of swindlers and they're trying to cover their backs by claiming he was cheating." The old man sounded pleased with himself, like he reckoned he'd gotten the better of Fierro.

"And so he traveled here for a visit with an old friend? That's what you're saying?" Johnny stalked across the room.

"What other reason would he have for coming?" Guthrie locked eyes with him.

Johnny paused, just long enough to have them hanging, waiting on his words. "Did you ever offer him a share in this place
or a job here?"

Guy's head jerked up in surprise. He looked even more
surprised when Guthrie nodded slowly. "Not exactly a share as
you put it. But when we first arrived in the States together, we
discussed employment opportunities. We were, as he mentioned,
doing all sorts of jobs to make ends meet while I decided what I
wanted to do in the future. I had a considerable sum of money
to invest in some form of enterprise and considered various options. We did talk in a very broad sense about a possible partnership if I bought a ranch or a farm. As Ramsey mentioned during dinner, his father was the factor on our estate in Scotland.
An estate manager, I suppose you could call it. Ramsey had
been brought up on the estate and was starting to learn about
the business from his father when he, Euan, and I decided to
come to America. As a result Ramsey knows a lot about running big estates, so yes, a deal of some form was a possibility. I
thought he might have something to contribute to the manage-
ment of a big spread like this."

"Like I said, he owes money all over town, and God only
knows where else." Johnny settled himself on the arm of one of
the chairs. Dios, he loved this. Knowing this was his game and
it would play out just as he intended it to. "He ain't here by
chance. He's been telling everyone in town he's getting a piece
of a ranch—and I'll lay money he's thinking of this one. And
hell, let's face it, with the money he owes, he needs it."

Guy jerked forward even as the old man gave another of his
exaggerated sighs. When Guthrie spoke he sounded like he
didn't believe a word of it. "And you believe these tales? It's
probably people trying to get you worked up. They're merely
trying to cause trouble."

Yeah, that figured. Nobody in town could be believed because

Burnett was as pure as the fucking driven snow.

"You just admitted you offered him something—"

Guthrie cut across him. "I said it was discussed, that's all, and then we mentioned it again a few years later but we never formalized anything. It was an idea that we kicked around and it never went further than that. The offer was never made in writing." He stood up, and started pacing around the room. "The second time we discussed it was long before you came home. It was back when Guy seemed to be more interested in staying in Boston and building a future for himself there. I didn't have a segundo at the time and thought maybe Ramsey might have been interested in the job, but he turned the offer down. But I certainly wouldn't have given away a share of the ranch that I have worked so hard to build. It's the sort of foolish thing one considers when one is young. Later on, I realized that the differences in our backgrounds would have made a partnership between myself and Ramsey inappropriate. And he'll understand that there's no question of that particular job being offered now. You two boys are here, and Alonso has been segundo for a good many years and I have no intention of replacing him. He's too good a man to lose."

Johnny ducked his head. His father's voice had the ring of truth. He hadn't expected Burnett and seemed genuinely surprised by the notion that his old friend had come for anything other than a friendly visit. "Well, you'd best tell him the offer ain't on the table no more. Kind of make it plain that the deal's off."

"I said he'd realize that circumstances have changed. If you'd stayed this evening and become acquainted with him, instead of walking out in the middle of dinner, you'd know that he's an honorable man. You need to get to know him," snapped Guthrie.

Dios. Know him? He'd got him pegged already and the man was a slimy piece of shit. Didn't trust him an inch. Him or his fucking bonnomy. He gave Guthrie an icy look. "I had business in town. But you need to set him straight. Because he ain't getting a share of this ranch or a job on it. And whatever you promised him, it ain't yours to give no more." He wished Guy would say something. Agree with him. Back him up. Mierda. Was Guy just going to sit there like he was weighing everything up, before he put in his two cents' worth?

Guy met Johnny's gaze and sighed heavily. "Johnny is right, sir. If it was just a general discussion, it's not binding. It certainly doesn't form any type of contract. And obviously your circumstances have changed substantially since then."

Johnny felt a little of his tension slip away. Harvard had taken his time, but he'd come through finally. But boy, he sure put things in a fancy way. Always sounded good.

"I'm well aware of that, Guy. I will repeat myself," the old man sounded like he was talking through gritted teeth. "Ramsey will realize that things have changed. But I'm sure it had never entered his head to even think about our old discussions of a partnership, or the subsequent job offer when he came by. I dare say he's forgotten all about it. As I said, it was a long time ago."

Johnny managed to stop his mouth dropping open. How the hell had the old man managed to build a successful ranch when he was so useless at reading people? The man was a total sucker, too trusting by a long way. That was his problem. Thought everybody was as honest as him. Unless they were gunfighters . . . Shit, Fierro, don't start thinking like that now.

"I'll speak to Ramsey tomorrow. I'm turning in now. Tomorrow's going to be a long day with the party in the evening. Goodnight, boys." The old man paused in the doorway. "And, Johnny, get to know Ramsey. I'm sure you'll like him and rub along splendidly. He's great company."

Johnny turned and looked at Guy as Guthrie headed off

upstairs. "So, Harvard, what do you make of all this?"

"I confess, I was puzzled as to quite why you were so worked up when you came in, but in the light of your revelations, I can understand it now."

Could Harvard ever answer a question like normal people? Never use one word when he could use ten or twenty. Johnny huffed out a sigh. "So? What d'you make of it all? Him even thinking of offering someone who ain't family, a share of his ranch! Or even offering a fellow who ain't no cattleman, a job as foreman. And don't say nothing about us not being here. Fact is, Harvard, he always knew where you were, but he didn't offer nothing to us until Chavez was breathing down his neck."

Guy raised an eyebrow. "It's what I like about you, Johnny. You always go straight for the jugular."

Johnny frowned. "What the hell are you talking about?"

Guy smiled. "It's your killer instinct. And no, before you start thinking I'm getting at you because you were a gunfighter, what I mean is, you get straight to the point. You don't mince your words." Guy paused, staring down into his glass like he was looking for a silver dollar in the bottom. "You have, of course, hit the nail on the head. Whereas he could be excused for not knowing where you were, he sent me away to live with my mother's family because of the Indian raids when I was a child. But when things quieted down again, he never pressed me to return home. He visited occasionally, and we corresponded, of course, but he seemed content for me to stay in Boston. Even after the war he never made an issue of me coming home, not until the business with Chavez started to simmer. It was only then he became more insistent. I suspect it was more to do with feeling my military experience would be useful to him than any great desire to have me home again."

Johnny bit his lip and shook his head. The old man was stubborn, though. He'd probably hated to admit that he wanted

44

Guy to come home. And God only knew what went on in his head sometimes. Seemed a bit simple at times. All that faith in his fellow man. When everyone knew that most folks were shit. "So, you going to ask him about it?"

Guy laughed, but it was a kind of sad laugh. "Let's just say I don't feel the time is right yet. Or, alternatively, we could just say I'm afraid of the answer I'll get. But you can sleep easy tonight. Our partnership agreement is binding and he can't give anything away and neither can he offer jobs to people without our consent. That's what you're really worried about, isn't it?"

Johnny grinned. His brother was no fool. "Well, I have to admit that I was starting to wonder if it was all nice and tight and legal. After all, you know how I like to stay on the right side of the law."

At least Guy laughed then like he meant it. "Yes. I know! And Burnett? What do we make of him?"

Johnny poured himself a shot of tequila and raised his glass. "What do we make of him? Hell, Harvard, we don't trust him an inch."

CHAPTER FOUR

No matter how hard he tried to make himself scarce, Peggy kept tracking him down to do odd jobs to get the place ready for the damn party. He thought he'd be safe in the barn or out in the corral but she always managed to find him.

She had him draping long pieces of colored cloth around the place. Called it bunning or bunting or something like that. He felt like he'd spent the day teetering at the top of ladders, while she issued orders from the ground clutching a list of jobs she wanted doing. "No, Johnny, not like that. I want it in cascades and swags." What in hell's name were swags anyhow? Do this. Do that. He'd be glad when the damn thing was over.

He'd even tried to sneak off to town. He figured he could go and see Delice and the girls and tell Delice about his talk with his old man the previous evening, but Peggy had spotted him and dragged him out of the barn by his arm. "You're not showing any interest in this evening. Aren't you looking forward to it?"

"I told you, I ain't coming. No way am I spending an evening with a load of folks I don't want to talk to, and a band playing that godawful music. Sounds like a catfight."

"But you've got to come, Johnny." Shit, any second she'd burst into tears and that would be his fault too. "All my friends want to dance with you." Her lower lip trembled but it wasn't going to work.

"I don't dance." A picture of all Peggy's friends floated in front of him. Dios. Those pasty-faced girls with their giggles and whispers, all batting their eyelashes at him. They looked like sheep, but not as smart. "You listening, Peggy? I don't dance and I ain't coming. Your friends can all dance with Harvard. Anyway, their fathers sure wouldn't want them dancing with me."

"But it's you they want to dance with." The lip was wobbling again.

Course it was only natural that the girls would prefer him to Harvard, but they were just kids and no fun at all for what he liked doing. "Like I said, their fathers wouldn't want me nowhere near them. And I reckon that them shooting me might kind of spoil your evening. I ain't coming and sure as hell ain't dancing."

She went off in a sulk. He rolled his eyes. What was it with the female of the species? They sure were dumb. One moment they wanted to prove they could do the same things as men and the next minute they were playing at being helpless. 'Specially when it came to putting up damned bunning or whatever it was called.

"Johnny! A word, please."

He closed his eyes briefly as his father strode across the yard. They'd been avoiding each other since the previous evening, both making out they were far too busy to speak to each other. So, what did the old man want now? Was he going to start on about Burnett? Or was he going to chew Johnny's ear off and order him to attend the party?

"Johnny, I just wanted you to know I spoke with Ramsey. I had a long chat with him to explain how things had changed now because you and Guy are full partners. It was much as I thought, he didn't come here looking to discuss a job—he merely wanted to catch up on old times. He's looking at some business opportunities and thought he could talk them through with me and get my advice. He'd forgotten all about our old conversation about a job. You of all people should know better than to take the word of a bunch of highbinders."

He couldn't think of a damn thing to say. Catch up on old times! Oh yeah. Come all the way along the Santa Fe Trail way to catch up on old times. Dios, the old man seemed a real innocent at times. If ever a man was after something it was Burnett. Guthrie was waiting, looking at him like he expected Johnny to admit he'd been wrong. It would be a cold day in hell before that happened. "Well, he ain't going to admit that he owes money in town, is he? Not to you."

Guthrie grunted like he was trying to keep his temper. "Why can't you just admit, Johnny, that you were wrong? I know Ramsey and when you get the chance to know him as I do, you'll see what sort of man he really is."

Johnny choked back a laugh. Hell, he knew what sort of man Burnett was. It was the old man who had a shock coming. He'd bet a month's wages that Burnett would spring something. Why couldn't his father ever trust Johnny's judgment? Just this once? He kicked at the dirt with the toe of his boot. Yeah, like that was ever going to happen.

"Anyway, Ramsey is going to stay for a few days. It means he'll join us at our party this evening. You'll have a chance to get to know him a little better."

"I ain't coming to your party." Johnny stared down at the ground, waiting for the old man to blow his top.

"You're not coming?" Guthrie sounded surprised, but not mad. Which was kind of strange. "We've been planning this for quite a time, Johnny. It is a tradition on this ranch, a reminder of my youth in Scotland. My father used to hold an annual party for the estate workers and I like to do the same for the ranch hands and their families. We are very privileged to have land and wealth, and it is our duty to treat our employees well and show them that we appreciate what they do for us. Our friends and neighbors always attend too. And because of that, I see this as a good opportunity to mend some fences with them."

Yeah, like he cared about the damn neighbors. "You ain't really expecting me to come and be friendly with people who'd rather see me dead, do you?"

Guthrie sighed. "I do understand how you feel, and I can't say I blame you for feeling like that. But the fact of the matter is we still have to do business with these people, we have to get along with them. I was hoping this evening might be a start along that road."

Johnny laughed softly. "I guess the ones that hate me most won't come. And the rest? Well, it'll be much better if I ain't there, and if you're honest, you know that's true. Guy can sweet-talk them, he's good at that. Hell, it's what he does best. Turn Guy loose on them, give them lots to eat and drink, and I'll stay out of the way. Leastways then some people might have a good time. 'Cause I can guarantee that me being there will really mess up the evening. I'd be about as welcome as a rainstorm at a fancy wedding."

Guthrie viewed him silently and then shrugged. "You're not going to change your mind, are you?"

"You're learning, Old Man. Nope, I ain't. But I reckon I'll have plenty of chances to get to know your friend over the next few days. And I don't care what you say, the talk in town is right. He's a fraud."

Guthrie's mouth tightened. "Ramsey's not like that. I grew up with him. We came to this country together. I know the man."

Johnny shook his head. "No. You knew him. People change and believe me, it ain't always for the better. He's bad news. I know he is."

"I'm not going to waste my breath arguing with you. I'll see you at dinner." The old man turned and stomped off toward the house.

Johnny hauled himself up onto the corral fence and sat with his feet on the middle rail. What did Burnett want? He'd probably figured he wasn't going to get no share of this spread, but he was staying for a few more days. Why? The man was up to something, he was hanging around for something, but what?

A cloud of dust rose up on the horizon. Screwing his eyes up against the sunlight, he could see a rider heading back in to the ranch. Coming from the direction of the big rocky outfall, where the hillsides were dotted with caves. No cattle were grazed there because it was such poor ground and there were so many rock falls, so what the hell was a vaquero doing out that way?

The rider slowed to a walk as he neared the ranch, his features becoming clearer. Burnett—the son of a bitch. What the hell had he been up to? There was nothing out there. Just rocks and hard soil with no graze. What was it Harvard called it? A strange geologic feature, or something like that. But it was different from most of the land on the spread. Not much good for anything, except maybe hiding in. Or hiding something in. And Burnett had been snooping round out there.

And right now Burnett was riding straight toward him.

"Johnny." Burnett reined in next to Johnny. "Looking forward to the party this evening?"

Johnny raised an eyebrow, why the hell would Burnett ask about that, unless it was to detract attention from whatever he'd been up to. "Nope. Like I told my old man, I ain't going."

Burnett's mouth curled into a sneer. "It's probably for the best that you're not going. You wouldn't fit in. You're an embarrassment to your father. He told me all about it. It's humiliating for him, you being here. You've no breeding, no manners, and no conversation. The biggest favor you could do him is to leave. He just doesn't know how to tell you. I dare say he'd willingly pay you off if it meant getting you out of his life. It would be for the best for everyone. God only knows why he married your mother. A man with your father's social background didn't need a half-breed for a wife. She was an embarrassment to him too. He should have just paid her off when he heard there was a kid on the way. In my experience it's the best way to deal with unwanted encumbrances, and that's exactly what you are."

Johnny's fists clenched, like they had a will of their own, even as he fought to keep his expression blank. "Well," he drawled. "I guess if my old man has a problem with me, he'll tell me himself. I don't need no jumped-up servant from his past telling me what to do. Because it don't sound to me like you were ever much of anything. And your pa was only a servant too. And I tell you, Burnett, you're going to stay that way, because there ain't no way you're getting a piece of this ranch."

Burnett's jaw tightened. "Your father and I have a long history together. I think you'll find that I have plenty of influence with him. Don't get too comfortable here." He jerked his horse around and spurred it into a lope, kicking up a cloud of dust.

Johnny watched Burnett ride into the barn, wishing he could just put a bullet in the man. Hell, not just one bullet—right now he'd happily empty his gun into him. And had Guthrie really told Burnett that his younger son was an embarrassment to him? That he'd rather his son left? He knew his father was ashamed of Fierro, but was he ashamed of Johnny Sinclair too?

Peggy's voice broke into his thoughts. Calling him. "Johnny! I need your help. Now."

He shut his eyes briefly, even though a tiny part of him was glad of the distraction. Fucking parties. He'd make damn sure he was away for the next one. Anywhere but here. Hell, he'd even go to Albuquerque and put up with the damn lawyers and bankers. Anything was better than this. He jumped off the rails, and slowly, very slowly, headed over to see what she wanted doing now.

★ ★ ★ ★ ★

He slunk into the kitchen to try to scrounge some of the scraps that weren't being carried out to all the guests. He'd done pretty well at avoiding them all, except for a small band of Peggy's friends he'd collided with when he slipped in the side door. The girls had all turned bright red. Kind of like beets after cooking. Very red. And they didn't seem able to talk right or get their words out. They must be simple or something. How could so many of them be simple? Guy had told him once that interbreeding produced idiots. Interbreeding? Or inbreeding? Was that what Guy had called it? Well, whatever the hell it was, maybe that was why the girls couldn't talk normal. Kind of sad really. And the way they all stared at him, like he'd got two heads or something.

He glanced around the kitchen to make sure that Carlita wasn't there. She'd been in a foul mood all day, complaining loudly, and to anyone who'd listen, about how much cooking she had to do. She sure wouldn't be happy if she caught him thieving food. But it seemed it was his lucky night. She wasn't anywhere to be seen and somebody had left a huge meat pie on the table. Kind of a shame to leave it there to go to waste. He hacked off a big chunk and scooted out before there was any chance of her catching him. She'd probably tell him to go and join the dancing.

From the sound of the music and voices, the thing was in full swing. He stood in the shadows, near the door, listening to the music. The band only seemed to know two tunes. Still, by the time people had a few drinks and some of Guy's punch, they probably wouldn't mind about the music. He'd sneaked some tequila into the punch earlier. Harvard had been fussing over it like it was a newborn foal. Insisting the recipe had to be just so. Well, now it was just so with some added punch. He grinned. Yeah, the punch would pack a punch now. And maybe it would taste better too.

Footsteps echoed along the path by the house. Harvard, gussied up and carrying his gloves. Why the hell did he need gloves?

"Johnny." He gestured towards where all the noise was coming from. "Are you coming to join in the festivities? These annual parties mean a lot to Father. He wrote about them in some of his letters."

Johnny leaned back against the wall. "Nope."

He could feel Harvard's eyes boring into him like he was trying to read Johnny's mind. "Are you still worried about Burnett? With that many people there, it will be easy to avoid him."

Johnny hesitated. He hadn't told his brother about his earlier run-in with Burnett. Hadn't wanted to tell anyone what Burnett had said . . . Burnett might have been telling the truth . . . Instead, Johnny shrugged. "No. I don't like crowds, and I sure as hell don't like our neighbors. Anyway, you'll have a lot more fun without me there." He gave a brief laugh, but Guy just looked uncomfortable. Awkward, like he didn't know what to say.

"Well, I'll see you later." Guy slapped his gloves against his thigh and shrugged before turning away.

Had Guthrie held parties like this when Johnny had lived here as a child? Probably. From what his father had said earlier, these parties were a long-standing event, not something he'd only started recently as a fond reminder of his days in Scotland. Had Johnny's mother danced here? She loved dancing. When he was a child she was always telling him how popular she'd been and how men had always wanted to take her in their arms. Had that been here? Probably. He shut his eyes, picturing her. She'd been so beautiful. Sometimes she would whirl around their shack snapping her fingers and stamping her feet in time to some long-remembered music in her head from another, happier time. Maybe from here? She'd lift her skirts up and show her legs as she twirled about. And sometimes she just danced naked, because she felt like it.

He loved watching her dance, but was always afraid that she'd pull him out from wherever he lay watching her, to join her in a dance. She'd tell him he was no good. And if he trod on her toes, her mood would change and she'd scream at him. He'd loved watching her brush her hair too. He shut his eyes again briefly, remembering. He could see her now, when she would sit brushing her hair, the sunlight through the window making it look as glossy as a raven's wing, while he crouched in the corner of the room, watching her. Such beautiful hair. He always wanted to touch her hair. But more often than not, when she saw him watching her, she'd throw something at him. Tell him to get lost, to fuck off, she had a man coming to see her. But other times, she'd demand he brush her hair for her, and then she'd want him to rub her shoulders and neck real slow and plant kisses wherever she pointed . . . Now, he couldn't help but wonder what else she'd have wanted him to do to her if she'd lived till he was just a little older. He huffed out a bitter laugh. Mierda. Some mother.

He shook himself, irritated. He might as well ride into town and get away from this place for a while. He sure as hell didn't intend joining the party. And if he went to see Delice and the girls, maybe it would stop him brooding over Burnett's words, which were eating away at him. Couldn't get them out of his head.

He prowled across to the corral, stopping briefly to grab a halter. Moving slowly between the milling horses, he slipped it over Pistol's head before leading the horse to the barn where he saddled him and then headed out toward the town.

He was riding through the big gates that marked the entrance to the ranch when he saw horsemen coming toward him.

Chapter Five

Johnny peered through the fading light at the riders. "Stoney! Don't tell me you're going to join the party?" He jerked his head in the direction of the strains of music.

The sheriff shook his head. "Nope." He pointed to the other two horsemen. "Figured I'd best bring some backup. I reckon you'll be pleased to hear that I'm heading up there to arrest that friend of your pa's. I did some checking on him, like I told you I would, and there's some serious paper out on the son of a bitch." Stoney's teeth flashed suddenly. "And I bet that's the best news you've had all day."

Johnny let out a whistle. "Hell, yes! But what did you find out about him? What's he been up to?"

"Well, I kind of expected gambling debts, but he's also accused of being caught up in some big land fraud down near the border. But the clincher . . ." Stoney paused, as if for effect. "The clincher was finding that he shot a fellow during a poker game and seeing as how the man wasn't armed, it didn't go down too well."

Hell, he'd known Burnett was no good! But even as he felt a surge of delight, Johnny pushed the thought away. This was going to hit his father hard. Real hard. He'd been friends with Burnett all of his life from the sounds of it, but he sure was a lousy judge of men.

"So you going to ride in with us and see the fun?" Stoney sounded very cheerful.

Johnny shook his head slowly. "No, I reckon I'll pass, Stoney. If the old man sees me, he'll be certain I've had a hand in this. He don't think too much of me, I guess." Johnny tailed off, remembering Burnett's words.

Stoney huffed out a sigh. "Whatever you think best. Come on, boys." He urged his horse on, signaling for the two men to accompany him.

Johnny leaned forward resting his hands on the saddle horn, and watched the three riders head up the long driveway to the hacienda. He continued to sit there even when they were out of sight. Part of him wanted to ride in with them and see Burnett taken down, but the other part of him didn't want to be there when his father would be shamed in front of all his guests. In front of his friends . . . With a grunt of irritation, Johnny urged Pistol on toward the town.

He hadn't even ridden a couple of miles when he heard the sharp crack of gunshots ring out in the still of the gathering night.

And they came from the ranch.

He wheeled Pistol around and spurred him into a reckless gallop, charging through the darkness toward home. As he approached the courtyard, lit by flares, he could see all the guests milling around, and a handcuffed Burnett, flanked by Stoney and his two temporary deputies, who were deep in conversation with Guthrie.

Guthrie glanced across even as Johnny swung himself out of the saddle and pushed through the throng of people who were gawking and gossiping like they didn't want to miss the excitement.

Guthrie walked slowly toward Johnny but didn't look him in the eyes. He cleared his throat and gestured vaguely toward Stoney. "The, um, sheriff, um, informs me that um, my old friend is wanted for some, um, business down near the border—"

"I told you he was no damn good," snapped Johnny. "But you didn't want to hear it, did you? I told you there'd been trouble in town, but you didn't want to hear that either, did you?"

Guthrie finally looked him in the eyes, looked like a damn dog begging for scraps. "He's an old friend, Johnny—I stand by my friends."

"But not by your son?" Johnny shook his head. Hell, he should know by now that he was at the bottom of the heap with his father.

"Don't be ridiculous—"

Johnny glared. "I told you what sort of man he was, but you didn't believe me. Seems you never believe me. Course, if Guy had told you Burnett was trouble, it would have been different. You always listen to Harvard but you never damn well listen to me." He took a deep breath, trying to rein in the angry words before he said too much. Shouldn't let his father see how riled he was. Just keep cool, Fierro. Never let them see they've scored a hit.

Guthrie shook his head, like he didn't believe that. "That's not true, Johnny. Surely you can see—"

"It is true! And I tell you something else, Old Man, Guy agreed with me about Burnett. He could see right through him too." Johnny took a breath, had to calm down. "Anyway, what the hell's been happening here? I was on my way to town when I heard the gunfire."

Guthrie bit his lip, and looked at the ground and then around the courtyard—anywhere it seemed, rather than look at Fierro. "The sheriff rode in to arrest Ramsey. Ramsey tried to make a run for it. I guess he was scared. He's not a bad man."

Johnny raised an eyebrow. Yeah, he'd just bet that Ramsey

had tried to get away. He threw his father a sharp look, seemed he was real reluctant to get on with the rest of his tale. The man was shuffling his feet and still chewing on his lip. Dios. "And?"

Guthrie swallowed. "He . . . He fired off a couple of shots. I don't think he meant to hurt anyone . . ."

Johnny rolled his eyes. The old man was such a pushover. "And?"

"Guy was hit—"

A chill swept through him at his father's words and his guts clenched up like someone had punched him hard in the stomach. Shit, no! Not Guy. He couldn't lose Guy. The words came tumbling out, hot with rage. "Guy's been shot and you're standing there defending that bastard Burnett?" Couldn't remember being so angry. Or so frightened. He turned to run toward the house, even as his father put out a restraining hand.

"He's fine. It's only a flesh wound. A scratch—"

Johnny turned briefly, his lip curling. "Take your hand off me." His voice came out as cold as he felt. And as soft as falling snow. His father stepped back, like he sensed the threat behind the words.

"Johnny. He's going to be fine . . ."

Johnny didn't stop to hear more. He shoved his father to one side and tore toward the house. He paused only at the sight of Stoney and Burnett. It felt like all the rage inside him was bubbling up. Like he was going to burst into flames. Johnny moved to block their way. "If my brother doesn't make it, Burnett, I promise I'll kill you. You won't ever get to Santa Fe to face a jury because I'll kill you first. And I tell you, I'll enjoy it. So you better start praying that my brother's OK."

Burnett staggered backwards, paling. Stoney leaned forward with a grin and spoke low to Burnett. "Yeah, you'd better start praying, because Johnny Fierro always follows through on a threat."

Johnny pushed past them, not waiting to see Burnett's reaction to the name of Fierro. He sped to the house, praying that it was only a flesh wound. Praying to God. And he hadn't done that in years. Please God, let Guy be OK. Don't let him die. He shoved the door open and heard voices in the living room. His heart seemed to leap into his mouth—it was Guy's voice. He tore into the room, breathing fast. Guy was sitting on the couch while Peggy crouched over, bathing a wound on his arm.

"Let me see." He pushed in front of Peggy, ignoring her squeak of protest. "Let me look at it. I know about bullet wounds. Believe me, I know all about bullet wounds."

Guy gave a muffled snort of laughter. "Never a truer word, brother. But, in your vernacular, I am fine. It's only a flesh wound."

"Flesh wounds can turn real nasty." Johnny paused, looking closely at the wound. Wound? Barely a graze. His body felt lighter again and he found he could breathe better. "Damn it, Harvard—I thought you'd been shot."

"He has been shot, Johnny! And he had a very nasty bang to his head when he fell to the ground." Peggy sounded crotchety. She tried to elbow him out of the way.

He grabbed the bowl of water and the cloth out of her hands. "I'll see to it, Peggy. You go make him some of that nice tea of yours. You know, the sort you made for me when I was shot up."

Guy jerked forward, almost knocking the bowl out of Johnny's hands. "No! Please! Not the willow bark tea."

Peggy put her hands on her hips, and pursed her lips. "Guy Sinclair! That's downright ungrateful!"

Johnny grinned at her. "Go on, Peggy, make him some of your tea. I'll make sure he drinks it. And don't worry, I'll tend to his bullet wound." He pushed her, still protesting, out of the room, before turning back to Guy. "Bullet wound! I thought you'd been shot!"

"I was shot. Luckily it just grazed me. Were you worried?"

Johnny curled his lip and waved his hand in the air. "What? Worried about you? Hell no, but I figured I might be in for half a ranch instead of a third. Still, I guess it just wasn't my lucky day."

Guy leaned back, grinning. "Sorry to disappoint you. Looks like you're stuck with me. Ouch! Careful with that stuff, it stings."

Johnny grunted as he swabbed away the last traces of blood. "Shoot you myself one of these days, Harvard."

"So, I hear Burnett was already wanted for a shooting down near the border." Guy's expression was serious.

Johnny paused with the swabbing. "Yeah. We were right about him. And the old man was wrong. But even now, even after the bastard shoots you, our father's still making excuses for him."

Guy sighed. "I suppose he hates to admit that he misjudged his friend. It must be a hell of a thing to find out that he's got it so wrong."

Johnny lifted his head and looked at Guy. "I didn't tell you, but I saw Burnett earlier. He'd been riding around out on the range. God knows what he was up to out there, but I swear he'd been up to something. Anyway, I spoke with him when he rode in." Johnny hesitated. Part of him didn't want to admit what Burnett had said, but another part of him longed for Guy to tell him it had been bullshit. That Burnett had been stirring trouble, nothing more. "He said . . . He said Guthrie told him I was an embarrassment to him, that you'd all be better off without me here . . . Burnett said the old man just wanted to get rid of me, but didn't know how to tell me."

Guy eyed him, like he was considering a problem. Didn't say anything for a few seconds and then shook his head slightly. "And you believed Burnett?"

Johnny shrugged. "It sounds like the kind of thing the old man would say. He sure didn't want Burnett to know about my past."

Guy huffed out a sigh. "Why do you always imagine the worst? He was trying to make trouble, that's obvious. You wouldn't dream of believing anything else Burnett told you, but you're prepared to accept that at face value. You always leap to the conclusion that you're not wanted here, and that Father wants to get rid of you. And what makes that even stranger is that in every other respect you always consider things very carefully and weigh up all the possible connotations. But never with our father. You always believe the worst where he's concerned."

Johnny frowned. Why did Harvard always use such tricky words? Was Guy saying that maybe Guthrie didn't want to get rid of him? All very well for Guy. The old man respected him. Trusted him. Listened to him. But not Fierro. Not that he could blame his father. Nobody would want Fierro around except when it suited them. Like when a ranch was threatened by the likes of Chavez and Wallace. Fierro was useful then. But when the shooting was over?

"He does want you here, Johnny. You're forgetting that it wasn't so long ago he beat up some of his other old friends when they dared to accuse you of involvement in that lynching." Guy cocked his head, and raised an eyebrow. "I would say for him to do that, it was a huge gesture of affection. Love, even."

Johnny turned away. Tried to swallow the huge lump in his throat that felt like it was going to choke him. Love? Nobody would love Fierro.

Guy laughed softly. "Even now, you can't accept it, can you? Even when he showed that level of faith and trust in you, and broke all his strongly held codes of behavior, you still have to see it all wrong."

"Nobody would want me. Not if they knew what I've done. The things I've done." He spat the words over his shoulder. Couldn't face Guy. Not till he figured things out. His head was buzzing, like there was a huge swarm of flies in it. Or a thick fog. Love? That was a joke. He doubted even his mother had ever loved him, never mind a father who was a stranger.

Guy's voice, soft as a butterfly landing on a flower, broke into his thoughts. "You haven't finished cleaning my bullet wound. I'm still bleeding here. And I need a sling for my arm."

Johnny sucked in a breath. Tried to clear his mind, before turning back to his brother. His compadre. "Bleeding? You don't even do that right, Harvard!" He kept his eyes down, fixing them on the graze as he put a small dressing on it. Then he made a sling out of the cloth that Peggy had left there even as he felt Guy's eyes boring into him.

"What the hell happened to you, Johnny? What was it that makes you doubt everything? Everything is black with you. But out there." Guy gestured towards the window. "Out there, there's a world full of light and hope. And people who care about you. Including our father."

Johnny sat back on his haunches and stared down at the floor. Funny, he'd never noticed how threadbare the rug was. When he'd first arrived here, he'd thought everything looked incredibly grand. It sure had seemed that way. But lots of the things were kind of worn out, just like him. And yet all these things belonged here. Could he? Could Guy be right about the old man? Trouble was, if his father knew about Fierro's greatest sin, if he ever found out . . . Dios. But perhaps he'd never find out. Maybe it would stay between Fierro and God. He knew there'd be no redemption. Didn't deserve it. But maybe he could belong here for a while. Maybe he could find a little peace. And God only knew how he wanted some peace. A chance to rest. As long as his family never discovered the worst of him.

"So? Do you believe me?"

Johnny shrugged. "Never let up, do you, Harvard? Not even when you've been shot."

Guy grinned. "I thought you said it didn't qualify as a gunshot wound."

Johnny stretched slowly, getting to his feet. "It don't. But I bet that won't stop you milking it for all it's worth." He paused, and shook his head slightly. "You really believe what you just said?"

"Or did I just say it to make you feel better?"

Johnny nodded. "Yeah. D'you really believe it?"

"Yes, I do. And, I'd lay money on the fact that you two fought outside and you stormed away, leaving him wondering what the hell he'd done wrong. He's not the sharpest knife in the block when it comes to judging others or their reactions to his words."

"He's sure lousy at choosing friends."

The sound of voices and horses outside broke the moment. Stoney was calling out that they were heading back to town with the prisoner.

Guy rose carefully to his feet, flinching as he did so. "Come on, I think we'd better see the man off."

Johnny followed him out to where Guthrie and Peggy stood watching Burnett being helped, with handcuffed hands, onto a horse. Johnny hauled himself onto the wall to watch.

Burnett sat shaking his head, staring down at his handcuffs, his mouth a thin tight line. He huffed out a big sigh. "Who'd have thought when we came to America all those years ago that it would end up like this." The man shook his head again.

Guthrie seemed to be finding the ground around his feet particularly interesting. He stood stiffly and shuffled his feet. "Aye, this is a sorry day, Ramsey."

Burnett forced a smile. "Don't believe all that you hear, Guthrie. Please."

The old man seemed to be getting more of a grip now. He drew his shoulders back and looked at Burnett. "I'll try to track down Euan and let him know about this. And, if you need financial help, I'll go to Santa Fe. Pay for a lawyer, that sort of thing. We'll do everything we can to help you."

Johnny ground his teeth. We? That was rich. Fierro wouldn't be lifting a finger to help Burnett. Fuck that.

Stoney swung his horse toward the gates, with the two deputies flanking Burnett. They rode away as his father stood looking kind of lost. Johnny hopped down from the wall, the chink of his spurs breaking the silence.

Guthrie shook his head. "I can't believe any of this. I've known Ramsey all my life. It's unbelievable that he could end up like this. We were good friends, and despite the difference in class, my parents allowed him to accompany us to our old hunting lodges for our shooting trips. We shared so many adventures as boys. If I'd thought anyone would end up in trouble it would have been Euan, he was the reckless one, a daredevil and a bit of a show-off. But not Ramsey—he was loyal and good. It's sad that he never married. Maybe that's part of the trouble. He's been alone for far too many years." Guthrie sighed heavily. "A man needs a family, it keeps him grounded. But without family, without anyone to care . . ." Guthrie trailed off, and still shaking his head, he turned toward the house. He looked older suddenly.

Guy and Peggy followed him back into the hacienda, leaving Johnny outside. When a man's alone, when he's got no family . . . His father's words played over and over in his head. Fierro had been on his own all his life pretty much, and there'd been few enough people who cared about him. But maybe Guy was right, and here there were people to have a little faith in Fierro and to care about him.

He swung himself back onto the wall and watched the riders until they faded into the night. The moon was huge and golden, almost as bright as day. It lit up the surrounding mountains and the range spreading to the east. His landscape. His ground. Maybe, just maybe, where he could finally belong.

As long as his past never caught up with him.

Chapter Six

"The date has come through for Ramsey's trial. It didn't take long for them to move on that." Guthrie took another sip of coffee while he carried on reading the letter that one of the hands had brought back from a trip into town.

Guy helped himself to some more bacon before commenting. "Were you thinking of going?" He kept his tone neutral but even as he spoke he could still feel a slight twinge from where Burnett's bullet had found its mark. What his brother had dismissively described as a scratch. Scratch or no, he certainly didn't feel any sympathy for Burnett.

He glanced across the table at Johnny to gauge his reaction to their father's announcement. But Johnny's face gave nothing away. It was almost as if he wasn't listening to the conversation or didn't know who they were talking about. But Guy suspected that Johnny's apparent disinterest was very far from the truth.

Guthrie set his coffee cup down with a clatter. "But of course I'll be going to the trial. I must support him and do whatever I can to help him. I told him I would and I'll make sure he has the very best legal representation."

Guy stole another glance at Johnny but his face was still an impassive mask.

"Ramsey was a good friend over the years. We go back a long way and he's not a bad man. It was circumstances that were against him."

Circumstances? Guy almost choked on his own coffee at that

little gem. Would he ever understand his father, never mind understanding Johnny? It was beyond him how Guthrie could be so accepting of Burnett's activities but so quick to criticize Johnny. While he appreciated that Guthrie didn't intend to be callous or insensitive, it was hard to believe that the man could be so oblivious. He could be quite breathtakingly blind at times.

"I gotta go check on that sorrel mare. She's about ready to drop her foal." Johnny pushed back his chair with a clatter. He walked swiftly from the room, pausing only to grab his hat, which he thrust onto his head, pushing it forward to cast a dark shadow over his face.

Guy waited till he'd gone, slamming the door behind him. "Sir, it might be advisable to exercise a little tact and diplomacy when discussing Burnett in front of Johnny."

Guthrie's eyes narrowed slightly and the man clenched his jaw before appearing to compose himself. "What point exactly are you trying to make?" There was just a touch of sarcasm in his voice.

Guy ignored it. He wasn't going to rise to that. Instead he kept his voice level and moderate. "Simply that Johnny warned you about the sort of man Burnett was but you reacted as though any opinion of Johnny's was worthless."

Guthrie snorted derisively. "Nonsense. And anyway, Burnett's not a bad man. He just got in over his head."

Guy raised an eyebrow. "Well, I think perhaps we'd best agree to differ on that. But I did tell you after Stoney arrested him, how Burnett behaved very differently toward Johnny when you weren't around. He was extremely offensive."

Guthrie clenched his jaw again and swallowed hard. "I'm sure that Johnny simply misunderstood. I'm certain that Ramsey intended him no ill will. And I'm sure that when he fired off his gun, he never intended to hit you. It was just a desperate attempt to get away."

"Hmmm."

Guthrie threw him a sharp look, before speaking in a voice that almost sounded like he was pleading. "I have to stand by him. I've known him for years. He was a good friend. Surely you can understand that?"

Guy sighed. "I understand that you feel loyalty to an old friend, but I'm afraid that I don't share your faith in his essential character. My arm certainly doesn't! And I'm sure that Johnny shares my views."

Guthrie bowed his head briefly. "Ramsey and I have known each other all our lives. We grew up together."

There'd be no reasoning with his father over this. And while Guy admired loyalty, he couldn't help but feel that this time it was misplaced. He was simply wasting his breath.

"How long will you be away?"

Guthrie's face cleared, as if relieved that Guy wasn't going to push him further. "I thought I'd tie it in with a visit to an old friend in Texas. Bob MacDonald—he has a spread down in the Panhandle. His herd has excellent bloodlines. I'd like to introduce some new strains here, and I'd be interested to see if he has any bulls that he is willing to sell. But it does mean I'll be away for some time. However, I'm sure that you and Johnny can hold the fort in my absence."

Guy nodded. "Of course. When do you plan to leave?"

"I thought the day after tomorrow."

Guy left Guthrie fussing over organizing his packing for the trip and headed out in search of Johnny. He was in the largest barn, sitting in the straw, cradling a mare's head in his lap and talking to her in soothing tones. He glanced up as Guy walked in but looked away almost immediately. It never failed to amaze Guy how good Johnny was with animals. All animals, it seemed, but he had a particular affinity with horses. It was a shame that Johnny didn't have the same affinity with people.

Johnny spoke in a low voice, but avoided meeting Guy's eyes. "So he's going to Santa Fe to help Burnett. That'll be nice for him. Give him a chance to see his dear friend."

Guy scratched his chin, wondering how to respond to his brother's bitter tone. "He's loyal. I suppose that's an admirable trait."

Johnny grunted in obvious disgust. "Loyal! To that asshole? What about you? Hell! Burnett shot you."

"I remember it well!"

Johnny was silent for a moment. He stroked the mare gently, fondling her ears, before sighing softly. "And the old man still won't believe bad of him. Seems he's prepared to forgive him for anything. But he always thinks the worst of me . . . Kind of funny really."

Guy didn't think it funny. "Father's going to combine the trip with a visit to some old rancher friends in Texas. He'll be away some time."

His words were rewarded by one of his brother's broad grins. "Now you're talking, Harvard. Sounds like we might have some fun."

"Peggy will be here." Guy spoke mildly but was heartened to see how Johnny's mood had improved.

"Peggy? We'll send her off to stay with her friends." Johnny waved his hand dismissively. "She won't be here all the time, it'll be easy to get rid of her for a while." Johnny's eyes lit up. "I can wear my spurs in the house, drink tequila with dinner, and go to town without him moaning. Hell, Harvard, we'll have fun!"

Guy shook his head, laughing at Johnny's glee. "You're a man of simple tastes, Johnny, and easy to please."

Johnny grinned. "Yeah, Delice's girls know just how to please me."

★ ★ ★ ★ ★

As the day for Guthrie's departure approached, Guy had to wonder if their father trusted them at all, or maybe thought they were children. The man drew up countless lists of instructions for every possible eventuality. And issued orders. Lots and lots of orders. In fact the only bright spot was watching Johnny become more and more irritated with each new directive that emerged from Guthrie's desk. Johnny started grinding his teeth, and his fingers twitched constantly, as if he was having trouble restraining himself from shooting Guthrie.

Peggy, wisely, left them to it, announcing her intention of going to stay with old friends east of Cimarron. Guy almost envied her, even though he thought the friends in question were crashing bores. But at least her departure brought a brief smile to Johnny's face before the scowl returned. One down, one to go.

"Ain't you done yet, Old Man?" Johnny's fingers tapped ominously on the table at breakfast on the day their father was due to leave. Guthrie had been outlining the numerous reasons for calling a horse doctor out, in addition to detailing the even more numerous occasions when such action would be a shameful waste of their money.

Guthrie frowned, his brows drawn close together, and then gave Johnny the dubious benefit of one of his sternest glares. "These things are important, young man. Even if you don't think so. We cannot afford to fritter money away on luxuries."

"Yeah, yeah. I know, and you sure as hell don't trust us not to mess things up while you're away."

Guthrie sighed, obviously exasperated by his son's attitude. "It's just that this is the first time you and Guy have run things on your own for any length of time."

"And you don't trust us." Johnny sounded very scathing. Guy tried to smother a soft sigh as it seemed that the two of them were about to start yet another fight.

"Don't be ridiculous. Of course I trust you both."

Johnny leaned back in his chair and smiled sardonically. "Maybe you shouldn't. Maybe we'll sell it all out from under you while you're off seeing your good friend Ramsey Burnett."

Guy gave a soft sigh. An audible one this time. Why did Johnny do it? He really seemed to go out of his way to annoy Guthrie. Constantly pushing him. Never letting up. Was he testing Guthrie in some way? But if so, why? One thing was certain—it was incredibly wearing and he was fed up with being caught in the middle. The sooner Guthrie left for his trip, the better.

Guthrie seemed to think so too. Pushing his chair back, he gave Johnny another thin-lipped glare. "Johnny, I have a stage to catch. I am not going to rise to this. I must get going."

As Guthrie stomped upstairs, his heavy footfall echoing around the house, Guy shook his head in despair. Johnny sat sipping his coffee, but the fingers of his gun hand still tapped incessantly on the table.

Guy glared at him. "Why do you do it? You know he fusses about the ranch. He was bound to behave like this when he's leaving his precious baby in our care."

Johnny shrugged. "Just don't see why he's so fired up to help Burnett, is all." Johnny paused, biting his lip. The fingers tapped faster. "Would he support me like that? If it was me in Santa Fe, accused of killing a man, would he be there then? All fired up over me? I bet he damn well wouldn't." There was a flash of pain in Johnny's eyes. Gone almost as quickly as it came, but there just the same.

"Let it go, Johnny. It's not worth worrying about."

Johnny shrugged, pushing his chair back with a clatter. "Just don't see why he's so fired up over Burnett is all." With a curt nod Johnny stalked out of the room, pausing only to grab his gun belt.

His brother was jealous. That was the only explanation. Jealous of Guthrie's loyalty to an old friend. God, Johnny was a complex man. All bravado and swagger on the surface, but underneath the veneer was a very different man, a boy almost. A boy who seemed to doubt everyone and everything and was painfully unsure of his place within his newfound family.

Guy didn't see him again until much later. Johnny had been out with a work party mending fence lines when Guthrie had finally departed. Guy had heaved a huge sigh of relief when the stage had clattered out of town. He smiled at the memory of his father's final instruction to be sure to look after his brother. As though Johnny needed looking after. What a ridiculous notion. But perhaps now he and Johnny could relax a little and settle down to running the ranch together.

"Peaceful, ain't it?" Johnny grinned as he rooted around in the liquor cabinet searching for something to his liking. "Drink before dinner, Harvard?"

"I'll have a Scotch, thanks." Guy reached out to accept the proffered drink. "I thought he was never going to leave. I don't know why you should mind him going to see Burnett. It means we can have a bit of peace! And you can go into town whenever you like."

Johnny grinned over from where he now sprawled, stretched out on the couch, with his spurs much in evidence. "Yeah, that had occurred to me, 'specially while Peggy's gone. Don't have to make up any excuses."

They enjoyed a leisurely dinner, sharing a bottle of Burgundy from the cellar. Although Johnny was usually dismissive of wine, it amused Guy to see he was more than willing to partake of the Aloxe-Corton while they planned the work schedule for the coming week. He seemed far removed from the hardened and bitter gunfighter who'd ridden in a few months earlier.

"How about a game of chess, Harvard? Or can't you handle

being beaten?"

"I'll rise to the challenge and give you a run for your money!" Except, of course, Johnny would beat him. Johnny always won and the concept of being magnanimous in victory hadn't apparently occurred to him. Competitive didn't come close to describing him.

Johnny was dozing and Guy was pondering his next move when he heard the sharp rap on the door. Before he could haul himself to his feet to answer it, he heard Carlita bustling to open it and the sound of muted voices.

Curious to see who could possibly be calling this late in the evening, Guy struggled to his feet from his prone position on the floor by the chessboard, even as Stoney came into the living room, with two strangers close behind.

It seemed a strange time for a visit, but politeness dictated a warm welcome. So Guy smiled as though delighted to have his evening interrupted. "Stoney! This is a pleasant surprise."

Johnny's eyes opened in surprise. "Stoney? What the hell you doing here this time of night . . . ?" His voice tailed off as he eyed the two strangers.

"Um, a drink, gentlemen?" Guy felt that whatever the reason for the visit, he should play the gracious host.

Stoney shuffled his feet awkwardly and twisted his hat in his hands. Guy couldn't recall ever seeing anyone look quite so embarrassed and ill at ease. "No, thanks. This ain't exactly a social visit." As he spoke Stoney looked at Johnny with a strangely hurt expression. "It's business. These two fellows here," he gestured towards the two hard-faced men. "Well, they're lawmen and . . ." He paused, looking again at Johnny. "Well, they've got a warrant to arrest Johnny. On a charge of murder."

CHAPTER SEVEN

It was funny in a way. Somewhere, deep inside, Johnny had always known this moment would come. Sometimes he'd allowed himself to think that the past really was just that—past and gone. He'd tried to kid himself that everything would be OK. That at worst, the only thing he needed to worry about was people wanting to gun him. Yeah, tried to tell himself those things, but he'd never believed it—not deep down. So he'd known, the second he saw the men with Stoney, that his past wasn't past and it had just come back to bite him. They were men with hard faces, tired faces, like they'd traveled a long way. Searching for Fierro. And now they'd found him. And that warrant was their trump card.

Guy had stopped trying to play the good host. He looked kind of stunned. Even paler than usual. And even though he'd opened his mouth to speak, nothing came out. Like the words had got stuck somewhere between his brain and his mouth.

"What do you mean? Murder? A warrant? For Johnny? What the hell is this all about, Stoney? You waltz in here at this time of night to arrest Johnny, all on the say-so of two strangers?"

Stoney shook his head, kind of like it was all too much for him. "This fellow is a deputy marshal, and the other fellow is a deputy sheriff, Guy, and they got a warrant. It's all legal, believe me. It's signed by a judge."

"There must be a mistake. Did you say murder?" Guy sounded like he just couldn't believe what he was hearing.

Stoney looked at Johnny for a moment. Kind of looked like a whipped dog when its owner kicks it. "Yeah, Guy, I said murder. Ain't nothing wrong with your hearing."

"Murder." There was a vein pulsing now in the side of Guy's head. Just like the old man had when he got riled. "And exactly who is he supposed to have murdered? And where was this alleged murder, for heaven's sake? There must be a mistake. Johnny's a gunfighter and my understanding is that gun fighting is not illegal. Am I right?"

The marshal stepped forward. "Gun fighting ain't illegal when the players follow the rules. But this ain't nothing to do with any gunfight. This is cold-blooded murder we're talking about."

"And exactly where is my brother supposed to have committed this cold-blooded murder?" Guy didn't sound too impressed.

The second lawman smirked. "In Utah. That's where we've come from. Four years ago, it was. We thought Fierro was dead, but when we heard he was alive and kicking, we went and got the warrant. Murder ain't something we ignore. 'Specially one like this."

"Utah!" Guy looked kind of pleased. "I wouldn't think my brother has ever been to Utah. It's far too far from where he was raised. Isn't it, Johnny? Tell them, you've never even been there, have you?"

He couldn't look at Guy. And he sure couldn't look at Stoney. It was easier to look at the lawmen. He shrugged. "Sorry, fellows, but as anyone who knows me will tell you, I've always worked around the border. Ain't nobody ever paid me to go to Utah."

"See!" Guy sounded like he'd just won a battle. Was he dumb enough to think the men would just go away?

"We got a warrant to arrest you, Fierro, and that's just what we're going to do." The deputy had taken his gun from the holster and had it trained on Johnny.

Johnny's stomach seemed to have got itself into a tight-knotted ball but he shrugged again, and laughed softly, like he was real relaxed about it all. "Well, I reckon you fellows just got the wrong name. But seeing as how you got yourselves a warrant, I guess we'd better go and straighten this out."

Stoney wrenched his hat again. Any second he'd tear it in two. "Yeah, Johnny, you'll have to go with them. And," he paused again, shuffling his feet. "You gotta stand trial. Nothing I can do to help you, boy. Not this time."

"I want to see this warrant." Guy held his hand out.

The deputy reached inside his pocket for a piece of paper. Just one sheet. Simply one piece of paper but it was Fierro's death warrant. Shit. All those men who'd tried to face him down and failed. But that one sheet of paper . . .

Guy was reading it, real careful, like he didn't want to miss anything. Except he didn't need to use a finger to follow the words. Then his shoulders kind of sagged. "It looks legal to me, Johnny. Seems we haven't got any choice but to go to Utah with them."

He couldn't breathe, and the knots had suddenly gotten a lot worse and he felt chilled all over. He glanced down at the floor trying to get himself together before looking across at Guy. "We?" Johnny curled his lip. "I think I'll manage this on my own, Harvard. Don't need both of us to straighten this out." Dios. The last thing he wanted was Harvard tagging along. Hell, no. God only knew what he'd find out about Fierro. Too much, far too much, that was for sure. Couldn't take that. No! Couldn't bear the thought of Guy's disgust when he found out the truth about Fierro. Anything but that.

"I said we, and I meant we." Guy's voice was kind of steely. The sort of voice he used when he'd made his mind up. Well, old Harvard had a shock coming, because no way was he coming along for the ride this time. And Fierro would do and say whatever it took to make sure that Harvard stayed put on the ranch. And as far away from Utah as possible.

"Someone needs to stay here and run the place." Johnny could do steely too. Except it sounded even colder when he did it.

The marshal interrupted. "You can argue about that later. Right now, we're taking you to Cimarron and locking you up. We leave the day after tomorrow. Search him, Carter. On your feet, Fierro, and move real slow."

Johnny got slowly to his feet, and raised his hands. Somehow, it felt worse because of being in the house. Raising his hands outside wouldn't have seemed so bad. But in his own house . . . And all the while Stoney was looking at him like Johnny had let him down. No surprises there—Fierro let everyone down. Sooner or later.

Carter ran his hands over him, searching for any weapon. "He's clean—nothing on him."

The marshal rubbed his chin, like he was thinking hard. Dios! He hated lawmen who actually thought for themselves. Never a good idea. "Check his boots. People like Fierro usually have a knife. Take your boots off, Fierro."

"His name is Sinclair and is this really necessary?" Guy was looking really pissed and the vein was still pulsing.

The marshal ignored him. "Take the boots off. And move nice and slow."

"Yeah." The deputy still had the unpleasant smirk. "No sudden movements. I'd hate to have to shoot you. Can't cheat the hangman, can we, Fierro?" He smiled around at them all, like he'd made a funny joke.

Johnny sat down on the couch and tugged at his boots. Carter felt inside them before smirking and pulling out the fighting knife. "You were right, Ford."

Johnny could feel Stoney's eyes boring into him. Dios. Did Stoney know about the other knife in his boots? Had he ever told him about it?

He gave Stoney a quick look. The sheriff's eyes were narrowed and he was looking way too hard at Johnny. Now he was looking at the damn boots again and back at Johnny. Shit. "Can I put my boots back on, now? Or ain't you done yet?" Johnny tried to sound relaxed and kind of bored. It worked, because Carter tossed him the boots.

"Yeah. Put 'em on and then we're heading into town." Carter took a pair of cuffs out of his jacket.

"My brother will need a coat. You can't expect him to ride into town at this time of night in just a thin shirt. Stoney, surely Johnny can have a coat?" Seemed Guy was going to behave like a mother hen. Dios. Did he think Fierro was some little kid?

"I'm fine, Harvard, and I don't need no coat . . ."

"Get him a coat, Guy." Stoney glared at Johnny. "And you, just pipe down. Seems to me you're in enough trouble already without catching your death of cold."

"Yeah. Can't cheat the hangman." And Carter laughed again.

"I understood that in this country a man is presumed innocent until proved guilty." Guy sounded as cold as a north wind in the winter, but kind of polite at the same time. "I'll ride into town with you. I'd like to ensure that my brother gets there safely."

Johnny shut his eyes briefly and sighed. Guy didn't have the first idea how to treat lawmen. All he'd do is piss them off. Stoney sure looked put out by Guy's words.

Stoney's jaw jutted out. "I'll be riding into town, Guy. It's my jail that Johnny will be in and I swear no man ever came to any harm in my custody." Yep. Guy had upset Stoney. Real smart.

The marshal was butting in now, Ford was it? "Mr. Sinclair,

while Fierro is in my care, everything will be done by the book. I'm charged with taking him back to Utah to stand trial, and that's exactly what I intend to do."

Guy didn't look too bothered that he'd got them all riled up. Just curled his lip. "See that you do. But I'm still riding into town with you."

"Ain't no need for that, Harvard. I don't need a damn nursemaid." Maybe, if he was real nasty, Guy would back off. But Guy strode off and came back with the jackets—his and Johnny's. So much for hoping that Guy would stay at the ranch.

Carter ran his hands through the pockets of Johnny's jacket before tossing it over. "OK. Put it on, then I'll cuff you. And get a move on."

Johnny shrugged himself into the jacket and then held his hands out. His stomach lurched as Carter clamped the iron cuffs around his wrists, the metal cold on his skin. He glanced at Guy. "Well, I guess if you insist on riding escort into town you'd best bring my saddlebags. I'll need them for the trip to Utah. And I'll sure as hell need them for the trip back."

Nodding, Guy scooted off to hunt out the bags and Johnny followed the men outside where they had their horses ready and waiting—including an extra one for him. Carter and Ford bundled him, none too gently, onto the horse and they headed off towards Cimarron, leaving Guy to catch up.

The lawmen rode either side of him as Stoney led the way into town. The new moon didn't cast much light and the road was hard to follow in the dark. Would this be the last time he ever made this ride into town? His horse stumbled slightly, but despite the cuffs he was able to keep his balance. How the hell was he going to stop Harvard coming to Utah? Because one thing was certain, he had to be stopped. Johnny couldn't bear the thought of Harvard being there for a trial—or a hanging. And if Guy found out about his past, how could Fierro ever face him again? Guy was too smart by far. He might put two and two together and figure things out. Maybe he'd even figure out what had happened when Johnny was a child. And Fierro couldn't face the shame of that. He knew it was his own fault. That he'd asked for it in some way. His mother had always told him it was all his own fault. Shit. He had to stop Harvard coming to Utah. And he could only think of one way of doing that . . .

The sound of hooves dragged him back to the present. Guy had caught up, and had the saddlebags with him. "Can you manage with your hands cuffed, Johnny?" He sounded concerned. Johnny tried to swallow the lump in his throat. He hated the thought of what he'd have to say to his brother, but couldn't see no way round it.

"I'm fine." He kept his voice cold. He'd talk to Guy once they'd locked him in his cell. Guy was bound to stay and talk to him alone. Hell, he even knew what Harvard would say. He'd be telling him how everything would work out fine. That they'd get a good lawyer. That they should send for Guthrie . . . Madre de Dios. Anything but that. It'd be even worse than Harvard finding out about him.

He could see the lights of Cimarron ahead. Faint strains of music from the saloon were carried on the breeze. He could picture the saloon and the bordello, full of smoke and people laughing and drinking. People who could walk out of the door and go home to sleep in their own beds. Or Sadie's bed. Would he ever see the girls or Delice again? It was dumb, but he wished he'd had a chance to say goodbye to Delice. One last visit to her and the girls, in case he really didn't come back. In case this ride to Utah was the last ride he'd ever make . . . Mierda! He had to stop thinking like that. He needed to start planning. He sure as hell didn't intend to hang.

They reined in outside Stoney's office. As the others

dismounted, Johnny swung his right leg across the saddle horn and then steadied himself before sliding down. He stumbled, but at least he didn't fall. He'd be damned if he'd let them see him fall. By the time he got into the office, Stoney had already gone through to the back and opened up the cell. Ford unlocked the cuffs and pushed him in. At least it had a tiny window high up to let in a patch of light in daytime. But it was real small. Bars on three sides and a low metal-framed bed with a straw mattress, so thin it could hardly be called a mattress. The only other thing in there was a bucket to piss in.

Stoney looked kind of awkward. "Ain't up to much, I'm afraid. I'll get you some blankets and stuff." He pushed the cell door closed with a clang and turned the big key in the lock. "You staying a while, Guy?"

Guy nodded. "Yes, I'd like to talk to Johnny, if that's OK?"

"I'll leave you to it." Stoney left them alone and went to join the lawmen in the office, closing the door behind him.

Guy still looked pale and uncomfortable, shifting his weight from one foot to the other. If he was waiting for Johnny to say something, he'd be waiting a long time. Johnny sat on the edge of the bed. He could wait. He wasn't going nowhere. Not yet.

"I know you said you'd take care of it, but I am coming with you." Guy sounded determined. "Firstly, because I want to ensure you arrive there safely, and secondly to find you a good lawyer and make sure you get a fair trial." Johnny could feel Guy's eyes fixed on him, but he didn't bother answering. "Did you hear me? Johnny, are you listening to me?"

Johnny stared down at the stone floor. Big slabs of cold stone. "Johnny, did you hear me?"

He looked across at Guy, hating himself for what he was going to do. "Yeah, I heard you, Harvard. And I seem to remember telling you I don't need you to come with me. But maybe you got something wrong with your hearing. I don't want you to come and I sure as hell don't need you. Why the hell should I? I ain't a kid, so stop treating me like one. Just go on back to the ranch and stay there." Guy didn't look too bothered by his words. Damn, he was going to have to be more brutal. A lot more brutal.

Guy rolled his eyes. "It's not a case of treating you like a child. I want to come and support you for all the reasons I mentioned, and because you're my brother and that means a great deal to me."

Johnny swallowed. Narrowed his eyes. "Brother! Don't make me laugh, Harvard. So, we share the old man's blood. That don't mean nothing. We sure as hell don't share nothing else. You don't mean nothing to me and I don't want you tagging along behind me looking like the dumb son of a bitch that you are. You and your stupid Eastern ways. You should see yourself now. What fucking use do you think you'd be? You're just a Boston dandy with Sunday manners. You ain't a real man and I reckon you ain't much good for anything. You've given me a few laughs since I been here. Hell, I've had a lot of laughs about you, but now why don't you just piss off back to your books at the ranch and leave me alone?"

Guy flinched, almost like he'd been struck, and he took a step back, kind of like he had no control over his body. His mouth clamped shut in a thin line. And the pain in his eyes . . . He turned abruptly to go into the outer office, slamming the door shut behind him.

Johnny shut his eyes tight. And he hurt deep inside and it felt like he could barely breathe. He should never have stayed here in the first place. Should have taken his money and left. And how had Guy done this to him? Gotten to him the way he had? Dios, it hurt. He'd been so scared when Guy was shot, scared that he'd lose him. Well, he'd sure as hell lost him now, because even if he got off at the trial, no way would Guy ever want to have anything to do with him again. And who could blame him? But better to have Guy hate him, than be disgusted by him . . .

He sat slumped over, wrapping his arms around himself. Stoney would be in with blankets and stuff. Couldn't let Stoney see that he was hurting. Keep the mask in place. How many times had he told himself that? Never let them see you hurting . . .

The door swung open, and Stoney staggered in with an armful of blankets and a couple of pillows. "It can get chilly in here so I fetched you some extra blankets." He paused, and looked at Johnny sharply. "Where was Guy rushing off to? He almost knocked me over in his hurry to get out of here."

Johnny shrugged, playing for time. "Dunno. Back to the ranch, I guess."

Stoney dropped the blankets next to the cot. "Well, it looked to me like he was kind of riled up over something. I thought maybe you'd had words."

Shit. Since when did Stoney get so damn smart?

Stoney scratched his chin, like he was thinking hard. "The thing is, Johnny, I reckon it's time you and I had a talk, because what I want to know is whether you were expecting a visit from Utah sooner or later? When I first arrived in town, I asked you to be straight with me. And you told me you weren't wanted anywhere."

Johnny glared at him. "If you want to know if there was a wanted notice out for me that I knew about, the answer's no." He'd suspected there might be, but he wasn't telling Stoney that.

"You didn't ask those fellows any questions, which makes me wonder if it's because you already knew the answers." There was an edge in Stoney's voice, like he wouldn't take no bullshit.

"I didn't know they were coming, OK? And I figure I'll hear all the details of whatever they're accusing me of on the way to

Utah. I can wait."

"Thought maybe you didn't want your brother to know about it."

Dios! Stoney just had to be so fucking smart. Johnny gritted his teeth, and tried to relax his shoulders, which were tensing up. "Leave it alone, Stoney. We ain't talking about this. And I don't want no visitors in here, neither. That's my right, isn't it? Don't have to see people, do I? Well, I don't want to see anyone, including my brother. Got that?"

Stoney was silent for a few seconds, scuffing up the toe of his boot, before looking across at Johnny. "No visitors? Yeah, it's your right. But that brother of yours is OK. You told me that yourself. About the same time you told me that nobody was after you." He paused again, chewing on his lip. "I don't like being lied to, Johnny, 'specially by you."

"I didn't lie!" He'd bent the truth but he hadn't told an outright lie. "You so sure I'm guilty, Stoney? I worked down around the border, you know that and you know me."

Stoney shook his head slowly. "No, I don't know you, Johnny. I wonder if anyone does. But I tell you something, you're going to need that brother of yours. It's going to be rough in Utah and you're going to need all the help you can get."

Stoney turned to leave, but paused again. "Something else. You once told me you always carried two knives."

"Notice you didn't say so in front of them lawmen." Johnny spat the words out.

"I thought about it. But figured I'd give you a chance. I ain't going to ask you if you still carry two, I simply want your word that you won't use one on a lawman doing his job."

Johnny gave a brief laugh. "You mean you'd trust me?"

"Just want your word, Johnny."

Johnny looked at Stoney, feeling oddly moved. The sheriff still put some trust in him, even though Johnny had done nothing to earn it. He sighed, wondering what Stoney would say if he knew about the guard Johnny had killed to escape from the jail down in Mexico. "No, I won't use a knife on a lawman just doing his job. But, if it came to it, Stoney, I ain't going to hang. I sure as hell ain't going to hang."

Stoney nodded. "That's what I figured." He opened the door to go back to his office. "No visitors, I know. But you need to think on whatever you said to that brother of yours, because I'd bet good money he didn't deserve it."

The door slammed shut after him and Johnny fell back onto the bed, feeling like his guts had been torn from him.

CHAPTER EIGHT

Guy stumbled from Stoney's office and swung himself onto his horse. All he wanted was to ride back to the ranch as fast as possible. It was as though he was being swept down a mountain in an avalanche of emotions and right then the strongest one was rage. And if he didn't get out of town, he might be tempted to shoot Johnny and save everyone the bother of an expensive trial.

Had he really been totally taken in by Johnny, all these months? To think that Johnny had been laughing at him all the time hurt more than he could bear to admit. His brother's insults still rang in his ears. The tone of his voice, that sneer, the curl of his lip, the disdain and mockery. And he felt angry. Furious. Furious with himself that he'd allowed himself to be so taken in by Johnny, that this so-called brother had the power now to hurt him this much.

Throughout his childhood he'd always mourned Johnny, believing that his younger brother was dead. Although his aunt and uncle had loved him and welcomed him into their home in Boston, he'd missed not only his father and home, he'd missed his brother too. And finally discovering that Johnny was, after all, alive had meant so much. He'd hoped they could enjoy a close brotherly relationship, but now it seemed that Johnny's friendliness had all been a sham.

He spurred his horse on, riding far faster than was wise at night. But he was past caring. The lights of the hacienda shone out a welcome in the distance, beckoning him home.

The house was deserted when he got there. Carlita had presumably gone home to tell her family that men had taken her precious Juanito away. She'd always indulged his brother: cooking him spicy tamales, giving him extra helpings of meals, and baking him special Mexican cookies, which she kept hidden away for Johnny alone.

Guy strode to the liquor cabinet and poured himself a very large measure of Scotch. The open bottle of tequila stood next to it, where Johnny had casually slapped it down before lounging on the couch earlier. Guy picked the bottle up and hurled it at the fireplace. The shards showered across the hearth and the liquid spread over the floor, like Donovan's blood had spread across the floor when Johnny had moved so fast to protect Guthrie, just weeks earlier. When the rancher had pulled a gun on their father, Johnny had reacted with lightning speed and gunned Donovan down.

He sank onto the couch. His head was thumping, the pain concentrated above one eye. And there was a twinge from where Burnett's bullet had grazed him. Burnett's bullet. The memory gave him pause to think and to calm down. He leaned back, taking a swig of Scotch, remembering how Johnny had reacted when he'd heard that Guy had been shot. He remembered the way Johnny had looked when he'd torn into the room, pushing Peggy to one side, wanting to reassure himself that Guy was OK. And although Johnny had been dismissive of the wound, he'd been very gentle bathing and dressing it. Not the actions of someone who professed to despise everything about his Boston-raised brother.

Other memories flooded his mind now. Johnny leaving himself wide open to take a bullet in the shootout in the bar in Bitterville in order to save Guy—the night that Johnny's old friend Eagle had fortuitously arrived and saved Johnny's life.

And how, very early on in their relationship, before Johnny had ridden into town for a gunfight, he'd looked at Guy as though he was trying to memorize his face and the brief admission afterwards that it was difficult to concentrate in a gunfight if there was somebody watching who you cared about.

Had all of that been a pretense? He shook his head slowly. No. If there was one thing he was sure of, when Johnny had rushed in to check on him after Burnett had shot him, that fear he'd seen in Johnny's eyes had been real.

He took another sip of his drink. And if that had been real, what was he to make of his brother's words earlier that evening? Such cold, cruel words. Cruel enough to drive anybody away . . .

Cruel enough to drive anybody away.

With a heavy sigh, he heaved himself off the couch and trudged up the stairs and along the corridor to Johnny's room. It was large and impersonal. There were no books piled on the table next to the bed. No pictures on the walls or photographs on the desk. A well-worn boot had been thrown down in one corner of the room but there was no sign of its mate. And a shirt was bundled up and lay under the utilitarian wooden chair. But the shirt and the boot were the only signs that anyone even used the room. It was almost as though Johnny Sinclair had never been there.

The second drawer of the heavy chest next to the window protruded slightly and Guy moved to close it. It jammed awkwardly, causing him to pull it out to set it firmly on the run-ners. His mouth dropped open. The drawer was full of boxes of bullets. Lots and lots of boxes of bullets. Surely more than any man could use in a lifetime. Each box was carefully laid in its place.

Curious, he opened the small top-left drawer to find that filled with boxes of rifle shells, again all meticulously laid out.

On further investigation, the right-hand drawer contained what he knew to be Johnny's "fighting" gun, together with its special cutaway holster. Both were carefully wrapped in chamois cloths and a bottle of gun oil was stored in such a way that it couldn't tip over. The other two drawers contained just two spare shirts and some long johns.

Stunned, he sat down on Johnny's bed. It was crazy. How could anyone need that many bullets? The answer, of course, was they couldn't. It certainly couldn't be normal to stockpile ammunition like that. His brow furrowed as he sat remembering the numerous occasions that Johnny had visited gunsmiths because he "needed a few bullets." And whenever they had to buy ammunition for the ranch, Johnny always got an extra box for himself, almost absentmindedly as an afterthought. It was as though his brother couldn't walk past a gunsmith without buying bullets, and although he'd always thought that Johnny seemed to buy a lot more than other men, it had never really registered quite how many Johnny bought. Why would he do it? Some men collected stamps or coins, maybe Johnny collected bullets . . . He shook his head at the ridiculous notion. No, that made no sense whatsoever.

He was surprised to find that he no longer felt angry. His rage had dissipated and now he just felt bewildered. He leaned back against the headboard, taking in the appearance of the room. It struck him suddenly as sad that after all these months there was nothing of Johnny's character imprinted on the room; it was as though it was unoccupied. Until, of course, one examined the contents of the drawers. And that in itself was disturbing. Was Johnny crazy?

He shook his head slowly. No, Johnny was strange, but eminently sane—cynical, clever, and calculating, but definitely sane. Clever and calculating? Now there was a thought. Because if Johnny had wanted to stop Guy going to Utah with him, his words were calculated to force Guy to abandon the idea. Johnny was shrewd enough to know that Guy wouldn't feel that his first duty was to the ranch. No, Johnny would have guessed that Guy would insist on going with him. And so he said what was necessary to ensure that Guy did indeed abandon his plan.

Quite why Johnny didn't want him to accompany him to Utah was harder to fathom. Johnny wouldn't commit cold-blooded murder, of that he was certain. Johnny had never been to Utah. Was Johnny frightened that they'd convict him anyway and didn't want Guy to see him hanged?

He sighed. This wasn't getting him anywhere and his head was hurting even more. He struggled to his feet, resolving to talk to his brother the next day and sort things out. He gave the chest of drawers another puzzled glance but didn't feel up to solving the conundrum of why Johnny needed his own private arsenal.

"What do you mean, he's not seeing visitors?" Guy stared at Stoney in disbelief. "He's in jail, for heaven's sake, he's not some king from a bygone age holding court and deciding whether he's in the mood to receive visitors."

Stoney scratched his head as though confused by Guy's analogy. "I don't rightly know about kings or bygone ages, all I'm saying is he ain't seeing anyone. Thought that would be clear enough." Stoney paused, screwing his face up as if reluctant to say what was coming next. "And he was real strong-minded about you being the person he'd least like to see."

"And you intend to pander to him over this?" Guy couldn't keep the sarcasm from his voice.

Stoney narrowed his eyes slightly as he stomped across the room to make himself a mug of coffee from water bubbling in a battered frying pan. "Ain't a question of pandering to him," he growled. "He's a prisoner, and if he don't want no visitors, that's his right."

Guy tried to quell his rising irritation. There was little point in annoying Stoney. The sheriff wasn't the kind of man to cave in to bullying. Stoney—who'd known Johnny in the old days, before his brother had come home. Quite suddenly he remembered something Stoney had said the previous evening, which had intrigued him at the time. "Last night, Stoney, when you came to arrest Johnny, you said you couldn't help him. *'Not this time'* were your words—what did you mean? When did you have to help him before?"

Stoney busied himself with adding sugar to the foul-smelling coffee. His shoulders were hunched and he seemed very tense and reluctant to answer.

"I know you and Johnny were friends, so what did you mean?"

Stoney shrugged. "Don't rightly remember."

Guy shook his head. "Oh, come on! You don't think I believe that, do you? Tell me, how well did you know Johnny? Were you close friends?"

The sheriff stomped back to his desk and banged his mug down, spilling the coffee over a pile of wanted posters. "I hardly knew him at all. Happy now? I met him once when he was a kid and I spent two or three days in his company when he was older. That's it. So he's as much of a puzzle to me as he is to you." Stoney turned away, looking almost distressed, as though regretting his outburst.

Stoney's words triggered something in Guy's memory. It was like alarm bells going off, telling him these words were important. Why did those words sound so familiar? He chewed on his lip as he wracked his brain trying to bring whatever it was to mind. Spent two or three days in Johnny's company but hadn't seen him then since Johnny was a kid. Why was it so familiar? There was something, just out of reach in his mind. Why?

"Good God! It was you!" The words burst out of Guy as the memory flooded into his consciousness even as he felt almost stunned by the realization.

Stoney looked at him, frowning. "What the heck are you talking about? What was me?"

"The best day of Johnny's childhood." Guy spoke softly, enjoying the look of bewilderment on Stoney's face.

"Damn it, man. What the hell are you going on about?"

Guy smiled. "I'm talking about a man who rode into a border town and found a young kid being kicked on the ground. And that man picked up the kid and took him to a doctor and got his back treated. Ring any bells?"

Stoney flushed, and busied himself with straightening his pile of wanted posters. "Don't know what you're talking about."

"Yes you do. But what you might not know is that Johnny described that day as the best day of his childhood. A gringo sat him on a horse and took care of him, and even bought him a meal afterwards. Wouldn't have been much of a day to most children, having to go to a doctor and being kicked around, but to Johnny it meant everything—because on that day he felt like he mattered."

"Damn." Stoney spoke quietly, and sat down heavily in his chair. He gave Guy a sharp look, before staring down at the floor, shaking his head. "What else did he tell you?"

"That he met the gringo years later, bought him a meal in return, and spent two or three days in the man's company."

The sheriff looked up, concern evident now in his face. "But he ain't told you it was me? Damn."

Guy frowned, slightly puzzled by his reaction. "No, he didn't tell me it was you. Does it matter?"

"Shit, yes! Of course it matters. Ain't you learned anything about that brother of yours these past few months? Just don't . . . just don't tell him you figured it out. And for God's sake don't tell him we've spoken about it." Stoney sighed, before adding gloomily, "I'd like to live a few more years."

Stoney looked genuinely concerned and Guy suspected that it wasn't an act, but it puzzled him just the same. "Johnny wouldn't hurt you. He's grateful for what you did for him. That day stands out in his memory as the best day ever when he was growing up."

Stoney snorted. "Didn't stop him threatening me. He sure as hell didn't want you to know it was me."

"He threatened you?" Guy could hardly believe this. It was crazy. Why should Johnny care if Guy found out that Stoney was the man from his youth who helped him?

"Yeah, he threatened me." Stoney fumbled in his pocket and pulled out a plug of chewing tobacco. "He's a secretive bugger and he's always planning his next move, staying one jump ahead of folks. Guess it's how he stayed alive so long." The sheriff shook his head and paled slightly, a faraway look in his eyes. "When I first saw him, Christ! The state of his back . . ."

"That bad?" Guy tried to quell the first signs of nausea in his stomach. He hated to think of what Johnny might have suffered as a child.

Stoney looked at him. "Yeah, that bad. It was running sores from where he'd been whipped and there were maggots crawling in it. And thin! Could see every dang bone in him. Don't believe anyone had ever done a damn thing for him." Stoney shook his head in obvious distress. "And that mother of his . . ."

"Did you meet her?" Guy was curious to learn anything about Gabriela. His own memories of her were hazy. All he remembered was her beauty and her fondness for throwing things. Certainly he'd never heard Johnny say a word against her.

"Nah, never met her. But I did ask around a bit and heard a few things . . . Let's just say there were better mothers in this world. To be honest it sounded like she was crazy." Stoney shrugged. "But like I said, he's a secretive bugger and he'd be mad as hell if he knew we'd discussed this." Stoney jerked his head, nodding towards the heavy oak door. "Good thing that door is so heavy and he can't hear us."

Guy scoffed. "I can't believe he'd really mind."

Stoney glared at him, and shoved the plug back in his pocket. "Like I said, you don't seem to have learned much about him. Anyway, he sure as hell don't want to see you right now and he don't want you going to Utah with him."

"I don't understand that. It makes no sense. Why wouldn't he want me to go?"

Stoney stared at him, his mouth slightly open. "Why the hell d'you think he don't want you to go? For starters you'd learn way too much about Johnny Fierro."

"He's never even been to Utah. He said so."

Stoney looked at him through narrowed eyes, and shook his head slightly as if he thought Guy was stupid. "No, he never said that. He's real smart. Think on it."

Guy thought back to the previous evening and his brother's words. What was it he'd said? That nobody had ever paid him to go to Utah. That was it! "You mean what he said about not being paid to go there? That was just his way of expressing it, Stoney. I don't suppose it even occurred to him that the words could be interpreted differently."

Stoney laughed sardonically. "Believe me, Johnny Fierro thinks of everything."

"You think he's guilty, don't you?" Guy shook his head in disbelief. "You think he did it."

Stoney looked at him, a strange expression in his eyes, almost pity. "I dunno if he's guilty or not, but I sure as hell wouldn't underestimate him. Don't get me wrong, I like Johnny, and I know better than most what a rough life he had. Rougher than he ever deserved. But a life like that, well, it leaves its mark on a man and Johnny is a very tough hombre. The toughest son of a bitch I ever met. And the most devious."

Guy glared. "Well, I know Johnny wouldn't commit murder and I don't believe he's ever been to Utah. And whether he likes it or not, I'm going to Utah too. I intend to see that he gets a good lawyer and we clear his name. And I don't give a damn what he thinks about me going." Guy turned on his heel, pausing only at the door as Stoney spoke again.

"I'm glad you're going. For his sake I'm glad. But I tell you, he ain't gonna be happy about this." Stoney paused. "And for what it's worth, if he did do it, he must have had one hell of a good reason."

CHAPTER NINE

"Your brother was in." Stoney passed a mug of coffee through the bars. "But I told him you weren't seeing nobody. He didn't seem too impressed and stomped out a while ago."

Johnny grunted and reached out for the coffee. Least it was hot. Something to warm his hands around. "Tough. Don't want to see anyone, Stoney. Just as long as you understand that."

"He says he's going with you, no matter what you say."

Despite the steam rising from the mug, Johnny suddenly felt icy all over. What the hell did he have to do to make that dumb son of a bitch stay at the ranch? Surely he'd been brutal enough to make Guy never want to see him again. What the hell was wrong with that man? Anyone else would have gotten the message but no, not Guy, he had to be a pain in the ass.

"Can't you arrest him or something? Lock him up, that'll stop him going." Johnny looked angrily at Stoney. "If I got the right to say no visitors, don't I have the right to say he can't come?"

Stoney didn't look none too impressed. "It's a free country, and trials are open to all—even your brother. Anyway, you should be grateful that someone cares enough to go with you."

"I don't want him to go. I sure as hell don't want him around on this trip. I don't need nobody, Stoney, you hear me? 'Specially some dumb Boston dandy. I done OK all these years on my own and I sure as hell don't need nobody now." Johnny slammed the coffee down. Dios, even his hands were shaking.

Stoney looked him straight in the eyes. "Who you trying to convince? Me? Or you?"

"Why don't you just get out and leave me alone." Johnny slumped down on the cot, glowering at the sheriff who looked unconcerned. He sure as hell wouldn't look so easy if Fierro wasn't locked in a cell. Be different then. But as it was, Stoney just strolled out like he didn't have a care in the world.

Johnny pulled his knees up and wrapped his arms around them, hunched over. If only he could sleep. He needed to sleep while he had the chance because he knew he couldn't risk sleeping on the journey ahead, not with two lawmen there. He might talk in his sleep and that would never do. Couldn't chance whatever he might give away. He'd have to stay awake as best he could. But he was so damn tired. Tired of fighting. And it just never ended. The past never went away. Maybe he should just give in and take what he had coming, because he was too tired to fight any more.

He'd like to be lying out somewhere, with the sun on his face and a woman in his arms. His own woman. His very own woman. Someone smart and funny with legs up to her armpits and maybe green eyes. Yeah, like that was ever going to happen! Who the hell would ever want him? Only time he'd had a woman of his own, she'd upped and left. She'd seen through him. But Guy would have it all one day. A woman of his own. He'd be a good husband, a good father to a whole bunch of kids, and have a real good woman who didn't fuck for money. Guy deserved all of that. But Fierro? No, sinners didn't deserve nothing. Hell, Mama had told him often enough he was no damn good, that he'd never amount to nothing. If she could see him now she'd laugh and say how she'd been right all along.

The cell was suddenly flooded with light. The sun must have reached a point where its rays finally reached the tiny window. He shifted so that he could feel it on his face and shut his eyes, enjoying the warmth. If he tried hard he could imagine riding Pistol with the breeze ruffling his hair and the sun on his back. Riding back to the hacienda for a good meal and maybe a game of chess with Harvard . . .

He shook himself angrily. Harvard. He had to think of some way of stopping Harvard coming on this trip. One thing was certain, even if Fierro got off, Harvard wouldn't never want to play chess with him again, not after the things he'd said. Odd that Stoney said Harvard was still planning on coming along. Why the hell would he want to come? Unless now he just wanted to see Fierro swing.

He shook his head slowly. No, that wasn't Guy's way. He wasn't a man who'd be happy to see someone else in trouble. Which still left the question of why he was coming to Utah. Couldn't figure that one at all.

The heavy oak door creaked open and Stoney shuffled in, chewing on his lip and avoiding Johnny's gaze. "You got a visitor."

"Shit, Stoney. I told you I wasn't seeing anyone. I don't want any damned visitors. Are you too dumb to understand that?"

Stoney flushed as though he was angered by the accusation. "This one wouldn't take no for an answer." Stoney threw his hands in the air like he hadn't had any say in it. "I'll leave you to it." He stood back to let the visitor in.

Johnny leaned forward, ready to hurl a few more insults at anyone who'd come to jeer at him, to see a pair of cool green eyes watching him.

He huffed out a sigh. "Delice, what the hell are you doing here?"

She pursed her lips and tilted her head to one side. "Oh please, honey, don't get up on my account."

He could feel the heat flooding his face and he swung his legs off the cot to get slowly to his feet. "Told Stoney I didn't want to see anyone."

She raised an eyebrow and her lips twitched like she was trying to stop herself from laughing at him. "Oh believe me, I know. He told me so. Frequently."

Johnny frowned. "So how come he let you in?"

She shrugged. "How come?" Her lips twitched again. "I guess he just didn't dare say no."

Johnny had to smile at that. It was true. Stoney was scared to death of Delice, same as most men seemed to be. "What you got there?" He gestured towards the small box she was carrying.

"I'm like the Greeks, I come bearing gifts."

Johnny tilted his head and stared at her. What the hell was she going on about? She was as bad as Harvard, and may as well have been talking Greek for all he understood. "Greeks?"

She sighed. "Just a classical reference. When the girls heard about your . . ." She hesitated, like she was trying to decide what to say. "Your unfortunate predicament, they decided to bake you a cake."

"A cake!" He grinned. He'd enjoy some cake and it would be better than the food Stoney had offered him.

"Oh don't get your hopes up, honey. They made three and managed to burn all three. Just as well they're whores—they'd make lousy housewives. So, sorry, no cake, but there are homemade cookies." She pushed the box through the bars to him. "Cookies, but sadly no hidden file to saw away at the bars—Stoney checked for that."

Lifting the lid he could see at least three varieties of tempting cookies and not a burned one amongst them. "Thanks, Delice. Who made them? They look real good."

She waved a hand as if it wasn't important. "Oh, just someone in the kitchen. At least they'll be easier than a cake for you to carry on this trip."

And there it was. The first mention of what lay ahead. He

couldn't look at her now. He turned away and put the box down by the bed. "Yeah, I guess so."

He could feel her eyes on him. Felt like she was looking right inside him, in his head and in his thoughts. Shit, why did he always feel that she could read him?

"Murder, they say." She made it sound like a question, fishing for more information.

He shrugged. "Dunno what it's all about. I'll hear soon enough."

"You mean you haven't asked them?" She sounded like she found that real hard to believe. She shot him another piercing look. "Unless, of course, you already know what it's all about."

He glared at her. "Told you, they'll tell me soon enough."

"And you're not remotely curious?" The way she said it sounded like she didn't believe a word he'd said. Damn it. He never could fool her. She was way too smart. He shrugged because it was a hell of a lot easier than looking at her or saying anything.

"I saw Guy earlier. I bumped into him on my way here."

He felt a tightening in his chest. He turned away, determined that she wouldn't see that her words bothered him any. And he didn't say a word, just fiddled with the box of cookies.

"He seemed somewhat agitated."

Dios, she just wasn't going to leave it alone. He shrugged. "Dunno why."

"Well, you wouldn't, would you? Seeing as you'd refused to see him." She struck her head with her fingers like she'd just thought of something. "Oh, silly me, maybe that's why he was so upset! Because you won't see him."

He clenched his jaw and glared at her. "OK, so we both know exactly why he's pissed with me."

"So what are you going to do about it?"

He glared again, irritated by the tone of her voice, like she thought he was dumb and didn't know what was best for him. "Nothing. OK? Nothing. I ain't gonna do nothing about it. Not my problem."

"You're simply going to let him sweat?" She didn't sound too impressed.

He shrugged. "Like I said, it's not my problem. Don't have to see him . . ." He almost added that he didn't have to see her either, except it seemed that he did because Stoney was too chicken to keep her out.

"He's worried about you."

Johnny looked at her briefly, but looked away. Those cool eyes were way too good at seeing inside him. "Don't know why. Anyway, that's his problem. I sure wouldn't worry over him."

"Ah, yes, because Johnny Fierro doesn't care about anyone or anything." She was using that voice again, like she always used when she thought he was talking bullshit. "So, why won't you see him?" He opened his mouth but she held up a hand. "And please don't tell me it's because he doesn't mean anything to you. We both know that's a lie."

He could feel the heat flooding his face again. It irritated the hell out of him the way this damn woman always saw through him. How did she do that? She was only a woman, damn it.

"Well?" Her voice sounded steel-edged and as sharp as the knife in his boot.

"Just don't want to." The look on her face said he wasn't getting off that lightly. He threw his hands in the air. "OK! This ain't no place for someone like him."

She shook her head. "No. Sorry, honey, but your brother isn't some frail little flower who would find it too distressing to visit a man behind bars. So, let's talk about the real reason."

"Don't know what you mean." He sat back on the bed. Maybe if he lay down, she'd leave. He stretched himself out. She pulled up a chair and sat looking in at him, obviously not planning on going anywhere any time soon. So much for that idea.

"And do sit up when you speak to me. I don't relish addressing the soles of your feet."

He looked at her and scowled. "You never give up, do you?" With a sigh he hauled himself back into a sitting position, drawing his knees up and wrapping his arms around himself. He glared. "Well?"

She didn't answer for a moment. Just watched him in silence like she was considering the worth of some damn horse at an auction. "You really are a very difficult man." Her voice was soft, and kind of gentle now. "You really hate the thought of Guy seeing you in here. And you hate the thought of him finding out too much about you, so you push him away. It won't work. He's very determined under that suave exterior."

Hell! The words she used. Where did a whore learn all those fancy words?

"He's going to go to Utah with you whether you want him to or not. There's not a thing you can do about it. He's determined to get you a good lawyer and a fair trial."

"I ain't a kid. I can get myself a lawyer. Don't need him hanging around."

She pursed her lips and narrowed her eyes. "Hmm. Hanging. But there's the crux. Does the thought of him seeing you hang scare you more than the hanging itself?"

The question rocked him. He had to say something. "They ain't found me guilty yet." He glared at her again but she didn't seem too bothered. Why? People usually backed off when he gave them his coldest looks.

"I'm well aware of that. But knowing you as I do, I would bet good money that in the event of you being convicted, you're more scared of Guy being there than you are of hanging."

"I ain't scared of nothing." He wondered how many times

he'd said that.

She smiled. "Honey, we're all scared of something. And I'd say in your case it's allowing yourself to get too attached. Or letting people get too close to you. And, for what it's worth, I think you're afraid of disappointing them." She sat back, like she'd had her say and was waiting for him to say something. Except he couldn't think of a damn thing to say. He fiddled with the Apache bracelet he always wore on his wrist, spinning the beads around. Why did she always wear that ugly gray dress? And scrape her hair back like that? She sure didn't do herself no favors. Did she ever wear jewelry? Funny, she was the whore but he was the one with the bracelet.

"Well?"

He couldn't look at her. He shook his head. "Just don't want him to go. Maybe you could talk him out of it?" Why the hell did he ask her that? Knew what the answer would be. And there was a huge lump in his throat and he felt so damn tired. He ran his hand through his hair. Too damn tired for what lay ahead, that was for sure.

She rolled her eyes. "No, I won't try and talk him out of it. You're going to need somebody with you and he'd be a good man to have by your side." She sighed. "Not that you'll accept that. You'll spend all your time pushing him away. Be careful. One day you might push too hard."

It hurt. The thought of Guy hating him really hurt. But the thought of Guy despising him for his past was even worse. Johnny swallowed. "Why did you come here? It wasn't just to bring me cookies."

She smiled, but she looked kind of sad. "I came because we're friends. I've told you that before." She gave a soft laugh. "And of course to tell you to hurry back, I really can't afford to lose a good customer. Even a difficult one."

"And you think I'll be coming back?" He said it casually, trying not to give away how much he needed to hear her say yes, that he would be coming back, that everything would be OK. Pathetic. God, he was pathetic. But it was like all the fight had gone out of him. Maybe if he could sleep . . .

"I certainly hope so!" She sounded amazed that he'd asked. "The girls will sulk most terribly if you don't. I find it very trying when they all sulk. They flounce around and it gives me the most blinding headache. Really, it plays on my nerves. And, like I said, I always hate losing good paying customers. I have my profit margins to worry about. And heavens, just imagine if all of the girls sulk, en masse as it were, it might cause me to lose other customers who'll take their business to the saloon at the other end of town." She leaned forward, like she was telling him some big secret. "And believe me, honey, the girls at that place are not nice. Not nice at all. And they're none too clean, either. Between you, me and this cell door, I do swear that a man could pick up some very nasty infections there. Very nasty indeed."

He could feel the smile threatening to break out, so he gave in and started to laugh. She smiled back at him. "That's better. I swear you were starting to depress me. I was feeling positively maudlin."

"Delice, I reckon you know as many fancy words as Harvard. D'you go to some fancy school too?"

"None of your business." Her smile faded. "Just make sure you come back to us. This town is a whole lot more boring when you're not around." She paused, pursing her lips as though she was trying to figure out the best way to say something. "It seems to me that Utah is an awfully long way from Johnny Fierro's usual haunts."

"Yeah, well, that's what I told them." But he couldn't look at her as he said it. He spun the beads on the bracelet round and round, making them go fast so that all the colors merged and he couldn't tell one from another.

She stood, pushed the chair back, and walked slowly to the door. He could feel her eyes watching him. "Utah is pretty much a long way from anywhere and if someone had made a trip there, I think he'd have had to have had a good reason for doing so."

His head jerked up, even as the color flooded his face. She smiled and winked. "Take care of yourself and be nice to your brother. And don't be gone too long. Hurry back to us. Have some consideration for my poor nerves. And my business."

He sat back as she left with a cheerful wave of her hand. And he realized he was smiling. And he didn't feel so tired. How did she do that? Because all of a sudden it felt like he'd got his fight back. It was time he stopped mopin' around feeling sorry for himself and started planning. Because he was damned if he'd swing for this. Fuck that. Johnny Fierro wasn't through yet.

CHAPTER TEN

"On your feet, Fierro. It's time to go." Carter's rasping voice startled him. He must have been dozing.

Smothering a yawn, Johnny struggled slowly to his feet. Maybe he'd been at Sinclair too long anyhow because he was sure getting soft. His back was aching from sleeping on the narrow cot. He winced as he stretched and moved his head from side to side trying to ease out the crick in his neck. His neck. Kind of funny really. Maybe he wouldn't be needing to worry about his neck for much longer.

"You can wipe that smile off your face, Fierro. Believe me. You ain't got nothing to smile about."

He narrowed his eyes, looking Carter up and down real slow. The man was puny for a lawman, with watery blue eyes and a thin straggly beard, like he wasn't man enough to grow a proper one. "I reckon I'll have the last laugh, when I walk out of your courtroom a free man. You'll look like a real jackass then." He paused. "You got my saddlebags? Like I said earlier, I'll be needing them for the ride back."

Carter smirked and scrabbled in his pocket like he was looking for something. "Yeah, I got your saddlebags—had to check them for any hidden weapons. And looky here at what I found." The smirk grew bigger as he held up a gold nugget, waving it in Johnny's face. "I found me a big piece of gold hidden away in the bottom."

Pity he'd promised Stoney he wouldn't use his knife on no

lawman because right then he was tempted to slit the grinning man's throat from ear to ear. He clenched his fists tight to stop himself taking a swing at the man. It would feel so good to smash a fist into that fellow's face and splatter his nose right across it. But probably wouldn't be too smart. He needed to get to Utah in one piece. "That's mine." He spoke real soft and easy. "And if you got any brains you'll put it right back where you found it."

Carter laughed. "How do I know you didn't steal it, Fierro? Maybe you're a thief as well as a killer. After all, a killer like you wouldn't think nothing of helping himself to other folks' belongings."

"That's enough, Carter." Ford stood scowling by the cell door. "Give Fierro the nugget and let him check his saddlebags." He glanced at Johnny, raising an eyebrow. "You found that nugget, Fierro? Is it yours, fair and square?"

Johnny nodded, looking him right in the eyes. "Yeah. It was years ago. I was messing about doing some panning, and I found it. Carried it in my bags ever since." And the day he'd found it, he'd sworn that one day, if he ever had a woman of his own, he'd make her a ring from it. Kind of dumb, really. Chances were nobody would ever want him, but if they did . . .

Ford nodded. "That's good enough for me." He turned as Carter stomped back in carrying the bags. "Give them to Fierro, let him check them."

"Ain't much in them . . ."

Ford sighed like he'd had enough of his companion. "That's not the point. Just give him the damn bags, Carter."

Johnny grinned. "Much obliged." He tried not to flinch as Carter thrust them at him, whacking him in the stomach in the process. Instead, he took the nugget and pushed it back down into the corner of the bag where he always kept it and had a quick glance through the other things in his bags. Nothing else had been disturbed. But trust a son of bitch like Carter to find the gold.

"I'll make sure your bags get loaded on the stage. Carter, get him cuffed and bring him on out." Ford held his hand out for the bags, and walked out, slinging them over his shoulder, leaving Carter to snap the cuffs round Johnny's wrists. Dios, they were tight. Way too tight, but if he said anything Carter would make 'em tighter. He was that type.

Carter gave him a shove in his back, pushing him out of the cell, and then drew his gun. "Outside, now, Fierro, and don't try anything clever because I will use this gun if I have to. In fact, it would be a real pleasure. Except I'd hate to cheat the hangman."

Johnny walked through into Stoney's office and out onto the street, the chink of his spurs sounding like a death march. There was a small group of people huddled together whispering and pointing at him. He recognized some of them as the ladies of the sewing circle who spent most of their time sniping at people they didn't approve of. He gave them one of his broadest smiles. "Now don't you ladies go worrying yourselves about me. I'll be back real soon, so you just all rest easy in your beds."

It shut them up. They turned away, looking like angry old hens when the rooster gets too close. Johnny glanced along the street and hissed in a breath, because riding right on down the middle of the street toward the livery stable was Harvard. Shit. What the hell did he have to say to that man to drive him away? Didn't think he'd ever known a man as thick-skinned as Harvard. Why couldn't he just back off and leave Fierro alone?

Guy reined in next to the hostler and dismounted smartly like he was still in the damn cavalry. Everything he did was like a reminder that he'd served in the army. Everything was just so with him. Never a hair out of place. Always kind of clean and tidy. Fucking officer and gentleman, that was Harvard. Johnny could feel the dry heat of rage now, growing inside himself, and he was glad of it. It was easier to say what he had to say if he was angry. And he was angry. Tired of telling his brother to butt out. He breathed in deeply, and he would have clenched his fists but the damn cuffs were cutting into his flesh and there were damn all links between them so his hands were too close together.

Harvard passed the reins of his horse to the hostler before walking over, standing straight like a damn soldier. Johnny sneered. "Come to see me off, have you?"

Guy raised an eyebrow, just a touch, like he always did. Any minute now he'd start with his damn gloves. "No, Johnny, I haven't come to see you off. I believe I'm heading in the same direction. I have a ticket for the stage." He waved a small slip of paper at Johnny.

"Why the hell don't you take off, Harvard, and leave me alone?" His voice came out as a hiss. But Dios! He had to stop Harvard coming. Couldn't cope with Harvard finding out . . .

Guy just raised his eyebrow again. And then he leaned forward to whisper in Johnny's ear. "It won't work. Sorry, brother, but I can see right through you. And I don't believe a word of it."

Johnny just managed to stop himself jerking forward. It wasn't supposed to play out like this. What the hell did Fierro have to do to make him stay away? He swallowed hard, and tried to keep his expression blank, because he couldn't let Guy see the fear.

Guy flashed him a smug smile, kind of like he knew he gotten the upper hand. "So, I'm coming too. Unless, of course, you'd prefer me to send for Father?"

This time Johnny couldn't stop himself, his head jerked up even as he felt a cold shock of horror. No, not the old man. He couldn't stand the thought of that. It was like he didn't have any control left over anything. And he had to be in control. Had to be . . .

"No?" Guy smiled, like he was hoping Johnny would say something. But he couldn't say a damn word. "I'll take that as a no, then. And so it seems you're stuck with me. Whether you like it or not." He turned away and tossed his saddlebags to the shotgun rider who piled them in with the rest of the luggage on top of the stage. "I must say, I'm glad the first bit of this journey will be in the stage." Guy glanced up at the threatening clouds. "Because it looks like it's going to pour down at any second." He hopped up into the stage, settled in a corner seat, and proceeded to take a book out.

A book? Madre de Dios. Harvard was going to sit and read? Johnny sucked in some air and stood straighter. He'd be damned if he'd let anyone see that Guy had gotten to him. Still, at least things couldn't get no worse.

A gravelly voice called out behind him. "You got room for another passenger? I don't mind riding up top. I can squeeze in beside you and the shotgun rider."

Johnny bit back a groan. He'd been wrong. Things could get worse. He glared at Stoney, who was all wrapped up in his big tartan coat and shambling over to talk to the stagecoach driver.

Johnny shook his head, almost in despair now. What was wrong with them all? Why wouldn't they just leave him be? "Not you too, Stoney? I don't need a damn nursemaid."

Stoney shrugged. "Figured your brother could use the company."

Johnny would have thrown his hands in the air if it wasn't for the damn cuffs. But why, in the name of God, did these two stubborn men want to come all the way to Utah? Pity he hadn't got a gun! Because right now he felt like shooting the pair of them. And what good did they think they could do once they got there? Bribe the fucking jury? And God only knew what they'd think when they heard the details . . . Oh hell! It couldn't get any worse than this. He huffed out a sigh. Yeah it could. It would be even worse if the old man was there. Thank God for Burnett. Which was kind of funny really. Never thought he'd see the day when he was grateful to that slimy piece of shit. Oh boy, and here was Mayor Tandy puffing his way along the street. The man would be crowing like an old rooster at seeing Fierro in a scrape.

"Sheriff Rockwell. Sheriff Rockwell! Where do you think you're going?" Tandy was red-faced and breathing hard from the effort of getting off his fat butt and hurrying. Made a change from sitting in his store, counting his money.

Stoney didn't look too bothered. "I'm taking a few days leave, Mayor Tandy. What is it to you?"

"What is it to me?" Tandy puffed out his chest. "I'm the mayor and I must remind you that you have a responsibility to this town."

Stoney laughed, like Tandy had made a real good joke. "Well, as the town ain't paying my wages, I reckon the town can't complain if I take a few days off. It managed to struggle along before I came, so I reckon a few days won't make no difference."

"You're not planning on accompanying that . . . that . . . desperado . . . that ruffian?" Tandy pointed an accusing finger at Johnny, who promptly smiled. A big wide smile that would really irritate the hell out of that tub of lard.

Johnny stepped toward him. "Now don't you go fussing yourself, Mayor Tandy. I'll be back real soon and be able to sort out any of them outlaws you get so bothered about. A man your age shouldn't get so worked up. You're getting yourself in a state and that ain't good for your health. Don't you fret none. Soon as I straighten out this mess, I'll be right along back to this nice little town of yours. I know that'll be a real comfort to you."

"Why, Fierro . . . Fierro . . . I—"

Johnny gave him another broad smile. "Don't worry, there ain't no need to thank me. I know how grateful you are. And I know how much all you folks will miss me. Like I said, I'll be back real soon." Tandy looked like a big old fish. Opening and closing his mouth. Hell, he never thought he'd see the day, but he reckoned old Tandy really was finally lost for words. And it was almost worth getting arrested just to see that. Maybe life wasn't so bad. He turned to clamber up into the stage, which was kind of tricky with his hands cuffed, but he'd manage with no help. Wouldn't take no help from anyone.

He'd got one foot in, when Ford pulled him back. "Those cuffs OK, Fierro? They look kind of tight."

He shrugged. Be damned if he'd complain. Ford was looking at him real hard. Reaching for the keys. "I'll ease them off a bit. They look too tight to me."

Johnny frowned. In his experience marshals were usually bastards who didn't give a damn about the comfort of prisoners. And why should they? So what was it with Ford? He sure wasn't like most marshals. He was kind of thoughtful. Maybe he bought into all that crap of Harvard's, about a man being innocent till he was proved guilty.

Ford leaned over and loosened the cuffs, then jerked his head towards the stage. "Go on and get in now. It's going to be a full house on this ride. You might as well make yourself comfortable."

Couldn't think of a damn thing to say, so he scrambled up. Guy had taken the corner seat on one side, so Johnny sat on the opposite side, knowing the lawmen would want to sit either side of him. Guy glanced up, all casual. "Ah, you've arrived. I imagine we'll be off soon. Did I hear Stoney asking for a ride too?"

Johnny stared at him, suddenly knowing how Mayor Tandy

had felt when he couldn't think of anything to say. He forced himself to nod. "Yeah. I guess so. I think he's got to ride up top. I reckon we've got other passengers."

"Yes, I believe the others joined the stage earlier. They're in the hotel, taking refreshments at present." And then Guy buried his nose back in his book like he was heading off on a business trip. Not to see his brother hang.

Madre de Dios. When did his brother learn to act so cool? And Guy didn't even seem to notice that Johnny was staring at him. Shit. Maybe Guy and Fierro had something in common after all. And that was kind of worrying. Because maybe it meant that Harvard would come all the way to Utah, and whatever Fierro said wouldn't make no difference. Johnny shook his head slowly. Seemed like too much to think about right now. He needed to plan ahead, and quit worrying about Harvard.

The stage rocked violently as Ford and Carter climbed in and took the seats either side of him. And then two sour old biddies in drab clothes were given a hand in by the stage driver. Dried up as old prunes. Oh boy. He hated stages at the best of times, but he had a feeling that this was going to be a real shitty journey.

CHAPTER ELEVEN

The stage set off with a jolt, clattering along the street, throwing him against Carter and causing Harvard to make a grab for his book. It was an awful big book. Like the ones he'd noticed Harvard reading when Johnny had been laid up in bed after being shot in the battle with the mine owner Wallace when he tried to seize control of the Sinclair ranch. Johnny had pretended to be asleep, but Harvard had often sat in the corner of the room reading. And Johnny had wondered why the hell this stranger had cared enough to spend all that time sitting with him. Later, Johnny had made barbed comments to Harvard about him reading such big books.

Harvard glanced across at him, and his mouth quirked in a smile, almost like he was remembering the same thing.

Johnny bit his lip and looked away quickly, trying to ignore the sudden pang that the memory brought. And trying to ignore the sudden lump in his throat and the tight pain in his chest. He hated the way Harvard had gotten under his skin. How the hell had Fierro allowed that to happen? It was odd though, how he'd sensed exactly what Harvard had been thinking then. Wasn't the first time either. They often seemed to think the same things. See things the same way. Was it because they were brothers? Bound by blood?

But what the hell would Harvard think when he heard all the details about what had happened in Utah? He'd be disgusted then. Yeah. Disgusted. Johnny swallowed hard. He hated the thought of letting Guy down. Of disappointing him. Disgusting him. But now it was all going to come out. Every sickening detail would be bandied around that courtroom. And there was nothing he could do to stop it. Felt like he was on a runaway horse. Everything was outside his control. And he hated not being in control. All he could do now was to play his hand as well as he could and hope that his ace in the hole was enough. Enough to save him from the hangman.

"What crime has he committed?" The sour old cow sitting next to Harvard was looking at Johnny with the kind of look she'd have if she stumbled over a rotting steer. She had straggly gray hair that was fighting to escape from under an ugly brown bonnet. And her thin lips were pressed together around a mouth that he'd wager had never sucked a cock. Not surprising though. She'd probably been real ugly even when she was young.

Carter leaned forward, obviously keen to share the details. "Murder, ma'am. He's nothing but a cold-blooded killer."

She let out a little cry and fell back in her seat fanning herself. Too bad the shock didn't silence her permanently.

The other woman, who looked like a school marm, was made of stronger stuff. "Who did he kill? Is it safe for him to be traveling with good, decent, law-abiding folk?"

Carter smiled, showing the gaping holes where his front teeth had once been. Probably some pissed-off prisoner had punched 'em out. He'd sure like to buy that man a drink, whoever he'd been. "Well, ma'am, there's no need to fret yourself. He's cuffed good and tight, and he won't ever be hurting anyone ever again. And me and my friend here are both lawmen. We're taking him back to Utah to hang him, even though there's some that say hanging's too good for him. He deserves worse than that."

Ford snorted at that. "No. We're taking him back to Utah for a trial. He ain't been convicted of nothing."

"Who did he kill?" The woman leaned forward, clasping her

hands together and licking her lips, like the idea of a killing excited her. Old hag.

And Guy paused in the middle of turning a page, kind of like he was waiting on the answer too.

Carter leaned forward, obviously keen to share his tale. "Oh, a real nice gentleman. Quiet and very amiable, he was. Hadn't been in our little community long, but he stepped right up and even offered to help out at the local orphanage with the little kiddies. Yep, a good man. He built himself a nice little house on the outskirts of our town, and then this fellow." He paused to jab Johnny with his finger. "This fellow killed him. That poor man was in his own home when this desperado came along and brutally killed him." Carter shook his head. "Vicious it was. In all my years as a lawman I ain't never seen the like of it. But I can't tell you more, ma'am, the details ain't fit for a lady's ears."

"Oh." She sounded disappointed and her shoulders drooped. He almost wished Carter would tell her. It would sure shut her up.

"Of course, look at the color of his skin, he's obviously a breed. You can't expect anything else from his type." The first old prune seemed to have recovered from her shock.

The other woman nodded repeatedly. "Oh, my dear, I so agree. It's bad blood. It's what comes of mixing blood. Breeds, well, they're not like normal people."

Guy slammed his book shut, making them all jump. "Madam, firstly, this young man has not been convicted of any crime and therefore has the right to be presumed innocent until proven guilty. Secondly, the matter of his parentage is hardly your concern, but the fact that he is of mixed heritage certainly has no bearing on his character, which, I might add, is wholly admirable and will easily withstand close examination."

Holy shit! Old Harvard might use ten-dollar words but the

meaning was clear enough. And it felt good to hear it. Trouble was, Harvard wouldn't say all that if he knew the truth. And he was going to find out the truth all too soon.

"You are acquainted with this unfortunate creature?" The school marm sounded real surprised.

Guy looked at her, didn't say nothing for a second, almost like he wanted his words to count more. "Yes, ma'am, I'm proud to say he's my brother."

The old prunes' mouths dropped open. They stared at Guy, wide-eyed, and closed their mouths and then opened them again, but they didn't say a word. And he couldn't blame them for that. He was kind of speechless himself. He stared too, trying to sort things out in his head. Harvard held his gaze briefly and then winked at him as he opened his book once more.

Johnny frowned. Would he ever understand Guy? He knew he didn't deserve his brother's support but it had sounded so good to hear Guy defend him. Real good. Be nice if he had the chance to get to know Harvard better. Maybe Guy wouldn't believe the things he was going to hear in Utah. Maybe Fierro would get lucky and get away with it. After all, everyone knew the devil looked after his own. And the devil had kept him alive this long, maybe his luck would hold a while longer. Maybe.

He leaned back, shuffling against the hard seat in an effort to get comfortable. His eyes felt heavy and he'd have loved to doze but it didn't seem worth the risk. Didn't want to give nothing away. Couldn't take the chance of talking in his sleep. Not with a coachload of witnesses.

The coach jolted over a particularly bumpy bit of track, throwing Ford, who'd been dozing, against him. "Sorry, Fierro." The man settled himself back in his corner and shut his eyes again. Johnny frowned. It was strange how Ford looked out for him and treated him right. Unusual in a marshal. Seemed a nice enough fellow. Not like Carter—he was a real piece of shit.

Ford didn't seem to like Carter either. Acted like he wanted nothing to do with the man.

The nervous old prune was staring at him. Her eyes were wide open like saucers. Acting like she thought he was going to attack her or something. He grinned at her. "Ma'am." He spoke real soft and easy but the way she jumped was like he'd leapt at her and held a knife to her scrawny throat. One thing was certain, she'd never been a beauty.

She fanned herself with a tattered scrap of handkerchief. "Marshal, make him stop talking to me." Her voice was shrill and set his nerves on edge.

Carter jabbed him hard in the ribs. "You heard the lady, Fierro. Don't speak to her. She don't want nothing to do with the likes of you."

"Fierro?" The school marm jerked forward. "Did you say Fierro?" She fixed Carter with a piercing look.

Carter nodded. "That's right, ma'am. Johnny Fierro."

She gasped, her faded blue eyes shining with excitement, and shook the other woman's arm. "Oh my goodness, Mildred. Did you hear him? That's Johnny Fierro. He's famous."

Johnny bit back a smile. Mildred didn't look none too impressed. Confused more like.

"You know, Mildred." The school marm sounded irritated, and she nudged her friend with her elbow. "The gunfighter. We've read about him. He's very famous." She frowned at Harvard. "I wouldn't have expected him to have a brother."

Harvard sighed and put his book down. "Why ever not? Why shouldn't a gunfighter have a family like other people?"

Mildred looked more interested now and had to have her say. "Fierro? Oh yes! I remember the stories now. He's the spawn of the devil, that's what he is, Ethel. A brutal killer! Hang him, that's what I say."

"Ladies." Ford opened his eyes. Maybe he hadn't been sleeping after all. Maybe he just didn't want to talk to nobody and who could blame him? But he looked mighty pissed off. "Mr. Fierro has not been found guilty of any crime . . ."

"As yet," Carter butted in, smirking.

Johnny ground his teeth. He'd love to wipe the smile off that man's face. All in good time, Fierro, all in good time.

Ford scowled at Carter. "As I was saying, Fierro hasn't been convicted, and as such, deserves to be able to travel in this stage without being abused. Now, if you've all quite finished, I would like to get some sleep."

The old prunes flushed an ugly brick red and sat back whispering to each other. He could make out some of the words, like disgraceful and offensive, and how they'd expect a marshal to be more civil.

Guy glanced out from behind his book and winked at him again. And before he could stop himself, Johnny found himself grinning back. Damn. He really was getting soft. He'd been so set on scowling at Harvard all the way to Utah but it was harder than he expected.

Johnny settled back in the hard seat. The stagecoach was rolling and rattling and it felt like every bone in his body was being shaken out of place. It was going to be a hellishly uncomfortable journey through rough country. The stagecoach was following the Old Spanish Trail route, which would take them through the corner of Colorado before heading into Utah. Ford had mentioned that they'd have to complete the last part of the journey on horseback and right now that couldn't come soon enough.

They made only brief stops; the driver's schedule meant he pressed on through day and night. But at least they'd get a longer break once they reached Mancos.

Johnny had lost track of time. The skies had been unrelentingly gray since the start of this journey. And now, rain had set in as a steady downpour. Poor old Stoney—he'd be getting soaked riding up top. Bet he was regretting his decision to come now. But why the hell had he come? Johnny shook his head—he'd spent hours brooding over that and was still unable to think of a good reason. Couldn't figure any of this at all. First Harvard. Then Stoney. What was it with those two? Just as well Delice hadn't decided to come along for the ride. That would have been too much to cope with. Damn woman. Always thought she knew best. Still, the cookies were good . . . Surely she hadn't baked them herself? No. Why the hell would she waste her time making cookies for a gunfighter? After all, she didn't like gunfighters—she'd told him that when they first met. And where did she learn all them fancy words she was always using? How come she became a whore? Smartest whore he'd ever met. And he'd sure known a lot of them. And fucked a lot of them over the years. Would he ever have another woman? At least he'd had more women in his short life than most men managed in a lifetime, so he shouldn't complain. Still, he'd have liked one last visit with Sadie . . .

The rain was coming down harder now. Splattering in through the rough covers at the windows. And the wind was getting up, buffeting the coach and making it roll from side to side. Harvard closed his book with a sigh, like he couldn't read in these conditions. Johnny studied him through half-closed eyes so Guy wouldn't realize he was being watched. Funny how he'd taken him for a real dandy when they'd first met. But now he could see that the outlandish Eastern clothes that his brother wore for social occasions were almost like a disguise, masking the man beneath. Back then, Johnny hadn't noticed the determined set of Guy's jaw and those steady eyes. Which was odd, because he could usually read a man real well. But he'd been too busy laughing at Guy to notice that he wasn't a man

to back down or give in without a fight. A loyal man. And right
now it seemed that Guy figured his brother needed his loyalty.

Couldn't barely remember anyone who was so . . . so . . . ?
True? Maybe that was the word. Loyal and true. Even the
thought of it brought a lump to his throat. He couldn't
remember anyone having such faith in him before now, apart
from Luke. And that made it all worse somehow. The thought
of Guy finding out what Johnny had done. Madre de Dios! The
shame of it.

A deafening crack of thunder spooked the horses, and sent
them skittering sideways, causing the stage to lurch violently.
The women squealed in fear as they were thrown sideways
before the coach steadied and carried on.

"Surely this isn't safe, Marshal?" Mildred trembled as she
spoke, and more of her untidy hair made a bid for freedom
from her sludgy brown bonnet. She looked a real bad color too.
Kind of like she was going to spew her guts up at any minute.
Johnny moved his feet in closer to his seat.

Carter didn't look none too good either. Mierda. That was all
he needed. Carter and the old dame spewing over him. He'd
known this would be a shitty journey.

Carter leaned out of the window but whatever he yelled at
the stage driver was lost in the still strengthening wind.
Lightning forked across the dark sky, casting an eerie and ever-
changing pattern of flashes in the gloom. And the air seemed
heavy, making it hard to breathe. It stuck in his throat, choking
him, like a hangman's noose. The hairs on his neck stood on
end. It was like some dark force of nature had taken over and
everything was out of control.

Another deafening crack of thunder sent the horses skittering
again. The coach lurched violently, the women screamed again,
and then the world went tumbling over. He glimpsed the white,
staring face of the school marm, her mouth forming an O before

they hurtled into each other, thrown together as easily as rag dolls. Guy's book hung suspended briefly before thudding into Carter, who was thrown half out of the window as Ford and Guy cartwheeled through the air and then everything went still. Except for the wind.

CHAPTER TWELVE

"Any last requests?" The bearded man, reeking of sweat and whiskey, placed the noose over his head, taking care to position the knot so it would break his neck when they opened the trap. Made from coarse fibers, it irritated and rubbed his skin.

He couldn't speak. He shook his head a fraction. And looking down at the sea of faces, all he could see was Guy watching him, his eyes full of contempt. Fierro was finally getting what he deserved.

The hangman positioned him over the trap and lifted his hand to give the signal. The drop jolted him and seemed to go on forever—surely his neck should have broken by now? Then all he felt was cold water, like someone had thrown a bucketful over him. His head felt like he'd been kicked by a mule. And his mouth was full of dirt. He struggled to open his eyes even as he pulled his face away from the choking mud. Where the hell was he?

A clap of thunder overhead brought him to with a jolt. Madre de Dios. The stage. He'd been on the stage and then the world had spun upside down. With a hiss of pain he struggled to his feet and stood swaying as he tried to focus on the wreck. And what a wreck it was. The axles and pole were smashed and the coach itself lay crushed on its side with one wheel still slowly spinning. The luggage was scattered all around and God only knew where the horses were. How the hell he'd survived seemed like a miracle. But then, everyone knew the devil looked after his own.

He stumbled closer for a better look, wishing the world would stop spinning, never mind the damn wheel, before stopping abruptly. The school marm—Ethel—was lying on her side, wedged in the door staring from sightless eyes. Her skirts were bundled up around her waist, exposing a pair of faded gray bloomers stretched across her ample backside.

Memories flooded his mind now. Guy. Where the hell was Guy? He scrambled around the woman, trying to see past her into the wreckage. Maybe Guy was in the stage. He manhandled her out of the way, cursing the cuffs, which made the task damn near impossible. Her head lolled sideways on her broken neck and her eyes looked at him accusingly. Dios, she was heavy. Dead weight. But leastways he didn't need to worry about being gentle. Gritting his teeth he gave another big heave, wishing he had the full use of his hands. Another backbreaking tug and he'd have her clear. He grunted with the effort and fell back to the ground as he finally hauled her free of the door. He staggered back to his feet and tried to pull her skirts back into place to make her decent. It seemed wrong to leave her uncovered.

He stumbled back to look in the stage. Guy had to be all right. He had to be . . . His heart plummeted with a sickening jolt as he peered inside. Ford was slumped over, his arm twisted at an impossible angle, and the other old dame was sprawled across the seat. But Guy wasn't there. Where the hell was he? Had he fallen clear?

Screwing up his eyes to see through the driving rain he scanned the ground around the stage. "Guy. Guy!" His voice sounded hoarse. He strained to hear some reply, but there wasn't a sound except for the wind and the rain.

Again he peered in the coach. Had he missed something? No. Just Ford and the woman. He fell to his knees and tried to scramble under the coach but there was nothing there. Clambering to his feet he retraced his steps, tripping as he kicked the luggage out of his path trying to get a clearer view of the ground. Guy had to be here somewhere.

He could feel fear overwhelming him like water closing over his head. Guy had to be safe. He couldn't lose him like this. Please, God, make him be safe. He shook his head. This was what God did. Any time Fierro started to care for anyone, God took them away.

"Guy!"

Frantically he tried to remember the events. He vaguely recalled Carter falling from the stage but Guy had been sitting on the other side. Shutting his eyes, he took a deep breath and then another, trying to slow his racing heart. Damn it! He needed to get back in control. When he opened his eyes he found he could focus better and the world didn't seem quite so wobbly. He lifted his hands to wipe the wet from his face. Damn rain. But when he dropped his hands back down he saw they were covered in blood. Moving slowly, he made his way round to the far side of the stage and then he saw Guy, lying crumpled with part of the axle resting across him. Johnny felt lighter suddenly, warmer, and his legs worked better and he found himself running to Guy's side.

He fell to his knees beside Guy, bending over him. His heart lurched again. His brother was awful still. God, no. Johnny stared at Guy's chest, hoping for some movement. Some sign of life. And then it moved. He was sure it moved. The shirt rippled even as he watched. But his heart plummeted once more as it hit him that it was the wind moving the shirt.

He lowered his ear to Guy's chest, listening for something. Anything. But all he could hear was the sound of his own fear rushing in his ears. And the damn wind. And then a beat? Maybe? "Guy! Can you hear me? Guy!" But Guy made no sign of having heard.

A flash of lightning lit up the sky as another clap of thunder shook the ground he crouched on. Johnny tried to fight his rising panic but his chest was tight like it was being crushed. What if Guy didn't wake up? Shit, no, not that. He shook him by the shoulder.

"Why did you come? Why couldn't you have stayed at the ranch?" He was yelling, but Guy still didn't move. "Why? You shouldn't be here. You should be safe at the ranch. You had to be fucking stubborn. Why?"

"Hell, is he hurt bad, Johnny?"

The voice startled him. Johnny swung round to face Stoney who'd come up behind him. "I don't know . . . I think maybe . . . You check him."

Stoney grunted. "Shift over. Let me get a look at him. And clear some of that damn wreckage away from here. Can't see what I'm doing."

"He ain't moving, Stoney. He ain't moving. You hear me, Stoney?" His voice sounded strange to his own ears.

"Yeah, Johnny, I hear you. Just get out of the way, damn it, and let me see him." Stoney ran his hands over Guy and then bent so he could listen to Guy's chest. "Well, he's breathing OK. Heart don't sound bad at all." He looked at Johnny, narrowing his eyes. "Dunno why you couldn't hear that. Anyone might think you were panicking. Ain't like Johnny Fierro to panic."

Stoney bent again, running his hands along Guy's arms and legs. "Well, I ain't no doctor, but I don't think he's broke nothing, or nothing too serious anyway." He gently tilted Guy's head to one side. "It looks like he's had a mighty crack to his head, though. Look." He pointed to a bloody patch on the back of Guy's head.

"He's awful still, Stoney."

The sheriff sighed in irritation. "Course he's still, he's unconscious, you dumb son of a bitch." Stoney leaned down and, grunting with effort, hefted Guy over his shoulder. "Reckon he'll be OK. I'll put him in the stage. Leastways he'll be out of the rain." He shot Johnny a piercing look, his lips twitching slightly, like he was trying not to smile. "Seems to me that for someone who didn't want his brother to come on this trip because he means nothing to you, you're awful worked up about him now."

Johnny narrowed his eyes, glaring at Stoney. "Just look after Guy, and stop trying to be so fucking clever. Not much wrong with you, at any rate."

Stoney grinned. "I jumped clear as it started to roll. Hurt my ankle, is all." He limped off, bent almost double under Guy's weight, before easing Guy gently into the shelter of the stage.

Peering inside, Johnny saw Ford was awake, although he looked kind of green, and the old dame was huddled in the corner, shaking like she'd got the ague or something. And now Guy was moving too. Letting out a sigh of relief, Johnny pushed forward to lean over Guy, who let out a low groan as his eyelids flickered. Johnny dropped to his knees. "Harvard. Hey, Harvard. Can you hear me?"

Guy winced and opened his eyes slowly. "Johnny?" He struggled to sit up, and then went even paler. "Hell. You look awful."

"Me?" Johnny scoffed. "I'm fine. More worried about you, Harvard. But stay still for a moment, will you? We need to check there ain't nothing broke." Johnny raised his arms trying to brush the blood and water from his own face so he could get a better look at Guy.

"I've just got a pounding headache, and I feel a bit bruised. But nothing worse." Guy pushed Johnny's hand away. "I'm more concerned about your head than mine. You're covered in blood."

"Damn it, Guy, I'm fine. But you take it easy and don't move too fast. Don't want you passing out again."

He could feel the old dame watching him. He glanced at her. "You hold still there, ma'am, make sure you feel OK before you move around too much."

Her eyes opened wide and she shuffled rapidly along the seat, farther away from him. What was it she'd called him? Spawn of the devil? Yeah, spawn of the devil. "You got a name, ma'am?"

She jumped like she'd been burned. She turned to Ford. "Shouldn't he be tied up or something? He could escape."

Ford sighed softly. "He's wearing cuffs. I don't reckon he'll be going too far." He screwed his eyes up, looking harder now at Johnny. "You're bleeding bad, Fierro. You OK?"

Johnny grunted in irritation. Why did people make such a fuss about a bit of blood? "I'm fine, just fine," he snapped. "I'd better go see if I can find the others. Stoney, you rest up here if your ankle is troubling you. Look after these people and I'll be along."

"Someone should go with him and watch him." The old dame didn't trust him at all. "He may try to escape. And my friend is out there somewhere. He may frighten her if she sees him loose."

Johnny shook his head and sighed. "I'm real sorry, ma'am, but your friend . . . Well, she didn't make it. She was hurt bad falling from the stage when it rolled. If it's any comfort I don't think she suffered."

The old dame paled and shrank back into the corner, looking frail and smaller suddenly. Her lower lip started to tremble and her eyes filled with tears. "We'd known each other all our lives."

"I'm sorry, ma'am. I truly am." He shifted awkwardly, uncertain of what else to say. "I'd best go look for the others."

"Hold up a minute, Fierro." Ford fumbled in his pocket. "Let me undo those cuffs. Be easier for you to manage with your hands free."

Johnny felt a rush of surprise. And confusion. For a brief moment he couldn't think of a damn thing to say. Couldn't remember a lawman ever trusting him in the past. "Ain't you worried about me escaping?"

Ford shrugged, wincing with pain. "Don't reckon you for a coward. Only cowards run." He nodded towards Guy. "And you got your brother here. Nope. I ain't worried about you escaping. Reckon you'll be back. Besides," he paused, smiling weakly. "I guess the horses have long gone in this storm. You won't get too far on foot."

Johnny nodded briefly and headed back into the storm, trying to see through the driving rain sluicing down from a leaden sky. Hell. What a mess. At least one dead, and God only knew what had happened to the stage driver and his sidekick. Or Carter. He gritted his teeth as he thought of Carter. The man was a nasty son of a bitch. If there was any justice it would be Carter lying with a broken neck instead of the old school marm. Justice? Hell, he'd seen little enough of that during his lifetime.

He pulled his jacket collar up round his neck. Maybe he'd find his hat. Damn rain. God, he hated rain. Keeping his head down, he scanned the ground ahead and could just make out the shape of two figures in a tangled heap. And they weren't moving. He crouched down, gently turning the men over to get a better look at their faces. The driver and the shotgun rider. They were both dead. They must have taken the force of the impact as the stage went over. Poor devils. But it meant that Carter was still out there somewhere. And Fierro would probably catch his death of cold hunting for him.

A flash of lightning forked down and struck a tree close by, causing him to jump sideways. It burst into flames, lighting up the gloom. It was too damn close for comfort. Never mind catching his death looking for Carter, he'd probably get struck by lightning instead. Hunching down into his jacket he retraced the path of the stage. Another flash of lightning lit up a gully falling away from the main track. Straining his eyes he tried to gauge how deep it was. The low-growing brushwood at the edge was broken and crushed. As if someone had rolled down there.

He grimaced. Carter had to be down there. It was tempting to simply return to the stage and say he couldn't find the man. Very tempting. He shook his head briefly and with a sigh started making his way down the gully.

The sides were steep and slippery and he lost his footing, sliding several feet before grabbing at some branches to slow his descent. Should have brought a rope. Guy would have thought of a rope. If Carter was injured it would be damn near impossible to get him back up without one. Maybe Carter would be dead and he wouldn't have to bother. The thought cheered him and he scrambled down the last few feet. He stood trying to catch his breath when he heard the crack of a twig behind him. Whirling round he found himself face to face with Carter and looking down the barrel of the deputy's gun. Carter gave a low laugh and cocked the gun.

CHAPTER THIRTEEN

"Well! I guess I just got lucky. Found me a killer on the loose." Carter grinned like he'd won the pot at the poker table.

"I ain't on the loose. I was looking for you." Johnny kept his voice casual.

Carter snorted. "Is that so? Planning on finishing me off, were you? I got news for you, Fierro, I think I'll finish you off and save the hangman the trouble. And it'll be a real pleasure, you sick son of a bitch." He cocked the hammer.

Shit. The bastard was loco enough to do it too. Johnny huffed out a sigh. "They know I'm here. Ford turned me loose to look for you. He figured you were lying hurt somewhere."

Carter narrowed his eyes. "Ford would have looked for me himself. He's a fool, but I don't reckon he'd have let you go. Kill him too, did you?"

Johnny shrugged. "He's hurt. His arm's broke. If it was up to me I'd have left you for dead, but he wanted me to look for you." Could he take Carter? It had to be worth a try. The bastard was going to shoot him either way. Leastways it was better than hanging. And if Carter killed him, Guy would go back to the ranch and never find out about Utah . . . He'd never discover how bad Fierro really was. It was a way out. Maybe the best way out.

"Start saying your prayers, Fierro."

Johnny smiled. "I told you, his arm's broke. He did send me to look for you. And I reckon he'll be pissed if you shoot me."

Carter laughed. A big laugh showing the gaps in his teeth. "I don't give a damn if he sent you to find me or not. I killed you when you went for me. That's all anyone needs to know. Hell! I'll be a hero. The man who killed Johnny Fierro. And trust me, when people hear about what you did in Utah, ain't nobody going to be bothered you're dead."

Carter aimed the gun at Johnny's chest, even as he hurled himself at the deputy. The explosion almost deafened him as the bullet seared a path across his hip. Trying to ignore the pain, he wrestled Carter to the ground with a bone-crunching thud that knocked the breath from him. He heard Carter's breath hitch too, but Carter still had hold of the gun and was struggling to bring it around while Johnny fought to grab hold of it. Shit. Johnny felt the barrel push against his ribs and threw himself sideways as Carter fired again.

Johnny tried to scramble sideways but Carter's fist aimed a blow at his head, throwing him backwards against a boulder. Johnny took a step to fight back but his feet were wobbling and the world was spinning around. But not enough to blot out the view of Carter grinning and leveling the gun at his head.

"Drop it, asshole."

Stoney? Was that Stoney's voice? Or maybe he was imagining things. His head felt like it was full of Peggy's knitting.

"I said drop it!"

He could hear rocks sliding as someone scrambled down the gully. Screwing his eyes up, he could make out the shape of a man. Two men. Except they both looked like Stoney. And the two Stoneys had their guns trained on Carter.

"Fierro was trying to escape. He went for me. I was protecting myself. Ain't no law against that, Rockwell."

The other man grunted like he didn't believe it. "Went for you? When he didn't have a gun? You really are a slimeball, Carter. Ford's injured and Johnny came to look for you. If he wanted to escape, he sure as hell wouldn't have bothered coming down here to try and save your sorry ass."

Johnny tried to get to his feet but stumbled back as the world went spinning around him again. His head was hurting bad and his hip felt like it was on fire from Carter's bullet. He could feel blood soaking his shirt. Dios. What a mess. Should have let Carter kill him. Would have made life a damn sight simpler. Life? Death? He laughed out loud. It seemed real funny now.

"Hell, Johnny. You look rough, boy. Hold still and let me look at you." Surely that was Stoney's voice but it seemed to come from a very long way off. He tried to focus but dammit, now there were three Stoneys. And he wanted to puke. Could feel it rushing up from his gut. Hell. What was wrong with him? Wasn't like he'd taken a bullet. Had he? Shit. He was going to puke. And his head was throbbing.

He was gagging on a mouth full of vomit. And the world was spinning again. And there was something in his head hammering to escape. Pressing real hard to get out. Had he been shot? Maybe Donner's bullet had got him. Or was it Mendoza? Or maybe Chavez had got a shot off at him.

But why was Stoney here? Maybe it wasn't Stoney? He puked again. Smelt like last night's dinner but worse. And the thing inside his head was still trying to escape, hammering at his skull. Dios. Just wanted to close his eyes and have everything go away.

A voice came from far away. "Johnny. You just sit back there while I look at your head."

Somebody was pushing him back. He fumbled at his hip. Mierda. Where was his gun? Where the hell was it? He needed his gun. How could he have lost it? He needed to stop Wallace. Had to stop him. And the world was spinning awful fast. If only it would stay still. But it was going faster and faster . . .

★ ★ ★ ★ ★

He could hear the drone of voices. Where was he? He could feel something soft and itchy under him. Maybe a blanket? Yeah, seemed to be lying on some blankets. He guessed he should figure out where he was but it seemed too much trouble. All he really wanted was to sleep. If only they'd all stop talking. Just shut the hell up. And his head hurt. He tried to open his eyes but everything was swaying and it made him want to puke again. Easier to keep them closed. If only they'd all quit talking . . .

The bed sure was hard. It wasn't his bed at the ranch, so where was he? His head felt fuzzy and like it would explode any minute. Had he been shot? If so where'd he been? And who the hell shot him? If only he could remember . . .

"Johnny?"

Strange. That sounded like Harvard. He opened his eyes and tried to focus on the figure next to the bed. Yeah. It kind of looked like Harvard. If only the man would stand still maybe he'd be able to get a better look at him.

"You've had us all worried, brother."

Brother? Yeah. Had to be Harvard. Johnny tried to speak but his mouth felt as dry as the desert. He licked his lips and tried again. "Donner." It came out as a whisper. "Did he get me? What's happened?" Yet even as he spoke the words he had a feeling he'd got things wrong somehow. Maybe if his head stopped thumping and the pain in his ears would go away, he'd be able to figure things out.

"Donner?" Harvard sounded puzzled. "Johnny, where do you think you are?"

Why did Harvard have to ask such a damn silly question? Didn't he know where they were either? If Harvard didn't know, and he was awake, how the hell did he expect Johnny to know? Dios, his head hurt. Everything was all muddled. And it felt like someone had a long knife and was stabbing deep inside his ear. Flinching, he tried to pull away from the stabbing pain. Yeah, like that was going to work.

"Johnny." Harvard was talking again. Didn't the man ever shut up? "Where do you think you are? Can you open your eyes and look at me?"

"Sleep. Want to go to sleep." Johnny rolled over. Shit! His hip hurt real bad. Had he been shot in the hip?

"Don't go back to sleep yet. I need to know what you can remember."

Harvard's voice sounded like it was coming from a long way off. Sleep. He needed to sleep. Maybe he'd be able to figure it all out later . . .

He opened his heavy eyes slowly. A figure was snoring softly in a chair by the bed. Harvard. But where the hell were they? He didn't recognize the bed or the room. This was a plain room. There were no pictures and it sure didn't look like the ranch. He gave a hiss of pain as the thing in his head launched another attack on the inside of his skull.

Harvard stirred, opening his eyes and sitting forward sharply as he met Johnny's gaze. "You're awake at last."

Trust Harvard to state the obvious.

"You've been out of it for a couple of days."

Two whole days? What the hell had happened to him? "Wallace?" But even as he said the name he knew it didn't feel right.

Guy frowned and looked worried. "Wallace was killed months ago, Johnny."

"Yeah. Yeah, I knew that." He tried to make his voice sound casual. All relaxed, like he really had known that. But months ago? What the hell had happened between then and now? If only Harvard would just tell him. But he wasn't going to ask.

Fuck that. It would show weakness. Never let anyone see your weakness. All he could do was bluff his way through.

"What's the last thing you remember, Johnny?"

Why did Harvard have to ask these questions? 'Specially ones Fierro didn't know the answers to. He shut his eyes briefly, struggling to remember something. Anything. He had to remember . . . Rain. That was it. Surely it had been raining? He'd been wet. Soaked through. Yeah. It had been raining real hard.

"Well?" Harvard never knew when to quit. Damn man should have stayed at the ranch. Stayed at the ranch? Where did that thought come from? Felt like bells were ringing in his head now, telling him this was important. Should have stayed at the ranch. Damn it. If only he could remember why it was important. If only thinking didn't hurt so much.

"Was I shot?"

"Carter's bullet grazed you."

Carter? Who was Carter?

"But you had a very bad bang on the head." Guy paused and smiled, kind of like he was joking. "I rather hoped it would knock some sense into you."

Carter? The old man had a rancher friend called Carter. Had it been him? No. That didn't feel right. This was a different Carter—he was sure it was. But if so, who was he?

"So, what do you remember?"

Seemed Harvard wasn't going to give up. "Um . . . well." Play for time, Fierro. He shrugged, and then wished he hadn't because it hurt. "Carter shot me."

Guy gave a big sigh. Like he was irritated. "I just told you that. What happened before that?"

"I got a real bad headache right now. Can we do this later, Harvard?"

Guy shook his head. "No. We need to establish what you can

remember. So?" He folded his arms and sat back in his chair.

Johnny sighed softly. "It was raining. Wasn't it?" Suddenly he even doubted that. Maybe the rain was from some other time. Life seemed very confusing right now. He felt a surge of relief as Guy nodded and smiled like Johnny had just won a prize.

"Yes, it was raining. Quite a storm, in fact."

A storm. Thunder. He'd been on a stage, hadn't he? Yeah, he'd been on a stagecoach. Maybe.

"We were on the stage." He tried to sound certain, not like he wasn't sure about things.

Guy beamed. "Yes. We were on the stage and it crashed."

It crashed? Well, maybe that little snippet would help. The stage crashed. He frowned, trying to remember. A woman. There'd been a woman who died. "One of the passengers died. Some old woman." Even as he said the words he could see her face. The way she'd looked in death. Those eyes staring at him.

Guy nodded enthusiastically. "See you're remembering. Yes. One of the passengers died—an elderly woman who'd been traveling with a friend. What else do you remember?"

Shit, no! The memories came tumbling into his head, flooding it, threatening to overwhelm him. To drown him. He shut his eyes trying to block out the horror. Not Utah. Oh God! Not Utah. And he could feel the color rushing to his face, making it feel like he was on fire, as the shame swept over him, wrapping him in its clinging shroud. He couldn't look at Guy. Hell, Guy shouldn't be here. He should have stayed back at the ranch.

Carter. Damn it. He remembered Carter now. One of the lawmen. There'd been two of them and Carter was the asshole.

"So?" Guy leaned forward, alert, looking like a hound dog on the scent of a rabbit. "What else do you remember?"

Johnny shrugged, wincing with pain as he did so. "I know you should've stayed at the damn ranch. I ain't a kid and I don't need no minder."

Guy rolled his eyes. "We've had this argument before, but I take it that you remember everything now. You had me worried when you were asking about Wallace. I was concerned that you might have amnesia."

Amnesha? What the hell was amnesha?

"In case you're wondering, we're near Mancos. A fellow came along with a wagon. That's how we got you here. Ford has had his arm set—luckily it was a clean break. And Stoney is limping around mad as hell with Carter."

Stoney. Damn it. He'd forgotten about Stoney. Dios. Stoney and Guy. Could things get any worse? He ran his fingers through his hair, and then wished he hadn't. His head was so tender it hurt to even touch it with his fingertip. He sighed. "Is Ford fit to travel?"

Guy grinned. "Probably not, but he's a damn sight fitter than you are right now. The doctor doesn't want you moved. You had a bang to your head when the stage crashed but then you gave it another severe bang in the tussle you had with Carter. You're very lucky it didn't fracture your skull."

Another pain shot through his ear, causing him to flinch away from it. He could see concern flash across Guy's face. Dios. Why did Guy have to come? He didn't want him here. "Guy, will you do me a favor and go on back to the ranch? I'll get myself a lawyer. I'll be fine and somebody needs to be at the ranch making sure it all runs smooth. It'll keep the old man happy." He spoke real soft. Maybe if he asked like this, all gentle, maybe Guy would agree.

Guy's shoulders were hunched up and he was staring at the floor like he'd lost a silver dollar down there. Then he shook his head real slow before looking up, meeting Johnny's gaze. "No. Sorry, Johnny, I know you don't want me to come, though for the life of me I can't think why, but I'm coming anyway. Like it or not, I'm coming. My place is with you, not back at the ranch."

"Why?" The question burst out before he could stop himself. But he had to know why the hell Harvard was so set on coming too.

Guy smiled, tilting his head to one side. "Maybe for the same reason that caused you to panic when you thought I'd been seriously hurt in the crash. Stoney mentioned that you were a little overwrought."

Over what? He'd kill Stoney one of these days. Him and his big mouth.

"You still don't get it, do you?" Guy spoke gently. "You're the only brother I've got. And I don't intend to lose you. We did that once already—I'm not going to let it happen again." He paused, screwing his face up like he'd just remembered something. "Funny thing, when Father left his last words were to tell me to look after you. I never imagined it would be necessary."

The confusion was back, fogging his brain. He couldn't figure any of this. "That the reason then, Harvard? You're doing this because the old man told you to?"

"You're not listening, Johnny. I'm doing it because you're my brother and I care about you. I certainly don't need our father to tell me to look after you. I'm doing it because I want to."

There was a lump in his throat. God only knew where it came from but it sure was big. Shit. He couldn't look at Guy so he picked at a loose thread in the blanket, watching it unravel and wishing the lump would get smaller. "I ain't worth it, Harvard. Trust me, I really ain't worth it."

Guy laughed. "I'll beg to differ. You're stuck with me, Johnny, so you might as well give in gracefully and accept that I'm coming too. I'll brook no arguments so you might as well save your breath."

Why did Harvard use such odd words? And so many of the damn things? "I mean it, Guy. I don't want you to come. I really don't want you there."

Guy sighed. "Why? What are you so afraid of? I wish you'd confide in me. Carter and Ford wouldn't give me any details of what you're accused of, other than it's murder. But I know you're innocent, Johnny, that's all that matters. And we'll clear your name together."

Innocent? That was a joke. He'd never been innocent. Not since he was a tiny kid. And if Guy knew half the things he'd done he'd never want anything to do with Fierro again. And yet it felt so good to have someone believe in him. Made him feel warm. And he wanted to grab the thought and hold onto it real tight. But Guy would hate him when he heard what happened in Utah and that would make losing Guy's friendship even worse. But there didn't seem to be any way out. Guy was going to come no matter what Fierro said. Because he cared. Did Stoney care too? Was that why Stoney had come along? Stoney hadn't told the lawmen about the knife in Johnny's boot. He'd trusted him not to use it on Carter and Ford. And seemed to understand that if it came to it, Johnny would use it on himself rather than hang.

Maybe it was a good thing that Stoney was there. Leastways he'd be able to help Guy when they learned the truth about Fierro. And they would learn the truth . . . He sighed. "I guess it's better you than the old man."

Guy grinned and stood up, stretching slowly. "I was tempted to send a telegram to try to track Father down, but I thought you might shoot me if I did that."

Johnny grunted. "Hmph. I would have. Believe me, Harvard, I would have."

"I'll go and tell the doctor that you're awake. And I'll see if I can rustle up something for you to eat."

Guy turned and strode out of the room. Johnny swallowed the lump in his throat and shook his head. Things didn't normally get to him like this. Must be the bang on the head that was making him so pathetic. But it looked like he was stuck with Harvard and Stoney. For the time being.

He glanced around the room. It wasn't a welcoming room. Kind of bare, really. A small table stood in the corner and there was a chair next to it where all his clothes were laid out. His boots were next to it. A feeling of unease crept over him. There was something wrong. Something was missing. If only he could remember but his head still hurt like hell and the stabbing in his ear was back. But something was missing. Maybe if he slept he'd be thinking better when he woke up. He huddled down under the blankets.

He jerked upright again. Fuck no! His saddlebags. His saddlebags weren't there.

CHAPTER FOURTEEN

"He's awake." Guy grinned at Stoney, who was sitting and resting his injured foot on a stool.

Stoney scratched his chin before tilting his head and looking up. "He remember anything yet or is he still carrying on about Donner?"

"He remembers the crash now. I've told the doctor that he's awake so he's going to check on Johnny and decide when he'll be fit to travel." Guy sank down into a chair. "I'll admit, Stoney, he had me really worried."

Stoney smirked. It was the only way to describe the look on his face and it was enough to irritate anyone. "What?" Guy glared at him but Stoney didn't seem bothered. The smirk just got bigger. "Why don't you just say what's on your mind, Stoney, instead of sitting there looking pleased with yourself?"

The smirk grew even bigger. "Worried? Don't think I ever saw a man in such a state about his brother." Stoney laughed. "Except maybe the way Fierro was when he thought you were hurt."

Guy felt the color rushing to his face. "You say he was in a state but you should have heard the things he said to me before we left Cimarron. You wouldn't think he had any feelings at all if you'd heard that."

Stoney shrugged. "Just Fierro's way. He don't let anyone get too close. He's one tough son of a bitch. And he sure didn't want you along on this ride." Stoney paused and looked across

142

at Guy. "And don't that make you wonder why?"

Guy didn't answer immediately. Why wouldn't Johnny want someone with him? It made no sense for him to face whatever lay ahead alone. "Why do you refer to him as Fierro? He's Johnny Sinclair now." He knew he was sidestepping Stoney's question but he wasn't sure he knew the answer.

Stoney looked at him with a strange expression on his face, almost like pity? "Right now, he's Johnny Fierro again. I guess he left Johnny Sinclair back at the ranch. And I'll put my money on him staying Fierro until all of this is over. One way or the other."

Guy felt an icy clutch of fear in his stomach. "One way or the other? You really think he's guilty, don't you? You think he's going to be found guilty and they're going to hang him. Well, I know Johnny wouldn't commit cold-blooded murder. I know it."

Stoney didn't look up. He seemed more interested in studying the contents of his coffee cup. "Don't you find it kind of odd that Johnny hasn't asked for any details of what he's been accused of? Ain't natural. A man always asks what he's meant to have done."

"Maybe he's spoken to Ford about it when we haven't been around. All I know is my brother is not a murderer." Guy could feel the heat of anger in his face but damn it, Stoney was supposed to be Johnny's friend.

Stoney shook his head slowly. "I asked Ford. Johnny ain't asked him nothing. And Ford's no fool, he'll recognize the . . ." Stoney paused, his brow furrowed as if he was searching for the right word. "The significance of Johnny not asking. It's time you faced up to the possibility that there's something behind this accusation." He held his hand up as Guy opened his mouth to protest. "I get it—I understand you don't want to believe it, but Fierro ain't no angel. He's not a man to cross. He's a real hard son of a bitch. Oh I know he can turn on the charm when he has a mind to, and don't get me wrong, I like Johnny, but I sure as hell wouldn't underestimate him." He paused, giving Guy a hard stare. "And neither should you."

Guy took a deep breath, trying to quell the anger building inside him. "Johnny Sinclair is a good man."

Stoney shook his head as though exasperated. "That's as maybe, but we ain't talking about Johnny Sinclair. We're talking about Fierro, and I ain't too sure you've ever met him. I have."

"You talk about them as if they are two totally different people."

Stoney sighed. "Trust me, they are. You've only seen one side of Johnny."

"I've seen Johnny in gunfights so don't sit there telling me that I don't know what he's like." Guy contented himself with glaring at Stoney, although his hand was itching to hit him. How dare he speak of Johnny in this way?

Stoney grunted dismissively. "Yeah, but fact is Johnny knew you were there so I doubt you've really seen him at his worst. And I doubt you realize how dangerous he really is. I know you don't want to hear this, I understand that, but damn it you didn't know him when he was younger. And this business in Utah happened when Johnny was a kid, maybe about sixteen or seventeen. And believe me, when Johnny was that age he was wild and very dangerous." Stoney paused and scratched his chin again, his eyes narrowed as though remembering the past. "Yeah, even back then he always seemed to be very controlled, but he was damn dangerous too. No mistake."

Guy sat with his head bowed, unable to look at Stoney. What had Johnny been like when he was younger? Not capable of a vicious murder, of that he was certain. Johnny had grown up the hard way without any of the trappings of luxury that Guy had enjoyed, but he was a good man. So, it followed that he must always have been good—Q.E.D. "I know he had a hard time of it when he was young."

"Hard?" Stoney threw his hands up. "Hard! You got no idea—no idea at all. I told you about the state of his back but it was far more than that. I don't believe anyone had ever paid him much mind since the day his mama lit out from your ranch. He hadn't been taught anything. He was like a wild animal. The kind that'll let you pet it if it thinks you'll give it food but will turn and bite your hand off as fast as a rattler striking if you ain't careful. He was full of more hate than I've ever seen in anyone. Guess that kept him alive. It sure wasn't love and devotion from that mother of his that kept him living." Stoney ran his fingers through his hair. "He was already old when I first met him—but he couldn't have been more than nine or ten then. But his eyes were old. And I guess there wasn't anything much he hadn't seen by then. Don't that tell you something?"

"I'll grant you that he's cynical . . ."

"Cynical! When are you going to stop kidding yourself? Oh I know you served in the war, Johnny told me, and I reckon you think you've seen most things. But Johnny . . ." He paused, shaking his head. "Johnny's seen things we can barely imagine. Life at its worst."

"I thought you said you didn't know him that well." Guy felt resentment flooding over him like a wave. How could Stoney know so much if he'd only met Johnny a couple of times?

Stoney sighed. "Guy, it's in his face. You must see it. Anyone who knows what to look for can see it and I don't think you're that dumb. You just don't want to see it. But you need to start facing up to things. He's had the luck of the devil for years but it could be that this is payback time for Fierro."

Guy sat with his head bowed, staring down at the worn wooden floor. Was Stoney right? Was he really kidding himself and only seeing what he wanted to see in Johnny? Why had

Johnny been so set on Guy staying at the ranch unless he had something to hide? Guy shut his eyes briefly and tried to quell the seed of fear growing inside him. Johnny was a good man. Wasn't he?

All his brother's past warnings flooded his memory. Warning Guy that Fierro was dangerous, that he'd done a lot of things he would never want anyone else to know about . . . Done things he couldn't even tell a priest. No! Johnny couldn't have meant murder.

Other memories came like a deluge. Johnny fretting over what might have been in the Pinkerton report. Johnny saying that when he started out he hadn't been too fussy how he got a reputation as long as he got one. But Johnny had risked his life for the women on the ranch when he took on Donner and Wallace. There was a core of goodness running through Johnny, he was certain of it. Wasn't he? Damn it, he wasn't going to have Stoney planting seeds of doubt in his mind. Johnny was his brother and he was innocent.

He stood up. "I'm not discussing this, Stoney. You're wrong. I thought you were Johnny's friend, maybe I was mistaken."

Stoney gave a grunt of irritation. "I am his friend. But I ain't afraid to face facts. Seems to me that you are."

Guy bit back an angry retort. There was no point in falling out with Stoney when they still had a long journey ahead of them. He made an effort to sound calm and controlled. "If you were a friend, you would believe in him. You'd believe he was innocent."

"I ain't saying whether he's guilty or not. But I do know if he is guilty, if he did do what he's being accused of, he would have had a damn good reason for killing the man. Johnny don't kill for the thrill of it. That I'm certain of."

"Johnny was a gunfighter. Not a murderer. And that's an end of it." Guy paused, his heart feeling as though it was going to burst out of his chest as he fought to keep his temper under control. "I'll go up and see how he's doing and hopefully find out what the doctor had to say. Are you coming?"

Guy led the way through the doctor's house to the room occupied by Johnny, with Stoney hobbling along after him. Scrambling down the bank to help Johnny and restrain Carter had worsened the injury to his ankle. Guy couldn't deny he felt immensely grateful to Stoney for saving Johnny from Carter's bullet; for having heard Stoney's account of what happened in the gully, Guy was certain that Carter would have killed Johnny. Although proving it was another matter altogether. Ford and Stoney both said they could do nothing about Carter's actions because there had been no independent witnesses. Stoney had come on the scene too late. It was Carter's word against Johnny's, and Guy was realistic enough to realize that no jury would take the word of a gunfighter over that of a lawman. All in all it was a damnable mess. It looked as though there would be no alternative but to continue the journey with Carter in tow. Guy didn't trust him an inch.

He pushed open the door to Johnny's room and stopped dead in his tracks, causing Stoney to walk smack into him. Johnny looked far worse than earlier in the day. His face was ashen and he was sitting shaking on the edge of the bed. "You're not supposed to be out of bed, little brother." He tried to sound light-hearted, but his stomach clenched at how sick Johnny looked.

"I'm fine." Johnny was staring fixedly at his clothes and boots in the corner of the room. "You got my saddlebags, Guy?"

Guy's brow furrowed. "Your saddlebags? No, I haven't. I shouldn't worry. If they're lost I'll buy you some more . . ."

"Damn it, Guy, I don't want new ones, I want mine." Johnny tried to stand but stumbled back onto the bed flinching and holding his ear.

"Maybe Ford has them—" Even as Guy hurried to Johnny's side, his brother interrupted his words.

"He hasn't, he was in a while ago. He ain't seen them." There was an unfamiliar note of desperation in Johnny's voice. "I need 'em, Guy, I got stuff in them. Stuff I need."

Guy placed a hand on Johnny's shoulder hoping to calm him. It must be the head injury causing his brother to fret. "I'm sure we can replace anything that you need, Johnny. It'll be fine." His words didn't seem to reassure Johnny, who sat shaking with hunched shoulders and staring again at the clothes in the corner. Johnny turned his head as though noticing Stoney's presence for the first time.

"Have you got my saddlebags, Stoney?" There was a note of urgency in his voice and a spark of hope in his eyes.

Guy turned toward Stoney, who just shook his head. "No, sorry, I don't rightly recall seeing them. I thought we got all the luggage scattered around and brought it to town." Stoney shrugged. "Ain't worth getting all fired up over some saddlebags, Johnny. Probably time you had new ones. They looked like they'd seen better days."

His words didn't seem to reassure Johnny. Guy felt a knot of fear again. Maybe the head injury was more serious than he'd thought. Johnny was behaving most oddly; his hands seemed to be shaking and his brow was glistening with sweat.

"I think you need to get back into bed, Johnny. Did you see the doctor? He said he was going to look in on you."

Johnny stared at him, apparently confused by the question. "The doctor? Yeah, I think so. But my saddlebags, Guy . . ."

Stoney sighed. "What the hell is in these bags, Johnny, that's got you all fired up?"

The question seemed to throw Johnny. He shook his head and ran his hand through his hair before flinching away from his own touch. "Just stuff, Stoney."

"Stuff?" Stoney raised his eyebrow sardonically. "Stuff. Well if it's just stuff, I don't see what all the fuss is about. Unless there's something special in them bags of yours that you ain't telling us about." He limped over to the chair by the bed and sat down heavily. "Dang, my ankle is sore."

"No. Nothing special." Johnny's voice was barely a whisper. Guy moved closer and lifted Johnny's legs to help his brother back into bed. He felt another pang of concern. In the past, even when he'd been very badly hurt, Johnny would never have accepted help without a fight but right now it seemed that he had no fight left. Guy shot a look of concern towards Stoney, who just shrugged. Fat lot of help he was.

"I think you need some rest, Johnny. I'll go and have a word with the doctor. Did he say anything about when you could be moved?" Guy spoke gently, hoping maybe he could get Johnny's mind off the damn saddlebags.

Johnny fumbled with the blanket, unraveling the wool and twisting it around his fingers. Had he even heard the question? "Johnny? Did the doctor say anything?"

Johnny looked up, his eyes glazed as though he was hardly aware of Guy and Stoney. "What?"

"The doctor, did he say anything about your traveling?"

Johnny frowned and shrugged. "I don't recall." He bowed his head and continued unraveling the blanket.

Defeated, Guy turned away. At this rate there wouldn't be a blanket left. "I think I'll go and have a word with the doctor myself. Coming, Stoney?" He jerked his head toward the door. "I think Johnny needs some sleep."

Stoney muttered an oath as he struggled back to his feet and hobbled over to join Guy by the door. As they left the room Johnny spoke again. Guy strained to catch the words. "Nothing special. Nothing important."

Guy closed the door behind them. "I'll go and see the doctor and find out what I can. To be frank, I can't believe Johnny will be fit to go anywhere any time soon. He seems very confused. And he's getting himself in an awful state about his saddlebags. I guess I'd better go and buy him some new ones."

Stoney shot him a sharp look. "And you think that'll make everything OK?"

"Do you have to be so perplexing? Can't you just say what you mean?" His patience was fast running out where Stoney was concerned. The damn man acted as though he always understood Johnny better than anyone else.

Stoney shrugged. "Ain't my place to say what I think."

When did that ever stop him? The uncharitable thought leapt unbidden to Guy's mind. He bit his lip. "You volunteered to come on this journey, Stoney, nobody forced you to. Right now, my primary concern is Johnny. I'll go and see the doctor and talk to Ford." Guy turned on his heel, leaving Stoney standing as though lost in thought outside Johnny's door.

It was sometime later before he sought Stoney out back at the hotel they'd checked into. He'd had frustrating talks with the doctor and Ford.

"The doctor feels that Johnny could travel if we get a wagon for the first part of the journey. I can't say that I'm happy about it. I think he's far from ready to travel but I know Ford wants to get going and he feels that he can cope despite his injured arm. I suspect he's simply anxious to be rid of Carter's company as quickly as possible." Guy paused, glancing around Stoney's room. It struck him how tidy it was, with none of his gear strewn around as there had been on previous occasions when Guy had called in for a talk. Then he spotted Stoney's things packed and piled neatly in the corner next to the door. He raised a quizzical eyebrow. "Going somewhere, Stoney?"

Stoney shrugged. "My ankle is paining me real bad. I don't

feel up to making the trip to Utah. You'd best go on without me. I'm heading back."

Guy felt a twinge of guilt. Was this really more to do with the way he'd spoken to Stoney earlier? "Look, Stoney, I'm sorry if I was a little sharp before. I guess my worrying over Johnny is making me short-tempered."

Stoney hobbled across the room, his limp more pronounced now than earlier. "Understandable. But I'm still heading back. Like I said, my leg's bad so you'll be best off without me." He stooped to pick up his bags and with a nod left Guy alone in the drab little room.

CHAPTER FIFTEEN

The wagon jolted violently as it struck yet another deep rut in the track, throwing Johnny off balance and against the canvas cover, jarring his shoulder. He felt sick and his head felt odd. At times it was like there was something inside it trying to escape and at other times like there was something outside pressing to get in. And the stabbing pain in his ear came and went in waves. Along with the dizzy spells. Dios, he felt like shit. And this wasn't a good time to be feeling like shit. Not that there was ever a good time to feel sick but right now he needed his wits about him and he could hardly even think straight.

He needed to figure out how he was going to fight the murder charge, 'specially now everything had gone wrong. Losing the saddlebags had thrown all his carefully laid plans out the window. Fuck. And he'd thought he'd got it all figured out as well as he could. Life was a real bitch and it sure didn't help when he didn't have God on his side, not that that was anything out of the ordinary. But it seemed even the devil was letting him down now and surely he was supposed to take care of his own.

What he really wanted was to lie down and rest his aching head and sleep but he couldn't take the risk of talking in his sleep and giving something away. And although anything he said might not mean anything to Harvard, he'd bet that Carter or Ford would make something of it. Carter never stopped watching him. Every time Johnny glanced up, Carter would be there eyeing him with an unpleasant smile on his ugly face. Bastard. Looked like Fierro would have to make do with naps. Oh well, he'd be a long time dead, there'd be plenty of time for sleeping then—if it was possible to sleep in hell. And it looked like it wouldn't be long now till he got there. Unless he could come up with a new plan.

He flinched away from a new wave of stabbing pains in his ear. Sure made it hard to concentrate and plan his next move. Like how to play the jury. Trouble was, juries didn't pay much heed to gunfighters. They tended to think the worst. And more often than not they were right. But they sure wouldn't think much of a breed gunfighter especially when there was some hard-assed fancy lawyer prosecuting. Best thing was to destroy any witness. But that was easier said than done. And then a lot depended on the judge. Some judges were just assholes.

He screwed up his eyes as another wave of pain swept over him. Mierda. He really didn't need this. Opening his eyes once more he met Guy's concerned gaze.

"Are you all right?"

Johnny rolled his eyes. Harvard did ask damn stupid questions. Of course he wasn't all right but he'd never own to it. He scowled. "I'm fine, Harvard. Just fine."

"You don't look fine." There was a deep furrow between Guy's eyebrows. "I knew you weren't fit to travel. I spoke to the driver we hired and this trail's not going to get any easier."

Johnny shook his head and wished he hadn't. "Like I said, I'm fine."

"Don't much matter how he is, they're going to hang him whatever state he's in." Carter snickered, like he'd just made a joke. "No jury's going to let you off, Fierro, you sick son of a bitch."

Johnny raised an eyebrow and laughed. "Wouldn't count on that if I were you, Carter." It came out more cocky than he felt, which was exactly how he wanted it to. "And then, Carter, when I walk out of your court a free man, you and me, we got a score to settle, don't we?" And he laughed again. He was pleased to see Carter pale, just a touch, but enough to show that Johnny had gotten to him. That the threat wasn't lost on the bastard. Yeah, Fierro still had the touch, even when his head felt like shit. Hell, he had to walk out of the court just so he could make sure that Carter got what he deserved. He smiled. He was going to enjoy payback time.

"You got nothing to smile about, Fierro." Carter was trying to sound full of himself, but there was an edge now to his voice. Yeah, Fierro really had gotten to him.

Johnny laughed and leaned back, shutting his eyes. The light made his head hurt more so it was easier to shut his eyes. Just as long as he didn't fall asleep.

"Why don't you do us all a favor and just keep quiet, Carter?" Guy snapped. "I think you've caused enough trouble on this trip. It's your fault my brother is injured and I'd like to remind you that a man should be presumed innocent until—"

"Innocent!" Carter laughed. "Trust me, Sinclair, when you find out what your brother did, you'll be wishing I had killed him." Carter paused. He had a sly look on his face, like he was enjoying baiting Guy. "Ain't you curious, Sinclair, to hear what he done?"

Johnny swallowed hard, trying to quell the rising nausea, even as he watched Guy's reaction through half-closed eyes. Half of him was hoping Guy would ask for details and the other half was praying he wouldn't. In some ways, it might be better if Guy did. Get it out in the open now. Guy could see Fierro then for real. Not some painted picture of a gunfighter from a dime novel, but the real Fierro—for the bastard he was. But somewhere deep inside, a tiny part of Fierro was screaming that maybe, just maybe, he could get away with all of this. That he could fool Harvard into believing he'd been right all along that Fierro was OK, not a rotten and maggoty apple to be squashed underfoot, as Harvard turned away and headed back to hearth and home.

What the hell was Harvard thinking? Wasn't he gonna say anything to Carter?

"I'm really not interested in hearing your warped views on this so-called murder of which Johnny is accused. You have the wrong man, as we will ably demonstrate when we get to Utah. So, Carter, I suggest you keep your opinions to yourself and stop trying to stir up trouble." Guy sat back and closed his eyes.

Carter sniggered. "You got one heck of a shock coming, Mr. High and Mighty Sinclair. We got us an eyewitness, ain't we, Ford?"

Guy didn't stir, but Johnny could see Guy's body tense up, like Carter's words had finally gotten to him.

Johnny gritted his teeth. He needed to act calm. He'd be damned if he'd let them see he was bothered. Never let them see they got you on the run. Play it cool, same as always. And hell, it wasn't like Carter's words were any great shock—he'd always suspected there'd been a witness.

"Hear that Sinclair? We got ourselves a witness. And he can't wait to testify." Carter laughed.

Guy opened his eyes and looked at Carter but kind of like he was bored. "An eyewitness? We'll see." Harvard sounded like he wasn't interested, but for a brief moment his gaze flickered over Johnny. And Johnny saw the glimmer of shock in his brother's eyes. And something else. Maybe doubt?

"Yeah." Carter smirked. "Bet you didn't know you was seen, did you, Fierro?"

Johnny yawned, a real big yawn, and rubbed his eyes like Carter had woken him up. "Don't you ever stop jawing, Carter? I'm trying to get some sleep here. I got a bad head. Some dickhead of a deputy hit me. So, just shut up and let a man sleep, why don't you?"

"I second that." Ford aimed a kick at Carter. "I'm sick of the sound of your voice, Carter. If I could fire your sorry ass I would after the stunt you pulled back there. And even though I can't fire you, I will be giving a full report on your actions to those who do have the authority to kick you out."

Johnny allowed himself a small smile. Good. Carter was the sort of man who should never wear a badge. God only knew who'd appointed him in the first place, but whoever it was had sure made a bum decision.

He settled back against the canvas, wishing the damn wagon would stop jolting around. But he noticed that Guy was sitting staring into space, like he was deep in thought. And there was a deep frown on his face.

Johnny breathed a sigh of relief when in the late afternoon they finally stopped at a small way station. They'd be able to change the horses and spend the night in some comfort. A hotel with a nice soft bed would be better but this would have to do. His head was pounding and the stabbing in his ear seemed to come and go. And every time he stood up he had a dizzy spell. Right now he'd like to put a bullet between Carter's eyes.

He sat in the corner of the small room set aside as a kind of dining room, picking at the rabbit stew. He didn't feel hungry but he knew Harvard was watching him. The man never took his eyes off him. Pity it wasn't Harvard who'd left instead of Stoney. He could have coped with Stoney.

Stoney . . .

It was odd that Stoney had lit out the way he had. Probably didn't want to be anywhere near Fierro. Stoney would see through him. He knew way too much about Fierro. Johnny jerked his mind back to the present as his brother walked over to him.

"You've got to eat, Johnny."

Johnny rolled his eyes—the man was like a mother hen. "Ain't hungry, that's all. I guess the trip wore me out." He could have bitten his tongue off—why say something like that? It was only going to make Harvard fuss even more. And sure enough his brother pulled up a chair next to him, like he wanted to talk. But Guy didn't say anything at first, he just sat fiddling with the buttons on his shirt. Johnny sighed softly as he waited for his brother to spit out whatever was bugging him.

"Carter says they have an eyewitness." The words came out in a rush.

His stomach shrivelled into a tiny ball. If it got any tighter he'd puke all over the floor. How to play it? What the hell should he say? One thing was for sure, he needed to act relaxed as if he hadn't a care in the world. "Yeah—I heard him. I was there in case it's slipped your memory."

Guy took a deep breath. Then he fiddled with the damn buttons again. Then he took another breath, like the first one wasn't big enough. What the hell was he plucking up the nerve to say?

"Why haven't you asked them about the circumstances surrounding this accusation? Surely you want to know the details of the charge?" Guy's face was pale. Even paler than usual. And sort of tight. Like there wasn't quite enough skin to cover all those worry lines.

"I'll find out when we get there." Johnny tried to sound casual, like he was bored by the whole thing. Even though every nerve in his body felt like it was pulled tight to bursting point.

"Men always ask, Johnny. They always want to know what they're being accused of doing."

Johnny raised an eyebrow. No way would his brother know anything about what men asked when they got arrested.

Someone had to have put that idea in his head.

"Well," Johnny drawled, "I guess I ain't like other men. I got all the time in the world and I'll find out soon enough. But right now my head's aching, so if that's all, Harvard . . ."

"Johnny, they say they have an eyewitness . . ."

"I heard you the first time. And like I said, I heard him say it. What of it?" Johnny paused, sat back, and stuck his hands in his belt. How to play this, that was the question. Relaxed. He had to seem relaxed. "You got something to say, Harvard, then say it."

Guy bit his lip, and then his face hardened, his mouth set in a grim line. He glanced around, as if to make sure that nobody could hear what they were talking about. "I want to know if there's something you're not telling me about this business in Utah."

Madre de Dios. Something Fierro wasn't telling him. If he only knew . . . God almighty. Even if he could bring himself to own to what happened there was no way he could tell Harvard. Couldn't plead not guilty then. And Fierro would fight this all the way. No way would he let that bastard, Doe, win. And if they hanged Fierro, that animal . . . No! That piece of human shit would have won. The word animal was too good for that bastard. Johnny stared down at the floor briefly. Couldn't show any expression, couldn't risk giving anything away. He glanced back at Guy, gave a soft laugh. "I told you before, Utah's way out of my territory. Ain't nobody ever paid me to do a job there."

Guy swallowed hard, like he'd got some of that damn stew still stuck in his throat. "The question is, Johnny, have you ever been to Utah? Not whether you were paid to go there."

Felt like he'd been kicked in the gut. It was bound to come. Guy could see through him. He had to have seen through him. Finally seen Fierro for what he was. And it hurt. It fucking hurt. Worse than any knife or bullet. But he couldn't let Guy see the pain. All he could do was keep up the pretense. After all, it was all his life had ever been and he wasn't going to cave in now. A lifetime of pretending. So he smiled, all casual. "Is that what you think of me then, Harvard? That I'm just a cold-blooded murderer?" Except it hadn't been cold-blooded. That aching for revenge had been hot, burning into his very soul and consuming him. And even though it meant he was damned, he could never repent. So many things he regretted, but not Utah. Never Utah.

"I don't know what to make of you."

Johnny bowed his head and stared down at the floor, anything to avoid Guy reading his eyes. Those words, an echo of what Guthrie had said to him more than once on the numerous occasions when they'd stood face to face arguing. At times he thought he'd traveled a long way since coming home. But that had been a pretense too, because here he was right back where he started. He should never have stayed. But he'd let himself be seduced by the lure of family and a different life. This sham of a life. The local doctor had once told him that he had to take a chance on this new life. And so he'd gambled and he'd taken the chance and all it was doing was leading him straight to the hangman's noose. Well, fuck them all. Who needed family? He sure didn't. Did he?

He looked up, feeling the fire of rage flooding his body. "Think what you like. Nobody asked you to come on this trip. Now get the hell out of my face."

CHAPTER SIXTEEN

Well, he'd wanted Guy to stay away from him on this trip and it sure looked like he'd succeeded in driving him away. They'd barely exchanged ten words since the night at the way station.

Guy had asked about his head a couple of times. But that was it. End of story. He'd expected to feel relieved when Guy finally backed off. But instead, he just felt empty inside. Like there was a big gaping hole, a part of him missing. And he hated himself for his behavior but there hadn't seemed to be any way out. Part of him was screaming that Guy's questions didn't necessarily mean he'd finally seen through Johnny. That all Guy had wanted to do was get things clear in his head. Get the facts. Because facts and logic seemed real important to Guy.

But another part of him said Guy had seen through him and Fierro had to protect himself. Just like he'd been doing ever since he could remember. Not that he'd always made a very good job of it. Hadn't stayed out of the way of some of Mama's men as often as he should have. And he sure hadn't been able to protect himself in the prison. But that had been the turning point for him. It was then that he'd sworn he'd never trust anyone, and that he'd never let anyone hurt him again. He'd already been well down the road to Johnny Fierro when he was thrown in the prison, but by the time they let him out . . . He shook his head slightly, lost in the memories. By the time they let him out, he was determined to be the hardest and fastest gunfighter anyone had ever known. There was no turning back then. It was the only way to be sure that nobody ever hurt him again. He'd spent his life being everybody's whipping boy. But prison had changed him. Made him harder than ever. Never again would anyone use him. For anything.

But of course they had. Every time he hired out someone was using him. Not in the same way as before, but still using him. The only difference was they paid him. Just like they'd pay a whore. Funny, it'd taken him a while to see it. Dios, he'd been so damn cocky. Thought he was finally calling the shots. But he wasn't. People were still using him for their own ends. Making sure someone else did their dirty work. The work they hadn't got the stomach for. So, yeah, they paid him, but they were still fucking using him.

He glanced around the way station. It was much like the last two they'd stayed at. The most he could say about it was it was dry. He wanted his own bed. He wanted his home. How soft was that? The trouble was the place had gotten to him. And he'd let Guy get under his defenses. When the hell did that happen? He sighed. It was time he admitted exactly how much Guy had come to mean to him. He'd finally met a man who he really trusted—the first since Luke. A good man. Honorable. And look how Fierro treated him.

He looked across to where Guy was dozing. He was slumped, snoring softly, in a big, sagging armchair close to the potbellied stove. Yeah. A good man. And still here. Even after Johnny had spat the hot words into his face two days before, Guy had merely retreated, like a wounded cub. But he hadn't lit out. He was still here, obviously determined to stay with his brother no matter what. Because he cared. Johnny shook his head again. Who'd have thought this educated Easterner would care about a no-good breed brother? Especially one as sharp-tongued as Fierro.

And they'd been getting along so well before all this had

come back to bite him. He'd felt easier with Guy than he'd ever felt with anybody he'd met in years. And Guy didn't seem to notice that Fierro hadn't got the fancy education or that his skin wasn't quite the right color. He just treated Fierro like a brother . . . Hell, life was such a bitch. Fierro finally had something good within his grasp. Even recognized it was good and worth having and holding on to. He'd touched it for a brief moment before God swept it away from him. *Your sins will find you out.* The words of a long-forgotten padre echoed in his ears from some half-remembered preaching in a dim adobe mission where the sun had lit the dust floating in the air. He could see it clearly in the picture book of his memory. He'd hidden in the back, a child sheltering from some forgotten foe, and tried to catch the dust in his fingers.

Well, it seemed the padre was right. Fierro's sins had sure found him out. But he couldn't tell Guy the what or the why of it. Couldn't tell anybody about it. He lived with it. But he'd never tell a living soul about the purgatory he suffered in prison. And if Guy knew about it, he'd be disgusted. Johnny shook his head and sighed. Guy would be revolted when he learned at the trial what Fierro had done. But he'd be more disgusted if he ever found out why.

If only Stoney hadn't lit out. Johnny had a feeling Guy was going to need someone to lean on when this was over. And even if Fierro succeeded in fooling the jury, chances were he wouldn't fool Guy and the man wouldn't ever want anything to do with Fierro again.

"Do you ever sleep, Fierro?" Ford's voice shook him from his thoughts. The man jerked his head towards Carter and Guy, who were both sleeping. "I don't believe I ever see you sleep."

Johnny laughed. "Plenty of time for sleeping when we're dead, wouldn't you say?"

Ford looked at him for a long moment. "You should rest."

His voice was surprisingly gentle. "You're going to need to be sharp for what lies ahead. I'll . . ." The man paused and bit his lip, like he couldn't quite decide to say whatever was on his mind. "I'll wake you if you talk too much. So get some rest."

Time stopped. He could hear his own heart beating. He opened his mouth but all he could hear was his own breath. No words. Just his blood pulsing like the world had stopped turning and he was suspended in time. Why would Ford say that? What did he know? But he couldn't ask . . . That would leave Fierro exposed. Never let the defenses down.

"Like I said, Fierro, get some rest." Ford picked up a book, and turned away like what he'd said meant nothing. Except it did.

Johnny slumped down on the couch. He was so damn tired. Did Ford mean what he said? Was it a trap? No. Somehow Ford didn't seem like the sort of fellow to lay a trap. He'd played fair right from the very start. Looked out for Fierro, if Johnny was honest. Which could only mean . . . Mierda. All this thinking made his head hurt more. He could feel the pressure building inside it, starting to push on his skull, trying to escape. Maybe, just maybe, he should stop trying to outsmart everyone and get some rest. Even though it meant trusting someone he barely knew. A smile pulled at his mouth. It would sure be a first.

He awoke in the early gray light of dawn. He'd actually caught some sleep. Could hardly believe it. He must have crashed out almost straight after Ford's words. And that was very strange. Normally he'd have lain awake for hours overthinking everything, worrying away at it like a dog with a bone. Must have been the bang on his head making him careless. He glanced across the room. Ford was busy brewing coffee, managing well despite one arm being splinted up. Guy and Carter were still asleep, both snoring.

Ford turned as though sensing he was being watched. He

raised the pot up in a questioning sort of way. "Coffee?"

Johnny nodded. "Yeah, coffee would be good." He stood, stretching to ease the crick in his neck, before taking a mug of coffee in his cuffed hands. He eyed Ford thoughtfully as he sipped the strong brew. Who the hell was this fellow? And why would he be watching Fierro's back? "You been a marshal long?" It seemed as good a question as any to ask.

Ford's mouth quirked, like he was amused by the question and knew what lay behind it. "Almost nigh on twenty years, I reckon."

Johnny frowned. Somehow he hadn't expected that. He didn't know what he had expected, but not that. It meant Ford was established. Recognized and accepted as a steady lawman, not somebody new to the job with a personal motive or score to settle. But he'd lay money that Ford wouldn't tell him anything so asking would be a waste of breath. So, play it cool, Fierro, same as always. "How much farther 'til we get there?"

"A couple of days' hard riding. You think you're up to it? We can take a day to rest up, if you're feeling too rough. I reckon I agree with your brother, the doctor was a quack and you weren't fit to travel."

Johnny narrowed his eyes. "I'm fine, just fine." He felt a pang of guilt. No need to snap at the man. Ford had sounded like he was genuinely concerned. Johnny spoke softer now. "Really, I'm ready to ride. I guess I just want to get there now. Get on with it all, if you know what I mean."

Ford nodded, scratching his stubbled chin. "OK. If you're sure. But I'm sorry, I can't take the cuffs off to make it any easier for you."

"Don't expect you to take 'em off." Johnny grinned. "Carter would go loco. He's crazy enough to shoot the both of us."

Ford grunted. "Ain't that the truth?"

"More to the point," Johnny nodded toward Ford's splinted

arm, "Are you fit enough to do two days of hard riding?"

Ford shrugged. "I can manage fine. I picked me a good steady horse and the arm isn't paining me too much." He glanced across to where Guy and Carter were starting to stir. "I'd best make some more coffee."

Johnny sat back in an easy chair, watching Ford go through the motions of brewing fresh coffee while Harvard sat forward sniffing the air, looking like a dog on the scent of a bitch in heat. "Coffee, I smell coffee."

"Coming right up." Ford passed him a mug. "Don't be too long getting ready. We need to get a move on. I'd like to be there by tomorrow night."

Guy glanced over at Johnny. "Are you sure you're up to making this ride? How's your head?"

"My head's fine, Harvard. I just want to get this trip over with."

Carter sniggered. "Shouldn't be in too much of a hurry, if I were you, Fierro. Sooner you get there, the sooner they'll hang you."

"Well, we'll just have to see about that, won't we? But I wouldn't bank on it, Carter. And you and me, well, we got a score to settle, don't we?" Johnny smiled, raising his mug in a salute to Carter, easy like he hadn't a care in the world.

"Fuck you, Fierro." Carter glared across at Johnny before shuffling over to the door. "Ford, I'll go and get the horses ready. Make sure that bastard, Fierro, is well and truly cuffed. I don't want him escaping—I'm looking forward to seeing him swing."

Johnny smiled as Carter slammed the door. Yep, Fierro was really getting to the man. Payback would be real sweet. No way was Fierro going to hang. That would never do—not when he needed to get even with Carter. He'd think of some way of getting off. But it sure would have been a mite simpler if he'd got his saddlebags.

The next two days were hell. The only high spot was Ford and Carter falling out over whether Johnny should have his hands cuffed in front or behind. Guy had gotten involved in that, too. Arguing that his brother couldn't possibly be safe riding if his hands were behind his back. Ford agreed with him. In the end his hands were cuffed in front of him. Even Carter had to admit that it meant they could move faster that way. But Carter had fixed them on too tight, with a nasty sneer on his face. Johnny didn't flinch, even though the cuffs hurt like hell. Wouldn't give Carter the satisfaction.

The first signs of the onset of winter were all around them. The leaves had disappeared from the trees, their bare branches reaching out to the leaden sky as if begging for warmth and sunshine. But instead of sunshine the rain fell, more like sleet than rain. It was cold. Fucking cold. Madre de Dios. If they had to take him all the way to Utah, couldn't they have waited until the spring?

He rode with his hat pulled well down to try and to keep the stinging damp from his face. Any minute it would turn to snow. Who the hell would want to live in Utah? Scorching hot summers in parts of it and bitter winters in other parts. The heat was one thing, but the cold . . . He hated being cold. It seemed to eat into his bones and flesh, gnawing away at him like scavenging rats.

If only he had a warmer coat. But hell, there'd be no need to worry about the trial—he'd fucking freeze to death before they got there. And what riled him even more was that the cold didn't seem to bother the others much. Ford and Carter must be used to this weather and Harvard had once told him how cold the winters were out east. Well, wasn't that just fine and dandy for them? He hunched his shoulders over, shrugging himself deeper into his jacket. He thought of Stoney's big tartan coat. He always thought it looked damn stupid, but right now he'd sell his soul for a coat like that. Except, of course, he'd sold his soul a long time ago.

It was carried on the wind, just a whiff, but he could smell a town. It couldn't be too far now. He could always tell when he was close to a town. He could smell the stench of people and their dull little lives. He wanted it now. He wanted to get there and he wanted to get on with the whole damn business—it was time to end it. He'd take his chance, play the jury and hopefully play a winning hand. He wasn't done yet and he'd be damned if he'd let Doe win. Because if they hanged him Doe would have won. The man had tried to break him all those years ago, but Fierro didn't break that easy.

He pulled his shoulders back and sat taller in the saddle. Didn't give a damn now about the cold. Fierro was riding in to win.

He could scent wood smoke. The town had to be real close. They were almost there. He realized he was smiling. And oddly, he found he was looking forward to this. Fierro was getting his edge back.

He could see the smoke now, rising from a small settlement nestling in the curve of the hills. It had been a few years, but the place looked the same as it had before. Didn't seem to have grown much. But then it was pretty much a dead-end kind of a place. It was maybe a touch bigger than Cimarron, but Cimarron would grow. This place would probably never change.

They slowed the horses to a walk as they approached the main street. The town couldn't get many visitors because they seemed to be creating a lot of interest as they rode in. People came out of the shops and lined the boardwalks—the word must be going out that the lawmen were back with Fierro. And all the eyes were on him. He kept his eyes straight ahead, just a whisper of a smile playing at his lips. If these folk thought they were going to get a hanging they had a shock coming. He knew he could do this. He knew he could win. Fierro was back in control.

CHAPTER SEVENTEEN

Guy could feel the color flushing his face. Everyone was staring at them. He tried to block out the faces of the people gathering to watch as they rode in and attempted to keep his eyes focused straight ahead, but he was failing miserably. It was odd though, because although he couldn't remember ever feeling quite so self-conscious and embarrassed, when he looked across at Johnny he'd swear that his brother was smiling.

It wasn't an obvious smile. It was more like the ghost of one. He felt a pang of concern. Of fear, if he was honest. It was as though Johnny was enjoying the attention. No. That wasn't possible. Johnny couldn't enjoy being the center of attention in circumstances like this. Could he?

The whole thing was obviously the most dreadful mistake. Wasn't it?

Stoney's words echoed in his head. The sheriff had made a valid point. Why hadn't Johnny asked any questions about the murder charge? Every time he thought about Stoney's words he felt a heavy lump of dread weighing him down. Stoney was right. It wasn't natural. Any man would want to know what he was being accused of doing. Wouldn't he?

Ford reined in outside a building marked as the marshal's office. The man had done well to make this journey considering he had one arm out of action, and although he must have been in considerable pain, not once had Guy seen him even wince, let alone complain. Guy had been impressed by Ford's steadiness throughout. He had an air of quiet confidence and Guy suspected that he would be a very good man to have by his side in a battle.

Guy glanced once more at Johnny. His brother didn't seem to be in any hurry to dismount. He was just sitting on his horse with the strange half-smile pulling at his mouth as though amused by the whole ghastly business. It was almost as though he wanted to draw attention to himself.

Guy dismounted and went to stand by Ford and Carter, who were hitching the reins around the rail running the length of the building. Johnny swung his leg over the saddle horn and paused briefly before jumping gracefully to the ground. Damn it! His brother really was trying to draw attention to himself. It was blatant. Most men wearing cuffs would have been more hesitant, careful. But no, Johnny was all show.

The action wasn't lost on Carter either. The deputy gave Johnny a hard push. "Just get on inside, Fierro." Johnny didn't move. He just turned toward Carter, smiling all the while, but the smile sent a chill down Guy's spine.

Johnny leaned toward the man. "Don't push me, Carter. And trust me, you don't want to piss me off any more than you already have, because I'll make you wish you were never born."

How did Johnny do that? He could smile and speak so softly but seem so deadly and menacing at the same time. However he did it, it seemed to have quite an effect on Carter. The man paled and took a step back.

Johnny paused and scanned the crowd before turning and walking into the office. Guy followed him in, happy to finally shut the door on all those prying eyes.

It was a fair-sized office for a small town. A row of rifles were locked and chained to a gun rack and a heavy oak door separated the office from the cells at the back. Ford jerked his head towards the cells. "Come on, Fierro, in the cell and then I can take those cuffs off you."

Johnny strolled into the cell, looking for all the world like he was just heading into a bar for a drink. As Ford clanged the metal cell door closed, Johnny bent and tested the mattress, before springing onto it and stretching himself out with his hands behind his head. He looked like he did stretched out on the couch at the ranch.

Guy ground his teeth. He couldn't figure his brother's mood at all. Johnny seemed far too relaxed about the whole business. It was as though everything was just a minor inconvenience, an irritation that would be swept away in no time. He certainly didn't give the impression of a man concerned about being tried for murder.

"Something you wanted, Harvard?" Johnny sounded amused. "You'd best go book yourself into a hotel if you're figuring on staying in this territory."

"Of course I'm staying." Guy took a deep breath. "I will go and find you a lawyer and then I will check into a hotel. Is there anything you need?"

Johnny gave him that strange half-smile again. "No, I'm just fine and dandy. I got everything I need right here." He waved his hand around the cell, as if to emphasize the point. "But Harvard, I don't need no lawyer."

Guy could feel anger building inside. Why the hell wasn't Johnny taking this seriously? "This is not a game, Johnny. There's going to be a trial—that inconvenient truth is not going to just disappear. You will be on trial, for your life. And, if I recall correctly, you have not qualified as a lawyer. And it is, oddly enough, advisable to have a lawyer fighting your case when you're on trial for murder."

Johnny laughed. "Murder? Hell, it's just a mix-up. They got the wrong man is all." He hesitated. "A case of mistaken identity. That's the phrase, ain't it? I'll deal with it myself. I don't need no fancy-assed lawyer. They charge a fortune and they'll screw you as soon as look at you."

Guy glared at him through the bars of the cell. "Stop being so obtuse. I am here to ensure that you get a good lawyer and a fair trial. And that is exactly what I intend to do."

Johnny returned the glare. "And I just told you I don't need one. And I sure don't trust no fancy lawyer to be worrying about my skin. The only person who's going to look out for me in that courtroom is me."

"Tough." Guy felt the last vestiges of his patience disappear. "I'm getting you a lawyer whether you want one or not and that's it. The matter is not negotiable." He stalked to the door, secure in the knowledge that just for once he could have the last word. "I'm going to go and organize it now, so you'd better start getting used to the idea. I'll see you later." He slammed the door shut behind him.

Ford looked up at him from the desk, where he was sorting through a pile of paperwork. "Anything you need, Mr. Sinclair?"

Guy grimaced. "More patience!"

Ford grinned. "Giving you a hard time, is he?"

Guy perched on the edge of the desk. "That's putting it mildly." Guy hesitated. How to phrase the question that was gnawing away at him? He sighed. The easiest thing was just to spit it right out. "Has Johnny not asked you anything about this murder charge? Anything at all?"

Ford bowed his head, seemingly intent on shuffling the paperwork. "Not that I recall."

Guy frowned. "You're certain you haven't forgotten anything? It seems most . . ."

"No." Ford's response was abrupt to say the least. Guy eyed the man curiously. There was something in his demeanor that struck Guy as evasive. It was obvious that Ford wasn't going to be drawn on the subject.

Ford walked over to the rifle stand and checked the locks as if to indicate the conversation was over. He glanced at Guy over his shoulder. "So, anything else you need, Mr. Sinclair? There's a hotel along the street on the right, next to the small cantina. It's not too fancy but it's clean and the food isn't bad."

No, he definitely wasn't going to be drawn into conversation about Johnny. Guy sighed. "Before I check into the hotel, I need to know where I can find a lawyer for my brother. Does the town have one? I should have thought of it when we were on the trail and wired ahead. But with the stage crash and Johnny's injury, I totally overlooked the matter."

Ford nodded. "Yeah, we got a lawyer. His office is at the far end of the town. The other end from where we rode in. He's not . . ." Ford hesitated. "He's not an easy man, our lawyer. A bit of a law unto himself, if you ask me."

Guy felt a twinge of misgiving—that was all he needed. If the lawyer was difficult, it would make Johnny even more difficult, and he really didn't think he could cope with his brother being even trickier to handle than he was at present. He sighed. "Right, thanks for the warning. I guess I'd better go and pay him a visit, and I will endeavor to be charming!"

Guy strode to the far end of the town, only too aware of the interest he was attracting. He kept his head down, but he could hear whispers as he walked, and Johnny's name seemed to be on everyone's lips. He heaved a sigh of relief when he spotted a big brass plate on the wall announcing the lawyer's office. Horatio D. Wilson, Esq.

Guy pushed open the door to see an elderly man with wispy white hair, putting some papers into a worn leather bag. Guy made a slight bow. "Mr. Wilson?"

The man peered at him, fumbling in his pocket for a pair of wire-framed spectacles. "I am he. What can I do for you, young man?" He continued to fill the bag with more papers, before looking up impatiently. "Well? I am a busy man, get on with it."

Guy smiled and inclined his head. "My name is Guy Sinclair. I've traveled here from New Mexico to accompany my brother. He's to go on trial here, accused of murder. He obviously will need legal representation and I should like to retain your services to represent him, please."

Mr. Wilson looked up, his shaggy white brows drawn close together. "Murder? You mean your brother is Fierro?"

Guy nodded. "Yes, but his real name is Sinclair, and, as I said, he needs a lawyer."

The lawyer gave what could only have been described as a snort of derision. "Hmph. You can say that again." He adjusted his spectacles. "However, I must regretfully inform you, young man, that however much your brother may need the services of a lawyer, he won't be receiving mine. Now, if you'll excuse me, I have to lock up."

What? For a brief moment Guy couldn't think of a single thing to say. But then the words tumbled out, as though falling over themselves in a headlong rush. "What do you mean, he won't be receiving your services? You're the only lawyer in town, I believe, and my brother needs a lawyer. We can afford to pay you, if that's what you're worried about."

"Whether you can afford to pay me is of little consequence. I am choosing not to represent your brother. Good day." The man picked up his bag and then pointed with his hand for Guy to leave.

Guy moved across the doorway, blocking it. "No! I'm not just going to leave it at that. You have a professional duty to represent my brother . . ."

The man bristled with indignation, puffing his chest out. "I have no such thing. I am not a doctor bound by a strict oath to treat people, whatever their morals may be. I am perfectly entitled to turn down a case, and believe me, I am turning this one down."

"Every man is entitled to a defense. To be presumed innocent until proven guilty. Do you have so little concern for justice?" Guy could feel the heat in his face, but the man's attitude was insupportable. Guy was not giving in without a fight.

"Justice?" Mr. Wilson spat the word out. "Justice for whom? There was certainly no justice for the victim in this sordid case. However, Mr. Sinclair, I do not have to explain my motives to you. Let us merely say that this is one case I prefer not to accept. Now, I am leaving town for a few days and I wish to lock up. Good day to you."

There was a look of steely determination on the man's face. Guy knew intuitively that nothing he said would change the man's mind. And who wanted a lawyer whose heart wasn't in the job? Particularly in a case such as this. "Well." Guy couldn't keep the note of sarcasm from his voice. "If it's not delaying your departure too much, perhaps you would be good enough to tell me if there are any other lawyers in this area?"

The man inclined his head as though prepared to concede an answer to that question at least. "The nearest lawyer, a man called Pearson, is a good three or four days' ride from here, but he's usually drunk. Good day, Mr. Sinclair."

He knew when he was beaten. Guy just nodded and walked wearily back out to the sidewalk. Dusk had fallen and lamps were being lit, shining out a welcoming glow from the windows of the houses. But Guy had the feeling that there was no welcome for him in this dull town of small-minded people.

He trudged toward the hotel, stopping to collect his saddlebags from the livery where the horses were already bedded down in comfort and enjoying what looked like steaming bran mash. The sight of it made him realize how hungry he was. At least the hotel food would be edible if Ford was right.

The hotel was quiet. There was nobody manning the reception desk so he rang the bell and waited patiently until a coarse-looking blonde woman emerged from a back room. "Sorry to keep you, dearie. I'm Mrs. Nixon, the proprietor . . ." She paused, her hand flying to her mouth and her face paling. "Oh my! You rode in with the marshal and that killer. Are you a lawman too?"

"No, I'm . . ." He bit back the words that would declare him as Johnny's brother. The woman would probably refuse him a room if she thought he was connected with "that killer." He smiled—the most charming smile he could muster when he was tired, dirty, and hungry. "No, ma'am, I'm not a lawman. I'm a businessman in need of a room and your establishment has been highly recommended. And from what I hear, I understand that you serve excellent fare. I am full of eager anticipation and even on first glance I can see that your charming hotel can equal anything that cities such as Boston and San Francisco have to offer."

It worked. She positively preened. "Oh, my, you're too kind. Boston! Oh my goodness." She fluttered her hand in front of her heavily made-up face, and then adjusted her hair. She leaned forward, resting her ample bosom on the counter. "You mean you are familiar with Boston?"

Guy inclined his head graciously. "Familiar? Madam, I was raised there and I assure you, your hotel is as delightful as any hotel in that city."

Her smile grew wider and the flush started on her quivering chest and worked its way up over her face. She reached for the registration book and then a key. "I'll put you in number five. It's our very best room. And what name is it please?"

He hesitated. "Eliot. Guy Eliot." It wasn't a total lie—it was his middle name. And it was definitely prudent to avoid making any connection between himself and Johnny, just in case the name Sinclair came up.

He followed her up the stairs, trying to avoid staring at her vast backside, which appeared to be trying to escape from its prison of pink silk. The dress was straining so tightly that he feared her buttocks would make a successful bid for freedom and the dress split wide open. He shuddered as he conjured up the picture in his mind's eye.

She left him in "the best room" promising that dinner would be ready in twenty minutes. He shut the door, leaning weakly against it as he took in the full horror of the room. Pink was very obviously her favorite color. Pink satin drapes framed the window and a vast pink canopy covered the bed. There were vases filled with purple and pink feathers and a pink velvet chaise longue stood at the end of the bed. In one corner there was a statue of a large pink bird, standing on one leg. The overall effect reminded him of a tart's boudoir. But not as classy.

He breathed a sigh of relief that at least Johnny couldn't see the room. His mouth quirked in a rueful smile as he thought of what Johnny's sardonic comments would be about the accommodation.

Ford had been right about one thing—the food wasn't bad. In fact, it was a surprisingly good meal that he would have enjoyed under any other circumstances. Instead his mind was filled with a maelstrom of ideas while he tried to formulate a plan to help Johnny. The trouble was, he couldn't think of any way to do so. The drunken lawyer whom Mr. Wilson had mentioned didn't seem like a good idea.

He sat back, sipping his coffee, reflecting on Stoney's words back in Cimarron, when the nightmare journey had started. He recalled Stoney's horrific description of his brief glimpse of Johnny's childhood. Guy shuddered, suddenly visualizing a starving, blue-eyed wild boy.

He set his coffee cup down with a clatter. Johnny had been beaten and starving while Guy had lived the good life. Their respective childhoods couldn't have been more diverse. Childhood. He shook his head slowly. If Stoney was right, it didn't sound as though Johnny had ever had one. And as he thought about it, he realized that the few snippets Johnny had divulged about his past were like crumbs thrown to a dog. Johnny had actually told him very little while cleverly giving the impression of confiding in Guy. Hell, Johnny was so damned difficult to figure. And Stoney acted as though he knew so much about Johnny, but in fact, Stoney barely knew him at all.

The question was, did anyone really know Johnny?

Or what he might be capable of?

Guy shoved his chair back, trying to push the disturbing questions from his mind. He needed some fresh air to clear his head. He grabbed his coat from his room before heading out into the lung-chilling night air. He walked along the boardwalk with his hands thrust deep in his pockets for warmth. There were few people around. Anyone with any sense was inside in the warmth. Laughter echoed from the saloon, but even that was hardly doing a brisk business. Looking through the steamy windows he could see an elderly barkeep and a few customers. The laughter came from a group of young cowboys playing cards. They were joshing each other good-naturedly. None of them seemed to be weighed down by worry that their brother might hang.

Almost unknowingly he found himself standing outside Ford's office. He grimaced. He might as well admit to himself that all he really wanted to do was check that Johnny really did have everything he needed.

Pushing the door open he saw Ford sitting back in a big chair with his feet on the desk reading a newspaper, a half-finished bowl of stew discarded next to him. Ford raised his eyebrows slightly. "Something I can do for you, Mr. Sinclair?"

Guy shrugged, embarrassed. He didn't want Ford to think that he didn't trust him.

"He's fine, Mr. Sinclair. He had dinner and he's got plenty of blankets. It's as comfortable a cell as you'll find in any town jail and better than most." Ford's mouth quirked slightly, like he was biting back a smile.

Guy flushed. "I'm sorry. I know that you'll see he's treated well. It's just . . ."

"That you'll feel better if you have a word with him?" Ford stood up and gestured towards the door. "Be my guest."

Guy nodded his thanks and pushed open the heavy door that led through to the cells. Johnny didn't look as though he'd moved. He was still stretched out with his hands behind his head, a picture of a man at ease. And he still had that damned irritating half-smile on his face.

"You forget something, Harvard?" There was an edge of insolence in the question. Guy scowled at him. Johnny really knew how to irritate him.

"No. I didn't forget anything. I came to check you had everything you needed."

Johnny laughed. "I told you before, I got everything I need right here. Hell, I had a good dinner and I got me a nice big pile of blankets." Johnny looked at Guy with a speculative sort of look in his eyes. "You get checked into a hotel, did you? I was wondering if maybe they'd refuse to let you in, being as you're my brother an' all."

Guy met Johnny's gaze. "I didn't tell them. I thought it wise to not admit to the connection. I used the name of Eliot."

There was a flicker of something in Johnny's eyes, but it was so fleeting, gone so fast he couldn't read the emotion.

"So, is it a nice comfortable hotel? You got a nice soft bed?"

Guy smiled. "You'd like my room. It's all pink. It looks like a tart's boudoir. Knowing your propensity for whores, you'd feel right at home in it."

Johnny turned his head away with just the merest hint of a smile. "But I feel right at home tucked up in here too, Harvard. It's real cozy."

"If you say so, but I suspect you'd rather be tucked up with a whore."

Johnny didn't bite. "Anything else, Harvard?"

Guy grimaced. "I went to see the town lawyer, but he didn't want to take your case."

A broad smile spread across Johnny's face. But it didn't reach his eyes. "Now that is good news. Told you, I don't need no fancy lawyer."

Guy narrowed his eyes and huffed out a sigh. "I'm not having this argument again. I will find you a lawyer. It just might take a little time."

Johnny raised an eyebrow. "Maybe I don't have much time, Harvard. What you going to do then?"

Guy bit his lip. He'd never met a man who could sound quite as arrogant as Johnny.

He didn't bother answering. Instead he opened the door of the office and called to Ford. "I'd like your advice please, Marshal. I went to see the lawyer but he's refused to represent Johnny. Can you recommend somebody else?"

Ford ambled to the door, scratching his chin thoughtfully. "Circuit judge arrives the day after tomorrow. Reckon he'll want to start this trial right away."

Guy quelled the urge to snap at Ford. He struggled to keep his voice calm. "A man is entitled to a defense. Surely the circuit judge will adjourn the case until I find a lawyer for Johnny?"

Ford sighed deeply and stared down at the floor, avoiding Guy's gaze. "I wouldn't recommend that, Mr. Sinclair."

Guy looked at him sharply. "Why not? That has to be the

best thing for Johnny."

Ford shook his head. "Nope. The circuit judge arriving this week is Judge Denning. He's a fair man. Sound. Steady. He doesn't jump to conclusions like some judges are minded to. But if you go gallivanting off trying to track down a lawyer, Denning will move on. And the next circuit judge due here is Jeffries. Trust me on this. Fierro will be better off with Denning."

Guy shook his head. "I can't believe he'd be better off without a lawyer." He glanced over at Johnny who was lying back, still looking totally at ease. "You need to have a lawyer."

Johnny didn't answer immediately. He turned his head and looked hard at Ford. Raised his eyebrows in that odd way of his like he always did when he wanted a second to think something through. "Denning? That's the best man?"

Ford nodded. "He's the best man. Better than Jeffries. You really don't want Jeffries."

Johnny shrugged. "That settles it, Harvard. I'll go with Denning. And no lawyer." And as if to signal the end of the conversation, he rolled over with his back to them, pulling a blanket over himself.

Guy followed Ford into the office. "Surely you can see he needs a lawyer. He needs legal representation. Wilson said there's a fellow a few days' ride from here."

Ford threw his hands in the air. "Yeah, he's right, there is. But the man's a drunk. And you'll end up with Jeffries as the judge, and a drunken, no-good lawyer. Do you really care what happens to your brother?"

"Why the hell do you think I'm here? I didn't ride all this way for the fun of it. Of course I care." Guy took a deep breath, trying to keep control and not lose his temper.

Ford eased back into his chair and gave him a hard-eyed look. "Then trust me on this. Even without a lawyer, your brother's best chance is with Denning. Unless you want to guarantee that he hangs. They don't call Jeffries the Hanging Judge for nothing."

CHAPTER EIGHTEEN

So, it had begun. As the door slammed behind Guy, Johnny rolled over onto his back and lay staring at the ceiling. Guy Eliot. He laughed softly but he sure didn't feel too happy. Even so, it wasn't anything he hadn't expected. And he certainly couldn't blame Guy. The only surprising thing was that Guy hadn't given up on him a long time ago.

He hauled himself up and swung his legs around over the edge of the iron-framed cot. He reached in his pocket and took out the makings for a cigarette, grateful that Ford had allowed him to keep them. No point in brooding over things. He needed to concentrate on how to wriggle out of the murder charge. Because he sure didn't figure on being found guilty. To hell with that. Fierro hated to lose and he wasn't going to lose his life over this. Not for that son of a bitch. The court case had to play out the way he wanted it to. And it would be a hell of a lot easier to manage that if he hadn't got some fancy windbag of a lawyer. Seemed to him that all lawyers were in love with the sound of their own voices. He'd never met one who'd simply do as he was told in a court of law. So, even though it would be kind of handy to have someone around who knew the way it all worked in court, he'd probably be better off without some slimy gringo who'd treat him like shit. Because he'd bet good money that even if some lawyer took his case, they'd look down on the breed gunfighter. All they'd care about was their fee—and they got paid even if he hanged.

He struck a match and lit his smoke, and then, leaning back against the wall, he started to plot. Going over everything that happened in that shiny-as-a-new-pin house, so that he could prepare for anything the court might throw at him. No. He had no intention of just rolling over dead for this. He was going to win.

"We need to have a serious talk." Guy had sure been up early. Dios, he'd hardly given Johnny a chance to eat his breakfast before he'd turned up at the jail.

"Serious?" Johnny cocked his eyebrow.

"Yes. Serious." Guy sure sounded snappy. Didn't look too good either. There were lines of worry across his brow and shadows under his eyes.

Johnny shrugged, pushing away the twinge of guilt. "I told you to stay out of it. But you were so hell-bent on coming. Should have stayed at the ranch, Harvard."

"So you have said. On numerous occasions. And I have grown weary of hearing it." Guy sounded like vinegar. A whole bottle of vinegar.

Johnny shrugged again. "Told you I could handle things here. And I can. They got the wrong man." Except they hadn't.

"They have an eyewitness, Johnny." Guy sounded real pissed off.

Johnny scowled. "In case you've forgotten, Harvard, I was there when Carter said it. But it won't be the first time eyewitnesses have gotten confused. Ask three different people how a gunfight went down, and they'll all give you a different story. So, like I keep telling you, I can handle this. Why the hell can't you just stay out of it? Go on home, Guy. The old man would want someone there running things while he's off trying to save Ramsey Burnett's precious hide."

Guy set his jaw and scowled. "As you know damn well,

Alonso is more than capable of running the ranch in our absence. And I think our father would be a damn sight more concerned about saving your hide. If they find you guilty, they will hang you, do you understand that? It's not a game, Johnny. They could hang you."

He said the last words slowly, kind of like he was trying to make a point.

Johnny rolled his eyes. Dios, his brother could be an irritating son of a bitch at times. Why the hell did Harvard treat him like some little kid? He wasn't a kid and he'd seen a hell of a lot more in life than Harvard had ever seen. "I know that. I ain't dumb." The words felt so hot it was like spitting venom.

"So?" Guy's words were kind of hot too. "Doesn't that thought bother you at all?"

"We all got to go sometime, don't we?" Probably wasn't the smartest thing to say. Guy turned a nasty shade of red. Johnny took a deep breath. "It ain't gonna happen, Guy, they ain't gonna hang me." And wasn't that the truth? He'd use his knife on himself before he let that happen.

"You need a lawyer, Johnny. We can delay the trial while I track one down."

"No! I told you, I don't want some fancy-assed lawyer. I'll look after myself and take my chances with this Judge Denning." Johnny sat back on the cot, wrapping his arms around himself.

"Take your chances? Take your chances?" Guy's voice was getting louder by the second. "Does your life mean so little to you? What about how this affects your family? Did you ever stop to consider that? Have you even spared a passing thought for us while you're being so downright arrogant about looking out for yourself? Have you stopped for a single second to consider anyone other than yourself?" Guy was pacing up and down outside the cell, like he was trying to wear a trench in the floor.

Johnny cocked an eyebrow. "Getting kind of worked up there, Harvard, that ain't good for you."

Guy stopped pacing. Stood totally still for a beat, before turning his head and staring hard at Johnny. "Getting kind of worked up? Yes, Johnny, I am getting kind of worked up." He shook his head slightly, like he couldn't quite believe something. "God, but you can be an incredibly selfish bastard at times. Do you really never stop to think of anyone else's feelings?"

Johnny stared down at the stone floor. He'd never had to think of anyone else before. Hell, there'd never been anyone else to think of. Just himself. Alone. Like he'd been for more years than he could remember. But no way was he telling Guy that.

"Well?" Guy was looking riled up and wanting an answer. "Do you? Have you thought how it would be for Father? He goes off on a trip thinking he's leaving the ranch in safe hands and comes back to find you've been hanged for murder. Maybe I'd better try to contact him. Maybe . . ."

Johnny jerked forward. "You do, and I promise it'll be the last thing you ever do." His voice came out real soft. The one thing he couldn't take would be for his father to find out about this and come storming down. Fuck, no. Fierro couldn't cope with that. It would be the final straw.

"Are you threatening me, Johnny?" Guy's eyes were wide open, like a rabbit looked when it was caught in the light of a lantern at night.

"Yeah, Harvard. I'm threatening you. Send for the old man, and I really will kill you. Even if I'm stuck in here, I'll find a way." The dry bitter heat of anger was rising and felt like it was going to choke him. "I knew you couldn't handle this. Oh, I know you think you've seen everything because of being in the war and all. But let me tell you, you ain't seen nothing. So stop damn well telling me what to do all the time. I ain't dumb. I ain't a kid. And I sure as hell don't need the old man dragged into this. Just like I didn't need you dragged into it. I told you to stay at the ranch, but you wouldn't fucking listen. You just had to come too, didn't you? You couldn't keep your nose out of my business. And now I have to put up with all this shit from you when I got other things to think about. Like avoiding getting a fucking noose around my neck.

"I ain't gonna hang. I don't need no fancy lawyer. I don't need the old man. And right now, Harvard, I don't need you. So get the hell out of here."

Was Guy going to move? Or was he just going to stand there, with his mouth open like he was trying to catch flies?

"All I wanted was to help you."

Johnny shut his eyes briefly, hearing the pain and disbelief in Guy's voice. He felt ashamed now. And it wasn't like Fierro to lose his cool like that. He bit his lip. He didn't want to lose Guy but right now he couldn't deal with him. He had to keep his edge. He had to keep his mind on the job ahead, and he couldn't do that with Harvard breathing down his neck all the time. He looked up, meeting Guy's gaze. Could see the pain there. Johnny swallowed hard, guilt washing over him.

"Look." Johnny spoke softly. "I know you want to help. And it ain't that I don't appreciate it. But right now, Guy, I want to handle this my way. Trust me. I know what I'm doing."

"Trust you?" It was the tone of Guy's voice. Johnny felt his guts shrivel up. He'd blown it. He'd lost his brother.

"Trust you?" Guy sounded even colder now. "You're asking me to trust you, when you won't tell me anything? And why do I get this feeling that you know far more about this business than you've let on? Is that it, Johnny? Did you kill this man?"

It felt like a punch in the gut. Felt that all the wind was

knocked out of him. He couldn't lie—not to Guy of all people. But he couldn't tell the truth either. What to say? What the hell should he say? Couldn't think straight. He sighed, shaking his head. "Go home, Guy. Go on back to the ranch. I'll handle things here."

"Tell me you didn't kill him." The vein was pulsing in Guy's temple, just like it always did with the old man.

"I ain't telling you anything, Harvard."

"Which leaves me to think—"

He couldn't bear to hear Guy say it. "You think whatever you like. I told you, they ain't gonna hang me. Just go home and leave me alone."

His heart was thumping real loud, and the blood was pounding in his ears. Surely Guy must hear it? Was the man going to say anything or was he just going to stand staring? And the way Guy looked . . . It was like he'd gone a long way off— somewhere he couldn't be reached. What the hell was he thinking about? Because his expression was impossible to read.

Guy turned and opened the oak door before pausing. "You want me to go home? Trust me. It'll be my pleasure."

The door closed with a bang that echoed through the cells. Like the sound when they hammered the last nail in a coffin or a gallows. His gut twisted and before he could even make it to the bucket, he spewed his breakfast up all over the cell floor. It still looked like his breakfast but it stank. And that made him puke again. He kept on puking until there was nothing left. He was just gagging and dry and the pain in his chest felt like it was going to rip him in two.

He stumbled to the cot and sat rocking with his arms wrapped around himself. Rocking back and forth. And he hurt more than he'd ever hurt. He bit on his lip hard. He knew he had to get back in control. He had to hold it all together and win. Because otherwise the bastard would have won. The man might be cold in his grave but he'd still have won. And Fierro couldn't let that happen. Not just for himself, but for the kid too. Fierro had made a promise, and he always kept his promises.

But his promise had a high price. It had cost him his brother.

He shook his head. Nothing lasted. He knew that. Nothing ever lasted. Never trust anyone—it saved a lot of disappointment. He'd lived by that rule for so many years and these last few months he'd let it slide. And he hadn't even noticed it slipping. When did it happen? When did he let Guy get under his skin? And Guthrie? And the ranch and the land . . . Home. They'd all gotten to him.

Delice's words echoed in his ears. The words she'd spoken just before he left for Utah. The words warning him to be careful. Warning him that one day he might push Guy too hard. He'd often thought that she reckoned she was right about everything. But she was on the money now, because it seemed that day had come.

The big oak door opened and his heart seemed to lift in his chest where the hole had been. He looked up, barely hoping. But hoping.

"Just checking if you needed anything, Fierro?"

And he felt empty again. Ford was looking at him hard, looking at the puke on the floor. "Looks like you need to wash up, I'll get you some more water." Ford gestured at the floor. "And we'd better get that cleaned up too."

Johnny didn't move. Couldn't move right then. It was like he was forged to the bed. Cast in iron and forged to the iron cot. Guy really had gone.

Ford came back carrying a jug of water, and a mug hooked over one of the fingers of his good hand. He passed them through the bars, setting them down on the bench. "You'd best drink something. I'll get a bucket and mop."

Johnny watched him. But it was like he was watching from a

long way away. Like Ford wasn't talking to him but somebody else. Nothing seemed real. Everything seemed to have slowed and faded away.

Johnny blinked. Ford was inside the cell. And that was odd, because he hadn't noticed the marshal unlock it. But it had been locked before so he must have unlocked it. Even stranger, the marshal was swamping out, sloshing the mop around with his one good arm. Prisoners always had to swamp out. Clean up after themselves. But here was Ford doing it, despite his injured arm. Odd.

"Guess your breakfast didn't agree with you." Ford sounded kind of level. No tone in his voice. Flat.

Johnny shrugged, struggling to think of something to say. Anything to say. "Maybe it's my head. I was sick when I hit it, I remember. Yeah. I was sick then. Must be my head. Probably ain't quite over the bang yet."

Ford met his gaze. Didn't say a thing for a few seconds. "Yep. Figure you must be right."

Johnny watched him through dulled eyes as he carried on swamping. "Where's Carter? I ain't seen him since we got here."

Ford's mouth quirked in a smile. "I gave him a few days off. I didn't want you shot trying to escape."

Johnny laughed, even though he felt like shit. "Yeah. I guess there was a chance of that." He paused. "Who the hell ever made him a lawman?"

Ford grunted as he put the mop and bucket back in the corner beyond the cell. "Oh, some dumb mayor we had here a year or so back. Wanted a pet dog with a badge. So they got Carter. But we got a new mayor now, and Carter's going to be on his way shortly. I don't hold with men who abuse their position. Not when law-abiding, hard-working folk are paying good money to men who are supposed to uphold the law. Nope. Don't hold with it at all. There's a sight too many people put in jobs of trust, who . . ." He paused, running his fingers through his hair and looking like he'd gone far away. "Well. Anyway. Some folk are just . . ."

"Shit?" Johnny figured maybe he should help him out.

Ford nodded. "Yeah. I guess that sums up quite a lot of folk." He narrowed his eyes, looking hard at Johnny. "You going to be all right now? Anything I can get you? Some more smokes?"

"No. I'm . . . fine."

Ford pushed the cell door closed, turning the key. "Your brother. He left in kind of a hurry—never seen a man leave my office so fast. You want me to give him a message?"

Johnny shook his head, staring down at his boots. The sole was peeling away from the left one. Needed fixing.

"Fierro? You sure you don't want me to give him a message?" Ford's voice came from far away.

"No. No message." Johnny's voice came out as a whisper. Like it had got stuck down his throat somewhere.

He felt Ford studying him for a few more heartbeats—funny how his heart was still beating when it felt like it had been ripped out of his chest. Ford sighed, shaking his head kind of like he was irritated over something. "Well, if you change your mind, call me. I'll be in the office."

Johnny shook himself as the door closed after Ford. He had to get a grip. So Guy was headed back to the ranch. Who cared? Anyway, it was what Fierro wanted. It was for the best. And when the court found Fierro not guilty, well, he could go back to the ranch too . . . He sighed. Somehow, it wouldn't be the same. No. They could all go to hell. Maybe when this was all over he should head back for the border. And never let anyone get close again.

It was some time before the door opened again. "You got a visitor." Ford was holding the door to let someone in and Johnny looked up, hoping against hope . . .

"Who the hell are you?" His heart felt like it had sunk right down to his boots as he spoke the words, looking at the scrawny kid who'd walked in.

On second glance, the kid wasn't that much of a kid, whoever he was. He was probably about nineteen or twenty, but real puny. And pale. Like he spent too much time indoors and not enough time outside working up muscle. Had he come because he wanted a glimpse of a famous gunfighter? Wouldn't be the first time.

The kid coughed. Kind of like he couldn't quite decide what to say. And cleared his throat a couple of times. Then he shuffled his feet. And cleared his throat again.

Johnny sighed. "You got something to say, kid, say it."

"I was hoping I could be of some service to you."

For a second, Johnny couldn't think of a damn thing to say. He opened his mouth but the words got stuck somewhere. He scoffed and didn't bother getting up. "Sorry? You were hoping to be of some service to me? And what the hell use does a kid like you think you can be to me?"

The kid swallowed real hard. "I'm . . . I was the clerk to Mr. Wilson."

Johnny narrowed his eyes. "Wilson? Who the hell is Mr. Wilson?"

His visitor shuffled his feet again. "Sorry, I thought you knew. Mr. Wilson is the lawyer here in town."

Johnny laughed. "Well, kid, from what I hear, your Mr. Wilson don't want nothing to do with me."

"That's what I'm trying to explain." He paused, kind of like he was trying to figure out the way to say whatever was on his mind. And then shuffled his feet yet again—at this rate he'd wear a hole in the stone floor. "I have been offered an apprenticeship with a firm of lawyers out east. And I'm leaving town in a few days' time. But, it seemed to me that you might be in need of some assistance first. Unfortunately, Mr. Wilson doesn't care much about people having lawyers, unless he has a mind to act for them."

Johnny shook his head, trying to figure the kid out. "Let me get this straight. You ain't a lawyer but you want to pretend to be my lawyer?"

The kid's shoulders squared up. He bit his lip and flushed. Looked pretty pissed off. "I don't want to pretend to be anything. But I am a legal clerk. I do know how the courts work. And I am bright enough to have been offered a really good chance with a big Eastern law firm. And there isn't another lawyer for miles. Mr. Fierro, I'm the best chance you've got."

The kid was serious. He really was serious. Johnny bit back a smile. "And how much do legal clerks cost? In these parts?"

"I'm more interested in results."

Johnny felt the smile spreading. Couldn't stop it. The kid had something. Wasn't sure quite what, but he had something. "Hell, kid, you won't never do well in the law if you don't worry about the money. Seems to me that's what lawyers worry most about. Never met one who wasn't more interested in his bank account."

The kid looked him square in the eye. "It might be an old-fashioned notion, Mr. Fierro, but I care more about the idea of everyone being entitled to legal representation than I do about personal remuneration."

Hell. The kid knew as many fancy words as Harvard.

Johnny eyed him curiously. "You from around these parts, kid?"

The boy nodded. "I am. And the name is Sweetfoot, not kid."

Johnny chewed on his thumb as an idea started to form.

"You know anything about this eyewitness they're supposed to have?"

A puzzled look crossed Sweetfoot's face. "Yes, I know him. Everyone knows him."

Johnny leaned forward as a little seed of hope sprang deep inside. Maybe, just maybe, things were looking up. Wouldn't do no harm to have someone who knew how the system worked. And if he knew the eyewitness, well, things couldn't get much better than that. "If I hire you, kid, we do it my way in court. You ask what I want you to ask. It's my game. My show. Would you be prepared to go along with that?"

Sweetfoot nodded slowly. "I would be taking your instructions."

Johnny grinned. "Well, in that case, Sweetfoot, you got yourself your first ever client and we got a deal." He paused, enjoying the open-mouthed look of amazement on the kid's face. "And now, I want you to tell me everything you know about this eyewitness. And I mean everything."

CHAPTER NINETEEN

Guy dropped the key. His hands were shaking and the damn thing didn't seem to fit the lock. But after much fumbling, he managed to unlock the door at his third attempt. Slamming it shut behind him, he stumbled across the room and sank onto the bed. It wasn't just his hands that were shaking—he trembled all over like an aspen leaf in a fall breeze.

Rage was building in him. Fury. His pulse was pounding and his breathing was ragged. How could he have been so naive as to be taken in by Johnny? He'd been taken in from the very start. How could he have never noticed what a cold, selfish bastard his brother was? Well, Johnny could go to hell. Guy had managed for more than twenty years without a brother—he certainly didn't need one now. Particularly a cold-blooded killer. That was what Carter had called him. A cold-blooded killer.

It was odd though that Ford hadn't been as quick to condemn Johnny, but from the muted gossip he'd heard around the town, it seemed to be a foregone conclusion that Johnny would hang. The townspeople obviously knew all about the case. And hanging was a fitting end for a vicious killer.

Yes. Johnny had fooled them all. It seemed that their father's first gut instincts about Johnny had been right all along. Hell, Guthrie had warned Guy early on. His father's words echoed in his head. *"Johnny's reputation is fearsome and long-established. Even if he does sometimes do the decent thing, you don't get a reputation like his by being nice. We have to be realistic and assume that he has a murky past, to say the least, and that he has committed some appalling acts."*

Appalling acts. And that was the crux of it. Guthrie had been right and now Johnny's past had finally caught up with him. And everything else about Johnny had been a sham.

He ground his teeth thinking how amusing Johnny must have found it all while he was busy charming them. Fooling them. He'd certainly fooled Guy. And Johnny had probably enjoyed a good laugh at Guy's expense, thinking how easy it was to sucker the Boston dandy. Guy shook his head. God it hurt now to think of all the times he'd defended Johnny and stood by him, believing that Johnny was a good and decent man.

Guy hauled himself up from the bed. His legs still felt wobbly but he stumbled to the washstand and splashed some water over his face. Looking in the mirror, he barely recognized the face looking back at him. He looked ten years older. There were lines and shadows around his eyes and the creases between his eyes seemed to have set into deep furrows. He turned away sharply, cursing Johnny for doing this to him. Right now he'd happily do the hangman's job for him and send Johnny to hell.

Guy's saddlebags were lying on top of the chest of drawers. He felt a surge of revulsion. He needed to get out of this room. Out of this town. Out of the damn territory and back to Sinclair. He needed to be there in case Father returned sooner than expected. Guthrie needed to hear what had happened. Guy shut his eyes briefly, his gut churning at the thought of having to explain all this to his father. How would his father take the news? Would he take it badly or would he merely think that all his worst fears had been realized?

And what would happen if Johnny was acquitted? If he got away with it, as he seemed so certain he would? Guy shuddered, because something deep inside was screaming that Johnny was guilty. And right now he couldn't imagine wanting to be anywhere near his brother, never mind trying to run a business and be in partnership with him. Guy shook his head. He knew he'd have no option but to return to Boston, to do anything else would be rank hypocrisy.

But first he needed to leave here. And that meant he needed a horse. Yes. That was the obvious thing to do. Go and buy a horse and leave this damn town as quickly as possible.

Even making a small decision seemed to calm him. He grabbed the key, and locking the door behind him, hurried down the stairs and out into the town to buy a fast horse.

A biting wind was blowing down the main street. Tumbleweed whipped around on the currents, blown this way and that like ships floundering in heavy seas. Which was exactly how he felt. Except he wasn't merely floundering—he was sinking fast and the only way to save himself was to get as far away from Johnny as possible.

Closed.

He sucked in a shuddering breath as he read the sign on the door of the livery stables. Closed! Damn it, why did the place have to close early today of all days? The sign beneath said it wouldn't be open again until the following day. Which meant he was going to have to stay in this damned town for another few hours. It seemed that the fates were all conspiring against him.

Turning on his heel, he pulled his collar up and trudged back toward the hotel, his head down in an effort to keep the damn dust out of his eyes.

"Mr. Sinclair."

Guy faltered as he stumbled slightly against Ford. "Sorry, Marshal, I wasn't looking where I was going."

"Guess you got a lot on your mind right now." Ford shook his head slightly as he spoke. "It's a sorry state of affairs right enough. But I thought I'd better let you know that the trial should start late morning tomorrow. The judge will deal with

197

some trifling matters and then—"

"I won't be coming to the trial." Guy interrupted, knowing he must sound cold, but he really didn't want to be drawn into any conversation about his brother's sordid affairs.

Ford pushed his hat back, sighing softly. "Not coming?"

"No, Marshal, I shall not be coming. I've made a decision and I intend to return home in the morning. Now, if there's nothing else I'll be getting on." Guy moved to step around the marshal when the man spoke again.

"So, just like that, you're up and leaving him and heading back to Cimarron?"

Guy gritted his teeth, but couldn't stop the sharp retort that sprang to his lips. "Yes. I am heading back to Cimarron. Just like that. Although I fail to see that my actions are any of your business . . ."

"He was sick earlier. Really sick."

"Sick?" Guy felt a pang of unease. He pushed it away. He didn't give a damn about Johnny. "I'm really not interested . . ."

"He was in a bad way." Ford was looking at him hard, as though searching for some reaction to his words.

Guy bit his lip. So what if Johnny was in a bad way? Although that head injury had been serious . . . "It must have been that head injury. A recurrence of the symptoms. Perhaps he should see a doctor." What a damn stupid thing to say. It wasn't as though he cared whether Johnny was sick or not.

Ford narrowed his eyes and gave an impatient shake of his head. "This was nothing to do with his head injury."

"Well, in that case, I'm sure that it's nothing you can't handle." Guy moved swiftly now, anxious to get away.

"It was right after you left him." There was a certain tone in Ford's voice, as though he was trying to make a point.

"Marshal, I'm really not interested. I reiterate, I am returning to Cimarron tomorrow. Good day to you."

Guy wasn't quick enough. Ford blocked his path. "So, you're running out on him. That's some way to treat your brother." Ford was looking at him now almost with a look of distaste. "Fine. You run out on him. But Fierro's OK. Take it from me, he's OK." With a curt nod, Ford carried along up the sidewalk, leaving Guy staring after him in bewilderment.

What the hell did the man mean? "He's OK." How was he supposed to interpret that? That Johnny was no longer sick? Or something else? Guy watched the man striding up the street, acknowledging some of the townspeople as he passed. Damn man. None of this was any of Ford's business anyway. Hell, he'd probably been fooled by Johnny as well.

Guy hurried back to the hotel. It was too cold to stand around wondering about Ford's enigmatic remarks. He'd buy a horse in the morning and head home.

"Oh, Mr. Eliot. Mr. Eliot."

He paused with his foot on the first step of the stairs leading up to his room. He shut his eyes briefly before turning and sweeping his hat off. He forced a smile as Mrs. Nixon, clad in yet another violent pink dress, leaned across the desk in reception waving at him. She patted her hair and then fluttered her hands. "Will you be dining in this evening, Mr. Eliot? You've missed lunch, but I do like to know my numbers for dinner. The stage has come in and we're a lot busier."

Guy forced another smile. "I'm so sorry, Mrs. Nixon, it was remiss of me, I should have let you know. Yes, please, I will be dining in this evening." He moved to one side as a tall woman in a thick veil brushed past him and hurried up the stairs. How on earth could she see through it?

He moved to follow her up the stairs so he could return to the sanctity of his room when he heard Mrs. Nixon's voice again. "Judge Denning, how nice to see you. Did you have a good journey?"

Curiosity got the better of him, and he turned swiftly even though he knew he shouldn't stare. A dapper, gray-haired man with a neatly trimmed goatee beard was bent over, signing the register. Immaculately dressed, he was the type of man who wouldn't have looked out of place in Boston. There was something reassuring about his precise movements . . .

Reassuring? What a ridiculous notion. Irritated with himself, Guy returned to his room. Perhaps he could read to fill in the time until dinner. Or take a nap. God only knew he needed one.

He tried to read for an hour or two but unable to concentrate, he found he kept reading the same line over and over again. He slammed the book shut and laid it on the table next to his chair. *The Count of Monte Cristo* would have to wait. The sooner he got away from this town the better. And no matter how hard he tried to block them out, he couldn't get Ford's words from echoing in his head. *Fierro's OK.*

He leaned his head back. Maybe he'd have better luck sleeping. He might as well attempt a nap before dinner.

But that was no more successful than the reading. When he tried to settle to sleep, Johnny's face kept drifting in front of him. And the look in his eyes when he'd heard that Guy had used the name Eliot. The look that Guy had been unable to read.

It had been an odd look. Guy shook his head angrily. He didn't care. The very fact that Johnny had refused to deny killing the man told Guy all he needed to know. Didn't it?

Stoney's voice was in his head now. *"I ain't saying whether he's guilty or not. But I do know if he is guilty, if he did do this, he would have had a damn good reason for killing the man. Johnny don't kill for the thrill of it. That I'm certain of."*

Guy tried to push the words away. What did Stoney know anyway? It seemed he'd barely known Johnny, so he was hardly a reliable character witness. And anyway, it had been Stoney who'd said how wild and dangerous Johnny was when he was younger. That sounded closer to the mark. And after all, it was Johnny himself who had frequently warned Guy how dangerous Fierro was. It seemed he should have paid more heed to his brother's remarks.

He shivered. The room had grown chilly so he pulled the heavy drapes, shutting out the dusk. A fire had been laid in the grate; it needed but a match. Striking one off his boot, he held it to the paper and twigs, watching the flames licking up the chimney. Slumping in the chair at the fireside, he couldn't remember feeling so downhearted for a long time. If ever. The misery of the war had been different. In a perverse way there had at least been a kind of justice to it. Even in the most appalling conditions, there had been a camaraderie. It was the unfortunate lot of a soldier to suffer hardship and you had to grit your teeth and get on with it. But this . . . this despair he felt now seemed deeper than anything he'd encountered before.

"Fierro's OK." What the devil had Ford meant? The words were ambiguous. They could mean that Johnny had recovered from whatever had ailed him earlier in the day—immediately after Guy had stormed out of the jail, Ford had said. But there had been a certain tone in Ford's voice, as though he was trying to make some other point. Guy shook his head in disgust. If Ford wanted to say something, he should have come right out and said it and not talked in riddles. Damn it, Guy wasn't a mind reader.

What else could Ford have meant?

He tossed another log on the fire, watching the sparks fly as the dry wood caught. When he was a child he had loved watching fires and seeing pictures in the flames. When he'd first gone to live with his aunt and uncle, he'd sat mesmerized at times, dreaming up memories of the father he so rarely saw, imagining him riding up on a big white horse to claim him and take him back to the ranch. But there were no horsemen in these flames. No knights in shining armor. All he could see was Johnny on a gallows with a rope around his neck.

He wished now he hadn't said that he would dine in that evening. His stomach was queasy and he felt nauseated. But maybe it was because he'd been unable to enjoy his meal the previous night. And that had been Johnny's fault, he thought bitterly. All in all, Johnny had caused him nothing but grief since the day they'd first been reunited.

It seemed so long ago now. Months past. Before the shootout in Bitterville when Johnny had gone in search of revenge for the Mexican hands who'd been killed.

All those months ago. Before the battle with Wallace. The battle where Johnny took a bullet in the back after leading Wallace's men to a showdown at the ranch.

Before he'd gone looking for revenge on the men who'd raped poor Lizzie. And he'd made the townspeople pay so that Lizzie had a chance of a fresh start.

And before Johnny had shot Donovan when the man had pulled a gun on Guthrie.

Guy swallowed hard. There was a pattern emerging. But no. The man who'd been murdered had been unarmed in his own home. And there was an eyewitness to it. An eyewitness who had identified Johnny as the killer.

"I do know if he is guilty, if he did do this, he would have had a damn good reason for killing the man." Stoney's words echoed again in his head.

"Take it from me, Fierro's OK." And now Ford seemed intent on invading his head too.

Well, they'd all been taken in by Johnny; that was all. If Johnny had indeed had a good reason for killing this man, he'd have told Guy what it was. He would have explained, he would have wanted to justify his actions. But he hadn't explained anything, anything at all. And that could only mean that Johnny was guilty as charged.

The clock chiming broke into his thoughts. He might as well attempt to eat something. He had a long journey ahead of him and at least the food here was good.

He pushed the food around his plate. He speared a piece of beef but then laid the fork down, the meat untasted. He'd sat in the corner of the dining room, and now watched the other guests tuck in to their dinners with gusto. The judge appeared to be greatly enjoying his meal and he teased Mrs. Nixon good-naturedly. He was obviously a regular guest and there was an easy familiarity in their manner together. The only guest missing was the woman in the veil. She was presumably dining in private. He'd seen a tray carried upstairs by a maid. Maybe the woman had come to town for the trial. Maybe she was a relative of the victim and wasn't in the mood to eat in company, and who could blame her for that.

Guy sighed. This wasn't getting him anywhere, and he couldn't face finishing his meal. He had a long journey ahead of him, so he'd turn in early and try to capture some sleep.

He tried to sleep and failed miserably. Instead, he spent the night dozing as images of Johnny slid in and out of his mind. Johnny's eyes when he thought Guy had been badly hurt by Burnett's bullet. Stoney laughing about the state Johnny had been in when he thought Guy was hurt in the stagecoach crash . . .

And the look in Johnny's eyes in the cell when Guy had told him he'd checked in under the name Eliot.

Now he knew what that look had been, as it flashed once more in his memory. It had been a look of shame. And pain.

Guy threw the blankets off and sat up, sweat pouring off him.

Damn Johnny. Damn him for this mess. This godawful mess.

If only, just once, Johnny had talked to him and been straight with him. If only he'd explained what on earth this was all about. But no—that would be too obvious, too straightforward. Too normal. Johnny seemed to delight in being so damn tricky and secretive.

Well, whatever it was about, Johnny could get on with it. Guy wanted no more to do with him. He'd had enough. And if they hanged Johnny, it was doubtless deserved. Murder was murder. And if Johnny had killed this man, he deserved to hang.

"He would have had a damn good reason for killing the man." Stoney's words were back, echoing around his head. And so was the memory of Johnny dressing Guy's wound after Burnett's bullet had grazed him. And the words and the pictures wouldn't go away.

Guy shook his head, angry with himself and hating the cold, leaden ball of fear that seemed to be growing in his gut.

Damn it. Johnny didn't want him here, he'd told Guy often enough. Well, that was fine by Guy. He'd get a horse and ride out and Johnny could go hang . . .

CHAPTER TWENTY

He tried to unclench his fists. And release some of the tension building in his shoulders. He needed to be loose for the trial. Relaxed. And play it cool.

He rotated his head to try and ease out the cricks in his neck. Then he shrugged his shoulders up and down and tried once more to unclench his fists. But they balled up again right after . . . He stretched his fingers right out, studying them closely for any sign of a tremble. They were rock steady. Nothing to betray him. And if he could keep the mask in place during what lay ahead . . . That would be the toughest part of what lay ahead. Not reacting when they spelled it all out. When they spelled out his sins. But he mustn't react, he couldn't let anything show. Because if he did, he wouldn't need to be worrying about cricks in his neck . . . only a noose around it. And he had no intention of dying over this.

It was kind of odd. He wasn't scared of death. There were lots of things he'd willingly die for. And there'd been so many times in the past where he hadn't really cared one way or the other. But this . . . No. He was damned if he'd hang for this. He bit back a smile. It was sort of funny really. This was the one thing he would be damned for. Well, this, and a lot of other things. But the devil could wait. Johnny Fierro wasn't going to swing for this.

But even if Lady Luck was with him and he got away with it, what should he do next? He'd never be able to go home. He shut his eyes, trying to block out the memory of the way Guy had looked when he'd stormed out of the cell. But it didn't work. Whether his eyes were open or closed, Guy's face and all that hate kept showing right up. It wouldn't go away. The look in Guy's eyes. Dios. It had been hate and pain and anger all coiled around each other, like a nest of vipers. Fierro had finally blown it. Nothing ever lasted; he knew that. And these last few months at the ranch were the closest to heaven he'd ever get. But now it was over.

He shook himself. He had to stop brooding about Guy. He needed to deal with the court case first and concentrate on that. He could worry about the future later. If he had a future.

Would the kid do okay? What was his name? Tom Sweetfoot? That was it. A clerk, just a lawyer's clerk. But the kid was hungry. It showed in his eyes. He wanted a name for himself. A bit like Fierro had when he was younger. Except that Sweetfoot wanted to make a name with words and Fierro had wanted to make a name with his gun.

Which was why he was the one behind bars and the kid was walking free and could go off fucking if he had a mind to. Except he didn't look like he'd had that particular pleasure yet. Still, he seemed to know the way things would work in court, and right now that was all that mattered.

It was this waiting that was the worst part. It gave him too much time to think. To brood. Guy must be well on his way back home right now. Guy had finally seen through Fierro. The only surprising thing was it had taken the man so long.

Johnny sighed, grasping hold of the bars on the high window and pulling himself up to peer out. Yeah. Harvard would be well on his way by now.

The street was busy. People seemed to be hurrying along, all going in the same direction. And it didn't take no genius to guess where they were all headed. Leastways Guy wouldn't be in the courtroom to hear all about Fierro's sins. Fierro was spared that. And that was a good thing. Wasn't it? It was what Fierro had wanted. To keep Harvard as far away from this as possible.

He stretched himself back down on the bed. And then hauled himself up again and started pacing out the cell. And tried to unclench his fists again but no, they kept balling right back up. Dios. He wanted to get on with things now. Get the damn thing started. It was time to throw the dice and see how they'd fall. If only he'd still got his saddlebags. It was gonna be touch and go without those.

He could hear footsteps so he threw himself again on the bed, stretched out, like he hadn't a care in the world.

"It's time to go, Fierro." Ford held up a pair of cuffs. "The judge is dealing with the last of the other matters. You're on next."

His legs felt like they wouldn't work. And his stomach had shriveled. It was real. Somehow he hadn't really believed this moment would come. A tiny part of him had wondered if maybe this was all a dream and he'd wake up back at the ranch. And suddenly his mouth felt as dry as the desert he used to hide out in as a kid. Bone dry. Please God, let the voice work. Let the legs work. Don't let me stumble.

He yawned, like maybe he'd just woken up. Stretched, real casual. And then yawned again, covering his mouth with the back of his hand. "About time too. Ain't nothing to do in this cell except sleep." He hauled himself to his feet, and stretched again, holding his hands out for the cuffs.

They snapped around his wrists—heavy and cold against his skin. Somehow they robbed a man of his freedom even more than a cell did. They made a man smaller. A man couldn't defend himself in cuffs . . .

He smiled. "Well, I guess we shouldn't keep the judge waiting."

Ford looked at him, long and hard, before nodding and taking hold of his arm. "No. I guess not." Ford paused, chewing on his lip like there was something else he wanted to say. But then he shook his head, like whatever it was didn't matter none. "Come on, then. I guess we'd better get moving."

The wind made Fierro catch his breath as they walked into the street. Dios, it was cold. It tore at his skin, eating into him. There were people lining the sidewalks and standing in the doorways of the stores, all watching him. And they were all silent. He walked casually, not hurrying, despite the cold wind. And he held his head high, with just a small smile quirking his mouth. Like he had nothing at all to worry over.

Ford led the way to some sort of meeting room that served as a courthouse when the judge was in town. There were a hell of a lot of people in there. People of all ages and all shapes and sizes, but he was scanning the room for just one face.

One face in a hundred.

He swallowed hard and felt his heart sink lower. Guy wasn't there.

And fuck it. That was what Fierro had wanted, wasn't it? Didn't want him there. But somehow, now, he felt as if he was tumbling into a dark pit. Because, one tiny part of him had been clinging to the hope that his brother wouldn't turn his back on him . . .

But he had. He really had.

"You need to sit over here, Fierro." Ford was pushing him to a chair, by a table where Sweetfoot was already waiting. Johnny nodded at the kid. But even now, he couldn't keep himself from scanning the room although the last seed of hope had withered away.

Carter was there, smirking, and pointing Fierro out to the

people standing with him. There was a woman in a bright pink dress, which stretched tightly over her ample curves. There were some middle-aged farmers and their wives. Some old biddies and some young ones, all staring at him and whispering. There was a tall woman, sitting right up front, wearing a thick veil. How the hell could she see through that? There were some bent, old men with big curving pipes that filled the room with thick, choking smoke. And lots of other folks. But he wasn't there. And looking hard wasn't gonna suddenly make him appear.

Johnny sank onto the chair and tried not to slump. Ford was saying something, but he sounded a long way away. And now Sweetfoot was talking at him. Had to pull himself together. This was what he'd wanted, wasn't it? For Harvard to be as far away as possible. And now he was.

Blinking hard, he could see him and Harvard, slouched over, playing chess. Joking together. Working together, rounding up a herd . . . Voices. Voices were talking at him. He dragged his mind back from where it was drifting. He had to get a grip. He forced a smile.

"I was thinking maybe I should offer to leave you all to it. Hardly seems room enough for me in here." He grinned, like it was real easy. Hell. It was what he did best: hiding the pain. Always hiding the pain.

Ford was laughing. "I think it might be for the best if you stay put. Judge Denning will be mighty pissed off if you ain't here." He nudged Johnny with his elbow. "And this is him now."

Johnny got to his feet, and stood straight, staring right ahead. It was only now he noticed his jury, all lined up across the room from him. A mixed bunch, by the look of them. A couple of them looked like they'd rather be someplace else, but the others were staring right back at him. Sizing him up. Not knowing yet what to make of him.

He turned his eyes to the judge who was settling himself in his chair and balancing a pair of spectacles on the edge of his nose, setting them so he could see through them or over them. And now the man was surveying the packed courtroom, with his eyebrows raised, like he wasn't used to a full house.

"Order." The judge banged the table with a small tool that looked like a type of hammer, but too small to drive a nail in. "Order."

Denning. That was his name. Well, he didn't look like no devil incarnate. Kind of mild looking really. Tidy. And maybe a touch fussy. The type who'd be particular. Want to get things straight. Yeah, all things considered, Fierro could have done worse.

"Before these proceedings begin, I wish to make one thing very clear." Denning rubbed the side of his nose and then adjusted his spectacles. "I shall tolerate no interruptions. This is a court of law and we are here for a serious purpose, namely to find the truth. And to serve the cause of justice."

The door to the courtroom creaked open. And every head turned to see who the latecomer was. Johnny glanced over too and his heart seemed to stop beating. Everything stopped.

The latecomer looked right at him, acknowledging him with the briefest of nods, before struggling through the mass of people to lean against the wall in the corner.

And Johnny still couldn't breathe. His heart felt too big to fit in his chest. Felt like it was going to burst right out.

And even though he'd been telling himself this was the last thing he'd wanted, he found he could stand a lot taller now. It was like he'd grown a few inches. And he gave a brief nod back, just to acknowledge the man he needed so much to believe in him. The man who hadn't left Fierro to face this alone. A man in a thousand.

And it suddenly struck him that even if they did find him

guilty, he was still the luckiest man alive to have a brother like Guy.

"Mr. Fierro. Do you have any legal representation?" Denning was peering at him, his brow furrowed. "I do not see Mr. Wilson in the courtroom. Has he been delayed?"

Sweetfoot jumped to his feet. "I'm representing the accused, your honor."

Denning looked at him over the top of his half-moon spectacles, even more creases in his brow now. "Sweetfoot, isn't it? I did not know you were a lawyer. I thought you were clerk to Mr. Wilson."

Sweetfoot didn't flinch. "I was indeed Mr. Wilson's clerk, your honor, but I am leaving shortly to be apprenticed to a major law firm in New York."

Denning pursed his lips and didn't look none too happy. "Where exactly is Mr. Wilson? This is a very serious charge and a man's life is at stake. The accused should have, and is entitled to, proper legal representation. I mean no offense to you, Mr. Sweetfoot. A defendant may have anyone represent him if they are of good moral character. But given the very serious nature of this charge, I cannot help but feel that Mr. Fierro would be better represented by someone qualified to do so."

"Mr. Wilson is out of town. He is unfortunately unable to represent my client, whose name, your honor, is Mr. Sinclair. Not Mr. Fierro."

Johnny suppressed a smile. The kid was doing just fine. He'd told the kid not to let on that Wilson had refused to represent him—somehow he felt that wouldn't have made a good impression on the jury.

Denning turned toward Johnny. Mierda, the man had sharp eyes. The sort of eyes that would see through anything. "Mr. Fierro. You are entitled to proper legal representation. If Mr. Wilson is unable to represent you, I will adjourn your case while you seek an alternative lawyer. Another circuit judge will be here in a month's time. He would be able to hear your case then."

Johnny inclined his head. "Thank you for the advice, your honor, but I'd just as soon proceed with Mr. Sweetfoot talking for me. And my name is Sinclair, not Fierro, sir."

Denning sat back in his chair, shaking his head. "This is all most unconventional."

Johnny ghosted a smile. "I ain't a very conventional type of man, your honor."

Laughter echoed round the courtroom. Denning banged the table lightly with the hammer. "So it would appear, Mr. Fierro. Mr. Sweetfoot, do you believe your client to be of sound mind? Do you believe him to be rational enough to make this risky decision?"

Sweetfoot nodded. "I do, your honor. And his name is John Sinclair, not Johnny Fierro."

The judge took his spectacles off and rubbed them with a big red spotted handkerchief. "Is there anyone else who can vouch for Mr. Fierro? Perhaps someone who has known him for longer than you have."

"I can." The smooth Boston voice carried over the heads of the people.

The judge put his spectacles on and peered towards the back of the court. "And who are you, sir? And what is your relationship with the accused? Are you well acquainted with him?" The judge sounded kind of doubtful, like he wouldn't expect someone so educated to know the likes of a breed gunfighter.

"My name is Guy Eliot Sinclair. John Sinclair is my brother. I can vouch for him."

Out of the corner of his eye, Johnny noticed the woman in the pink dress getting all agitated and whispering to the person next to her. What the hell was her problem?

"Do you believe your brother to be of sound mind, Mr. Sinclair?"

Guy nodded. "My brother is perfectly sane, your honor, and more than capable of making a decision like that."

Denning tutted to himself. Then he took his spectacles off again and gave them another polish before balancing them back on the end of his nose. Johnny eyed them. How the hell did they stay put?

Denning pursed his lips, shaking his head. "This is most unconventional."

"As my brother said, he's a most unconventional man." Guy sounded real smooth and another wave of laughter echoed round the room.

Denning sighed. "Very well. But in the event of your being convicted, Mr. Fierro, no appeal would be allowed on the grounds of you not having proper legal representation. Do you understand that?"

Johnny flashed what he hoped was his most charming smile. "Perfectly, your honor. And it's Sinclair. Not Fierro." Get the jury thinking of him as Sinclair. That had to be the first move. Keep plugging away until nobody used the name Fierro.

Denning leaned back in his seat and eyed him over the top of his spectacles. "I assume from these repeated assertions that you wish to answer the charge against you under the name of Sinclair?"

Johnny smiled again. "I do, your honor. That is my family name."

"Very well. Mr. Lincoln, before we start the proceedings, would you be good enough to note that?"

A thin fellow stood up. "I have made a note, your honor, but I would like to confirm that the accused has also used the name of Fierro in the past."

Sweetfoot sprang to his feet. "My client did use the name Fierro at one time, but he now works on his family's ranch in New Mexico where he is an upright, respectable, and law-abiding member of the community. His name is John Sinclair."

Upright, respectable, and law-abiding? That was news to Johnny but it sure sounded good.

Lincoln didn't look too happy. The tip of his nose turned red.

Denning fixed Johnny with a piercing stare. "The defendant is accused of the murder of Joseph Doe on July 14, 1866. How does the defendant plead?"

Johnny looked straight at the jury. "Not guilty." And that was the truth. It wasn't murder, more like putting down vermin. Or seeing justice done.

Denning nodded to him. "You may sit, Mr. Sinclair, while Mr. Lincoln outlines the details of the case against you."

Lincoln shuffled his papers. The he coughed. And then shuffled the papers some more. "I wonder, your honor, if perhaps we shouldn't clear the courtroom before I outline the details of this heinous crime?"

Denning grunted in irritation. "I have read the papers concerning this case, Mr. Lincoln, and I do see where you are coming from on this, but this is a free country and trials are open to the public. Whether you like it or not."

Lincoln's nose turned red again. "The details of this case against Mr. Fierro are not fit to be heard by the fairer sex."

Sweetfoot was on his feet. "Objection. The defendant's name is Sinclair."

Denning narrowed his eyes. "Sustained. Mr. Lincoln, do not force me to repeat myself. As long as there are no disturbances in my courtroom, it is open to all. Anyone who is of a more sensitive nature may leave now." He looked around the room. Nobody moved. Not a muscle.

The only movement was Guy's eyes. Johnny could feel them boring into him. He crossed his legs, and leaned back as if very relaxed. Like he hadn't a care in the world. Like he didn't know what was coming. Like none of this was anything to do with him.

Denning sighed. "Get on with it, Mr. Lincoln."

Lincoln's nose turned a deeper shade of red. "Very well. The prosecution will prove that on the fourteenth day of July 1866, Mr. Joseph Doe was brutally murdered in his own home on the edge of this small town, by the accused." He paused and pointed across the room. "Johnny Fierro."

"Objection." Sweetfoot was on his feet. "My client's name is John Sinclair."

Denning sighed again. "Sustained. Mr. Lincoln you are going to irritate me if you continue with this ploy. I do not expect to have to mention it again. I would also remind you that your term of office is approaching review."

Lincoln gave a slight bow. "An unfortunate mistake, your honor, I apologize."

Denning grunted, kind of like he didn't believe a word of it. Like he knew exactly what Lincoln's game was. "Just get on with it, Mr. Lincoln."

"The prosecution will produce a witness who will give evidence that the accused went to Mr. Doe's home and brutally murdered him. But this case isn't a straightforward murder. Mr. Doe died as a result of a gunshot to the head. But that was not the full extent of the barbarous nature of this crime."

Lincoln paused. Johnny looked straight ahead. His stomach was churning now. And his heart was pounding. Surely everyone could see it thumping against his chest? He forced his shoulders to relax. Stretched his legs out and crossed his feet. A man at ease.

"The victim had been . . ." Lincoln faltered. "Shot repeatedly in the area of his genitals and his male organs were shot off."

CHAPTER TWENTY-ONE

Two women passed out as gasps of horror filled the room. Another woman swooned and then there was an uproar with all hell breaking loose. Men were calling to give the women air and trying to clear people away from them. Some of the other women were standing fanning themselves, kind of like they might be thinking about fainting but looking like they were enjoying the attention of their men folk fussing round them. Dios. People!

Part of him was itching to look to see Guy's reaction, but he couldn't. Because the other part of him wasn't sure if he wanted to see it. But he was sure of one thing, if he met Guy's eyes, Guy would recognize the guilt.

He sat back, trying to ignore the chaos. Tried to ignore old Judge Denning banging with that damn silly hammer. Everything around him faded away to a blur and then all he could see was himself in that tidy little house. That fucking house. Everything in it had been all new and shiny. Yeah, it had been squeaky clean and it had made him feel old and dirty. He hadn't been old. Just a kid really. But boy had he felt old. And that had made him real mad.

And God, how he'd wanted that bastard to suffer. It was something he'd dreamed of for so long. Even now he could taste the hate, and surely that should have gone away by now? After all this time. But, hell, it was as bitter now as it was back then. And he'd thought killing the bastard would end it.

He'd had it all planned out. Shit, he'd had it planned for years. Killing him slowly. Making it long and painful. But when it came to it, and the man was there whimpering on his knees in front of him, he couldn't do it. Not that way. Fierro had failed. He'd stood with his gun in one hand and the knife in the other and suddenly he'd felt even grubbier. It had overwhelmed him. Disgust. Disgust at Doe. But mostly with himself. And what he should have done was walk away. But he couldn't do that either. He'd promised . . .

"Order." Denning's face was bright red and he was banging his old hammer down real hard. "Order in the court. Gentlemen, please help any ladies who are indisposed out of this courtroom and everyone else can either sit down and keep silent or leave now. Otherwise I will hold them in contempt."

He had to hand it to the old boy, he sure had a way of dealing with people. Seemed most of them weren't planning on going anywhere and they all sat right down except for the men carting the fainting women out. And they weren't doing it none too gently. Kind of like they couldn't wait to get back in to hear all the details. Didn't want to miss nothing. Dios, but most people were shit. He'd bet they were the same the world over.

Denning took his spectacles off and gave them another polish. Then he perched them back on his nose and looked around his courtroom. Because it was his courtroom and everyone in there knew it.

Denning fingered his little goatee beard as his gaze roved around the room. It was like he was waiting for everyone's attention. Johnny bit back a smile. It seemed the judge was a bit of a showman.

The man banged his hammer suddenly, making most everyone jump. Yeah. A real showman.

"Mr. Lincoln, now that order has been restored, perhaps you would continue with your outline of the case."

Lincoln got slowly to his feet. The man didn't seem in no hurry to get on with anything. Dios. Now he was shuffling his papers. Were all lawyers showmen?

"Mr. Lincoln, in your own time." There was a certain tone in Denning's voice that said he didn't think too much of Lincoln's carryings on.

"Just collecting my thoughts, your honor." Lincoln gave a ghost of a bow towards the judge. "The disturbances interrupted my train of thought. But, yes, the case against Mr. Fierro . . ."

"Objection." Sweetfoot sprang to his feet. "Your honor, I must protest Mr. Lincoln's repeated use of that name and insist that you take him to task."

"Mr. Sweetfoot, I will thank you to remember that I do not need reminding of my duties." Denning's beard bristled, he looked so riled. "However, I sustain your objection. Mr. Lincoln, I have warned you repeatedly about this. I will not stand for it. You have made your point to the jury."

Lincoln made a bigger bow. "My apologies, your honor. An unfortunate oversight. As I said, the disturbances interrupted my train of thought."

"How very convenient." Denning glared at Lincoln, whose ears turned red. "Now, can we get on with this?"

"Yes, indeed. We will return to the events of the fourteenth of July in 1866. Mr. Joseph Doe was a fairly new resident of this small town. He had worked for his county as a prison guard, with the unfortunate and unpleasant task of dealing with the dregs of society. Thieves, arsonists, shootists, and other people of the lowest moral standards. And having worked hard all his life, he was looking forward to a quiet retirement. He built his own home on the edge of this town, and had made overtures indicating that he would indeed be a boon to this growing society by offering to help out in various aspects of the town life.

"He had indicated his willingness to help out at the town socials, to help out at the orphanage, and even to take small groups of the more troublesome boys in the town on hunting trips and such to try and raise their moral standards."

Johnny stared down at the floor to hide any expression from showing. He could just bet that Doe had been keen to take the troublesome boys under his wing. And then he'd have set about sorting out the bullies from the weakest. Yeah, Doe would have had himself some of his own special brand of sick fun.

"So, I think it is apparent to all what a very good man Mr. Doe was. But coming from a prison where he'd have had to deal with all sorts of scum, including gunfighters, it is all too easy to conclude that one of those former charges would have taken it into his head to come looking for Mr. Doe."

"Mr. Lincoln." Denning held his hand up, to pause the man. "Are you intending to produce evidence that the accused was in the prison where Mr. Doe had been a guard? I don't recall seeing that in the papers relating to this case."

"No, your honor, I wasn't." Lincoln's ears were turning red again.

"Do you have any evidence to suggest that the accused was in the prison? Or is this conjecture on your part?"

Lincoln shuffled his feet, like he'd been caught out in something. "No, your honor, I have been unable to find any evidence that the accused has ever been in prison."

Denning half-turned in his chair, like he wanted a better look at Fierro. "Do you have anything to say about this, Mr. Sinclair?"

Johnny got swiftly to his feet, with the most charming smile he could muster. "Well, your honor, I'm not at all surprised that Mr. Lincoln couldn't find anything. But I will confess that I've spent a few nights in town jails."

Laughter echoed around the courtroom. Denning banged his hammer and raised an eyebrow. "Town jails?"

Johnny grinned. "Yes, your honor, ashamed as I am to admit it. But I have occasionally been thrown in jail for the odd fist-fight." He paused, looking around the courtroom and then right at the jury. "I'm sure there's many men in this room who've taken a drink too many as a young fellow and spent a night sobering up."

The lead weight was back. Pressing down in his gut. But it was the only way to play it. He'd known they'd find no record of him in that prison's records. He couldn't even remember now what damn name he'd been using, but it hadn't been Fierro and it sure hadn't been Sinclair. He smiled as he held Denning's gaze for a few heartbeats. Mierda. Could the old boy see through him? He seemed to have very sharp eyes.

A small furrow set between Denning's eyes. "Mr. Lincoln, is there anything you wish to ask Mr. Sinclair?"

Lincoln shook his head. Johnny felt a little of the tension ebb away; he felt lighter again. Denning was going to leave it to Lincoln to do his own work. Johnny sat down even as another thought slid into his head. Hell. Harvard knew he'd been in prison. He'd made the mistake of letting it slip, way back when he'd been recovering from Donner's bullet. Yeah, just after the first time they'd played chess. Shit.

He didn't dare glance across to where Guy stood. But he could feel Guy's eyes boring into him. Shit. Shit. Shit. But maybe Guy wouldn't remember. No. Guy always remembered everything—every tiny detail of all sorts of things. Shit.

"Well, Mr. Lincoln." Denning's voice was smooth as silk. "If you have no evidence to present on that score, I would suggest that you do not dwell on the matter of precisely who Mr. Doe may, or may not, have met in prison. Now, may we get on?"

Lincoln gave another of his odd half-bows. "I was just coming to the matter of the events of that day in July, your honor." He shuffled his papers again, even as Denning gave a very loud sigh and leaned forward resting his chin on his hand.

"The heinous crime that was played out in that small house must have been terrifying for the victim."

Yeah. He'd been terrified all right. Shitting himself. Johnny felt the old familiar twinge of shame. He'd enjoyed it at first. Seeing that bastard so scared had given him a rush. He'd felt powerful and totally in control, and for a few minutes he'd loved that feeling of power. At first, revenge had tasted so sweet. Sweet as honey. And he'd enjoyed the look of terror in Doe's eyes when the man had caught sight of the knife in Johnny's right hand.

But when the man had been on his knees sobbing and begging and pissing himself, all Johnny had felt was horror and disgust. Quick and clean. That had always been his rule. And he'd only broken it on three occasions. But this was far and away the worst thing he'd ever done.

"But, unfortunately for Mr. . . ." Lincoln glanced down at his notes. "Mr. Sinclair, there was a witness to his presence in that house which Mr. Doe had worked so hard to build. And I will call that witness now."

Johnny sat straighter in his seat, suddenly alert. It was like all his senses sprang to life and everything around him was brighter and louder, and he prayed that everything Sweetfoot had told him about the witness was right. If Sweetfoot was wrong, Fierro could well be on his way to the scaffold.

"I call Joshua Jackson." Lincoln, along with everyone else in the courtroom, looked toward the door as an old man was shown into the court.

The old man shuffled across the courtroom, peering about him like his eyesight wasn't none too good. Johnny bit back a smile. Maybe, just maybe, this at least might play out okay.

The old man fumbled in his pocket as he took the stand and pulled out a pair of twisted, wire-framed spectacles before peering at the court officer. "You'll have to speak up, young man, my hearing isn't as good as it was."

The officer had to repeat the oath to Jackson twice before the old man was able to get it right. Johnny sat back in his chair, his cuffed hands resting in his lap. A man at ease.

Lincoln got slowly to his feet. Did he do everything slowly? "Mr. Jackson, would you like to tell the court about the events of July 14 in 1866 and what took you to the house of Mr. Joseph Doe that day?"

The old fellow glared. "Well, that's why I'm here, isn't it? I ain't here for my health, and that's not as good as it should be."

Lincoln's ears had a pinkish tinge to them and Denning was polishing his spectacles again. Lincoln smiled, but it didn't look like it came easy. "It is indeed why you're here, Mr. Jackson. Now, in your own time."

"Own time? If this was my own time I wouldn't be here. I'm doing my civic duty, that's what I'm doing."

Lincoln's smile was more of a grimace now. "Quite so, Mr. Jackson. Now, you had been working at Mr. Doe's house on that day, had you not?"

Denning sighed. "I would prefer that you did not lead the witness, Mr. Lincoln. We are here to see what he recollects without prompting by you."

Lincoln inclined his head. "My apologies, your honor."

The old man nodded hard. "Yep. I'd been working in his garden all that day. He was planning a small area for vegetables. Mind you, it wasn't in the right place. But he wouldn't listen. He knew best. Or thought he did." Jackson shook his head as if in sorrow. "I knew them beans wouldn't do well there, but you couldn't tell him anything. He always knew best. Why, there was the time we were discussing where his onions should be set—"

"Quite so." Lincoln interrupted. "So, you had been working on Mr. Doe's garden."

"That's what I just told you." Laughter rolled around the courtroom like a wave. Jackson shook his head as though irritated by Lincoln. "Did my day's work, and believe me, he got his money's worth out of me, and then I headed back to town. But then I had to go back. And I could have done without traipsing all the way back to his house. My legs aren't what they were, you know. But I'd left my hoe behind, you see. I was almost home before I realized I'd left it back there. And I needed it for my own garden. My beans are always a treat to the eyes." He nodded more to himself it seemed like. "Yes, sir, my beans always do well. That's because I understand how things should . . ."

Lincoln grimaced and then forced a smile. "So, you'd left your hoe at Mr. Doe's house and were returning for it. What did you find when you got there?"

Jackson had cupped his hand around his ear, straining to hear Lincoln's words. "What did I find? Well, I didn't find my hoe straightaway and that's a fact. Looked all over the place I did. And then I hunted near to the house, though how it could have got there I just don't know. A bit of a mystery, really. I hadn't been working right next to the house . . ."

"And what happened next, Mr. Jackson?" Lincoln sounded like he was talking through gritted teeth.

Jackson cupped his hand around his ear. "What happened next? Is that what you said?"

Lincoln nodded wearily. "Yes, Mr. Jackson, what happened next?"

"Well, that's when I heard him." Jackson nodded real hard. "Yes, sir. That's when I heard him."

"Heard what exactly?" Lincoln looked like he was having a

hard time of not yelling at Jackson to get on with it.

"Well, him." Jackson pointed a gnarled, and none-too-clean finger in Johnny's direction. "I heard him talking. And Mr. Doe was . . . well, not sounding like a man should sound. No, siree. Not like a man should sound at all. I'd say he was blubbering like a girl."

All the folks started whispering. And even though they were only whispering, with so many of them going at it, it was loud. Denning banged his hammer. "Order. If the public cannot keep quiet, they shall be removed. Mr. Jackson, please continue."

"So, I peeped in through the window, careful like because I didn't want anyone seeing me, and that's when I saw him." He swung an accusing finger in Johnny's direction. More or less in Johnny's direction. "I saw him, standing with a gun pointing at Mr. Doe. Oh, I saw him all right. I thought mebbe best thing I could do was go and get some help. So I hurried away. But I heard him say he was Johnny Fierro. And as I went away from the house I heard his gun go off. Made me jump it did. And then it went off again and again."

"So, you saw the accused with a gun and you heard him declare himself to be Johnny Fierro." Lincoln was smooth now. "Thank you, Mr. Jackson. No further questions."

Judge Denning leaned forward, glancing at Sweetfoot. "Do you wish to question the witness?"

Sweetfoot smiled. "I most certainly do, your honor. Mr. Jackson, you seem to recall all these events very clearly. You have a good memory?" Sweetfoot didn't raise his voice the way Lincoln had, just talked at a normal sort of sound. Exactly like Johnny had told him to.

"You'll have to speak up, young man. My hearing ain't so good."

Sweetfoot repeated the question but only a touch louder.

Jackson huffed. "I said speak up, young man. My hearing

isn't good."

Sweetfoot repeated it, but much louder this time.

"My memory? Well, I ain't getting no younger, that's for sure." Jackson's brow creased up, like he didn't understand the question.

"Well, what did you have for dinner last night, Mr. Jackson?" Sweetfoot smiled.

"My dinner? What's that got to do with anything? I don't know what I ate. I can't remember what I had for breakfast this morning, never mind for dinner last night."

Sweetfoot's smile grew. "And yet your memory of events which happened four years ago is so precise. I put it to you, Mr. Jackson, that perhaps your memory of the events of that day, is not as clear as you would like to suggest. I would suggest that perhaps the story has become embellished over time? I'm sure people locally have wanted to hear your recollections, and as we all know, stories tend to become exaggerated over time with each new telling."

Embellished? What the hell did that mean? And judging by the look on the old fellow's face, he was wondering the same thing.

"I don't know anything about that bellish thing, all I know is that's the man over there. Johnny Fierro. That's what the man said his name was and that's Johnny Fierro."

"So, as your recollection of these events is so clear, perhaps you would care to tell the court in which hand the gunman was holding his gun?"

Jackson screwed his eyes up, scratching his head. "Well, I don't recall. Yes! It was in his left hand because he was on the right as I looked into the room and the gun was in the hand nearest the window." Jackson beamed.

Sweetfoot nodded slowly. "Well, that's a very interesting thing, Mr. Jackson, because if this man was indeed Johnny Fierro as you assert, he wouldn't have been holding his gun in that hand. Everyone knows that Johnny Fierro was a right-handed gunman."

Everyone in the room started whispering and Denning banged his hammer again.

Jackson snorted in disbelief. "Well, young man, that may be so, but the gun was in his left hand."

Sweetfoot smiled. "Which leads me to think that whoever this gunman was, it couldn't have been the famous Johnny Fierro. He was, quite indisputably, a right-handed gunman."

Jackson huffed. "You ain't going to make me say that the gun was in his right hand. It was in his left hand." The man nodded. "And I'll tell you something else. He had a long scar on his arm."

Denning was polishing his spectacles again. But now he leaned forward. "Perhaps Mr. Sinclair would roll his left sleeve up so we can inspect his arm."

He'd known this would come. His mouth was dry and his palms were damp. But he nodded and smiled at the judge. "Your honor." He rolled up the sleeve and held his arm out. Gasps of shock echoed around the court as they looked at the scar, which looked vivid and red.

Denning looked at him long and hard. "Would you care to explain that scar, Mr. Sinclair? How and when you came by it."

"Sure, your honor. I was whittling, making a pipe rack for my father, a couple of months back. The knife slipped and I cut my arm. I had a witness. A Mrs. Edith Walsh, she is the widow of a respected rancher down near Cimarron and now runs the ranch herself. She's a well-known lady in those parts. She can vouch for me. She had to tie a tourniquet to stop the bleeding. And then she took me to the doctor, in Cimarron, and he stitched it up. If you send a cable to Mrs. Walsh she'll confirm that."

Just don't send a cable to the doc. Ben had noticed something wrong with the cut when he stitched it. He'd asked if there was a scar there before. Mierda! Just don't contact Ben. Whatever they did, they mustn't contact Ben . . .

Denning chewed on his lip and fidgeted with his little beard. "It certainly looks to be a recent thing. Marshal Ford, would you be so good as to send a wire to Mrs. Walsh and ask her to confirm Mr. Sinclair's story? I would like it corroborated by an independent witness rather than by the defendant's brother." He reached into his pocket to pull out a gold watch. "I feel that this would be an appropriate time to adjourn. The court will reconvene tomorrow at ten. Gentlemen." With a brief nod to Lincoln and Sweetfoot, Denning stood and walked briskly out of the room.

As soon as the door closed behind him, the room was full of voices. He couldn't even see Guy because everyone was on their feet and swarming like flies on a rotting steer. The noise was enough to give anyone a headache. And he had one hell of a headache. Sweetfoot was busy talking to Lincoln, and Jackson was still fumbling his way out of the witness stand. Ford leaned over. "Come on. Let's get you out of here and back to the jail."

Johnny followed Ford, who cleared a path through the crowd and out into the street. Even the cold wind seemed welcome after the airless courtroom and the stench of sweating people. There were more folks in the street, pointing at him, talking among themselves. He inclined his head towards them with a brief smile. That would puzzle them. Get them wondering if maybe he was a man with a clear conscience. And not a brutal killer.

The jail seemed almost welcoming. And peaceful. Even the iron cot looked inviting. Damn, but he was tired. Felt like he'd been trampled by a herd of Guthrie's cattle. All he wanted was to stretch out and sleep. For a hundred years. And then wake up and find out it was all over. And he was a free man.

But without his saddlebags it wasn't going to be easy. Jackson hadn't been as dithery as he'd hoped. Stuck to his story. No, it wasn't going to be easy at all.

He stood by the cot as Ford unlocked the cuffs. Dios, it was good to be rid of the damn things. He rubbed his wrists trying to rub the marks away. God only knew what it was like for men marked by leg irons—those marks never went away if a man had worn them long enough.

"Can I get you anything else?" Ford put a pitcher of water on the shelf by the cot.

Suddenly the question struck him as odd. Why was Ford always so pleasant? Always looking out for Fierro. It didn't make sense. "No, I got everything I need, thanks. But, tell me, you treat all your prisoners this well, Marshal?"

Ford didn't say anything at first. Seemed to find his scuffed boots real interesting, then he shrugged. "Let's just say, I believe in treating prisoners like they're human beings."

Johnny looked at him thoughtfully. Somehow, he got the feeling that there was a lot more to Ford than met the eye. Something he wasn't telling. Still, he was a decent man. Not like Doe. He'd never treated anyone like they were human . . .

Ford clanged the cell door shut and turned the key in the lock before heading back to his office in the outer room.

The cell felt cold and clammy and there was nothing to do except try to catch some sleep. Johnny stretched out on the bed, pulling a couple of blankets over him, even as the outer door creaked open. Ford called out, "You got a visitor, Fierro."

He sat up, feeling a surge of relief when he saw Guy in the doorway. But it faded real fast. There was an odd look in Guy's eyes. Something that said maybe this wasn't a social visit.

"Johnny. I think it's time you and I had a little talk."

CHAPTER TWENTY-TWO

"Guy." At least his voice came out normal despite his suddenly dry throat. And his palms were damp. That look in Guy's eyes . . . Nope. Guy wasn't here to pass the time of day. And what were the odds he was going to bring up the whole thing about the prison?

Johnny nodded to the chair in the next cell. A cell with an open door that a man could walk in and out of. "Why don't you pull up a chair and sit down?"

"I prefer to stand."

Dios. Guy sounded cold enough to freeze an ocean. Johnny stared down at his hands and started fiddling with his Indian beaded bracelet, anything to avoid Guy's eyes. "I thought you were leaving. Going back to the ranch. That's what you said."

"That is precisely what I intended to do." It was still pure ice.

Johnny couldn't look up. His fingers were starting to tense right up now. He spun the beads. "Why did you change your mind?"

"That's what I've been asking myself since I sat through that travesty of an act you put on in court."

Travesty? What the fuck did that mean? Well, whatever it meant, it sure didn't sound good. And what the hell was it with Guy, anyway, that made him use such damned tricky words? Was he trying to get one over on Fierro? No. He knew Guy wasn't like that. Guy used them because he thought Johnny was smart. He'd told Johnny that once. Sometimes Johnny took that memory out to hold on to when everything else seemed to be slipping out of reach. It had made him feel real good.

"Well?" Guy was standing with his arms folded, like he was waiting for Johnny to explain himself. How the hell could he explain anything when he didn't know what Guy wanted to hear?

"Well, what?" He knew he sounded sullen, but he wasn't going to ask Guy what he meant. Wasn't going to show that he didn't understand some words. To hell with that.

"Why did you lie in court? You didn't admit you'd been in prison." Guy sounded like he was talking through clenched teeth. Or like he was trying to stop himself yelling.

"I didn't lie." And that was the truth. He hadn't lied, he'd sidestepped the question, and Lincoln, being a dumb asshole, hadn't noticed. But Guy had noticed. Just like Johnny had known he would.

"It might have slipped your memory, Johnny, but you once admitted to Father and I that you had been in prison. It's where you learned to play chess, if my memory serves me correctly."

Yeah, like he didn't know that his memory was serving him correctly. Damn stupid expression. "I didn't say I hadn't been in prison." The words snapped out like a rattler's tongue.

Guy didn't say anything for a second, kind of like he was thinking it over. "No, I suppose you didn't. You were too clever for that." Guy gave an odd laugh, but it didn't sound like he thought there was anything much to laugh about. "Just like you were clever when Ford and Carter came to arrest you and you went on about working around the border and nobody had ever paid you to go to Utah. Yes, you were clever then, because my guess is you came to Utah without anyone paying you. You came to see someone you'd met when you were in prison." He gave Johnny a long hard look. "Do tell me, am I getting warm here?"

Johnny shrugged, keeping his eyes fixed on his hands. "I guess it slipped my memory." Yeah. Like Guy was going to buy that. Dios, surely Fierro could come up with something better than that?

Guy laughed again, like before. Real cold. "Yes, I guess it slipped your memory. You certainly have a very selective memory."

Johnny risked a quick glance at him, before staring back at his fingers again. They were making fists, and every time he opened them up, they tensed right back in again like they had a life of their own. And he felt so small. But he couldn't tell Guy. Couldn't tell anyone about it. They'd be disgusted. They'd think he was dirty. And right now, Guy had the look of a man who'd taken about as much as he could. But why had Guy stayed? He'd said he was going to go back to the ranch, but he hadn't. Just for a while back there in court, Johnny had allowed himself to hope it was because they were brothers. Because it meant something. Because he mattered to Guy.

"And then of course, we have the little matter of your arm."

Johnny's head jerked up. What the hell could Guy know about his arm? "What about my arm? You saw it the day I did it." It came out strong, like he thought Guy was crazy.

"What about your arm?" Guy still had that sort of amused tone in his voice. "You know, something always bothered me about that cut. There was something niggling away at the back of my mind that there was something not quite right about it."

"I told you I did it whittling." Johnny snapped the words out.

Guy raised an eyebrow. "Oh, I know you said you did it whittling. I remember only too well the amusement and disbelief of everyone over the thought of you whittling. But today, in court, it came back to me."

Johnny eyed him uneasily. He'd been careful to cover his tracks. What the hell could Guy know? "What came to you?"

He tried to sound like he wasn't really interested, but he couldn't look at Guy. Might give himself away. Guy might see the concern in Johnny's eyes. The fear.

Guy raised an eyebrow. "You want to know what came to me? Do let me enlighten you. After you were shot by Donner and were unconscious all that time, I used to go and sit with you sometimes. I'd sit there, still hardly able to countenance that you had, in fact, been alive when I'd spent all those years thinking you were dead. And I'd sit and think about how my little brother turned out to be a gunfighter. And although you were all bandaged up, I remember being appalled at the number of scars you carried. Not just the ones on your back, but others too."

Johnny's guts were tying themselves in knots, and he suddenly felt very cold.

"I noticed lots of old bullet wounds and I noticed the whip marks on your back. And I noticed other scars too. And guess what, Johnny?" Guy sounded like he was real surprised about something, except he wasn't, and he knew that Johnny knew he wasn't. "There was a long scar on your arm. It was a fairly old scar, but by some strange coincidence, it was exactly where that new scar is. Isn't that strange? I mean, brother, don't you find that very surprising that you managed to cut yourself in the exact same place?"

What could he say? It would be a waste of his breath to deny it. And Guy didn't deserve that, anyway. No, he couldn't lie to Guy. But he couldn't tell him the truth of it all either.

"Well?" Guy was pacing now, up and down outside the cell. "Are you going to say anything?"

Johnny wrapped his arms around himself, hunched over. "No." His voice sounded like a whisper from someplace else. But Guy deserved better than that. He raised his head, met Guy's gaze. "I can't, I'm sorry."

"At least tell me how you got the scar. Tell me something."

It was odd, but Guy sounded almost like he was pleading. "A fight. A knife fight." And that at least was the truth. And it was the damnedest thing but he'd only got into the fight because of that skinny kid. Been minding his own business in a saloon near the border and some fellow had been picking on the kid. Hadn't even noticed the youngster in the corner—wasn't the sort anyone would notice. But the bully at the bar had noticed him. And if there was one thing he hated it was bullies. It was kind of funny though, he got the scar because of the kid, and if he hadn't met the kid . . .

"A knife fight? Where? In Mr. Doe's house?"

Johnny's head jerked up. "No! If you must know, I got it in a bar fight down near the border. Fellow pulled a knife on me."

"What happened to him?"

Johnny laughed sourly. "Let's just say I won." Except, in the long run, maybe he hadn't. The jury was still out on that one. And right now it wasn't looking too good.

Guy looked at him sharply. "But this knife fight was before you went to see Mr. Doe?"

"I never said I'd been to see Doe." Johnny stared down at the stone floor. Wasn't admitting to anything.

Guy gave a soft sigh, almost like a breath of wind on a warm night. "No, you didn't. But you did see him, didn't you?"

It came from nowhere. The heat of anger welling up. "What do you want from me, Guy? No, I didn't tell fucking Lincoln that I'd spent a while in prison. I might as well put the noose around my neck myself if I did that and I ain't that keen to hang. And any rate, he didn't ask direct. Denning simply asked if I had anything to say. So I didn't lie and I'm sure as hell not going to help them hang me. Damn it, Guy, I was a kid when I was in prison. A kid! I stole some bread, got thrown in jail, and then knocked the sheriff out when I tried to escape. And so they put me in prison. I wasn't sent there for some fucking evil crime. All I wanted was not to starve. I was hungry. Fucking hungry. And you wouldn't understand what it's like to be that hungry. Hell, I'm glad you don't know what that's like. I wouldn't want you to know what it's like when you're so damn hungry that it's like there's rats gnawing away at you from the inside. And it never goes away when you're that hungry. It's all you think about."

He was on his feet now, pacing up and down the cell, but he couldn't remember standing up. "So yeah, I've been in prison, but I don't reckon what I did was so terrible. I just wanted to live a little longer. Is that a crime? But yeah, I guess it is, because I wound up in prison because of it. And trust me on this, Guy, no kid that age should be in prison. Whatever they've done, they shouldn't be in prison. And they sure as hell shouldn't be there just because they're fucking hungry."

He was shaking now. And Guy looked kind of pale. But maybe it was time Fierro told it like it was. And it was almost like he couldn't stop the flood of words. They just kept right on spewing out. "And I'll tell you something else, Harvard, there's too many kids out there like that. Hungry. Alone. And nobody cares. They carry on with their nice comfortable lives and they go to church and call themselves God-fearing. But they don't give a damn about anyone except themselves. They don't want to get their hands dirty. Don't want to risk soiling themselves by as much as talking to some kid scratching to stay alive out on the streets. God-fearing! They don't give a damn. Fucking hypocrites. And God help you if you're a breed with a bit of Apache in you. Because then you're even worse. It ain't only the gringos who hate you then. No. You get double the hate because Mexicans hate the Apache too. And you stand there, and criticize me for not telling that fucking lawyer I've been in prison? Maybe you want me to go and build the scaffold myself while I'm at it. Because if they find out I was in prison, they'll have me up there so fast my eyeballs will rattle. I ain't doing their job for them." He slumped down onto the cot, wrapping his arms around himself in an effort to try and stop himself from shaking.

He shot a quick glance at Guy but he couldn't figure out what Guy was thinking. Guy's head was bowed, so there was no way of reading his eyes. "So, why didn't you leave, Guy? Yesterday you were all fired up to go, but you're still here. Why?" He needed to know. Needed to know if he had ruined everything with Guy. Or maybe there was still a chance for the two of them. When Guy had walked into court earlier in the day, Johnny couldn't believe the huge relief he'd felt. But now the doubts were back. And he just wanted Guy to level with him. If only he could do the same for Guy.

Guy turned and pulled up a chair, next to the bars, and sank onto it, before lifting his head and meeting Johnny's eyes. Dios. He had the look of a man who'd taken as much as he could.

Guy ran his hand through his hair, like he didn't know what to say. "You know, yesterday I was trying really hard to hate you. I couldn't remember ever being so angry with anybody. And I knew you were . . ." He paused, like he couldn't quite figure how to describe something. "I felt you were being less than honest with me. And I thought you were being stagger-ingly self-centered. And there was a point when I'd have happily done the hangman's job for him."

Johnny swallowed hard.

Guy shook his head slowly. "I went to the livery to buy a horse, but it was closed until today. And so I spent the night go-ing over everything in my head. Everything you've ever said and done since you first came home. I thought maybe you'd been fooling me right from the start. That it had all been a sham."

Johnny bit his lip hard, shame wrapping itself around him.

Holding him tight in its clinging web.

"But you know, I kept seeing all the good things you'd done. And I kept hearing the words of something that Stoney said to me—that you don't kill for the thrill of it. And I remembered all the times I told Father that there's a good man under that cold exterior, that armor you hide behind. And when it came right down to it, I couldn't bring myself to ride on out, leaving you to whatever your fate is." Guy sighed. "And then, today, sitting in court, hearing all those things . . . Watching you evading questions, sidestepping things . . . I don't know what to think anymore." Guy looked right at him. "I guess I was foolish. I saw you as good. All these months I was convinced you were a good man. Then yesterday, I saw you as bad. And what's the truth of it?"

Johnny swallowed again. He shook his head and shrugged. "Guy, there ain't anybody who's all good, and I guess there ain't many who are all bad." Except maybe Doe. Couldn't think of a single good thing about that man. "I guess most folks fall somewhere in between." Except most folks in his experience were nearer bad than good.

Guy raised an eyebrow. "So the world is gray? But the question is, how deep a shade of gray are you?"

Johnny looked down as his boots. The sole had come away a bit more. But maybe it wouldn't matter none. If they decided to hang him he wouldn't be needing his boots for much longer. "I done a lot of bad things, Guy. Some of them I regret and some . . ." He paused, hell, some things he couldn't ever regret. "I'm a gunfighter. I'm good at my trade."

"You're supposed to be a rancher now." Guy sounded pissed.

"Yeah. But life ain't that simple. My past is always going to be there. It's not going to disappear like it never happened. And it'd be a fool who thought it would. And I tell you, Guy, every now and then my past is gonna creep right up and nudge me."

"Like this?" Guy was looking hard at him now, like he wanted to look right inside Fierro.

Johnny shrugged again. "This fellow says the gunman was holding his gun in the left hand. You know I'm right-handed." But he could use his gun in his left hand whereas he couldn't use a knife in that hand. Always needed his right hand for the knife, and God only knew he'd planned to use that knife on Doe.

"There you go. You're doing it again!" Guy sounded really pissed. "You sidestep everything. I just want a straight answer."

Johnny laughed, but it sure wasn't funny. "I'm sorry. I reckon I'm asking you to trust me." He ducked his head briefly. "I don't blame you if you can't, but I guess, if I'm honest, I'm still hoping that you'll try and trust me. And for what it's worth, I was real pleased to see you when you walked in this morning. Despite everything I said to you about wanting you to leave."

Guy's head jerked up at that. "Well, that at least is quite an admission from you." He paused, shaking his head. "Like I said, I just wish you'd level with me, Johnny. Is it really too much to ask?"

Johnny nodded slowly. "Yeah. Right now it is. I'm sorry. But . . . Well, I'm sorry." Johnny tailed off. He didn't know how to put things. If only he was better with words.

Guy was chewing on his lip, fidgeting like he was struggling too to find the right words. And he looked kind of red-faced. "Johnny, I'm not a total innocent. I mean, I know the things that some of the older soldiers did to young, weaker soldiers. Did Doe . . . I've been wondering, well . . . What I mean is . . . Did he do things to you? In the prison?"

Fear was back. His pulse was racing and his guts coiled. "No!" And that was the truth. He wondered what the hell Guy would think if he knew what Doe's game had been. 'Side from being disgusted by Johnny. "He never laid a finger on me."

"So you did know him?" Guy was fishing.

"I didn't say that."

Guy shook his head, kind of like he was irritated but didn't know what to do or say. "No, you didn't say that. See what I mean, Johnny—you'll never give me a straight answer. You're so damn tricky at times. Sometimes, I think that you've become so used to that mask you wear that you don't know how to drop it. It's too much a part of you now. I'm trying to find the man behind it, but I don't think you know who he is anymore."

What the hell was Harvard talking about? And he accused Fierro of being tricky. Dios. If the man would only talk like other folk, Johnny would understand him a whole lot better. But he had to say something. But what? "Sorry." His voice came out like a whisper. "I'd tell you if I could, but I can't. I really can't."

"But you'll be giving evidence? Taking the witness stand?"

Johnny shook his head. "No."

Guy's eyes widened. "That's not a wise decision, Johnny. You need to take the stand and tell the jury that you've never met Doe. That you didn't kill him."

Johnny shook his head. He felt very small now. Guy would crush him underfoot if he had any sense. "I'm not taking the stand."

Guy leaned back in his chair, frowning like he was deep in thought, trying to figure things out. And then his face went kind of pale, like he'd just thought of something he wasn't happy about. "But why aren't you . . . Oh, God." His voice was real soft and kind of shocked. "You're not taking the stand because you'd be under oath. You don't want to stand there and lie under oath. When someone pleads guilty or not guilty, they're not under oath, but when you're giving evidence . . ." Guy's voice tailed off and he sat there, pale and staring.

He hadn't thought Guy was that sharp. Never thought Guy would figure it out. But what the hell should Fierro say now?

Could hardly say, yep, that's exactly why he wasn't going on no witness stand. He drew the line at lying under oath. The thought of holding a bible and swearing to tell the truth and then lying . . . It would be a step too far. He'd done enough sinning, and didn't want to do any more than he had to. To hell with that. And now, all he could do was try to bluff Guy. "Just no point in me taking the stand. Ain't got anything to say. They want a left-handed gunman. What they got is the wrong man. I ain't a lefty and that's the end of it."

"And so you're relying on them not believing Joshua Jackson's account of things? Is that the best you've got? You were so certain back in Cimarron that you'd be acquitted. What changed, Johnny? Because if you're relying on the jury doubting Jackson's word, I have to tell you that your defense stinks." Guy didn't sound none too impressed. And he didn't sound like he could believe it.

Of course, it should have been different. If he'd had his saddlebags he'd have a chance. But right now it wasn't looking too promising. And Sweetfoot had slipped up on a couple of things. Should have made a bigger issue of Jackson's hearing. Maybe Jackson didn't hear the gunman right. And made a bigger issue of Jackson's eyesight. Maybe Jackson didn't see the gunman as well as he thought he'd seen him . . . Yeah, Sweetfoot had made some mistakes. He was too young, that was the trouble. "Guess we'll just have to see how it all pans out." Johnny shrugged.

"How it all pans out?" Guy sounded like he couldn't believe what he was hearing. "Johnny, are you aware of what the penalty is for murder in Utah?"

Johnny glared. "Yeah, Guy, I ain't dumb. They hang people for murder."

"Hanging isn't their only option."

Johnny stared. "How d'you mean?"

"Well, they can execute you by shooting you."

"Shooting? Like a firing squad, you mean?" His spirits rose. Well that wouldn't be nearly as bad as hanging. Hell, shooting was quick.

Guy narrowed his eyes. "Or beheading."

"What the hell d'you mean by beheading?" Johnny stared at Guy, puzzled.

"They cut your head off." Guy's voice was kind of even. But he was looking at Johnny real hard.

"Shit. They cut people's heads off in Utah?" Couldn't quite believe that somehow. How sick were people in Utah?

Guy nodded. "It is one of the options open to judges when they decide how the death penalty should be carried out."

Dios. Beheading. That would sure cure a crick in the neck. Mierda. The knife in his boot was getting more attractive by the second.

"So, Johnny, you do take my point about needing to improve your defense?" Guy's voice was still kind of even.

"I ain't taking the stand, Guy. Just have to hope that Sweetfoot can use the fact that Jackson's eyesight ain't too good or that his hearing isn't up to much. But I ain't taking the stand."

"Because you killed him and you don't want to lie under oath?" Guy said it like it was a question, but the look in his eyes told a different story. Guy knew he'd killed Doe, as sure as the sun would rise the next morning.

"I never said I killed him. I just don't want to take the stand." How pathetic did that sound? And who the hell was he trying to fool? His fingers were making fists again. "Are you staying for the rest of the trial?" And as he asked the question he knew, without a shadow of a doubt, that he wanted Guy at his side during what lay ahead.

Guy didn't say anything for a few beats. And Johnny tried to swallow.

"Do you want me to stay?" Guy was looking at him, his eyebrow slightly raised, like he wasn't too sure what Johnny would say.

Johnny bowed his head. Just this once, Fierro, be honest. Say it like it is and to hell with pride. Because Guy deserved one honest answer, especially when he had to put up with so much crap from Fierro. He raised his head and looked his brother straight in the eyes. "Yes, Guy, I want you to stay. Please." His voice was barely a whisper and now, he held his breath waiting for Guy's response.

CHAPTER TWENTY-THREE

He was afraid to breathe. Afraid to hope. Dios, but Guy was taking his time. He was simply standing there, staring down like he was lost in thought. Was he going to stay or go? He couldn't blame him if he didn't want to stay. Not after everything Fierro had done and said. Not after everything he'd done to keep Guy as far away from here as possible. Guy must know now that Fierro was a total bastard. But Johnny knew, without any doubt, that he needed Guy to stay. It would be a little easier to face whatever lay ahead if he had Guy by his side. He could stand taller then.

But Guy was taking too long. Fierro had ruined everything—ruined that closeness that had been starting to form between them. No, it wasn't just Fierro who'd destroyed it. Doe could carry some of this blame . . .

"I confess to being astounded." Guy's voice broke into his thoughts.

The moment of truth. He swallowed hard. "Astounded?"

"Well, you saying 'please.' I think it's a first."

Johnny's head jerked up. He could see it now. A softening in Guy's eyes. They still had the frown lines between them, but they looked softer. Hope was blooming now, like a cactus flower in the heat of the sun. He could feel it growing inside him. It was as if the sun was coming out and warming his bones. "So?" His voice was still a whisper though.

Guy raised an eyebrow. "So? Well, I will say that I think you are the most frustrating and confounding individual I've ever met. And I wish to God I knew half of what goes on inside that head of yours. But I think, as I started this journey with you, I'd better finish it with you."

Did that mean he was staying? And if so, why didn't he just say so? Damn it, he found Guy a puzzle. But it was a yes. Wasn't it? He chewed on his lip. "Is that a yes, Harvard?"

Guy gave a soft laugh. "Yes, Johnny, it is a yes. But we are going to have this out at some stage. I just wish you could find it in yourself to trust me. If you did, maybe we could fight your battle together. We're brothers. It means we're on the same side. Brothers should face things together. You're not alone in this."

The sun inside of him was doing a real good job of heating him up. On the same side? Like in a range war. But more so. Because they were brothers. Even the word brother felt good. When they'd first met, it hadn't meant a damn thing. Nothing at all. And now it meant everything.

"It's not that I don't trust you. But . . ." Johnny sank down onto the cot, shaking his head. "But sometimes, Guy, and you got to trust me on this, it's better not to know things."

Guy raised an eyebrow, like he wasn't buying that. "A sort of ignorance is bliss approach? I'm afraid that isn't quite how I see it. I think families should be able to be honest with each other. I grant you that we don't exactly fall into the conventional family mold given how many years we've been apart, but we have to strive to become a family. It'll take a lot of work and trust. But I'm going to trust my intrinsic belief that you are not a brutal killer. I do think you killed Doe, but I am also certain that you must have had a damn good reason for doing so. Because, try as I might to see you as a black-hearted villain, I know that you're not. And believe me, I tried awfully hard."

Guy paused, like he was thinking hard what to say next. "And you, Johnny, need to learn to trust us. I appreciate that this is difficult for you, but you're not on your own anymore. It's no longer a case of you standing alone against the world. You finally have allies. They're called family."

Johnny breathed out real slow. The words sounded so gentle, curling themselves around him like a soothing breeze on a warm evening. It sounded so tempting, this trust thing. But he didn't know how to do it. He'd spent his whole life keeping everything from touching him. He lived life at arm's length. Always on the outside. Always standing in the shadows. And all of his life his one rule had been to never trust anybody because they'd hurt you in the end. But it was the damnedest thing, because even though Guy had figured out that Fierro had killed Doe, he still seemed to have faith in Johnny. And that was pretty amazing. Yeah, this trust thing sounded real good, but it would take some learning. But maybe if he survived all of this it was something to reach toward, if it would only stay within his grasp.

He ducked his head, trying to think of something to say. But that was something else he needed to learn. He never had been much good with words. But then sometimes simple was best. He looked across at Guy and met his serious gaze. Nodded an acknowledgment. "Thanks, Guy. I'm glad you're staying."

Guy's mouth quirked. "I tell you one thing. Fraternal loyalty doesn't mean I'm going to spend the night in the cells with you. I had better go and see if Mrs. Nixon, who runs the hotel, is prepared to let me keep my room now that she knows I'm the brother of the infamous Johnny Fierro." His smile faded. "I wish you'd think again over your defense, Johnny. If you don't take the stand—"

Johnny shook his head. "No, I told you, I ain't going on the stand, Guy. And that's the end of it."

Guy rolled his eyes. "It could be the end of you if you don't take the stand. Have you thought of that?"

Dios. Guy sure knew how to give him pleasant dreams. "I

ain't dumb, I know how juries like to hear the man on the stand telling them how it's all a mistake, that he's innocent. But I ain't got anything to say."

Guy had started pacing up and down again, running his fingers through his hair. "What I can't figure, Johnny, is why you were so certain when we were back in Cimarron that you would walk away from this. You positively oozed confidence and arrogance. You must have had some reason for being so positive, unless that was all bravado. What changed, Johnny? You were being so cocky, telling me how you'd need your saddlebags for the ride home . . ." Guy's voice trailed off. His face paled, like he'd had a big shock. Or something had struck him. Shit—it looked like Guy had figured it out.

"Your saddlebags." Guy's voice was barely a whisper. "Why were they so important to you? You were set on not leaving them at the ranch. And then, after the stagecoach crash . . ." Guy's eyes were wide with shock. Like all the pieces of a puzzle were falling into place. Madre de Dios.

Guy caught hold of the cell bars, staring in. "What on earth was in those bags, Johnny? What was in them that was so damned important? It must have been something you didn't want to leave behind at the ranch because you thought you'd need it for the trial. What was it?"

Johnny shrugged. "Just like my own saddlebags is all."

Guy narrowed his eyes. The color was coming back in his face now. Except it was looking kind of pink, like he was getting riled up again, and the pulse was going in his temple. "No! Don't start all the evasion again. And don't lie to me, Johnny. I don't deserve that."

Johnny swallowed hard. Guy was right. He didn't deserve that. And Fierro didn't want to blow this. Guy was staying and whatever Johnny said, he didn't want to push Guy away again.

He sighed softly. "Yeah, there was something in them that I

thought might be useful. But it don't matter none now." He shrugged again. "The bags are gone and that's all there is to it. I can't do much about it."

"Why didn't you tell me?" Guy still looked angry. "If you'd told me, I would have gone back and looked for them. Why didn't you tell me, damn it?" Guy paused, and then laughed, but it didn't sound happy. "But of course you couldn't tell me, it would have meant admitting that you'd killed Doe. Damn it, Johnny, I wish you'd just level with me. Don't you understand I want to help you? God, I wish I knew why you killed Doe." Guy held his hand up, kind of like he wasn't going to let Johnny butt in. "And don't go denying it. I won't believe you." Guy sank back onto the chair. "But I suppose you wouldn't deny it, you'd perform one of your clever evasions. It's that rather perverse sense of honor you have. You won't lie to me, just like you won't lie on the witness stand, but you'll wriggle like a worm on a fish hook to avoid answering any direct questions. I have to say it's quite a talent."

Johnny kicked at the cracks in the stone floor with the toe of his boot. Couldn't think of a damn thing to say. Guy was getting pretty good at reading him—too damn good. But there was no point in brooding over the damn saddlebags; they'd gone and that was the end of it. And maybe the end of Fierro too. He could feel Guy watching him. He could feel Guy's hurt, like it was his own. And he hated hurting him. But what could he say without making Guy a part of Fierro's guilt? He sure as hell didn't want Guy carrying that weight. Or having the nightmares if he ever learned what Doe's game had been. "Guy, why don't you go on back and get that hotel room of yours straightened out for tonight? Just trust me on this, it's better that you don't know too much. If I could tell you, I would. But I'm . . ." He paused, feeling the color flood his face, the words were so hard to say. "I'm real glad you're here. And that's the truth."

Guy hauled himself to his feet. "Well, I suppose we have made some progress. At least we appear to be on the same side again, even if you are being damned difficult. It seems I will have to be content with this for now. And for the life of me I can't even begin to imagine where the damn bags could have gone. We picked up all of the luggage, I'm sure of it. There weren't any bags left behind." Guy paused, shaking his head like he was real irritated. "You should have told me. God, but you're an awkward individual. But I won't be letting you off the hook, Johnny. At some stage I want to know what the hell this is all about."

Yeah, when hell freezes over. "I hope you get your room back, Guy. I wouldn't want you to have to spend the night in here." Johnny gestured around the cell. "This ain't exactly got many home comforts. Still, the food's fine. So, it could be worse."

Guy gave him the ghost of a smile. "I'll take the hotel for preference. The food there is excellent. Is there anything you need me to do? Do you want to see Sweetfoot? Shall I go and look for him?"

Johnny sighed. "Yeah, I guess he and I had better talk about how we play tomorrow in court."

Guy nodded. "I think that would be a very good idea. I'll send him over. And I'll see you tomorrow."

Johnny raised a hand in farewell. "Yeah. See you tomorrow."

His demons yanked him from sleep that night. It was the worst of his dreams, the one he hated the most. Same as always he was striking out, and all he could see was Doe's face. Doe, smiling and laughing, and walking through the crowd of jeering men, collecting the money as they placed their bets. And then the faces all merged and he was back in that house with Doe whimpering on his knees. And Fierro shooting him straight between the eyes, like the mark of Cain. And then the unimaginable rage boiling over, because he'd failed to kill him slow, like he'd promised he would. Rage because, in the end, Doe had it too easy. Far too easy. And so Fierro had just blasted away with his gun, emptying the gun into Doe's balls. And the red mist of anger clouding everything.

Johnny struggled up, still striking out wildly at the memories. His breath was coming in short bursts, and sweat was pouring off him, so he sat on the edge of the cot, wrapping his arms around himself and rocking gently to try to calm his racing heart. What would it be like just to sleep—a peaceful, dreamless sleep? Couldn't imagine that anymore. A woman. He needed a woman. It always helped a little. He could lose himself then. Those few seconds of ecstasy always drove everything from his mind. And right now he longed for the scent and touch and feel of a woman. He laughed out loud. God only knew if he'd ever have another woman. Maybe the jury would find him guilty and that would be it. The end of everything.

Sweetfoot hadn't seemed too happy. He'd looked kind of awkward really. Like he knew he'd messed up. But heck, Sweetfoot was only just starting out, he was bound to make mistakes. Johnny had tried to make out it didn't matter, but they both knew it did. Best they could hope for was the jury not having much faith in Jackson. Yeah. Like that was going to happen.

Johnny pulled himself up by the bars on the window. The first streaks of dawn were showing, but it sure wasn't going to be a sunny day. The sky looked heavy and threatening, with banks of clouds building in the east. Dios, he missed the sun. He threw himself back down on the cot and waited for Ford to bring breakfast.

The courtroom was full to bursting. People were crowding in, their faces pink from the biting wind. Least all those bodies produced some warmth. He'd got damned cold walking to the courthouse earlier, but he'd still taken it slow. Walked down real casual, like he hadn't got a thing to worry over. He needed to look like a man at ease.

Guy had gotten there early. He'd snagged a seat for himself instead of standing at the back. He met Johnny's gaze, gave a nod, a slight smile. Johnny nodded back and felt some of the tension ease from his shoulders.

It looked like the same bunch of people as the day before. The woman in the thick veil had bagged the best seat again, right at the front where she could see every damn thing. And the man with the big clay pipe was still puffing out great clouds of choking smoke. The woman in pink had settled herself down next to Harvard, like she was an old friend. She kept nudging him and was talking away at him nonstop. Johnny bit back a grin. It looked like the smile on Guy's face was kind of frozen there, like he was struggling real hard to mind his manners.

Sweetfoot had a pile of books in front of him. Real big books. Surely it would take a lifetime and a half to read those. And Lincoln was looking smug, like he reckoned he'd got it all sewn up. Which he probably had.

Everyone who'd got a seat shuffled to their feet as Denning walked in and sat himself down with his little hammer at the ready.

He arranged the spectacles on the end of his nose and gazed slowly around the courtroom, kind of like he was taking everything in. Denning fixed Ford with a sharp-eyed look—those eyes didn't miss a thing. "Marshal, were you able to contact Mrs. Walsh?"

Ford nodded and scrambled to his feet. "Yes, your honor. I got a wire off as soon as we adjourned yesterday and by good luck Mrs. Walsh was in town when it arrived. She sent a wire back confirming the story. It was exactly like Mr. Sinclair told the court. She says that he lost a lot of blood and required several stitches. She drove him to the doctor in her buggy. I also confirmed with the mayor there that she is a respectable widow who has run her husband's ranch since his death, just like Mr. Sinclair said. I've got the wires here." Ford passed the telegrams over to Denning who read them carefully before handing them over to Lincoln.

Denning fiddled with his spectacles again. "Well, that certainly bears out the accused's version of how he came by that scar. Mr. Sweetfoot, do you have any more questions for the witness?"

Sweetfoot nodded. "I do indeed. I haven't quite finished my line of questioning, your honor."

Denning nodded, a hint of a smile playing at his mouth. "I rather thought perhaps you hadn't. Mr. Jackson, will you resume your place on the witness stand, please? And kindly remember that you are still under oath."

Jackson cupped his hand behind his ear. "What's that? My hearing ain't so good you know."

One of the court officers guided Jackson to the stand and Sweetfoot stood patiently waiting while the old man got himself settled.

Sweetfoot smiled across at Jackson. "Good morning, Mr. Jackson. I have just one or two more questions for you."

Jackson peered across the room. "What's that? You'll have to speak up, young man. I told you I don't hear too good."

Sweetfoot nodded and looked kind of pleased. "Yes, that's what I wanted to ask you about, Mr. Jackson. Your hearing really isn't very good at all is it?"

"That's what I've been telling you." Jackson glared as laughter rippled around the court.

"But although you admit your hearing isn't good, you are very convinced that you heard the left-handed gunman say his name was Johnny Fierro. I put it to you, Mr. Jackson, that you were so alarmed by the horror of the situation in which you found yourself, and were so understandably frightened and anxious to get away, that you misheard the gunman. I believe that you picked on the name of Johnny Fierro because it was a well-known and familiar name. I put it to you that with your poor hearing, and your panic, you could not have been certain what name the gunman gave and that the name of Fierro simply sprang to mind."

Jackson leaned forward. "My hearing might not be as good as some folks, but I know what I heard that day, you young whippersnapper. And I know what I saw. I saw that scar on his arm."

Sweetfoot shook his head. "Mr. Jackson, we all saw yesterday that you have poor eyesight in addition to your poor hearing. Can you really be so sure, that in what by your own admission was only a quick glimpse, the man you saw was the man sitting here today accused of this crime? I put it to you that your glimpse of the man with Mr. Doe was too brief for this court to be able to accept your testimony with any degree of certainty. That is the truth of the matter, is it not, Mr. Jackson?"

Jackson snorted. "I know what I heard and I know what I saw." He pointed across the court. "I saw him and I saw that scar on his arm."

Sweetfoot smiled smoothly. "In the light of Mrs. Walsh's cable, I believe that everyone here accepts how Mr. Sinclair got the scar, Mr. Jackson."

Jackson snorted again. "The killer had a scar in that exact same place. Maybe he's cut that arm more than once. It happens. I often get cuts in the same place when I'm gardening."

Dios. Was Sweetfoot going to let the man prattle on putting ideas in the jurors' minds?

Sweetfoot reorganized the pile of books in front of him and then spoke very softly. "And that is idle speculation. I think that's all, Mr. Jackson."

Jackson cupped his ear again. "What's that?"

"I said thank you, Mr. Jackson. That will be all."

Denning polished his spectacles with a large blue checked handkerchief. "Mr. Lincoln, do you have any further questions for your witness?"

Lincoln shook his head. "No, thank you, your honor. No more questions."

Denning perched the glasses back on the end of his nose. "I take it that you will now be calling Mr. Sinclair to the stand, Mr. Sweetfoot."

Sweetfoot shook his head, flushing slightly. "No, your honor. My client instructs me that as he has never been to Utah and is right-handed, he feels that there is nothing he can say which will contribute to this hearing. It is simply a case of mistaken identity."

Denning leaned forward, resting his chin on his steepled fingers. "Mr. Sweetfoot, I appreciate that you are very inexperienced, so I will give you some advice. I would most strongly suggest that you put your client on the witness stand." He looked over at Johnny. "Mr. Sinclair."

Johnny sprang to his feet. "Your honor."

"Mr. Sinclair, I feel it is my duty to point out to you the possible ramifications of not taking the stand. As I just indicated, Mr. Sweetfoot is inexperienced and I fear that he might not have fully clarified your situation to you. Mr. Sinclair, if you are convicted you will be executed. And as things stand at the moment we have an eyewitness to this crime who is standing by his story that it was you he saw in that house in July 1866. Juries always pay more heed to evidence given on oath, and I would strongly advise you to take the witness stand and give evidence on your own behalf."

Johnny inclined his head briefly before giving everyone in the room the benefit of one of his biggest smiles. "Your honor, I really appreciate your advice. But there's nothing I can add. Everyone who knows me would tell you that I spent all my time around the border. Utah is well out of my territory and everyone knows I'm right-handed. So, whoever Mr. Jackson saw that day, well, it wasn't me."

Denning shook his head. "I feel this is most unwise. Mr. Sweetfoot, do you have any other evidence you wish to call?"

Sweetfoot flushed a deeper shade of red. "No, your honor, we don't."

A chair scraped across the floor. Everyone turned to see who the hell wasn't interested enough in the case to stay listening, and there were whispers of surprise to see it was Ford who was on his feet, crushing his hat in his hand.

Johnny's brow furrowed. What the hell was Ford up to?

"Your honor." Ford's voice came out strong. "If I may, I have some evidence for the court to hear."

Chapter Twenty-Four

It was a deafening uproar again as everyone started talking but this time the name on everybody's lips was Ford.

"Order!" Denning banged his hammer. He'd turned bright red and his spectacles were jigging up and down on the end of his nose. "Order! Anyone who ignores the solemnity of this court of law will be removed. Everyone sit down or leave. Now! I will not countenance such disturbances in my court."

That sure shut them up. Nobody wanted to miss whatever Ford had to say. Including Fierro. Dios. He always knew there was more to Ford than met the eye . . . but what? Nothing he'd ever been able to put his finger on. Had he said something when he was sleeping? Had he given himself away and Ford had overheard something? Would the ramblings of a sleeping man be accepted as evidence? Mierda. Johnny chewed his lip.

Johnny glanced across the court to where Carter was sitting, red-faced and muttering to the fellow sitting next to him in an agitated way. Well, whatever Ford had to say, Carter was as much in the dark about this as Fierro.

Johnny stretched his legs out and leaned back, trying to look relaxed. Like he wasn't too bothered about whatever Ford had to say. But shit, how was Ford involved in all of this? He tried to push away the feeling of unease. He didn't like surprises. 'Specially when it was his neck on the line.

Sweetfoot looked puzzled too. He leaned over to whisper to Johnny. "Do you know anything about this?"

Johnny shook his head. "Nope. I ain't got a clue."

Lincoln was frowning and scanning his papers. Maybe that was a good thing. If Lincoln wasn't expecting this, maybe Ford wasn't taking that side. Which meant that maybe he was speaking up for Fierro's side? But no. That didn't make sense. Ford would have said something. Wouldn't he?

"Order." Denning banged his hammer again and then pulled out his handkerchief and started polishing his spectacles again. Dios. Did the man never do anything else?

Denning balanced them back on the end of his nose and then started rubbing his beard, like he was thinking hard. "Marshal, you have information that is pertinent to this case? You believe you could enlighten the court about the events that occurred at Mr. Doe's house?"

Ford wrung his hat a bit tighter. One thing was certain; he'd never be able to wear it again. "I have some information, your honor, about the victim. It might prove helpful."

Denning sat back in his seat and stared real hard at the ceiling. Dios. The man was a real showman. And boy did he know how to make sure everyone was paying him heed. He was going to keep 'em all waiting too. He didn't seem in a hurry to say anything.

Denning rapped the table with his fingers, like he was still thinking. "So, Marshal, you wish to make a statement? This is a somewhat unorthodox development. Mr. Lincoln, Mr. Sweetfoot, do either of you have any objections to that?"

Sweetfoot rose. "I would like to take instructions from my client." He turned to Johnny, looking kind of panicky and leaned forward to speak in a low voice. "What should we do?"

Johnny shrugged casually, like he wasn't bothered. "I guess we might as well hear what he has to say." He wasn't going to tell Sweetfoot that Fierro couldn't wait to hear what Ford had to say.

Sweetfoot turned back toward Denning. "We have no objections, your honor."

Denning pursed his lips. "Hmm. I rather thought you wouldn't. Mr. Lincoln, are you satisfied with this development?"

Lincoln paused and shuffled the papers again before nodding slowly. "No objections, your honor."

"In that case, Marshal, perhaps you would like to take the stand and tell this court whatever is on your mind." Denning sat back with his arms folded. But although the judge looked like he was relaxed, there was a real sharp look in his eyes, which said he wanted to hear this too.

Ford walked slowly to the stand. "Do you want me to take the oath?"

Denning pulled at his beard again. "No, I don't think that will be necessary, not at this stage, as this is not exactly a part of the formal proceedings. If I decide it is necessary, I will instruct you to do so."

There wasn't a sound in the courtroom. Could have heard a horse shedding.

Ford cleared his throat. "As most folk in this town know, I've been a deputy marshal based here for getting on for four years. I came up here from down south in Arizona. But what most folk don't know is that the reason I came here was to hunt for Mr. Doe."

Excited whispers came from all around the courtroom. Denning banged his hammer. It shut them all up.

"I'd been tracking him for some time. He had settled in another small town, much like this one, over in Texas, but he'd moved on by the time I tracked him to there. I followed his trail to here. However, when I arrived here, I heard that he'd been killed, so I suppose you could say I'd had a wasted journey." Ford twisted the hat again. "But the town needed law, and I was instructed to make this my base as a deputy marshal. I liked the town so I took the job and stayed on."

Denning leaned forward. "Pray tell us why you were tracking Mr. Doe. My understanding is that he was a guard in a prison. Were you being paid to trace him? And if so, why?"

The hat got another mighty wrench. Johnny frowned. What the hell had Ford been up to? He sure wasn't looking too happy about telling his tale. A nerve in his face was twitching, even though he must be used to giving evidence in his line of work. But something was making him real reluctant to tell this tale.

Ford cleared his throat again. "Mr. Doe had indeed been a guard in a prison. It was a well-paid job, which made it an attractive proposition to someone like Doe. He was fortunate in that he knew the right people and he was able to pull strings to get himself appointed. But unfortunately, Mr. Doe appears to have not been satisfied with his wages. He . . ." Ford faltered, like he couldn't decide how to say something.

But it sure seemed he knew a lot about Doe. Maybe too much.

"He abused his position as a guard. He . . . he manipulated people and was involved in accepting bribes. But that wasn't the full extent of his misdemeanors. He was also involved in the mistreatment of prisoners. He was a particularly brutal man who enjoyed seeing other people suffer."

And everyone started talking again. Except this time they didn't even bother whispering. Denning was banging with his hammer but everyone was ignoring him now; they were far too busy talking about this latest development. And Johnny could feel Guy watching him but he sure as hell didn't want to look him in the eyes. Didn't want Guy to start figuring things out . . . Not that he'd ever figure out exactly what Doe's game had been. Guy was too much of an innocent to even imagine what Doe had been up to. Unless Ford knew. But no, Ford would never tell it, not in an open court with women there.

He glanced around again, avoiding catching Guy's eye. The woman in the veil had turned her head toward Fierro. She'd tilted it to one side, like she was studying him. Who the hell was she? A relative of Doe, maybe? Johnny hadn't seen her talk to a soul in the court. He'd swear she didn't come with anyone. But she didn't miss much, he was certain of that.

"Order!" The hammer came crashing down with a big bang. "This is your final warning. Anyone causing a disturbance shall be removed from the courtroom." Denning gave them an icy glare, kind of like he really meant business. It shut them up. "Marshal, perhaps you could continue, please."

But Lincoln scrambled to his feet now. "Your honor, I must object to this unorthodox situation. I do not believe that whatever the marshal has to say can have any bearing on the case against Mr. Sinclair."

Denning grunted like he was running short on patience. "Mr. Lincoln, you had your chance to object earlier. I note your comment but I will thank you to sit down. I am most curious to hear what the marshal has to tell us about Mr. Doe. Then and only then, will I decide if it has a bearing on this case and will so instruct the jury of my decision." He paused, like he was waiting for Lincoln to sit back down. "Marshal, please continue."

Ford shuffled his feet and looked real awkward. Ford sure didn't want to be doing this. So why was he? And what the hell was he going to come out with next?

Ford wrung his hat a bit more. "Like I said, Doe was responsible for the ill treatment of many prisoners. Not that he ever touched them himself. He got other prisoners to do the hurting. He was very good at manipulating people. And he really enjoyed seeing people suffer. He used to take bets from the other prisoners on how long it would take for the victims to scream. He liked to see them scream, the louder the better. And he made a lot of money out of that. Many of his victims were very young. And as this is a mixed court, I'd rather not go into the details. They ain't fit for decent folk to hear."

Johnny shut his eyes even as there were gasps of horror in the courtroom. His palms were sweating and yet the rest of him was icy cold. He wanted to curl up in a ball—not sit and listen to this. The thought of it all being raked up—mierda. And he sure as hell didn't want Guy sitting listening to all of this, and he knew Guy was watching him. But somehow, Fierro had to sit here and whatever Ford said, he mustn't show any emotion. He had to try to look like none of this was of interest to him . . . But hell, it was easier said than done.

"The thing is, your honor." Ford's voice came out stronger now. "There would have been any number of men who would have wanted to see Doe dead. That's what I'm trying to say. Any one of them could have come to kill him."

Thank God. It looked like Ford was done and wasn't going to say no more about Doe.

Denning was tapping his fingers again. "And you, Marshal, what was your interest in Doe? What were you intending to do with him when you found him?"

Ford's face was blank now. No expression. "Bring him to justice of course, your honor. I had been asked to find him and bring him to justice."

"By whom?" Denning was looking real hard at Ford.

"By the family of one of the victims. But like I said, when I got here, Doe was dead. He'd been dead for a few weeks. But there's an awful lot of people would have had a darn good motive for killing him."

Denning leaned back in his seat again, pursing his lips. "That is a fair point, Marshal. But the fact remains we have an eyewitness who states that the person who came and killed Mr. Doe was Mr. Sinclair, who sits in this court accused of murder. I ac-

cept that your information does open up possibilities for many
people from the prison wanting Mr. Doe dead, but we don't
have any evidence whatsoever that anyone did come here with
that purpose in mind. It is my duty to point that out to the jury.
At the moment, all we have is Mr. Jackson's testimony." Denning looked at his pocket watch. "It is a little early, but this
seems an appropriate juncture to adjourn until after lunch. I
will use the lunch hour to consider whether there is anything to
be gained by putting you on oath, Mr. Ford, and pursuing this
line of enquiry." He glanced across at Sweetfoot and Lincoln.
"Gentlemen, I will expect your summation this afternoon.
Perhaps you might like to make one last attempt to persuade
Mr. Sinclair to give evidence, Mr. Sweetfoot." With a nod to
them, Denning stood up and left the court.

Guy was struggling through the mass of people to get to
Johnny. And Sweetfoot and Ford were heading toward him too.
Fuck. If only they'd all leave him alone. All he wanted right
now was to try to figure out where Ford fitted in all of this.

"Mr. Sinclair, I think perhaps you and I should discuss your
case." Sweetfoot's brow was creased up. "Things are not looking good for us."

Us? That was rich. Since when was Sweetfoot's neck on the
line? Madre de Dios. But right now he just wanted to get away
from everyone. Escape back to his cell for some peace and quiet.
And think things over.

"Johnny." Guy looked kind of pale. Shocked. Yeah, shocked
by what Ford had been saying. That figured. "We need to talk.
You've got to rethink your defense." He looked at Sweetfoot,
like he was hoping the kid would back him up.

Sweetfoot nodded vigorously. "That's what I was just telling
your brother, Mr. Sinclair. This isn't going well and I can see no
alternative but for him to go in the witness box and give
evidence on oath."

Johnny shook his head. "No, I ain't taking the stand. It's up to the jury. If they believe Jackson, nothing I say is gonna make a damn bit of difference." No way was he going to stand in front of God and lie on oath in that witness box. Couldn't do it. Not to save his own skin. Wouldn't be right. Hell, he'd been living on borrowed time for years. At least now he could die knowing what it was like to have family. He'd had a little bit of heaven for a time and that was as good as it was ever going to get. Nothing lasted.

"Damn it, Johnny . . ." Guy didn't get no further. Ford held his hand up, shaking his head.

"Mr. Sinclair, your brother looks done in. I think the best thing is for me to take him back to the cell for some lunch. Then maybe you and Mr. Sweetfoot can talk to him before the afternoon session. Why don't you go and get something to eat, and calm down a bit first?"

Guy chewed on his lip, looking like he wanted to say more. Then he nodded slowly. Didn't look none too happy but leastways it looked like Fierro could have some peace for a short while.

"Come on, Fierro." Ford steered Johnny through the folk still milling around the courtroom. He knew the woman in the veil was watching him walk out. Could feel her eyes boring into him. Who the hell was she?

They walked back to the jail through the biting wind. Tumbleweed was blowing along the sidewalks and the dust made his eyes sting. Maybe now he'd get the chance to pin Ford down. Because something told him that Ford knew a whole lot more than he'd let on in that courtroom. One thing was certain: Ford had chosen his words very carefully and been determined not to give too much away.

Ford let the door slam behind them in his office and Johnny went back to his cell as Ford reached for the keys to take the cuffs off him.

"I wouldn't mind a few answers, Marshal." Johnny spoke softly, watching the color flush the man's face. "You never let on to me that you'd been hunting for Doe."

"Hoped I wouldn't need to." Ford sighed and pulled up the chair outside the cell. "Not that it did you much good. I thought maybe it would put some doubt in the jury's minds. But I got to tell you, Fierro, your brother's right, it ain't looking too good."

Johnny tried to ignore the cold hand of fear inside of him. He shrugged. "We all got to go sometime, don't we? But I'd rather not go this way. Not for the kind of man you described today." Keep playing dumb. It was the only way. Still didn't know what Ford's game was. Would the man let on?

"The kind of man I described?" Ford smiled, like Johnny had said something real funny. "Between these four walls, Fierro, we both know that you know exactly the kind of man Doe was."

Johnny raised an eyebrow, gave a ghost of smile. "Sorry, Marshal, I didn't say I knew anything about the man. But I do wonder who asked you to hunt him down. And what you were planning on doing with him when you found him."

Ford sat with his head bowed, studying the floor real hard for maybe a minute before he replied. Johnny leaned back against the wall and waited. He'd got all the time in the world. Sure wasn't going anywhere right now. Not being as how he was locked back in the damn cell.

Ford threw his hands up and sighed heavily. "No one asked me. I was hunting him for personal reasons."

Johnny raised an eyebrow. "Personal reasons?"

Ford nodded. "Yeah, personal. And I was going to bring him to justice."

Johnny smiled at that. "Justice? You think the law would be interested in one of their own? In my experience folk like that close ranks, the law protects its own."

Ford laughed, but not like it was funny. "I didn't say the law. I said justice. Maybe like your version of justice, Fierro."

Johnny narrowed his eyes. "My version?"

Ford nodded. "Yeah. We both know that Doe was an animal. Sometimes, an animal is so dangerous it's up to a man to destroy it. Wouldn't you agree with that?"

Johnny smiled. "I've heard people say it." There was no way he was letting his guard down with Ford. And if Ford was hoping Fierro was suddenly going to admit to something, the man could think again. "So, you said personal? Just how personal?"

Ford stared down at the floor again, then shook his head kind of like he was sad. "You know, my brother had a son, his only child. The boy wasn't too bright, but he was a nice enough lad. But he was weak. He was the sort that always gets in with the wrong crowd. You know the kind."

Johnny nodded. And waited.

"Yep, he always got in with the wrong people. Easily led. And he wound up in trouble. He wasn't nearly old enough for it but he got sent to prison. No kid that age should be in prison."

"And that's where he met Doe?" Johnny could feel Ford's sorrow. It was wrapping itself around the marshal like a cloak.

Ford nodded. "Yeah. That's where he met Doe. And Doe liked the weak ones."

Dios, that was true. Doe loved 'em weak. Made his game so much easier. Yeah, the bastard had always singled out the weak ones. Just like he picked the tough ones to dance to his tune. And then stepped back to watch and take the bets. But Fierro had never made a sound. Never gave Doe the satisfaction.

"The things that happened to Dougie in that prison, well, he never got over it."

Johnny's head jerked up. "Dougie?"

Ford inclined his head and gave Johnny a knowing sort of

look. "Yeah—Dougie. You know, all of it broke Dougie. He couldn't live with what had happened—it just ate away at him, tearing him apart. And so one day, he went down into the orchard on my brother's farm, and he found himself a tree and hanged himself."

Johnny shut his eyes briefly. Fucking Doe. How many people had he destroyed?

"But you know, Dougie and I did talk a little before that day came. I tried so hard to get him to talk. Anyway, he told me how he was in a saloon one day, trying to drink himself into a state where he couldn't remember how much he hated himself." Ford shook his head. "Dougie did that a lot after the prison. Drinking to block it all out, I guess. Anyway, some fellow was goading him, trying to pick a fight. And what with the booze and all, the poor kid wasn't in no fit state to protect himself. But another man stepped in and came to Dougie's aid—fought the fellow and killed him in a knife fight. And then he and Dougie got to talking and it turned out they'd both been in the same prison. This fellow guessed exactly what had happened to my nephew. Anyway, he promised Dougie he'd take care of Doe. Said he'd make sure that Doe never hurt nobody else ever again. And Dougie believed him too. Said he was the sort of man who'd follow through, he wasn't the type to make empty promises."

Johnny swallowed hard. Tried to look relaxed. Yeah, like Ford would be fooled by that. "Dougie tell you anything else about this fellow?"

A ghost of a smile passed across Ford's face. "I reckon he did give me a name. But you know, I got one hell of a bad memory so I guess it's slipped my mind."

"You think it'll come back to you?" Johnny held Ford's gaze.

Ford gave a soft laugh. "I'll tell you one thing, it sure as hell won't come back to me in no court of law." He scratched his head thoughtfully. "You know, I reckon that man he met that day did follow through and I guess I owe him. And even though Dougie killed himself, I think he found a little comfort from meeting that man. He trusted him to keep his word, and at least he died knowing that probably nobody else would become one of Doe's victims. And I guess the fellow saved me from killing Doe myself. Because I sure as hell would have done it."

Johnny let out a long sigh. "Well, seems that Doe's killer did everyone a favor."

Ford nodded slowly. "I reckon he did. Trouble is, favor or no, your case ain't looking too healthy right now. Best chance you got is taking that stand and telling that jury what a good upright rancher you are and how you've never been to Utah."

Johnny shook his head. "I can't do that, Ford." He sighed. "Wish I could, but no, I ain't going on that stand."

Ford grunted in irritation. "They're going to find you guilty, boy. I never wanted to bring you in for this, but Carter had Jackson's testimony. And when he heard Johnny Fierro was alive and living near Cimarron, he went and got himself that damn court order without telling me. I reckoned the least I could do was bring you here safely. Carter would have shot you and not bothered bringing you to trial."

"Yeah. I reckon he would have done." Johnny swung his legs up and sat on the cot with his knees drawn up, resting his chin on them. "Well, I guess I'll just have to take my chances."

"I hate to say it, boy, but they ain't looking too good."

Johnny laughed. "Tell me something I don't know!"

The door to the outer office slammed. "Best go see who it is. Probably Sweetfoot or your brother." Ford stood and pushed the chair back into the next cell before going back into the main office.

Johnny groaned. Last thing he needed was to see either Guy or Sweetfoot. They were both going to start in on him. And right now he was likely to bite both their heads off.

He could hear muffled voices in the outer office and then Ford calling out. "You got a visitor, Fierro."

Johnny's heart sank. Hell, if only people would leave him alone.

CHAPTER TWENTY-FIVE

Johnny's head jerked up in surprise. "You! What the hell are you doing here?"

"Running around trying to save your butt, I reckon. And not for the first time."

Johnny narrowed his eyes. "Saving my butt? How you going to do that? I thought you'd gone back to Cimarron. With a sore leg, I heard."

Stoney grunted, and then leaned down to pick up something from behind the open door. "Figured you might be needing these." He held up some saddlebags.

His saddlebags! Holy shit. It felt like all the Christmases he'd never celebrated had suddenly all come at once. Good old Stoney. But how the hell had Stoney known to search for them? Johnny tilted his head and looked at him. "Why'd you go looking for them, Stoney? I never asked you to hunt for them."

Stoney gave him one of his looks, the kind that said he thought Fierro was being dumb. "You were real steamed up about them. And don't try telling me it's because you've had 'em a long time and are very attached to them. It might come as a surprise to you, but I really ain't that dumb. I figured, knowing what a slippery son of a bitch you are, that maybe there was something in 'em that you wanted. Wanted badly, judging by the way you were acting. And I tell you, if whatever you needed so badly ain't there, I sure as hell ain't going back to look again. I searched high and low for those in the damn rain. Lucky I didn't catch my death of cold. Not that anybody would have cared if I had upped and died."

Johnny grinned. "Don't be such an old grouch. You got no idea how pleased I am to see you, Stoney."

Stoney snorted. "Huh! Like hell you're pleased to see me. Don't give me that bullshit, Fierro. You mean you're pleased to see your goddamn saddlebags, not me."

Johnny bit back another smile. "Settle for you and the bags, OK?"

Stoney grunted again and pushed them through the bars. "Here you are. You'd best check them. And they'd better be worth all the effort I put in hunting for them. My leg is hurting like hell, Fierro, and if I spend the rest of my life limping, it'll be your doing." Stoney sank down on the chair next to the barred cell and rubbed his chin.

Johnny shut his eyes briefly at the touch of the worn old leather bags. Maybe, just maybe, he had a chance now. Because he really didn't want to die because of Doe. Just as long as he still had his trump card.

He opened them slowly, like he wasn't bothered one way or the other, trying to ignore Stoney's raised eyebrow and sigh of irritation. "You really are one irritating son of a bitch, Fierro. How the hell nobody's killed you before now, I'll never know."

Johnny flicked through the contents of the bags before setting them back down.

"Well?" Stoney had the grouchy tone back. "You got everything you need? Is everything there?" Stoney rolled his eyes dramatically. "Well?"

Johnny shook his head. "Nope. Not everything is there. There's a gold nugget missing."

"And you reckon I stole it?" Stoney sounded pissed.

Johnny laughed softly. "No, Stoney, I don't think you stole it.

But I tell you who did know it was in my bags. Fucking Carter."

Stoney sighed. "That figures. Those bags was hid. There was no way they got where they were by accident. I found them tucked down a crevice between the rocks, some way from where the stage crashed. That's why I've been gone so long. Took me two days before I found the damn things. Then, to top it all, my damn horse went lame."

Johnny looked up. "Two days." He felt warmer inside, like the sun had come out again. Stoney had spent two whole days searching because he wanted to help Fierro? "Stoney . . . I do . . . I mean, well . . ."

Stoney grunted, and waved his hand to shut Johnny up. "Yeah. Yeah. I know. Thing is, was the gold important?"

"Hell, yes! Of course it was important. I found that gold when I was messing around panning, years ago. I carried it ever since. Kind of like a lucky charm, I guess." Wasn't going to tell Stoney that he was planning on making a ring with it if he ever found a woman dumb enough to want to marry him. Stoney would reckon Fierro was really soft if he knew that.

Stoney stood up, pushing the chair back so hard it fell over. "You know damn well that ain't what I meant, Johnny. Hell, you're one tricky—"

"Son of a bitch?" Johnny grinned. "Let's just say that the gold is the only thing missing. Everything else is there."

Stoney shook his head, his face coloring up. "You ain't gonna tell me, are you? After all the trouble I went to?"

Johnny laughed softly. "Stoney, calm down. It ain't good for you to get so worked up. Like I said, the gold's the only thing missing. And trust me, if I get off the hook for this, I'm going looking for Carter and he'll wish he'd never been born. He's sure as hell not going to get away with my gold nugget. Fuck that."

Stoney glared. "Oh, wonderful. Yeah, that's a great idea. Get out of jail for one crime and then go right ahead and get yourself locked up in here again. You don't never learn, do you? Take a tip from me; sometimes it's better to walk away. Especially seeing as how Carter's a lawman."

Johnny snorted. "Lawman! He don't know shit about the law. Anyway, I already needed to get even with that bastard. Told him we'd got a score to settle. He's just given me another good reason. And I got a long memory, Stoney, a very long memory."

Stoney looked at him steadily. "Leaving that to one side for a minute, you said 'if you got off the hook.' Is that gonna happen? When I spoke to Ford, he said things weren't looking too good. Is that right?" Stoney kicked at the chair leg with his worn old boot. "I mean, what the hell has all this been about? Ain't like I've been here to hear the trial. From what he just said, I'm back in time to watch you climb the steps to the gallows." He looked across with narrowed eyes. "And if it's all the same to you, Fierro, I'd rather not see that happen. So tell me, what's all of this about? And don't go telling me you didn't kill this fellow, because I know damn well you did."

Good old Stoney. He never changed. He never pussyfooted around. He just spoke straight and right to the point. It was one of the things he liked about Stoney. Some people might mistake the sheriff for a fool because he acted vague and looked scruffy. But if they did they were the fools. Stoney was sharp as a razor, even though he didn't often use one. Maybe because he was so sharp he might cut himself. Johnny grinned at the thought.

Stoney grunted and threw his hands in the air. "Well, you gonna say something or just sit there grinning like a cat that got the cream?"

Johnny raised an eyebrow. "Kind of impatient there, ain't you, Stoney. Ford gave the court a bit of background on Doe. You missed that. He was a guard in a prison. According to

Ford, Doe abused the prisoners and took bets on things while all the other prisoners stood and watched . . ." Johnny tailed off. Didn't even want to think about those jeering men. Block it out. Maybe if he kept telling himself it never happened he might be able to forget it all. He tried to drag his mind back to now. He could feel Stoney's eyes boring into him. Seeing inside of him. Seeing all that dirt on his soul.

Johnny set his jaw. "Anyway, that's what Ford told the court." Yeah, cut it short. Don't give any more details. "And this eyewitness they got themselves, says he saw a left-handed gunman. And you and me both know I always use my right hand."

Stoney gave him another of those looks. "Well, I know for a fact you've been in prison, you told me so once. But I'll bet you didn't tell the court that."

Johnny shrugged. "Didn't see any point. I was just a kid back then." He tried to look Stoney in the eyes, but damn it, couldn't do it. Instead he fiddled with the catches on his saddlebags.

Stoney grunted in irritation. "Yeah, well, probably for the best that you didn't mention it in court. No point in helping them put a noose around your neck. I'm guessing you met this fellow, Doe, in prison then."

Johnny looked up sharply. "I never said I knew Doe."

Stoney raised an eyebrow. "I know you didn't say it, you dumb ass. But I'll bet my badge you did know him. Sorry, but I reckon I know you better than you think. I always figured you knew more about this case than you've let on. I was there when they arrested you—in case you've forgotten." Stoney looked at him in the sort of way he did when he was trying to make his point. "And you was clever then about avoiding the question of whether you've ever been to Utah. You are a slippery devil, Fierro. And you ain't never once asked what you were accused of doing. But you slipped up there. An innocent man would have been demanding to know."

He had to keep his face blank. He sure wasn't admitting anything—not even to Stoney. "If you're so sure of all this, Stoney, why ain't you running to tell the judge?"

Stoney looked at him hard. Didn't say a thing for a few beats. "Let's just say I never took you for a murderer. And this fellow you say they described in court . . ." Stoney shook his head slightly. "Sometimes, Johnny, doing things the legal way don't get the job done." Stoney chuffed out a laugh. "But don't tell that old windbag of a mayor in Cimarron that I said that."

Couldn't think of a damn thing to say. And it was real odd, but the two men who'd figured it out were both lawmen and both on his side. And yet, surely they were meant to be on the side of the law? But maybe that was it. They knew what crap the law was. That it didn't do much to protect those who couldn't protect themselves. That it tended to work best for people with power and money. He shook his head slowly. He'd known for a long time what a shit place this world was—full of small-minded, unpleasant people.

"Will the saddlebags help?" Stoney had a funny sort of half-smile on his face like he knew Johnny was figuring everything out.

Johnny chuckled. "Stoney. I ain't got a clue. I don't reckon I know anything anymore. Seems to me that everyone's full of surprises. But they might help, they just might. Guess we'll have to wait and see."

"Which means you still ain't gonna tell me what's so all fired important in them. Dang, but you're a stubborn son of a bitch. Don't know how that brother of yours puts up with you."

Johnny grinned at that. "Between you and me, Stoney, I haven't figured that one either. See you in court. You'd better go get a seat. It's been a full house since it started."

Stoney turned toward the door with a grunt. "You'll be the death of me one of these days, Fierro. See you in court."

"Stoney." Johnny moved closer to the bars, his voice soft. "Thanks."

Stoney paused and then gave a wave of his hand as he walked back into the outer room.

Johnny slumped down onto the cot. It was almost like his legs wouldn't hold him. So much had happened so fast. First finding out about Ford and where he fitted in, and then hearing about poor Dougie. And now Stoney showing up out of the blue with the saddlebags. He couldn't believe how fast his luck had changed. He'd thought it was all over. That Doe was finally going to win. The jury would find him guilty and that would be an end of it, he'd been all out of aces. But now the wind was shifting. Lady Luck had settled on his side of the table. And he had a ghost of a chance. Maybe more than a ghost. A chance to raise some doubts in the minds of that jury. Would Denning buy it? The judge was clever. Real sharp. But, surely Denning would have to think real hard about Fierro's trump card. Maybe it would turn out to be his ace in the hole. Thank God for Stoney. Seemed he made a habit of saving Fierro's hide. Johnny grinned. Yeah, the sheriff was a good friend. And he sure wasn't used to having friends but he seemed to be getting the knack of it now. He'd gotten himself a whole passel of them—Stoney, Guy, Ben, Delice, and maybe even Ford. Life sure was changing.

He never had brooded on the hand life had dealt him. A man simply had to play the cards the best way he could. He was happy that Guy had been dealt a better hand. Funny. He'd said that to Delice once. Least she'd be pleased that he'd sorted things out with Harvard. She'd warned him not to push Guy too hard. He grinned. Damn woman was always right. She was too smart by half. Especially for a woman. Back in Cimarron he'd had the sneaking feeling she'd figured he was guilty. But he'd also had the feeling she'd reckoned he must have had a damn good reason for committing murder. He shook his head.

Hell, it was like there were quite a few people trying to see the best in him. Who'd have thought it?

The heavy door from the outer office creaked open. "Sweet-foot's here." Ford's voice broke into his thoughts. "I'll send him through."

Johnny looked up with a grin. "Yeah, send him on in, Ford."

The court was a heaving mass of people. He'd have sworn it was even fuller than the previous sessions. Johnny gritted his teeth. It didn't take a genius to figure out why. They were cramming in because they knew that the jury would be having to consider its verdict. And on what had come out so far, everyone knew the jury would find him guilty. Dios, but people were sick. They just wanted to hear the old judge hand out the death sentence.

Johnny bit back a smile. Now that he had an ace up his sleeve, maybe he could upset the bloodthirsty assholes. Sure would be a pleasure. He glanced across at Sweetfoot. The kid had a spring in his step now and looked eager to be getting on with things. And who could blame him? He finally had something to work with. And Johnny had drilled him good. Told him exactly how to play it. What to say and when to say it. Told him what to say to everything Lincoln might throw at them. If the kid kept his cool, maybe, just maybe, Fierro would be sleeping in a proper bed before much longer. Preferably with some long-legged, green-eyed girl.

Guy was pushing his way through the crowd, the strain plain in his face. He looked older than before this had all kicked off. "Johnny, have you reconsidered your defense? You've got to do more. Say more. Things don't look good."

Johnny felt a pang of guilt as he looked at Guy's face. His brother never had that many lines before. And there were black shadows under Guy's eyes. He looked real rough. "It's okay,

Guy. Sweetfoot and me, we had a long session over lunch. We've got something lined up."

Guy gave him a look that said maybe he didn't believe that, but was kind of hoping it was true. "Well, I certainly hope so." Guy gave a start of surprise, and pointed across the room. "Good Lord, there's Stoney. I thought he'd gone back to Cimarron. He's the last person I would have expected here."

Johnny grinned. "Yeah. Last person I'd have expected too. But he came up trumps."

Guy shot him a sharp look. "Came up trumps? In what way?"

Johnny smiled, innocent like. "Oh, I just meant coming here to support me."

Guy opened his mouth to say something but Denning was in now, banging his hammer and Guy shot off to take the seat he'd bagged.

Lincoln was already seated at the lawyers' bench, looking smug, like he'd got everything sewn up. Boy, it was going to be fun wiping the smile off his face.

"Mr. Sweetfoot." Denning had his glasses balanced and was peering at Sweetfoot over the top of them.

"Your honor." He bounced to his feet. Yeah. Bounced. Boy was Sweetfoot eager. Couldn't wait for what was about to happen. Johnny grinned. He'd always reckoned that Sweetfoot was sharp and hungry. Maybe finally the kid would get a real chance to show the court what he was made of.

"Mr. Sweetfoot, I trust that you took advantage of the adjournment and have succeeded in talking some sense into your client. This is a matter of the utmost gravity. A man's life hangs in the balance. During the break for lunch I considered whether there would be any benefit in recalling Marshal Ford and putting him under oath, but I reluctantly came to the conclusion that it would be of little benefit to your client. His information is interesting, and perhaps the people of this town should be considering themselves fortunate that Mr. Doe didn't spend any longer enjoying their hospitality, but the fact remains that there is no evidence he can present. His statements tells us something of Mr. Doe's character and we may all speculate whether that would be a good reason for some unknown assailant to travel here to murder him. But, as far as relevant testimony goes, all we have is Mr. Jackson. It will be up to the jury to decide whether or not they are convinced by his testimony. So, Mr. Sweetfoot, where do we now stand? Is Mr. Sinclair going to take the stand?"

Sweetfoot gave a slight bow to the judge. "Your honor, I very much appreciate your taking so much trouble to consider Mr. Sinclair's position, but in fact, it will be unnecessary for Mr. Sinclair to take the stand."

Denning narrowed his eyes, and Lincoln, with the tips of his ears turning tomato red, swung to peer at Sweetfoot.

"Unnecessary?" Denning didn't sound like he believed that.

"Yes, your honor, unnecessary." Sweetfoot paused, and then glanced all around the court kind of like he was making sure he'd got everybody's attention. Not that there was much doubt of that. There was absolute silence while everyone seemed to stop breathing. It was almost like the world had stopped turning. Hell, it was so quiet you could have heard a flea fart. "Over the course of the lunch hour, new evidence has come to light which will prove, conclusively and beyond all reasonable doubt, that Mr. Sinclair is innocent of the charge against him."

CHAPTER TWENTY-SIX

Guy stifled a grunt at the sudden pain in his ribs. Mrs. Nixon was elbowing him excitedly, her face flushed and her eyes sparkling. "Mr. Sinclair, please do tell." She probably thought she was whispering but for heaven's sake, surely everybody must have heard her? "What's the new evidence? This is all very exciting. Our town is normally such a quiet little place. So, come on, what's happened during the lunch break?"

He struggled to smile politely. But yes, it was a very good question. What indeed? New evidence! During the adjournment! Damn Johnny! What the hell had he been up to now? And he'd left Guy out in the cold. Again. "Hush." He raised a finger to his lips, hoping she'd take the hint. But the courtroom was positively humming with whispered comments and asides. And Johnny, blast him, was sitting looking like the cat that had got the cream, with a hint of a smile playing around his mouth as though secretly amused by the effect Sweetfoot's pronouncement had made on everyone.

Guy gritted his teeth. One day he would take great delight in flooring Johnny. Even now his hand was positively itching to thump his brother. And his head felt as if it was spinning. So what the hell was this amazing new evidence anyway? And where had it come from? And why the hell hadn't Johnny told him? Out of the corner of his eye he could see Stoney leaning against the wall, a look of long-suffering resignation on his face.

Stoney!

Damn it! It had to be Stoney. Stoney, who'd supposedly gone back to Cimarron with his bad leg. What the hell had Stoney been up to?

"Order!" Judge Denning was banging the desk with his gavel, even as Guy remembered Johnny's damn saddlebags. And he remembered Stoney's caustic comment when Guy had said he'd buy Johnny some new saddlebags. *"And you think that'll make everything OK?"* Oh hell, it was obvious now. Stoney must have realized how important the bags were and gone searching for them.

"Order! I will have no more disturbances. Anyone who is unable to remain silent will be held in contempt. This is a court of law and shall be treated as such. I will not tolerate any further interruptions."

Denning polished his pince-nez and then settled back in his chair as the throng of people quieted down.

The judge waited until the court was silent. "Mr. Sweetfoot, you say that new evidence has come to light? I take it that you are asking the court to allow this new evidence to be admitted?"

Sweetfoot was back on his feet instantly. It was as though the young man had grown springs. He was brimming with enthusiasm, it was emanating from him in waves that surely everybody in the room must feel. "Yes, indeed, your honor. As you just pointed out, this is a case of the utmost gravity, and this new evidence sheds a very different light on the matter. As I said, it will prove beyond all reasonable doubt my client's innocence of the charge against him."

Guy could have sworn that Denning's lips twitched. It was as though the man was struggling to stop himself from smiling at Sweetfoot's unbridled enthusiasm. The lad bore an uncanny resemblance to a friendly and excitable puppy rushing everywhere wagging its tail.

Denning fingered his goatee beard as if deep in thought. He

nodded slowly. "Well, Mr. Sweetfoot, if this startling new evidence is that convincing, of course it must be presented to the court." His voice was grave but Guy was sure that there was something else there, definitely a hint of laughter as though he was entertained by the amazing transformation of the young clerk.

Even so, it was galling. Guy tried to refrain from grinding his teeth. But yes, damn it, it seemed that Sweetfoot and Stoney were both party to this amazing new evidence, while he was to be excluded. Didn't Johnny trust him? He pushed the thought away. He didn't want to believe that. And if it had only come to light during the luncheon adjournment when Stoney had turned up with the missing saddlebags, Johnny hadn't really had time to enlighten him. Maybe if he kept telling himself that, he might eventually believe it.

But knowing Johnny, and judging from the look on his brother's face, he was relishing springing this on everyone— Guy included. Johnny had been evasive and difficult from the very start of this whole ghastly business. And it didn't matter what Johnny said, Guy was convinced that his brother was guilty. He bit his lip. It hurt that Johnny hadn't been honest with him although at least Johnny had finally admitted that there was something in those damn saddlebags that could be useful in the trial. But he hadn't admitted killing Doe. No, he'd very cleverly evaded that issue.

Guy chewed on his thumb as he considered Johnny's behavior over the past few days. If he thought about it rationally, Johnny couldn't possibly admit his guilt to anybody without compromising himself and the person he confessed to. No, Johnny really had no choice but to keep professing his innocence. To keep lying. Certainly from what Ford had told the court, Doe didn't sound as though he was any great loss to anybody. But the big question was had Johnny been one of his victims? The idea of

Johnny being treated in that way was sickening. What was it Johnny had said when Guy had asked him if Doe had ever touched him? That Doe had never laid a finger on him. Which meant one of two things: that Johnny had never had any dealings with Doe, or that Johnny had indeed been one of the victims abused while Doe looked on. Guy shut his eyes briefly, trying to quell the feeling of nausea. God only knew what Johnny had suffered at the hands of brutal men. And he'd been a child when he was thrown in prison . . .

"So, Mr. Sweetfoot, perhaps you would be so kind as to share this startling new information with us all." Denning leaned back in his chair and folded his arms.

Sweetfoot nodded his head vigorously. "Yes, of course, your honor, it will be my very great pleasure to do so."

"Oh I have absolutely no doubt of that, Mr. Sweetfoot." Denning sounded very dry.

The only sound in the room was the rustling of the papers that Sweetfoot adjusted in front of him. It was as though everybody was holding their breaths.

Sweetfoot cleared his throat. "Since the very outset of this trial, I have been at great pains to point out that Mr. Sinclair is now a respectable rancher, living an upright and law-abiding life. And this is indeed the case. But perhaps now is the time to dwell on Mr. Sinclair's past. As my learned colleague went to so much trouble to point out"—Sweetfoot paused and made a slight bow to Lincoln—"the fact of the matter is that Mr. Sinclair has not always led a respectable life. For several years he was better known as the notorious Johnny Fierro. His speed and deadly accuracy were legendary. The tales of Mr. Fierro's prowess with a gun spread far and wide."

Sweetfoot paused again, glancing across at Johnny who was leaning back in his seat, apparently totally at ease. "Yes, there sitting in front of you, gentlemen of the jury, is the most infamous gunfighter of them all." Sweetfoot pointed dramatically to Johnny whose face was impassive. "Take a good look at him because I doubt that any of you will ever again get the opportunity to see such a notorious character at such close quarters."

Sweetfoot moved his papers around again. Damn it, would the kid never get to the point? Guy huffed out a sigh. The kid certainly had the entire room hanging on his every word. And now there seemed to be the faintest suggestion of yet another smile playing around Johnny's mouth. Guy shook his head. There was no doubt in his mind about who was pulling the strings in this performance. But what the hell was the kid going to conjure up to get Johnny off the hook? What on earth was this mysterious item from Johnny's saddlebag? It was obvious now that Stoney must have gone looking for the bags instead of returning to Cimarron. Guy remembered all too vividly now Johnny's insistence before they started the journey to Utah that Guy should fetch the bags for him. What was it he'd said? That he'd need them for the journey and he'd "sure as hell need them for the trip back." Guy ground his teeth. He'd be prepared to bet his share of the ranch that Johnny had been prepared for the possibility of this trial and kept whatever it was in those damn bags, possibly for a very long time.

Sweetfoot cleared his throat, and then took a sip of water, presumably to give everyone in the courtroom a chance to take a good long look at the *notorious character*. "And, as I'm sure everybody here can appreciate, people always pay lots of attention to Mr. Fierro. When Johnny Fierro rode into any town people noticed. He would be the sole topic of excited conversations from the saloons to the town sewing circles. In fact, I would go so far as to suggest that people would travel in from outlying settlements just to get a glimpse of Mr. Fierro. And human nature being what it is, part of his mystique, the reason people want to see him, is that they always hope they will see him in action."

Denning sighed. A long deep sigh and rapped his fingers on the desk. "Mr. Sweetfoot, is there a point to this lengthy discourse and if so, are you ever going to come to it?"

Sweetfoot beamed. "Indeed there is a point, your honor, and I am coming to that."

"Well, I'm very glad to hear it. Perhaps you could speed it up and put us all out of our misery."

Sweetfoot inclined his head. "Mr. Fierro's reputation being what it is, there is always somebody wanting to test him. Young guns who want to prove they're faster to the draw. And although Mr. Fierro usually tries to talk them out of their lust for a gunfight, he sometimes has no option but to defend himself."

Denning sighed. "How very trying for Mr. Fierro." The judge's tone was heavily laden with sarcasm.

Sweetfoot ignored it. Instead he bowed slightly to Denning. "It is very trying for him indeed. I'm so glad that your honor appreciates that. But although Mr. Fierro finds such situations most vexatious, he is not above vanity. He prides himself on the speed of his draw and his precision. By his own admission he was good at his trade. When he was working as a gunfighter he was a very expensive gun to hire. And a very vain one."

Guy frowned. Where the hell was Sweetfoot going with this? Because although he'd agree that Johnny was very vain when it came to women, he was never boastful about his prowess with a gun. In fact, quite the contrary. Johnny was matter of fact about it. It was just a part of him and certainly something he never bragged about. And that made Sweetfoot's claim very puzzling.

Sweetfoot paused, and adjusted his papers. "And so great is Mr. Fierro's vanity that one of his greatest pleasures is reading about himself and his exploits. As many of you must know, he is the hero of many a dime novel."

Reading about himself and his exploits? Guy tried to suppress a snort. Well, that was hogwash! Johnny hated dime novels. In fact it would be hard to find anyone more scathing about them. Johnny always said they were a "load of fucking crap" and he had been particularly rude when he'd once come across Guy reading one that featured Johnny as the hero. Guy had later found the charred remains of the book smoldering in the hearth.

"He also loves to read of his exploits as they are reported by the gentlemen of the press. And Mr. Fierro liked to collect such articles if they alluded to him. He amassed a veritable collection of press clippings." Sweetfoot paused and cleared his throat. Then he took another sip of water from the glass on the table. "And it is Mr. Fierro's vanity which shall prove to be his salvation." Sweetfoot bent forward and with a great flourish produced a slip of paper from the pile of documents and books in front of him.

"I have here, a newspaper cutting from a weekly newspaper which is published in Tubac, in Arizona. It is dated July 17, 1866. I will read this to the court."

"I rather thought you might." Denning leaned back in his chair, his arms folded.

Sweetfoot beamed and held the clipping in front of him, almost like a trophy, before starting to read aloud. "Our readers will already be aware of the lamentable events of Saturday, July 14. There was much excitement among the more undesirable element of our town at the news that the notorious gunfighter Johnny Fierro had ridden in the previous day. His arrival attracted the attention of a number of hands from the Bar C ranch. These same young men will already be known to many for spending a disreputable amount of time in the town's saloons at the weekends. Two of their number, W. McKinley and J. Adams, had over-imbibed in the Gold Strike Saloon and endeavored to start a fistfight with Fierro. The unfortunate incident degenerated into a brawl and McKinley and Adams challenged Fierro to a gunfight.

"The three men faced each other in the street and lively fire commenced. When the smoke cleared McKinley and Adams both lay dead. Fierro returned unharmed to the bar where he remained until leaving town on Monday morning."

Sweetfoot carefully laid the clipping back down and then pointed dramatically at Johnny. "I would ask your honor to accept my submission that my client, Mr. John Sinclair, couldn't possibly have been here in our town on that fateful Saturday because he was, in fact, engaged in a gunfight in Tubac, Arizona, as this newspaper cutting ably demonstrates. I put it to this court that the unfortunate Mr. Doe was killed by an unknown left-handed gunman. We have been at pains to point out during this trial that Mr. Sinclair is right-handed. We have also pointed out on numerous occasions that Mr. Jackson has poor hearing. We believe that Mr. Jackson misheard the name given by the assailant on that dreadful day. But one thing is certain beyond all doubt, that assailant was not my client. He has a demonstrable alibi for the crime. And therefore I would ask that the charge against Mr. Sinclair be dismissed."

Everybody started talking as Sweetfoot sat down and had another drink of water. Guy felt as though his head was spinning. This was just too incredible. Surely the judge would have to free Johnny now? And all because of a newspaper cutting. Newspapers . . . Guy bowed his head, frowning. There was something about all of this that was wrong, if only he could figure out what it was. There was something niggling away at the back of his mind, some memory just out of reach. Damn it. If only he could remember. Something to do with newspapers. Something Johnny had said.

"May I see this newspaper clipping, Mr. Sweetfoot?" Denning held his hand out for the slip of paper. He adjusted his pince-nez and read it carefully before handing it across to Lincoln. Denning pursed his lips, and sighed softly. "This was a most fortuitous discovery for your client, Mr. Sweetfoot."

Sweetfoot sprang to his feet. "It was indeed, your honor. As I said earlier, Mr. Fierro is a very vain man and he carried this and other cuttings in his saddlebags. These were mislaid on the journey here when the stagecoach crashed, but a friend of his, who is himself a sheriff, returned to search for the bags and only arrived with them today. Mr. Fierro was checking that his belongings were all there when he came across this cutting. It was a happy chance indeed."

"Indeed." Denning sounded very dry.

Out of the corner of his eye, Guy noticed Carter hurrying from the courtroom. What was he so fired up about? Surely the man would wait to hear whatever happened next? Especially now that according to the newspaper clipping Johnny had been in Tubac. And even as the thought flitted into Guy's mind, so did the memory. Hell, he could even hear Johnny saying it. It had been the night when he and Johnny had first ridden into town together. They'd visited the bordello, and upon their return Johnny had discovered Guthrie reading the Pinkerton report. And Johnny and Guthrie had argued and Johnny had stormed up to bed. But later, Guy had gone to talk to Johnny about the report and now the conversation came flooding back.

"Tell you one thing, I bet there's a whole lotta shit in that report. Never fails to amaze me how I can be in two places at once. You know, there I am thinking I'm in Sonora but I see something in the paper saying I'm in Abilene or Tucson. Hell, sometimes I'm in all three. I guess I just got real talent for spreading myself around."

That had to be it! Johnny had seen that newspaper report and been shrewd enough to realize it could be used as an alibi and save his life. Because if there was one thing of which Guy was certain, Johnny had killed Doe. He had been here, in this small town, and most definitely had not been in Tubac that fateful day. God, but Johnny was devious! Yes, devious, manipulative, and very clever.

"Mr. Lincoln, I thank you for your presentation of the facts in this case as you understood them, but this throws an entirely different light on the matter. In the light of this latest evidence, Mr. Sweetfoot," Denning paused to polish his pince-nez, "I believe that I must uphold your submission and dismiss the charge against Mr. Sinclair. It would appear to exonerate him. He is released from the custody of the court."

An excited clamor erupted all over the room. Sweetfoot rushed to shake hands with Johnny before remembering to shake Lincoln by the hand, which he did in a peremptory fashion before turning back to shake Johnny's cuffed hand again.

Mrs. Nixon started chattering loudly to the person sitting on her other side, her hands waving as fast as she talked. Guy stood and squeezed past her to make his way over to Johnny; as he did so, he collided with the veiled woman who was hurrying, with head down, toward the door. He uttered an apology, but he might not have spoken for all the attention she paid to him. He battled on through the throng to Johnny who was still having one of his cuffed hands pumped up and down by a very excited Sweetfoot.

"We did it. We did it! And my first ever case." Sweetfoot's face was flushed with pleasure. "We did it."

Johnny winced as he finally managed to wrench his hand out of Sweetfoot's grasp. "Yeah. You did real good, Sweetfoot. Not bad at all for a greenhorn. Be a real feather in your cap when you join that Eastern firm."

Sweetfoot's smile was so broad, Guy half-expected the young man's face to split in half.

"It really will, won't it? Oh my, I can't believe it, we did it.

Oh my! And to think that only this morning I really thought that we were going to lose . . ."

Johnny shrugged. "Yeah, well, we got lucky, I reckon. Good old Stoney came through. So, you'd best get me your bill, Sweetfoot." Johnny jerked his thumb toward Guy. "He'll pay it."

Guy sighed. "I knew I was here for something."

Johnny flashed him a quick grin. "Yeah, I know how you like to feel useful, Harvard. And so far on this trip you ain't had much to do. So just pay the man, will you?"

Guy raised an eyebrow. "It's so nice to know I can finally be of some use to you. And when I've paid him, you and I are going to have a little talk. Brother."

CHAPTER TWENTY-SEVEN

He'd done it. He'd got away with it. Madre de Dios! He'd really done it!

Guy was saying something in his ear. Something about needing to have a talk. What the hell did they have to talk about that was so all-fired important? And Sweetfoot looked like a rooster in a henhouse, and Stoney was yacking away in his other ear. And everybody in the damn room was talking at once so he couldn't tell one conversation from another. And he felt like everything was closing in on top of him and he was drowning. Shit! He needed some air. He needed to get out of this courtroom and get the hell away from this mass of people. He hated crowds. And he hated them even more when he wasn't wearing his gun. He needed his gun. Hell, any gun would do. Was there a gunsmith in this town? Yeah, that was the answer. Buy a gun and then get the hell out. Out of this town and out of fucking Utah. Before the judge could change his mind.

He tried to move away but Guy pulled him back, saying something about getting rid of the cuffs. He stared down at his hands—couldn't fire a gun with cuffs on. That was it, get rid of the cuffs and then go buy a gun.

Ford was fumbling with the key and then, with a loud click, the cuffs were gone. He felt lighter without their dead weight pulling on his arms. He rubbed at his wrists and Sweetfoot grabbed his hand and started shaking it all over again. Johnny jerked back from the contact. He needed to get outside. He needed air. Needed to breathe in and out. Needed to feel free again. And feel the comforting weight of a gun on his hip.

He stumbled toward the doorway where he collided with the woman in the veil who was also struggling to fight her way through the crowd. He muttered an apology as he pushed past her. And people were talking at him but he shut out the noise. Just wanted some air. Hell, he couldn't ever remember losing control like this before. Never. But it was over. It was finally over. It was crazy. For years now he'd spent nights tossing and turning, sweating and fretting, fearful that someone would arrest him for this particular sin. Did this really mean it was over? Was it done with now? Maybe he could finally move on. Unless the judge changed his mind.

The cold air made him gasp as he stepped outside. It was snowing heavily, blowing in all directions, and it burned his face and stung his eyes but he didn't care. There were no walls or bars out here. No clanging cell doors. He lifted his face up and sucked in deep breaths. Deep breaths of free air. Felt like he couldn't get enough of it. That there wasn't enough air in the world to fill his lungs. The snow was blowing onto his neck but it felt real good. He'd escaped the noose and that would have felt a hell of a lot worse around his neck. Dios. He was free. He was fucking free. Damn but that felt good.

"Are you all right?" Guy was by his side. Worry lines creased between his eyes.

"Yeah. Course I'm all right." Johnny pulled his shoulders back. Maybe nobody would notice that his breathing was harsher than usual. Or hear that his heart was thumping. "Just don't like crowds is all."

He scanned the people pouring out of the courtroom, all gawking at him. How the hell had they all managed to fit in there? He tugged at Guy's arm. "Come on, let's get out of here, Harvard. Is there some place quiet we can go? I want to get away from all these fucking people."

His brother nodded. "Good idea. We'll go to my room. You can wait there while I go and pay Sweetfoot."

Johnny followed Guy toward the hotel. But he couldn't relax and walk normal. Tension throbbed through his body, because without a gun he felt like he was naked. He had to get hold of a gun. Right now anyone could take him out. There could be somebody waiting in the shadows, leveling a gun at him . . .

Ford and Stoney had hurried ahead, and were already at the hotel, standing under the overhanging eaves, keeping out of the swirling snow. It reminded him of the way a woman's dress would twirl around when she danced.

Ford shot him a piercing look as they drew closer, the sort of look that saw right inside a man. "You OK, Fierro? You don't look too good."

Madre de Dios! What was wrong with everybody, first Guy telling him he didn't look good, and now Ford? He resisted the urge to snap at the marshal. Instead, Johnny shrugged. "Damn cold, that's all. How the hell do you stand living here? Freezing cold in the winter and hot enough to fry eggs in the summer." Johnny paused, biting his lip. "So I'm told."

Stoney and Ford exchanged looks, the sort that said they could see right through him, and Stoney grunted like he was irritated and grabbed Johnny's arm. "Just get the hell inside, Fierro."

A wall of heat hit him as Stoney pushed open the big heavy door leading into the hotel and hustled him inside. Glancing around, Johnny looked longingly at a group of battered old leather chairs by the hearth, where a fire blazed away, the flames licking up the chimney. It would be good to stretch himself out and let the fire heat his bones.

"Come on, I've got something for you upstairs. A surprise." Guy looked kind of pleased with himself. He was smirking like he'd won some contest. Johnny sighed and followed him up the broad staircase. The hotel was kind of grand for such a small town. Some sort of sparkling glass thing covered in candles hung from the ceiling. It must have been the devil to light, it was so damned big.

Guy opened the door to a room at the end of the corridor. He grinned at Johnny, and gave a sweeping bow as he waved Johnny into the room. "I told you the room was really something!"

"Holy shit!" Johnny put his hand across his eyes, pretending he was dazzled. Everything was pink. Every single damn thing. It was enough to put a man off his dinner. "It's like a bordello, Harvard."

"Well, you should feel right at home then." Guy was smirking.

There was a vast pink bed and Johnny threw himself down on it, closing his eyes as he sank into the feathery embrace. It would be good to sleep for a week. A year. He opened one eye and grinned at Guy. "You sure this ain't a bordello?"

"Sadly not. There isn't one in the whole town. Maybe they're strict about things like that in Utah. So, you'll have to wait until we get home." Guy was searching in a drawer as he spoke. "I told you I have a surprise for you. And you'd damn well better be grateful." Guy took out a package, wrapped in a soft cloth. The cloth looked oddly familiar . . . It couldn't be, could it?

He sat up slowly, hardly daring to hope. His heart seemed to have come up to choke him. He held his hand out for the package. A tidal wave of relief washed over him. It was. It really was. His gun belt. His gun. His fighting gun. Guy had brought them all this way, because he believed in Johnny. Even after the way Fierro had treated him back at Cimarron, Guy had still had faith. The words caught in his throat. He didn't know what to say or how to say it. Instead, he ran his fingers over the well-worn, supple holster. And the gun. His gun. Just the feel of it in his hand calmed his rapidly beating heart. He shut his eyes briefly, relishing the touch of the cold metal and the way the wooden handle fitted his hand. All this time it had been like a part of him was missing. Now he felt whole again.

He stood and fixed the gun belt around his hips. Real tight. And then he pulled it a notch tighter still. Then he carefully loaded the gun. And all the while he knew Guy was watching him. Johnny looked up and met Guy's eyes for a beat before speaking real soft, struggling for the right words. "Thanks, Guy. You couldn't have brought anything better."

Guy shrugged before flashing him a sudden smile. "I'll tell you one thing, I wished I'd brought the other gun. I only brushed a finger against the trigger of this one, and the damn thing went off. It scared the living daylights out of me."

Johnny bit back a laugh. "Kind of a hair trigger. It does go off too easy if you don't know how to handle it."

"And you certainly know how to handle it." There was something in Guy's tone. Cooler now.

Johnny spun it in his hand a couple of times. Making sure the action felt real smooth before slipping it back into the holster. "Yeah, Guy." He spoke soft again. "I know how to handle it. I thought you were OK with that."

Guy stood with his head bowed, like he was thinking real hard. He looked up. But Johnny couldn't read his expression. Guy opened his mouth to say something, and then shut it again. Instead, he turned suddenly toward the door. "I'll go and pay young Sweetfoot. As you say, I have to serve some purpose, particularly after traveling all this way."

It was his tone. Johnny felt a pang of guilt. "I'm real grateful for the gun . . ." But Guy had gone, the door slamming shut behind him.

Johnny sank back down onto the bed. Hell, what had he done

wrong now? Why was life so damn tricky? And why did he always mess up? Because he reckoned that Guy's tone said Fierro had messed up. He was useless at handling people—that was the trouble. Never knew what to say and he always put his foot in it. And it seemed he'd done it again. And he didn't even know what he'd done or said that was wrong. He'd only thanked Guy for bringing the gun.

He thumped his fist into the pillow. But it didn't make him feel any better. What the hell did Guy want from him? Because whatever it was, he didn't think he could give any more. And he was so fucking tired. Worn out. No. He just didn't have any more to give.

He hauled himself up. Right now he just wanted to get out of Utah. But he wasn't leaving without his gold nugget. He had a score to settle with Carter. And his head still ached from where Carter had thrown him back against the rock. So, two scores to settle. And Guy would have to put up with it.

The door creaked open as Guy came back in. "I saw Sweetfoot downstairs. Your debts are paid."

It was still there. That tone of voice. What the hell was Harvard's problem? Johnny bit his lip. Maybe it would be best to ignore it. Not rise to it. He had other, more pressing things to deal with. Like Carter.

He glanced at Guy's bags by the door. "So, we can go? You all ready? Because I want to get the hell out of here now."

Guy narrowed his eyes. His jaw looked kind of set. "All in good time. I think I'd like a few answers first."

What was it with Guy? Why did he always want to talk about everything? Some things, hell most things, were best left unsaid. But Guy never knew when to leave well enough alone. "Answers to what?" He knew he sounded aggressive but hell, why now? Why did they have to fucking talk now when all he wanted to do was get away from this town? Or get away as soon as he'd dealt with Carter.

"Like how long you've been carrying that newspaper cutting around?"

Johnny rubbed his chin while he tried to figure out what to say. Then he shrugged. "What the hell does it matter, Guy? I don't know how long I've had it. I came across it one day. Thought I'd keep it is all."

"Came across it?" Guy sure sounded like he didn't think much of that answer. "You just happened to come across it. Presumably that was seconds before you realized how it could provide an alibi for when you killed Doe."

Johnny shut his eyes briefly. Bit his lip hard. Because otherwise he might just bite Guy's head off instead. And he didn't want to fight. Not after everything they'd gone through. But if Guy thought Fierro was suddenly going to roll right over and confess everything, well, he could think again. "I never said I killed Doe. The cutting says I was in Tubac in a gunfight. Now, are you done, Guy? Can we go?"

Guy shook his head. "No, we can't go. And no, I'm not done. Not by a long shot. You see, I remember a conversation I had with you once. Not long after you first arrived at the ranch. You told me that you'd often seen reports of you being in places when in fact you were somewhere else. And I'm prepared to bet that's exactly what happened here, isn't it?"

Johnny smiled, real easy, like Guy's words meant nothing. Whatever happened, he mustn't rise to Guy's words. And he really didn't want to butt heads with him either. He shrugged. "It's happened sometimes, but I never said that was the case here. Now are you ready—"

"Damn it, Johnny!" The vein was pulsing in the side of Guy's head as he slammed his fist down on the table. "Just once. Just once, damn you, give me a straight answer when I ask you a question. I have had as much as I can take of your prevarication and your evasions. You never answer a question. Never. And I am sick to death of it."

It was rising now. That dull dry heat of rage. Tried to keep a lid on it but shit . . . Johnny lunged forward, his fists clenched by his sides. "What is it? What the fuck is it you want from me, Guy? You want me to stand here and tell you how many men I've killed? Is that it? You want me to tell you how sorry I am for all the things I've ever done wrong? Well, yeah, I've done lots of things I regret. A shit load of things I regret. And I've done things I won't ever regret. But I sure as hell ain't telling you about them. My sins are my business. Mine. God's business. The devil's business. But they're sure as hell not yours." His breathing was coming in short bursts. "So get off my back, Guy. I ain't got nothing to say about it."

Guy swallowed real hard. "Were you one of Doe's victims?"

He couldn't speak. Even if he'd known what to say. His mind felt like it was reeling, tossed one way and another and his thoughts wouldn't come straight. And he had to fight the desire to puke all over the floor and fall to his knees. Of all the questions for his brother to ask! And he didn't want to lie to Guy. But hell. Why now? Why did Guy have to do this now? He had no right. No damn right to know anything. Johnny took another step closer, so his face was just inches from his brother's. "I told you before. He never touched me." He didn't recognize his own voice. It sounded like a snake hissing.

Guy didn't flinch away, just carried on looking right at him. Like he was trying to look into Fierro's soul. "From what Ford said, Doe didn't touch any of his victims. He left that to others."

The bile was rising in his throat, choking him, but he swallowed it back down. He swung away. "I don't know nothing about it. Just leave it, Harvard. Leave it alone."

He met Guy's eyes briefly before looking quickly away.

Couldn't bear to see the expression in his eyes. Pity. They were full of pity. Fucking pity. Didn't want that from no one. And he sure as hell didn't want it from Guy. He'd expected disgust but not pity.

Maybe Harvard hadn't figured it? Maybe he hadn't guessed what happened to Doe's victims? Maybe he thought that the prisoners had just beat up on him. Yeah. That must be it. Guy must think that he'd been knocked around. That would explain the pity. Thinking of Johnny as a kid being beaten up. Yeah. That made sense. Because if he'd figured out what had really happened to Johnny there would have been disgust.

Dios. If only it had just been them beating him up. If it had only been that clean. He could take any amount of beatings. Those only left scars on the outside. They healed. It was the scars on the inside that never went away.

"You can tell me about it, Johnny. It's OK." And Guy's eyes were still sad, the pity overflowing.

Johnny looked at him, letting no expression show. "Let's get moving. But before we leave town, I need to find Carter."

Guy shook his head, kind of like he knew he was beaten. Fierro had won the battle. And Guy knew it.

Guy huffed out a sigh. "Why do you need to find Carter?"

Johnny smiled, but not like he meant it. "Because Carter and me have unfinished business. He took something of mine. And I want it back."

Guy frowned. "Unfinished business? I don't like the sound of that. And surely whatever he's got of yours can't be that important?"

"It is." Johnny spoke softly. "And he ain't keeping it." He turned and hurried out of the door, calling back over his shoulder. "I'll see you in the lobby. Ford told me where Carter lives. I won't be long."

He took the stairs two at a time. Needed to get away from

Guy. Away from his questions and his fucking pity. And hell, he could take all his frustrations out on Carter. Yeah. Take it out on Carter. He breathed in deeply and tried to focus on Carter. Focus on revenge. Because revenge had such a sweet taste. Like honey on peaches. He paused at the bottom of the stairs and felt a surge of excitement. He was going to enjoy getting even. Glancing across the lobby he spotted Ford talking to Sweetfoot. Looked like they were getting on well, jawing away together and far too busy to notice Fierro slipping out. But Stoney spotted him. Damn it, Stoney didn't miss a trick. And it looked like he wanted a word because the sheriff raised a hand and hurried across toward him. Johnny bit back a laugh as Stoney, in his haste, collided with the woman in the veil who was heading to the reception desk like she was about to check out. She went flying and Stoney landed on top of her. Seemed Lady Luck was still sitting at Fierro's side of the table because now nobody was paying him any mind at all.

He slipped through the door and headed out into the biting wind and snow. The icy blast almost knocked the breath from him. He took another breath and tried to concentrate on the job in hand. He had a pretty good idea of where he was headed. Ford had said Carter lived on the outskirts of the town, the last house heading east. Oh boy. He could feel the old familiar rush of the blood surging through his body. And it felt so good. Yeah, he was going to enjoy getting even.

He pulled his collar up. Then he pushed his hat down low to keep the driving snow out of his face, and to avoid the gaze of the few people still milling around who didn't seem to have any place better to be. Hopefully, he could catch up with Carter before the piece of shit skipped town. He'd sure had the look of a man worried about his own skin when he'd shot out of the courtroom earlier.

Johnny smiled. Yeah, Carter had been almost shitting himself when he realized that Fierro was about to walk. Well, one way or the other, Fierro was about to get even. Just like he'd promised Carter he would. And Fierro always kept his promises.

He knew the house as soon as he saw it. Although house was too grand a name. It was more of a shack. A rundown, scruffy place. There were broken hinges on the windows and the paint was cracked and peeling. It was the home of someone who didn't give a damn. Someone like Carter.

He felt good now. Felt whole again, with the weight of the gun resting against his thigh, and his gun belt tight enough to crush his guts. If he'd only had a chance to clean the gun, life would be pretty much perfect.

The shack looked deserted. Maybe he was too late to catch up with Carter here. Maybe Carter had already vamoosed and he'd have to track him. And yet . . . Maybe not. There was something. Something that was screaming at him that maybe the shack wasn't deserted. The hairs on his neck were standing on end. And he could smell something—the faintest trace of fear. He smelt it often enough to recognize it. There was someone in the shack. Someone who was afraid. He smiled. Didn't look like he'd have to track Carter after all.

He moved quickly into the shadow of the ramshackle porch and edged sideways to glance through the grubby glass window. There was a battered old table and a couple of chairs. And a doorway leading to another room. And he was certain there was someone in there.

Moving slow and careful he opened the door and slipped into the room, easing his gun from the holster. Wasn't taking any chances on Carter getting the drop on him.

There was a blur of movement from the doorway and he brought his gun up. The realization that his gun had jammed dawned even as something struck his head and knocked him off his feet. And everything spun around as he crashed to the floor.

Chapter Twenty-Eight

Silver stars. There were silver stars everywhere. They were dancing all over the place. And they sure as hell weren't badges on
Stoney's chest. These were smaller and filling his eyes, and it
didn't matter where he looked because they were all he could
see. He blinked hard, hoping to shut them out. And if wasn't
enough seeing stars, his damned ears were buzzing too.

Madre de Dios. How many knocks to his head could a man
take? Leastways the silver stars were sorta fading a bit now.

Mierda!

All things considered he'd rather have the stars than what he
was looking at right now. Which was straight up the barrel of a
fucking shotgun. With Carter's ugly face at the end of it. No
wonder his head was hurting if Carter had whacked him with
that.

And why the hell had his gun jammed? It had never jammed
before. Harvard. He'd had the gun last. Had to be Harvard's
fault. The man wasn't safe to be let out.

"You'd better start saying your prayers, Fierro."

Dios, but Carter was damned ugly. Johnny groped around,
fumbling for his gun even as Carter jammed the shotgun hard
into his chest. Carter laughed. "Looking for your gun, Fierro?
Tough! It ain't anywhere close, I kicked it to the other side of
the room. You're all out of aces. And I finally got you right
where you belong. At the end of my gun. Ain't such a hotshot
now, are you?"

Johnny scoffed. "You and me, we got a score to settle, Carter. How about you fight it out with me like a man? No guns. Just fists. Or ain't you any sort of man at all?" Shit, Fierro. That wasn't the smartest thing to say. Seeing as how Carter had a gun stuck in Fierro's chest.

Carter smiled, but it didn't reach his eyes. "You know what? I think I'll turn that offer down. I got me a gun and I reckon that gives me the upper hand. Ain't nobody coming to rescue you this time, Fierro."

Man had a point. Nobody was coming looking for him this time. It was funny really that it should end like this. Sitting on the floor looking along the barrel of a fucking shotgun. That would blow a hell of a big hole in a man. Big enough for an eagle to nest in. He'd rather go down fighting. But with that gun sticking in him, he sure wasn't going to be fighting for long. He bit back a snort of laughter. It had its funny side. He'd escaped the noose in Mexico. Escaped the noose here in Utah. Survived God only knew how many damn gunfights. And he was going to be sent to hell by some crazy coot of a deputy sheriff.

"Looks like you're holding all the trump cards, Carter. So, you just going to kill me in cold blood? That'll make you a murderer." Play for time, Fierro. Play for time.

"I don't reckon so. I'll just say you broke in here and I killed you in self-defense. Ain't nobody going to say different." Carter's smile spread. His finger was on the trigger now. Pulling the trigger back.

Fuck.

He knew he'd got no chance. But what the hell, he'd die trying. Johnny threw himself to one side as the explosion shook the small shack.

There was no pain. No pain at all. Surely the stupid bastard couldn't have missed?

And then he saw Carter. He was slumped at an odd angle with his eyes wide open. And blood was oozing from a hole in the side of his head.

What the hell—

"Is he dead?"

Johnny swung around at the familiar voice. His heart lurched as he saw Guy leaning against the doorway, ashen faced, his arm hanging limp against his side and a gun still hitched on his fingers. Even as Johnny watched, the gun dropped from his brother's hand, but Guy kept right on staring at Carter. "Is he dead?"

"Yeah." Johnny spoke softly. "He's dead."

"Are you . . . are you sure? Maybe he's just injured—"

Johnny glanced down at Carter. "No. He's dead, Guy. You got him right in the head. That tends to be pretty final."

"Oh my God." Guy swallowed hard. "I . . . I've never killed someone up close before . . ."

Johnny frowned. What the hell should he say to his brother? Dios, but Guy looked rough. Johnny scrambled to his feet and he shook Guy's shoulder. "Hey! You were in the army. You fought in the war. You must have killed lots of men then. And when Wallace's men attacked, you killed then."

Guy just shook his head, licking his lips before raising wild eyes to look at Johnny. "Different. That was different. That was war. This . . . this was—"

"War too, Guy. You did what you had to do then, and you did what you had to do now. No different."

Guy shook his head, but firmer this time. "No. You're wrong. It is different. You told me that yourself once. In war the law's on the soldier's side. But this? I didn't mean to kill him. I just wanted to stop him. I had to stop him. He was going to kill you." Guy's face was still pale.

Johnny chewed his lip. If only he was better with words. He

301

never could think of the right thing to say. Could hardly tell Guy that killing got a little easier after the first one. That sure wouldn't help none. And yet he could hardly believe this. Guy had killed a man to save *him*. Perhaps Johnny should focus on that—it might help Guy to feel better. Yeah. That would be best. "Like you said, Guy, he was gonna kill me. You saved my life." He aimed a gentle punch at Guy's arm.

Guy shook his head, and still looked kind of numb. "I didn't mean to kill him. I intended to just wound him, but I had to stop him." His eyes were wide with fear. "Will they hang me? Will they?"

The memories came flooding back. Johnny flinched, almost like Guy had struck him. Even now, after all these years, he could remember the taste of fear when his mother died. How scared he'd been then that they'd hang him.

He shut his eyes tight, trying to block out the picture that always came back to haunt him. He swallowed hard. "No, Guy, they won't hang you. You ain't done nothing wrong. He was going to kill me, you shot him. You ain't broke no laws. It'll be fine, you'll see. They'll believe you, I promise." He patted Guy clumsily on the shoulder. Knew he wasn't much good at this sort of stuff. "Honest. It'll be OK." He felt a stab of concern. Guy was still as white as death, shocked. His brother wasn't used to killing. Not like Fierro. "It'll be fine. Trust me." He gave Guy another pat on the shoulder. Tried to think of something else to say. Anything. He couldn't keep patting Guy on the shoulder—he'd wear a dent in it.

"What if they don't believe me?" Guy's voice was flat.

Johnny frowned and then smiled. "We'll tell 'em I shot him. They'd believe that."

Guy gave him the ghost of a smile. Not a big smile, but at least it was an attempt. "I think we'll stick with the truth, I think it's for the best." Guy paused, chewing on his lip. "He really was going to shoot you. I had to stop him. I'd followed you. I was worried you'd get into a fight with him, and you'd end up back in jail."

Johnny sighed. "I was planning on getting in a fight with him, Guy."

Guy held his gaze. "What sort of fight?"

Johnny bowed his head. Guy deserved some honesty, 'specially after saving Fierro's life. "Any kind of fight, Guy. But, I reckon if I'm being honest, I was hoping he'd draw on me. He was a piece of shit. And he stole something from me. And I guess I was mad about that. He'd tried to steal it before."

There were deep frown lines between Guy's eyes. "What was this thing that was so important?"

Johnny moved over to Carter and rifled through the man's pockets before turning back toward Guy. "This." He held up the big gold nugget. "I found it years ago. I was fooling around and thought I'd have a go at panning for gold. I never expected to find anything. But I did. I could scarce believe it when I found this. And I've carried it ever since."

Guy was still frowning. "But, surely a piece of gold isn't worth killing for?" He sounded puzzled. But leastways it had taken Guy's mind off the fact that he'd killed Carter. He wasn't brooding on that no more. No. He was thinking that Fierro would have killed a man over a gold nugget. Still, it was better Guy should be thinking like that than fretting over Carter.

Guy tilted his head. "I mean, it can't be worth killing over. You've got money now. You don't need that gold nugget."

Johnny ran his fingers through his hair. How could he explain it? His brother really couldn't understand what that gold had meant. He sighed. "Thing is, Guy, you've pretty much always had everything you need. You lived in a big house, you had food on the table. A bed to sleep in and warmth when it was cold outside. I was raised dirt poor." Dirt poor. That was putting it nice. "I never had nothing. And finding that gold, well, it might only be one nugget, but to me it was like finding a crock of gold at the end of a rainbow. I know it ain't worth a lot of money, but I found it fair and square. It's clean. Didn't kill nobody to earn it. It's solid, it's real and it's honest. And it's mine." He paused again. He'd gone this far and Guy was looking at him real serious. And hell, Guy had killed Carter, so Johnny owed him. Johnny sucked in a breath. "And, I always told myself that if I ever get a woman of my own, I'm gonna make her a ring from this." The words came out in a rush, and he paused, half-expecting Guy to laugh. But it was kind of odd, because Guy just nodded slowly, like maybe he understood. Johnny leaned forward and lowered his voice a touch. "And, Harvard, I ain't ever told anyone else about that." He paused again, and met Guy's gaze with just the ghost of a smile. "So if you ever repeat that to a living soul, I might have to shoot you."

Guy grinned. He had a touch of color back now. "Quite right, Johnny. We can't possibly have anyone suspecting that Johnny Fierro has a warm heart beating under that cold exterior." Guy huffed out a big sigh and looked across at Carter and shuddered. "I had to stop him. Whatever the cost, I had to stop him. I saw him there with his finger on the trigger, pulling it back. He was going to shoot you in cold blood. For no reason."

Johnny shrugged. "I reckon he was pissed because they let me go. Which reminds me, I really do want to get out of Utah before that Judge Denning has second thoughts."

Guy grinned again and Johnny felt the tension slip away. Yeah, Guy did look better. He looked like Guy again. "Johnny, you can relax. You can't be tried for the same crime twice. It's over."

Over? No. That couldn't be right. That would be too easy. Fierro never had things easy . . . Guy had to have that wrong. But Guy did know a hell of a lot of stuff. Johnny raised an eyebrow.

"It's over? Are you sure of that? Denning can't change his mind?"

Guy smiled, shaking his head. "No. I assure you, Denning can't change his mind. It really is over." Guy paused, and then tilted his head. "One thing puzzles me. Why on earth didn't you tell the court that there was a newspaper clipping that could save you? You never gave as much as a hint. But if you'd told the court about it, they could have got in touch with the newspaper and got a copy of the clipping you had. Newspapers keep all their old editions on file. Did you not know that?"

How to answer this? He wanted to give Guy something but he couldn't give too much. "I knew I had a few clippings from around that time but I don't remember all the dates on them, Guy." Shit. Fierro was doing what Guy had accused him of earlier. Prevarying or some long word like that.

Guy raised an eyebrow. Nodded sort of knowingly. Like he knew Fierro was prevarying again. "Ah, of course."

Johnny felt a twinge of guilt. He bit his lip. Oh hell, Harvard had saved his life, so he owed him. "And the paper closed down. The editor was a drunk."

"And you just happen to know this?" Guy raised a disbelieving eyebrow.

Johnny wriggled, felt like a goddamn worm on a hook. "Yeah. He was a drunk. And it seems he sometimes printed stories that weren't too accu . . . acar . . . that weren't right. Got things wrong, if you know what I mean?"

Guy nodded. "I think I am getting the picture."

Johnny nodded and felt the heat flush his face. "Yeah, well, the thing is, seems they printed something else to say the gunfighter in town wasn't Fierro. They got it wrong. Didn't really think that if the judge found that out it would help my case."

Guy nodded kind of seriously, but almost like he was struggling not to smile. "Sound judgment on your part. Very sound. Good move."

Johnny grinned. "Yeah. I thought so. But I was sure relieved to see Stoney." He reached out and jabbed Guy with his finger. "And before I forget, Harvard, what the hell have you done to my gun? It jammed on me. Do you really think Carter would have got the jump on me otherwise?"

Guy looked kind of surprised. "Done to your gun? I haven't done anything to it! I told you it went off when I brushed the trigger. It almost blew my nuts off! So I shoved some cloth in it to stop the damn thing firing again while I emptied it."

"Shoved some cloth in it?" Johnny's mouth fell open. "Shoved some cloth in it? Dios, Harvard, you got a lot to learn about handguns. It ain't a rifle where you pull something through to clean the barrel." He shook his head again. "I can see I got my work cut out with you, Harvard." He sighed. "Come on, we'd better go tell Ford what happened. Shouldn't worry about it if I were you. You've done Ford a real big favor. He hated Carter's guts. So did most people, I reckon. Probably loads of people out there who'll be real pleased to see him dead. Folks love baying for blood. You just gave them what they want."

"You really think so?" Guy looked kind of puzzled now.

"Yeah, Harvard. I think so. Trust me. It'll be fine." Johnny stooped to pick up his gun from the corner of the room. "Shoved some cloth in it! Mierda. Cloth! Pity it didn't blow your damn balls off." He dismantled it quickly and blew in it. Didn't know if it would do any good. Sooner he got back to the hotel and cleaned it, the better he'd feel. "Shoved some cloth in it." He shook his head again before grabbing a cloth from the table and throwing it over Carter. "Come on, Davy Crockett, let's go see Ford."

He grabbed hold of Guy's arm and pulled him from the shack. It had stopped snowing. And the clouds were scudding across the darkening sky. The first star was out. It always cheered him. 'Specially today. Back in the cell he'd got to thinking maybe he'd never walk free again. Never see the stars or feel the sun on his back. Never have another fuck. Pity there wasn't a bordello in this town. Another good reason for getting out of Utah as fast as possible.

At least the street was empty now. Everyone had gone back to the warmth of their homes, which was just as well. If the sound of muffled gunfire in the shack had brought them all running, Guy would have had a tough time handling that. It was lucky that Carter's cabin was right on the edge of the town with nobody around to hear what had gone on. But then again, Carter probably wouldn't have tried anything if it had been in the middle of town. Johnny glanced at Guy. Was he really OK? He'd gone awful quiet again. Looked lost in thought and was frowning. Johnny touched his arm. "Are you OK now, Guy?"

Guy pulled a face and shrugged. "I was just wondering about Carter." Guy stopped walking, his face half-lit by a lamp glowing in a window. "I mean, do you think he had family?"

"I dunno, Guy. Look, he brought this on himself. He started it all. It don't do no good for you to blame yourself. It's just one of those things. It happened. You did the right thing. And that's all you need to remember."

Guy sighed. "I know all of that. But it doesn't help. I'm here repeating all that to myself. But this was too close. It wasn't like a war. That I can deal with. Maybe it's because a war doesn't seem so . . . so personal. This was different."

Johnny stared up at the sky. Dios. Harvard did like to worry away at things. "Guy, this only just happened. I mean like minutes ago. It'll get easier. You know you did what you had to do." Johnny paused, trying to think of something to make it easier on Guy. "Look, I killed a lot of men in my life. Some of those killings I regret. And some of them, I don't regret. Hell, I guess there are quite a few things I done that I'll never regret. And I just have to live with it. Good and bad. But Carter, well, he's one of the killings a man doesn't regret. OK?" He scratched his chin, and kicked at the snow. "And I reckon . . . Well, I guess the fellow who killed Doe doesn't regret that killing either."

Guy didn't speak at first. Just looked at Johnny, thoughtful and then nodded slowly. "Thanks, Johnny. Come on, let's go and see Ford. And I suggest we leave this damn town first thing in the morning. I will be very glad to get out of this place. And I'm sure you will be too."

Johnny grinned. "Well, there are places I'd rather be. Like Sadie's bed. What the hell do the men here do? No bordello. No saloon girls. Mierda. Life just wouldn't be worth living here. It's probably why Carter was loco! Now can we please get moving? It's fucking freezing standing here." He pulled his collar up and hurried on back toward the jail. See Ford and then go find a bed. Any bed, in any room, as long as it didn't have any damn metal bars around it.

CHAPTER TWENTY-NINE

"Well, that all seems pretty straightforward." Ford put the pen down. He'd listened to Guy's story and scribbled some notes. Then he'd gotten Guy to sign a statement. He'd asked one or two questions of Johnny, but didn't seem bothered about the dead deputy. Which was just what Johnny had expected.

"Wouldn't bother yourself over him, Mr. Sinclair. He's no great loss. He was going to get fired later this week. The business after the stage crash was the last straw. He'd have killed Fierro then if Rockwell hadn't turned up when he did and it sounds like you were only just in time today. You've saved the county the trouble of firing him." Ford shrugged. "I never could stand the son of a bitch. And we don't need two lawmen in a town this size anyway. He was a waste of space and everyone knew it."

"Are you staying on, now it's all over?" Johnny regretted the question. Guy didn't know about Ford's involvement with Doe. Only that Ford had "been asked" to hunt him down.

Ford leaned back in his chair and put his feet up on the desk. "Yeah, I like this town. I've settled in." He smiled, more to himself it seemed than at Guy and Johnny. "Got me a nice young woman I'm courting. Figure it's time I settled down. A man needs roots, a wife and family. And now, well." He paused and shrugged. "It seems like a good time to take her to the altar." He shot a quick glance at Johnny. "Maybe it's finally time for you to settle down, Fierro. You got a nice home back there in New Mexico. And a nice family too." He nodded at Guy who sat clasping a mug of strong black coffee.

"Settle down? Hell, no. I ain't getting married yet. I got a whole lot of whoring left in me." Johnny glared as Guy and Ford started laughing.

"Respectable rancher. Isn't that what Sweetfoot called you in court? I know it's none of my business, but maybe it's time you lived up to it." Ford was looking at him hard, like he was trying to make a point.

Johnny stared at the blackness out of the window. Respectable? Him? Trouble was, folk had long memories and somehow he didn't see the people of Cimarron welcoming him with open arms any time soon. And settling wasn't proving easy. The work was hard and repetitive, and at times he missed his freedom so much that it became a physical ache deep inside him, ripping him in two. There were so many rules to live by now in this new life. Too many rules, if he was honest. Sometimes he yearned to just run wild and free like the horses on the range. And then he'd find himself brooding about whether this new life was worth all the sacrifices. Didn't always seem better. Just different.

He shook himself, trying to drag his mind back to the present. "It ain't that easy, Ford. There's always going to be someone coming looking for me. I don't see that changing any time soon." He could feel Guy's concern at his words. Guy didn't even need to voice it, it was that sudden tensing of the shoulders that gave him away and the worry seeped out of Guy like blood from a wound that wouldn't close up. Johnny flinched. He had to say something else. Something to ease Guy's mind. He forced a smile at the two men. "But I guess I just have to take whatever comes." Was that the right thing to say? Maybe not. Guy still looked kind of tight, hunched over, clinging to that coffee cup like his life depended on it. "Any rate, I'll be glad to get home."

Yeah, that should do it. It sounded better. But wasn't that half the trouble? It felt like he spent his life now worrying about what to say, when to say it, and saying it right. And more often than not he got it wrong—

"When are you leaving?"

He gave a start; he'd been drifting again. Ford was watching him through narrowed eyes, like he could see what Johnny had been thinking. Johnny glanced at Guy and raised an eyebrow. "Um. Tomorrow morning, I guess. Make an early start, won't we, Guy?"

Guy nodded. "Yes, we need to get going, before the weather gets any worse and winter sets in with a vengeance. But I'd like to thank you, Marshal, for all your help. You've been fair from the beginning, and I'm grateful. You've made a very unpleasant experience a lot more bearable."

There he went again. Talking came so easy to Guy. He always chose the right words and said what he wanted to. He envied Guy that way he had of being able to talk to anyone and put them at their ease. Was that the sort of thing they taught kids in school? Or just fancy schools out east? It was what other kids had done. Gone to school, learned how to live with rules. And all the while Fierro had run as wild and free as a mustang on the range.

"Just doing my job." Ford and Guy were shaking hands. But of course Ford hadn't been just "doing his job." He'd been looking out for Fierro because he knew what sort of man Doe had been. Yeah, Ford was a decent man. One of the few good men Johnny could remember meeting. He sure hadn't met many. But leastways he'd have two good men for company on the journey back. Guy and Stoney. He just hoped to God that Guy never found out that it had been Stoney who'd got his back seen to when he was a kid. He didn't want anybody finding out about that. Guy would be bound to ask Stoney questions. Guy always wanted to know about everything. He'd ask what Johnny had been like as a kid, and then he might find out exactly how rough things had been.

"Shall we go and see if there's a room for you at the hotel?" Guy stood at the door, ready to go.

"Yeah. Sure. And thanks for everything, Ford." Johnny clapped Ford on the back. "You just hurry up and marry that gal of yours. No point in waiting. Life's too short."

The clouds had gone, leaving the night sky clear, with millions of stars glittering bright as diamonds in the cold, clean air. The wind had dropped and the moon was rising. Johnny huddled down into his jacket, hating the chill in his bones. If he headed south toward Mexico it would be warmer. He ground his teeth. He had to stop thinking like this. He wouldn't be heading south, leastways not yet. He loved the ranch and the land. He had to keep fighting the pull of freedom. He'd thought it would fade. But it didn't. If anything it was getting worse. It was always there snapping at his heels. Or blowing in the breeze just ahead of him. Taunting him. Tempting him to just reach out and grab it or chase it, and to tell his old man to stuff his rules and his ranch. And much as he loved the fact that he was getting to know Guy, he still half-expected Guy to suddenly decide to go back to Boston. Surely someone as smart as Guy would get bored by a dumb brother and a difficult father. And by the hard life of ranching. Who'd be a rancher if they had something easier to do? Hell, Guy had been raised rich in Boston. Surely it was just a matter of time before the call of that life became too much. Because it must be calling to him. If freedom was calling so hard to Johnny, surely that cushy old life was calling Guy?

And surely it was only a matter of time before Guthrie threw Fierro out. Burnett's words echoed again in his head. Telling him that he was an embarrassment to his father. Maybe it would be best to leave. That way he could keep his pride. He didn't want to be broke to the plough by his old man. Hell, he couldn't even go whoring when he felt like it. Always had to wait for the weekend because otherwise it meant butting heads with Guthrie. They always butted heads if Johnny didn't toe the line. Wasn't allowed to think for himself—

"Come on." Guy sounded impatient. They'd reached the hotel and Johnny hadn't even noticed. Guy held the door open. "It's freezing out here. Get a move on, Johnny."

He followed Guy into the lobby. Stoney was sprawled in one of the big armchairs by the fire, his legs stretched out, snoring softly. He sure looked like a man at ease. What the hell would it be like to be able to relax like that in a public place? Stoney didn't worry about someone creeping up from his past to gun him. But then, Stoney wasn't Fierro so he could afford to just relax.

"Shall we wake him?" There was a hint of mischief in Guy's eyes.

Johnny grinned. "It sure is tempting. You were out saving my butt, and he's in here, all snug and warm, without a care in the world." Johnny paused, his mind replaying the events of the last couple of hours. "Maybe he got lucky with that woman he cannoned into when I was heading off to see Carter. Maybe that's why he's so exhausted." Johnny snorted with laughter at the thought. Stoney wasn't too good with women. "I don't think you saw that. Maybe you were still up in the room. But he was heading over to me and he collided with that woman in the veil. Knocked her clean over." His shoulders shook. "Anyway, who the hell was she? You know, the one who sat right up front. She didn't miss a trick at the trial. Paid more attention than the damn jury."

Guy shook his head. "I assumed she was something to do with Doe. She never ate her meals in the dining room with the hotel guests and I never saw her speak to anyone."

Johnny grinned again. "Well, if old Stoney got lucky with her, I reckon he'll tell us. Trouble is, Stoney ain't too good with women. He—"

Stoney opened his eyes, and scowled at them both. "I ain't got cloth ears. And, Fierro, just so as you know, I get along mighty fine with women."

"If that's the case, how come you're still on your own? A man your age." Johnny backed away, still grinning, as Stoney stood up with a mean look in his narrowed eyes. "So, come on, Stoney, tell us. Who was the mystery woman? You seemed to be getting to know her real well when I went out earlier."

Stoney scratched his beard. Damn, but the man could use a shave. And he had a kind of smug look on his face. Yeah. That figured. Stoney would love knowing he'd got an edge.

Stoney smirked. "Mystery woman? What mystery woman?"

Johnny glared at him. "The woman in the veil. You were lying on top of her when I left earlier. Getting on very well. It looked real cozy." He felt the smile starting to break out as he remembered the look of horror on Stoney's face when he'd collided with her.

Stoney shook his head, like he didn't remember no woman. "Woman? In a veil, you say? I ain't too sure that I recall any woman." Stoney's smirk grew wider.

"Aw, come on, Stoney. Who was she? Guy and me, well, we've been wondering who the hell she was. You got to tell us." Johnny gave Stoney one of his broadest smiles. "So. Come on. Spill it. Who was she? A relative of Doe? Who?"

Stoney had an irritating, smug look on his face. Looked like a cat who'd got a bellyful of cream. "Oh! The woman in the veil. That woman."

Johnny sighed in exasperation. "Yeah, Stoney. The woman in the veil. Who was she? You talked to her."

Stoney shrugged. "Yeah. Me and her, we had a nice chat.

And you know something, Fierro? Seeing as how you've caused me so much trouble these past few days, and I'm dead beat, I think I'm off to my bed. I got me the last room in the hotel. Guess you'll have to bunk in with your brother. Unless you want to ask Ford if you can bed down in that cell of his." Stoney limped towards the stairs.

Damn it, but Stoney could be an irritating son of a bitch at times. "Stoney. Who was she?"

Stoney started up the stairs without looking back. He paused halfway up them and called over his shoulder. "You know, I don't think I'm going to tell you. Man has to have some secrets. G'night, boys. Get some sleep. We got an early start in the morning."

Johnny turned to Guy. "He ain't going to tell us. You heard him, Guy. Can you believe that? He ain't going to tell us!"

Guy's mouth quirked. "So it would seem. Although, I must admit that I've been wondering a lot about that woman myself. There was something vaguely familiar about her. It's been niggling away at me since I first saw her. The way she walked. Her posture."

Posture? What the hell was that? Johnny stared at Guy, who was seemingly lost in thought.

Guy laughed suddenly. "I know who she reminded me of, but you'll never credit this! She reminded me of Delice. Same height. Delice is unusually tall for a woman."

"Delice?" Had Guy gone loco? "What the hell would Delice be doing coming all this way? And why would she hide herself away under a veil?" Johnny shook his head. "That's crazy." Yeah, Delice was tall. And kind of elegant the way she walked. But no, the whole idea was loco—Delice could never have kept quiet during the trial. She'd have been busy telling the judge how to keep order in his court. He sighed. "Stoney ain't going to come clean and tell us. And I sure as hell ain't begging him to tell us.

Won't give him the satisfaction. He's loving having one over on us."

Guy grinned. "I think you're right about that. Anyway, we won't ask him who it was. It'll drive him crazy. And to add insult to injury, he's got the last room. He's right; you'd better bunk in with me. At least I'll know where you are. It might keep you out of trouble. I'm really not sure that you're safe to be let out." Guy looked better now, more like himself. "Don't you get tired of people trying to shoot you? It must become very tedious. It certainly wears me out."

Johnny laughed, following Guy up the wide staircase. "Hell, no. It keeps life interesting, Harvard. Stick around and you'll get used to it."

The journey back was the hardest slog he could remember. It was bitterly cold with raw winds clawing at his face, and it felt as though it was eating the flesh off his bones. And every time he breathed in, it was like his lungs turned to ice. The only good thing was it stopped Guy from talking. They all had scarves pulled right up around their faces, so only their eyes showed. Made them look like a bunch of outlaws.

They didn't talk much at night either. The only high point was the look of irritation on Stoney's face that they didn't question him any more about the mystery woman.

They always broke their journey at a way station, but they were always deserted. Nobody else was loco enough to be out in this weather. Dios, it would be good to get out of Utah and back to a town with a saloon and women. He needed a woman real bad. It was getting that it was all he could think about. A green-eyed woman with real long legs would be best, but right now, any woman would do. He'd give anything to be stretched out in Sadie's bed with her tending to his needs. But he'd stopped mentioning it to Guy and Stoney after Guy had said that if he droned on about his needs once more, he'd put a bullet in him himself and finish what Carter had started.

"We'll be back in New Mexico territory tomorrow." Guy warmed his hands over the potbellied stove in the way station. Stoney was already asleep, snoring in his bedroll in the corner of the room. "You'll be able to find yourself a woman."

Johnny eyed him cautiously. But Guy looked more relaxed this evening. Maybe he hadn't liked being in Utah any more than Johnny had. Perhaps now was the moment to ask Guy the thing that had been bugging him for the past couple of days, the worry niggling away at the back of his mind. When he wasn't thinking about a woman. This was as good a time as any. "You know what you said, about Denning not being able to change his mind? Is that true? Are you sure about that?" He tried to sound casual. Like he wasn't bothered about it one way or the other. But he knew there was a note of something in his voice. Fear? Yeah, if he was honest the thought of it scared him. He didn't want to go through it all again.

Guy looked at him, and held his gaze before nodding. "Yes. I'm sure. You can't be tried for the same crime twice. It's written into our constitution." Guy's mouth quirked. "I know you think we're all just a bunch of stupid gringos, you've said so on more than one occasion, but we have one or two good things in this country. And our constitution is one of them."

Johnny felt a twinge of guilt. *"Our constitution."* Like Johnny belonged. Wasn't some breed who didn't belong either side of the border. But how could Guy be so certain? "Did you learn about things like that at your fancy school?"

Guy looked real serious again. "You mean Harvard? I guess we covered it there. But I had already learned about our constitution long before then." Guy paused, reached into his saddlebags, and pulled out a flask of whiskey, which he passed across to Johnny's already open hand. "Does my education bother you so much? You always refer to it as my 'fancy school.' I can't help but wonder whether you're jealous, whether you resent it."

Johnny took a swig from the flask, the mellow malt warming him as it coursed through his body. Did he resent it? Resent all the opportunities Fierro had never had? The warmth, the food on the table, a place to lay his head at night without wondering if one of his mother's men . . . Shit, there he went again. Why did those memories always come back? Why couldn't he simply bury them? A man just had to play the hand life dealt him. Whether it was a high card or a full house. Just seemed that Guy had been dealt a royal flush. He passed the flask back and then fumbled in his jacket for a smoke. He chuckled. "No, Guy, I ain't jealous. Kind of proud to have a real smart brother."

Johnny focused on rolling his cigarette. He bit his lip, trying to figure out how to voice the other niggling fear that he kept trying to push away. Because if he was honest, it was fear. "What's Guthrie going to say when he hears about this trip?"

Guy took a swig from the flask. "We just tell him." He paused and looked hard at Johnny. "We tell him that it was a case of mistaken identity. They got the wrong man. Didn't they?" Those eyes looked right into Fierro. Into Fierro's soul. "Denning freed you. Mistaken identity, Johnny. It's over. It's not coming back to haunt you. You can move on."

The lump in his throat felt like it might choke him. And his eyes were pricking. Not coming back to haunt him? The memories damn well would. But hell, it would be good if Guy was right and he could forget about the law coming after him. Because he couldn't forget Doe. What was it he'd said to Doe that day? "You should remember me. I sure as hell remember you. Yeah. I remember you, every waking hour and every fucking night." And there it was and there it would always be. Move on. Dios! Move on? If only life was that simple. Simple as dirt. But it wasn't. It was fucking hard.

But leastways Guy believed in him. Stuck by him through all the crap. And even killed a man for him. He could still hardly believe that. Guy gunning down Carter because he cared. Dios, but that felt good. Just to know that at least one member of his family cared that much. But what about his father? He'd bet Guthrie wouldn't have been so loyal and true. No, the old man had more loyalty to his old friends than to his son. Look how Guthrie had gone rushing off to support Burnett. And even now Burnett's words were stuck in his memory, eating away at the heart of him. Burnett telling Johnny that he was an embarrassment to his father. That the family would be better off without him. Maybe Guy was wrong. Maybe Guthrie really had said that to Burnett. He'd sure as hell wanted to help Burnett. To get him a lawyer. He hadn't believed anything Johnny had said about Burnett—but he believed every single lie that Burnett told him. His father excused Burnett's behavior as fucking circumstances. But he never excused Johnny's past. No. The old man was ashamed of his son. Well, his father could go to hell.

"Johnny." Guy's voice was gentle. "We put it behind us and we present a united front to Guthrie. OK?"

Johnny shrugged. "Whatever you say." But the knot was back. The knot that turned his insides all ways whenever he thought of his father's disapproval and the disappointment in the old man's eyes. He reckoned it was a dead certainty that the old man was not going to be happy about Fierro's latest adventure. And at times like this, the urge to just cut and run became almost overpowering.

"We'll find you a woman tomorrow." There was laughter in Guy's voice. Yeah, it was fine for Harvard. He wouldn't be tearing himself apart over what lay ahead. United front. End of story, as far as Guy was concerned. Why couldn't he be so easy about things? Be more like Guy? But for now, he'd content himself with a woman to fuck. Fuck hard. Block everything out. Lose himself in a few minutes of ecstasy when everything else faded away. Same as always.

"Just make sure she's pretty." Hell, who was he kidding? So long as she'd got legs to open, right now he didn't care. Any woman would do. "I'm beat. I'm turning in, Harvard. Need my energy for this woman you're going to find me tomorrow." He shrugged down into his bedroll and tried to block out images of Guthrie's eyes.

Guy had been true to his word. Found them a small scruffy town with a saloon and some worn-out women. He and Stoney had even given Fierro first pick. Not that there was much choice, but he'd been grateful for the gesture. So he'd spent a night under grubby sheets, sweating and grunting in the comforting embrace of a woman who'd seen better days. And he'd longed for Sadie's touch, her fingers soft and gentle as butterfly wings on his body.

They left Stoney at the fork in the road. He waved as he headed home to Cimarron. Johnny tried to crush the urge to ride in with him. To see Delice. It would be real good to listen to her talk in that crisp tone she always used when she thought he was being dumber than usual. She'd tell him how to handle his father . . .

Now they sat looking down on the ranch nestling in the valley, lights shining out a welcome in the dusk. He had a lump in his throat again. There'd been times these past weeks when he'd wondered if he'd ever see it again. The whitewashed walls of the hacienda were tinged gold by the lanterns lighting the courtyard. Smoke drifted from the chimneys, hanging almost suspended before slipping away on the whispering breeze. Maybe the old man wouldn't be back from his trip yet. Maybe it would be just

Peggy. Sick with worry for them, ready to pull them into a warm embrace with no reproach.

Pistol would be waiting, munching an evening feed in the barn. He'd nuzzle Johnny, pleased to see him. No reproaches from him. And Carlita would be excited and would cook them something special to welcome them back. Maybe tamales for her Juanito. Spicy tamales. No reproaches from her.

They didn't gallop down, like they did after a good day on the range. They walked the horses slowly. It had been a long trip, and their mounts were worn out. Bone tired—same as their riders. Yeah. Ride in slow and have a good meal. Figure out what to say to Guthrie later. He'd still be away on his trip. There was no need to worry.

As they rode into the yard, a couple of vaqueros hurried out, speaking warm, welcoming, kind words in that oh so familiar language of his childhood that sometimes made him ache for those lost and fearful days of discovery and danger.

Johnny and Guy smiled their thanks before walking together toward the hacienda. The door swung open before they reached it and their father stood framed in the doorway.

The face was stern, as if it had been carved from the land the man loved so much. Was there any softness in those eyes? Any welcome? It was too dark to tell. Too dark to read him right. Guy squeezed his arm lightly. Just the lightest touch, meant to comfort and reassure.

"Boys." The old man's voice rang out. "You two had better get inside right now. Because, believe me, the two of you have got some explaining to do. I go away, trusting the pair of you, leaving the ranch in your hands. Not too much to ask, I thought. But what do I find when I come home? I find an empty house and both of you missing. I hear that Johnny has been dragged away in handcuffs by a US marshal. Presumably something else from his past which never seems to leave this family alone. And

I find you've hightailed out after him, Guy. And not a word from you to let anyone here know what the hell has been going on. I want some answers and I want them now."

ABOUT THE AUTHOR

Adventurer and journalist **JD March** has tracked leopards in the Masai Mara, skied competitively, ridden to hounds, paddled dugout canoes on the Indian Ocean, and is an accomplished sailor. JD has lived in a series of unusual homes, including a haunted 12th-century house in Cornwall in Britain and a chalet in the French Alps. But a lifelong passion for the Old West means JD is happiest in the saddle, rounding up cattle on the Big Horn Mountains in Wyoming. www.jdmarch.com